PENGUIN CLASSICS

P9-CFO-829

HAWTHORNE: SELECTED TALES
AND SKETCHES

Nathaniel Hawthorne (1804–1864) was born in Salem, Massachusetts, where, after his graduation from Bowdoin College in Maine, he wrote the bulk of his masterful tales of American colonial history, many of which were collected in his *Twice-told Tales* (1837). In 1839 and 1840 Hawthorne worked in the Boston Customs House, then spent most of 1841 at the experimental community of Brook Farm. After his marriage to Sophia Peabody, he settled in the "Old Manse" in Concord; there, between 1842 and 1845, he wrote most of the other tales in this volume, first gathered in a collection entitled *Mosses from an Old Manse* (1846). His career as a novelist began with *The Scarlet Letter* (1850), whose famous preface recalls his 1846–1849 service in "The Custom-House" of Salem. *The House of the Seven Gables* (1851) and *The Blithedale Romance* (1852) followed in rapid succession. After a third political appointment—this time as American Consul in Liverpool, England, from 1853 to 1857—Hawthorne's life was marked by the publication of *The Marble Faun* (1860) but also by a sad inability to complete several more long romances. Ill health, apparently, and possibly some failure of literary faith finally eroded Hawthorne's striking ability to make imaginative sense of America's distinctive moral experience.

Michael J. Colacurcio is the author of *The Province of Piety: Moral History in Hawthorne's Early Tales* and of various essays and reviews in the field of American literature. He has also edited and contributed to a volume of *New Essays on The Scarlet Letter*. He is currently Professor of English and American Studies at UCLA.

SELECTED TALES AND SKETCHES

NATHANIEL HAWTHORNE

Selected and with an Introduction by
Michael J. Colacurcio

PENGUIN BOOKS

PENGUIN BOOKS
Published by the Penguin Group
Penguin Books USA Inc.,
375 Hudson Street, New York, New York 10014, U.S.A.
Penguin Books Ltd, 27 Wrights Lane,
London W8 5TZ, England
Penguin Books Australia Ltd, Ringwood,
Victoria, Australia
Penguin Books Canada Ltd, 10 Alcorn Avenue,
Toronto, Ontario, Canada M4V 3B2
Penguin Books (N.Z.) Ltd, 182-190 Wairau Road,
Auckland 10, New Zealand

Penguin Books Ltd. Registered Offices:
Harmondsworth, Middlesex, England

First published in the United States of America by Penguin Books 1987
Published simultaneously in Canada

21   23   25   24   22   20

Introduction and compilation copyright © Viking Penguin Inc., 1987
All rights reserved

The text of the stories in this collection is that established by the *Centenary
Edition of the Works of Nathaniel Hawthorne* published by the Ohio State University
Center for Textual Studies and Ohio State University Press. The selections are
from the volumes entitled *Twice-Told Tales, Mosses from an Old Manse, The Snow-Image
and Uncollected Tales*, and *Miscellany*. Copyright © Ohio State University
Press, 1974, 1987. All rights reserved.

Acknowledgment is made to The Library of America for their assistance in the
production of this book.

LIBRARY OF CONGRESS CATALOGING-IN-PUBLICATION DATA
Hawthorne, Nathaniel, 1804–1864.
Selected tales and sketches.
(Penguin classics)
Bibliography: p.
I. Colacurcio, Michael J. II. Title.
PS1852.C55 1987   813'.3   86-21247
ISBN 0 14 03.9057 X (pbk.)

Printed in the United States of America
Set in Garamond No. 3

CONTENTS

Introduction vii

A Note on the Text xxxvii

SELECTED TALES AND SKETCHES

The Hollow of the Three Hills (1830) 1

Sir William Phips (1830) 7

Mrs. Hutchinson (1830) 14

The Wives of the Dead (1832) 22

My Kinsman, Major Molineux (1832) 29

Roger Malvin's Burial (1832) 51

Passages from a Relinquished Work (1834) 74

Mr. Higginbotham's Catastrophe (1834) 90

The Haunted Mind (1835) 104

Alice Doane's Appeal (1835) 110

The Gray Champion (1835) 124

Young Goodman Brown (1835) 133

Wakefield (1835) 149

The Notch of the White Mountains (1835) 159

The Ambitious Guest (1835) 162

The May-Pole of Merry Mount (1836) 172

The Minister's Black Veil (1836) 185

Sunday at Home (1837) 200

The Man of Adamant (1837) 208

Endicott and the Red Cross (1838) 217

Night Sketches (1838) 225

Legends of the Province-House 232

The Hall of Fantasy (1843) 246

The Birth-mark (1843) 259

Egotism; or, The Bosom-Serpent (1843) 279

The Christmas Banquet (1844) 295

The Celestial Rail-road (1843) 316

Earth's Holocaust (1844) 336

The Artist of the Beautiful (1844) 358

Rappaccini's Daughter (1844) 386

Ethan Brand (1850) 421

Suggestions for Further Reading 440

Introduction

When Hawthorne recollected, in the often quoted Preface to the third edition of his *Twice-told Tales* (1851), that he had once found himself "the obscurest man of letters in America," he was speaking of a phase of his career that had long since lapsed. *The Scarlet Letter* (1850) had not yet had time to establish itself as the classic we now universally recognize—that miracle of meditation which transcends provincial origin and subject matter to become a standard of World Literature; but it was already a significant critical and popular success. *The House of the Seven Gables* (1851), which Hawthorne himself in some moods preferred to *The Scarlet Letter,* would further secure his reputation. And by the time *The Blithedale Romance* (1852) was making its way among reviewers and booksellers, a somewhat envious Herman Melville could write his recently estranged friend that "this name of 'Hawthorne' seems to be ubiquitous."

But if these three extended fictions—the "American Romances," as Henry James would name them in his critical biography of 1879—established Hawthorne in that rich and catholic world we treasure as "fiction in English," and also at the center of an ongoing critical debate we recognize as "novel versus romance," it remains true that those shorter fictions Hawthorne produced in the decades prior to 1850 amount to far more than a long foreground to worldly success. Indeed the total achievement of his earlier tales and sketches is so remarkable that Hawthorne would merit a place in the first rank of American authors even if he had written none of his longer works. Nor would the literature of any modern nation-state be anything but significantly enhanced if Nathaniel Hawthorne had happened to be born there and to have subjected its peculiar moral history to his unique style of fictional analysis.

Yet Hawthorne remains emphatically an *American* writer—self-consciously then and distinctively now. Most obviously: as no one escapes the pressures of history, so this notable descendant of the American Puritans could scarcely have eluded *all* trace of their conscientious and symbolic manner of taking the world. More significantly, his American-ness reveals itself in terms he consciously learned, by immersing himself, at the outset of his career, in the whole sequence of colonial and provincial texts which inevitably express the Puritan Mind and arguably control American Identity.

That is to say, Hawthorne did not merely inherit his status or assume his function as an "American" author; rather, he studied to recreate and meditated to judge the special quality of moral experience in his native land. More incisively than any writer of his generation, he placed the moral argument both for and against Calvinism. Further, he had the critical intelligence to discern how much of the familiar politics of mission and destiny was but the public face of a piety that flourished in America distinctively. And eventually, especially in the 1840s, he acquired the perspective to notice how much of the morale of his own generation of intellectuals was suitably understood as neo-Puritan, despite their vigorous rejection of the theological idioms of the older orthodoxy. The continuities are clear and strong enough to suggest that, after he had written out his account of the Puritan conscience, he deliberately turned to something like a moral history of his own times. Thus even Hawthorne's more contemporaneous tales maintain a firm sense of involvement in a reality that is both concrete and continuous.

From this observation it follows that the enduring, even dazzling achievement of Hawthorne's early fiction is not sufficiently appreciated in the terms modern readers find readiest to hand: not in that formalism which regards literary meaning as utterly internal to the work itself; and not even in those systems of psychoanalytic analysis which help us find, in literature as elsewhere, some structure deep enough to inform all possible experience of the world. For, contrary to the implication of both these famous critical schemes, the typical Hawthorne tale appears to insist that we *cannot* get along without historical reference. Not thematically, of course, as the tales frequently set out to judge the import of experiences that have been altogether real and definite. And not even formally—should we find ourselves insisting on that once proud distinction—for the reality of history usually introduces, quite deliberately, some contrary or discordant element into the otherwise smooth and plausible rhetoric of the Hawthorne tale itself. As *history* in Hawthorne usually signals *irony,* so we often find an entire reordering of values is triggered by some local but altogether strategic reference or allusion.

This is not to say, of course, that some subtle "historicism" may serve as our only system of critical notice. No one should fail to observe that Hawthorne's plots are often crafted for exquisite swiftness and precision of impact; or that his patterns of sight and sound are arranged with an artist's sense of repetition and difference. And only the studiedly naïve will resist the intimations of psychic complexity that lurk (even unconsciously) behind his most innocent-looking image or symbol. Yet the reader is also invited to pursue, with equal vigor and tact, the significance of allusions that seem to incorporate history into the imaginative world of the fiction. It might be too much to claim that we must always begin or end with such references. Yet it may be fair to suggest that Hawthorne *fully* emerges from his early obscurity only when the reader is determined to trace his art back to the real-life sources in the history that sustained it.

None of the works we might think to identify as Hawthorne's first significant literary production provides a full introduction to the precise historical demands we have been anticipating. His project of "moral history" begins quite early, but it does not appear to have been entirely aboriginal; and that fact seems always to have been part of our critical problem. Accustomed to identify moral "origin" with artistic "epitome," we have rarely thought to look for swift and significant historical development.

Fanshawe, a brief, seriocomic novel of sexual intrigue which Hawthorne managed to publish in 1828, is explicitly set in the previous century—in and about a "seminary of learning" located in a "retired corner of one of the New England states"—but its affinities are with literary traditions hardly to be identified with what Hawthorne's contemporaries specifically defined as "the matter of America." Scholars have patiently identified the influence of Sir Walter Scott, and of the so-called gothic and domestic or sentimental schools of English fiction; and though critics once claimed that this work predicted all that was really essential in Hawthorne's moral vision, no one has ever tried to link it very directly with the short fictions Hawthorne was also writing (and trying to collect) in the years immediately after his graduation from Bowdoin College in 1825. Indeed it now seems something of an embarrassment; not a false start, exactly, which the author subsequently tried to recall, as was once believed; but more like a bid to get *something* published, anonymously; something which lightly mocked even as it traded on the most popular of readerly expectations.

The case of the first of Hawthorne's several projected collections of brief tales is somewhat more complicated and suggestive, though even here the argument for the author's deep involvement in moral history, or in a fully studied art of allusion, would look a little premature. The title of the proposed collection, "Seven Tales of My Native Land," clearly suggests some patriotic motive, as does the prior fact of Hawthorne's membership in the more "nativist" of the two literary societies (the "Athenean") in existence at Bowdoin in the 1820s. Apparently Hawthorne began his career as a literary professional in substantial agreement with the widespread (though by no means universal) sentiment in favor of an American literature that should aspire to eventual greatness not formally, by imitating the established genres of British literature, but materially, by emphasizing those experiences that had distinguished American experience from all others. As earlier generations of independent-minded Americans had urged their constituents to "buy homespun," so American writers of the early nineteenth century were repeatedly urged to "use American materials." And we can easily imagine the author of the "Seven Tales" trying—in the words of one of Hawthorne's later, more ironic narrators—"to deserve well of [his] country by snatching from oblivion some else unheard-of fact of history."

Yet the literary image of the "Seven Tales" is blurred indeed. Part of the problem, quite simply, is that we cannot be sure of its precise table of contents, especially as this cardinal uncertainty is linked to some fairly strong evidence that a discouraged Hawthorne may have destroyed the majority of the tales intended for this first projected but never actually published collection. Well after Hawthorne's death (in 1864), his sister Elizabeth remembered reading, in the summer of 1825, a gathering of tales whose subjects she named as "witchcraft" and "the sea"; but she could mention only a couple of titles. One of these she referred to as "Alice Doane," and most scholars infer that "Alice Doane's Appeal" (1834)— whose clearly fictionalized narrator refers to the tale within his tale as one that chanced to survive some general literary conflagration—is in fact a dramatized redaction of one of Hawthorne's original "Seven." Beyond this one quasi-fact, however, most of the conditions surrounding Hawthorne's earliest attempts to market his tales remain indeed obscure.

"The Hollow of the Three Hills" (1830), which is surely about witchcraft in *some* sense, may quite possibly be a survivor from Hawthorne's first attempt at self-collection. So may be "The Wives of the Dead" (1832), whose setting and action at least partially invoke the sea. Nor is it entirely fanciful to suppose that "An Old Woman's Tale" (1830)—not included in this collection—might have been designed to serve as a sort of frame for some series or other; most suggestively, it identifies its source as the "strangely jumbled" memory of a cronelike old woman whose tale-telling habits have left "a thousand of her traditions lurking in the corners and by-places of [the narrator's] mind." All we can say with any certainty, however, is that the Hawthorne who returned in the summer of 1825 from Bowdoin College in Brunswick, Maine, to his native place of Salem, Massachusetts, had a mind to publish a *collection* of tales that subscribed, at least nominally, to the *nativist* literary program; and that he grew frustrated and even a little angry when he gradually inferred, by 1827, that publishers were not eager to publish his collection as such.

Yet it may be worth pausing a moment to consider the precise quality of Hawthorne's earliest published tale of his native land. For the temptation has been strong to identify "The Hollow of the Three Hills" as *indeed* a first; to decide that its subject recalls the infamous matter of the Salem Witchcraft, in which one of Hawthorne's remote ancestors had been deeply involved (as a surveillant but none too judicious magistrate); and to conclude with satisfaction and in haste that Hawthorne found his true "Hawthornean" métier almost immediately. The problem with this view is that it tends to establish a rather simplistic model of both the motive and the style of Hawthorne's involvement in history: gloomy ancestral wrong elaborated in a basically gothic manner. And while this account may almost serve for "The Hollow," it definitely reduces the complexity of tales like "Alice Doane's Appeal" and "Young Goodman Brown," in which Hawthorne's recreation of the past is much more than merely associative or tonal.

Anticipating just a bit, perhaps, the reader should notice that many features of "The Hollow of the Three Hills" are relatively conventional. The unspecified gloom of its setting amid "strange old times, when fantastic reveries were realized among the actual circumstances of life" contrasts quite noticeably with the sense of time and place so narrowly evoked in Hawthorne's two later witchcraft tales—the "Appeal" actually told on the "gallows hill" of the Salem executions, and "Brown" leaving clear traces of Hawthorne's reading of Cotton Mather's weirdly definitive *Wonders of the Invisible World* and deftly establishing a concrete sense of the moral psychology (and even the religious sociology) of the Puritan village. Furthermore, the literary effects of "The Hollow" seem a good deal more predictable than those which come later. The lonely grief of the dishonored father and mother, the madness of the deserted husband (complete with the insane laughter and rattling chains of his madhouse), and the most untimely death of the abandoned child all suggest that Hawthorne's loyalty to gothic and sentimental precedent is stronger than his fidelity to the motives and morphology of "Witchcraft in Salem." Even the witchery of the tale seems a bit more literary than the seventeenth-century record would justify: the old witch-woman who recreates the events of the tale is "diabolic" chiefly in her lurid enjoyment of domestic tragedy; and her supernatural powers, even if spurious, are largely those of some spiritualistic medium. The whole thing seems a little too pat, too trimly tailored to the taste of a nineteenth-century audience.

In general, then, it is no surprise that historical scholarship has had little to say about the "outré" events of this very early tale; or that existing criticism has analyzed its rhetorical and structural effects rather than elaborated its moral themes. It is as if Hawthorne were making trial of a tone rather than propounding an explanation; as if, in a way we have yet to consider, full seriousness entered a Hawthorne work only with an opening of some significant historical issue.

Nor do we have to wait *very* long for that implied event, as the tales Hawthorne intended for his second projected (but again unpublished) collection take us at once into matters which only a determined commitment to history can adequately follow. Again there is some uncertainty about the complete table of proposed contents. Possibly the tales which survived the fiery failure of the "Seven Tales" were to be included. And scholars have speculated that a number of historical tales published in the mid-1830s were originally written for this collection—the "Provincial Tales," which Hawthorne's letters clearly show him trying to publish in 1829. But here the ambiguities hardly matter, for a stable center quite plainly emerges. And with it a firm sense of the subtle direction Hawthorne's interest in American materials would take: not democratic patriotism or romantic nostalgia or even a moralized gothicism propels Hawthorne's literary fascination with "provincial" America but instead, and much more soberly, some fairly deep commitment to the project of culture criticism. The facts are the facts of history, and the spirit is that of irony.

At this stable center, then, lie three very significant tales, all of which were published eventually in an 1832 Christmas "gift-book," *The Token*. All are very pointedly historical and yet, significantly, each is immersed in materials quite specific to itself; and none deals with the ancestral (and also gothic) matter of the witchcraft. "The Gentle Boy" (omitted from this collection because of its length) takes up the issues of doctrine and religious psychology (piety) that appear to have divided, but also to have joined in mortal combat, the dominant sect of Puritans and their recessive but by no means quietistic antagonists, the Quakers. "Roger Malvin's Burial" leads us at once beyond the supposedly congenial confines of the original Puritan century and propounds a story of true and false heroism in the midst of a bloody but also representative or mythic "fight" for territory disputed by the French and the Indians, in the War which famously bears their allied name. And "My Kinsman, Major Molineux" appears to explore in advance the psychological and rhetorical conditions of the American Revolution, outrageously but deliberately reducing the one truly "majestic" event of American destiny to the contour and proportion of a rum riot, awkwardly occurring somewhere in the 1730s.

The range is surprisingly wide, as the past turns out to be more than a tonal alternative to the rational and recalcitrant conditions of the present; and the literary effects are anything but predictable, as the act of retelling is by no means an obvious or rule-ridden performance. Yet a common motive really does emerge: to insist that past experience is likely to have been far different from the image any present might wish, for whatever reason of identity or power, to project back upon it.

In one sense, of course, the range encompassed by these three tales is perfectly predictable, as theorists of American literary culture had already decided, quite early in the nineteenth century, that the store of peculiarly "American" materials consisted of three essential "matters": the matter of the Puritans, of the Indians, and of the Revolution. And at some level Hawthorne's three indubitably "provincial" tales merely take up each of these definitive historical matters in turn. Yet those same theorists were clearly calling for something much different from what Hawthorne was prepared to give them in his own highly, often wickedly unorthodox account of the American provinces. The Puritans, for example, were widely understood to be "bigoted"—persecuting the Quakers as fiercely as they had suppressed (and banished) "heretics" such as Roger Williams and Ann Hutchinson earlier, or as they later hounded the accused witches. But they were also supposed to represent a wholesome and valuable strain of dedication and purpose inseparable from the national character; and it was further assumed, more often than not, that their institutions actually contained, beneath the limitations of their own personal will, the seeds of liberal democracy. A fine theory, as Hawthorne surely must have felt. Yet what "The Gentle Boy" dramatizes instead is simply the pain and moral confusion of persons who, though clearly on opposite sides of *some* dialectic of history, all appeal in vain to an apparently uniform God beyond.

Nor are the other members of Hawthorne's tidy little trinity any more forgiving. "Roger Malvin's Burial" plainly announces that it has some reference to a 1725 episode of Indian warfare known as Lovewell's Fight which, though obscure to most modern readers, was widely celebrated on its hundredth anniversary as not only a triumph of advancing white civilization but also as a signal instance of frontier virtue and moral stamina. Well aware that the actual incident had been altogether ragged and unlovely, Hawthorne's response is clearly ironic and pointed, going straight to the express issue of courage and cowardice but also, with equal directness, to the suppressed one of lying about the logic (and even the events) of protective retaliation. And very few critics of "My Kinsman, Major Molineux"—including those who insist that its *real* interest is psychological or mythic—have been able to escape the impression that Hawthorne's version of the Revolution lacks all trace of ordinary American piety.

The psychoanalytic critics have a point, of course: "The Gentle Boy" does indeed suggest that persecuting sadists and suffering masochists have been let loose to play some terrible symbiotic game; and both "Malvin" and "Molineux" exhibit a deep structure it is hard to avoid calling Oedipal, in Freud's own most precise and father-murdering sense. Yet some other point seems just as true and more persistently provoked by the carefully appointed historical surface of these three tales: Hawthorne's provincial dramas are not set "nowhere," or even just "anywhere" in some remote and tonally appropriate past, but in those precise moments of historical crisis which Americanist theory had somewhat innocently identified as the young nation's most appropriate thematic space. The "Provincial Tales" clearly insist on their own historicity as the earlier "Seven" (as we know them) do not. Apparently something happened, between 1827 and 1829, to Hawthorne's sense of the project of American literature.

Literary maturity, we might safely suppose, is no less remarkably mysterious than any other kind: it comes, if at all, whenever it does; its forms may be structural, and therefore predictable, but hardly its causes. Yet it is difficult to resist the conclusion that the most important thing Hawthorne ever did for the maturing of his own literary career was to undertake, beginning in 1827, an exhaustive and fairly systematic study of American history in its colonial, provincial, and revolutionary periods. The early results of this program of purposive reading and imaginative "re-cognition" bear sharply on the historical density and difference of the "Provincial Tales."

The leading facts of "Hawthorne's Reading" have long been clear, for the surviving records of his borrowings from his local subscription library, the Salem Athenaeum, were published in 1949. This well-thumbed list, itself but a minimum suggestion of Hawthorne's voracious habits as a reader, clearly suggests that one of Hawthorne's principal and vital interests swiftly became something we might almost risk calling by the name of "American Studies." In an age when Everyman was, famously, "his own historian," Hawthorne merely fulfilled the role more faithfully than almost anyone else. In an age when *many* local institutions like the Salem Athenaeum were anxiously trying to preserve and collect everything that might shed light on the prerevolutionary identity of the nation's colonial experience, Hawthorne simply tried to read it all. Not only the obvious and crucial masterworks such as John Winthrop's *Journal* and Cotton Mather's *Magnalia Christi Americana,* which together form a magisterial frame around the original Puritan century, but more local and embattled texts as well: Edward Johnson's *Wonder-Working Providence of Sion's Saviour,* for example, which recapitulated the first two decades of founding under the urgent aspect of an immanent second coming; and Nathaniel Ward's *Simple Cobbler of Aggawam,* whose unwonted wit meant to instruct both New and Old England men in the more timely art of political compromise that yet stopped short of toleration; and *New England's Memorial* by Nathaniel Morton, the nephew and loyal redactor of William Bradford, whose own authoritative account "Of Plymouth Plantation" was piously folded into the larger "non-separatist" account of Puritan motive and meaning; and even William Hubbard's *Narrative of the Troubles with the Indians of New England.*

Nor did Hawthorne's reading limit him to one side of the story. Willem Sewel's *History of the Quakers,* which lies directly behind "The Gentle Boy," tells much that providential and filiopietistic history found it necessary to omit or gloss over. More significantly, perhaps, Hawthorne appears to have learned the meaning of the "radical" dissent of Roger Williams and of the "populist" loyalties of John Wise directly from their own works. He even appears to have known (though perhaps at some second hand) the aboriginal Anglo-naturalism of Thomas Morton, whose *New English Canaan*—or whose infamous outpost at Merry Mount—has enlisted the sympathy of so many who hate Puritanism by instinct. Thus criticism as well as myth went early into the Hawthorne mix.

Hawthorne clearly read George Bancroft's monumental but tendentious "libertarian" account of the Puritan contribution to the *History of the United States* as soon as the first volumes began to appear in 1834. But just as clearly he already knew much of the material on which it was based. Most importantly, perhaps, he was intensely familiar with the authoritative but not always "friendly" account it was supposed to supplant—the endlessly patient though often dull "constitutionalist" analysis of *The History of Massachusetts Bay* by Thomas Hutchinson, plainly the most fair and formidable of the Tory historians of prerevolutionary New England. Neither Hutchinson's secularism nor his loyalty to the king was lost on the Hawthorne who wrote "My Kinsman, Major Molineux," though for other purposes the mentality of Hutchinson would have to be supplemented by that of Benjamin Trumbull, whose *Complete History of Connecticut* everywhere privileges the "higher" considerations of piety, declension, and revival. And behind Hawthorne's alert response to these tomes lay his reading of the available local histories (of the towns of Boston, Salem, and Ipswich, for example, and of the regions of Maine and New Hampshire), and of dozens (probably hundreds) of local sermons and tracts. Apparently he even faced up to the available collections of legal and judicial proceedings from the earliest colonial years. The industrious graduate student is (cautiously) invited to attempt as much.

In the famously self-effacing letter to Longfellow of June 4, 1837, Hawthorne characterizes all this virtually archival reading as "desultory." And so it probably was, with regard to its available order and arrangement: who knew, in the 1820s, just how to re-cognize the colonial past? But Hawthorne appears to have read "religiously" as well, when we consider seriousness of purpose or efficacy of outcome. In one sense he merely did his required Americanist homework: before one could fairly "use" American materials, one had significantly to possess them. And in the end, what is often loosely referred to as Hawthorne's artistic *use* of history turns out to be something very like *history*.

Best recognized, of course, is Hawthorne's singular success in recovering the experience of those New England Puritans, whose piety and rhetoric have always advanced the most powerful claim to "founding" importance. And yet the evidence of the "Provincial Tales" suggests that it is possible to overstate and even misconstrue the place of Puritanism in the Hawthorne project. Hawthorne himself appears to have favored "The Gentle Boy" over "Malvin" and "Molineux," reprinting the one in the first of his *actually* published collections, the *Twice-told Tales* of 1837, while reserving the other two for later reissue. But modern criticism uniformly prefers the two "non-Puritan" tales in this group. And more significantly, perhaps, all three reveal a similar dedication to the shape and implication of moral experience in the relevant past. "The Gentle Boy" aptly reminds us that the notoriously puritanic theme of "weaned affections" contains a powerful theologic prejudice against what rationalists and romantics both called nature; but "Malvin" and "Molineux" exist to recall that the complex problem of American guilt and innocence has a significant political as well as a religious dimension.

The crucial issue lurking here, however, is probably biographical, as it involves the question of the personal or familiar bias Hawthorne may have brought to his study of moral history in America. As too many of the older biographies begin their account of this "Capital Son of the Old Puritans" with a highly dramatic account of "Ancestral Salem" in the seventeenth century, so, too, many literary interpreters have assumed that Hawthorne's penchant for and/or his quarrel with Puritanism was simply a given, with the implication that he wrote Puritan history either naturally or else by symptomatic retreat from an uncongenial present to a privileged past.

The facts tend to suggest otherwise. The Salem where Hawthorne was born (in 1804) was commerical rather than theologic in its dominant tone; and its religious cast was more liberal than conservative. His parents both belonged to churches that would become Unitarian when the "standing order" of Congregationalism was split in the 1820s; and all but one member of his extended family would favor churches teaching a decidedly un-Calvinistic understanding of sin and salvation. Accounts of Hawthorne's childhood all indicate that he was indulged rather than disciplined, in the formidable manner of puritanic "Christian nurture"; and the record of his early education reads more like a Novel of Enlightenment than any conceivable Narrative of Surprising Conversion. The (modest) record of the Bowdoin years (1821–25) indicates that Hawthorne neatly avoided all organized attempts to awaken his slumbering sense of sin and save his soul. Further, as we have already noticed, none of his first works indicates that he is merely expressing some Puritanism of nature or early training. When the Puritan mentality does authoritatively appear, in "The Gentle Boy," its context is one of learning and judgment: conscience and compulsion emerge as facts of the public rather than the private history.

Another way to approach the same fundamental point—that Hawthorne *learned* to do what he did with the past—is to notice that several other works published near the outset of his career also smell distinctly of the lamp of precise historical study. Three "sketches" of noteworthy historical figures, which appeared in the *Salem Gazette* in December 1830 and January 1831, all reveal a Hawthorne who is trying to be somewhat more precise about the import of the national "story" than he could conceivably have been in "The Hollow of the Three Hills" or "The Wives of the Dead." "Sir William Phips" deftly characterizes the political career and private morale of the man who had been the first governor of New England under its new, "Royal," and decidedly secularized charter of 1691. "Mrs. Hutchinson," besides predicting a certain "typic" identity for Hester Prynne in *The Scarlet Letter,* powerfully evokes the strain of theological feminism which mixes itself unstably in the religious recipe of Puritan prophecy. And "Dr. Bullivant" (omitted from this collection) aptly notices the puritanic expulsion of wit as but a merely naturalistic "humor," even as it elaborately meditates the cause and consequence of what a still unhilarious nineteenth century called gloom. Significant cultural achievements in their own way, each of these brief sketches serves as an important marker of Hawthorne's growing historical interest and precision.

Finally, of course, as even these three sketches tend to predict, it was on Puritanism that Hawthorne did choose to throw the light of his historical intelligence most fully and repeatedly. Yet clearly he must be thought of as *choosing.* Knowledge came from study and, as always, genius came from genius. But some considered project, provincial or otherwise, is clearly at issue in Hawthorne's repeated and increasingly subtle attempts to anthologize his early uses of American materials. So that, when the major tales of the Puritans do eventually emerge from the uncertain light of the famous "haunted chamber" of Hawthorne's family house in Salem—to which he returned, from Bowdoin, in 1825, and in which he read and wrote for the better part of the next twelve years—they must be thought of as coming as much from knowledge and conscious intention as from bias, as validly from the historical as from some other, more romantic form of imagination.

"Alice Doane's Appeal" self-consciously situates its gothic extravagance in precise relation to the mad logic of the Salem witchcraft of 1692: Leonard Doane does indeed, in the memorable formulation of Frederick Crews, "murder his personified wish"; but the rationale of this murderous aberration is specifically related to rumors of the Devil's insidious power of "spectral" simulation, so that the murdered man only seemed guilty of the deeds that tempted the fantasy of the murderer himself. "Young Goodman Brown" (1835) puts the capstone on Hawthorne's literary use of this peculiar Puritan theme of "specter evidence," as some pitiable yet far too culpably innocent protagonist "sees" absolutely everyone at a witch meeting that only he has verifiably set out to attend. All of this is somehow predicted by New England's own notorious witchcraft authority, Cotton Mather: the Devil can indeed appear "as an angel of light," or in the shape of an innocent person; God Himself may permit it as a test of the faith of the elect. All of this is superstitious or hysterical by the sober standards of enlightened reason. And yet before scapegoating Mather, Hawthorne appears to have felt, one had better decide if it expressed some fundamental tendency of human instinct or animal faith. Otherwise the past was all too simply *mad*.

Nor, as our argument has so far implied, is Hawthorne's psychology of witchcraft anything but a part of his total achievement in the area of historical re-cognition. "The Minister's Black Veil" (1836) and "The May-Pole of Merry Mount" (1836) stand out from the remaining "Puritan" group, providing (between them) as provocative and authoritative an account as we have had of the now cooperating, now contending styles of puritanic piety and politics. And there are other tales as well, just less significant in their *literary* power to do history. But most of these come along a moment later in Hawthorne's extended first period of artistic enterprise. And some account of Hawthorne's third and most complex project of organized self-collection may be required to get the full context and scope of their determined historicism.

Along with "Goodman Brown" and many others, Hawthorne's tales of the "May-Pole" and the "Black Veil" spilled forth as part of the virtual

flood of publications that followed the breakup, in 1834, of yet another
projected collection—"The Story-Teller." Once more, unhappily, a subtle
and multiform literary intention was atomized by editorial fiat; and once
more, maddeningly, its reconstruction lies just beyond the reach of surviving evidence. What does survive, however, clearly indicates that Hawthorne had labored very carefully, over a span of four or more years, to put
together a work which would collectively embody an extended commentary
on the emergent state of American culture. And though, as always, "the
might-have-been is but boggy ground to build on," all the signs suggest
that when certain arbiters of popular taste vetoed the publication of "The
Story-Teller" as such, American literature lost one of its most sophisticated
narrative experiments.

What Hawthorne delivered to a prospective publisher (early in 1834,
apparently) was the completed manuscript of a proposed two-volume work
in which many individual tales and localized sketches were all set within a
rather precise and dramatically significant frame: some concrete "narrator"—a well-identified personage, with a history and developing story of
his own—was to deliver each of the individual literary productions, and
each was to be associated with some particular and well-evoked though as
yet "unstoried" American place; furthermore, some unfolding thread of
travel and of story was to connect all the more specific manifestations of the
story-telling art. Perhaps Hawthorne was deliberately trying to domesti-
cate the example of Washington Irving's very popular *Sketch-Book* (1820),
which called up the storied places of England even as it borrowed a few very
old, probably archetypal folk tales for relocation in the Kaatskil region of
upstate New York. In any case, some principle of situationality or "world-
liness" was clearly trying to insist on itself, in relation to even the most
imaginative of literary performances. Evidently a mind haunted by reverie
and recollection was to be given a local habitation and a name.

But the collection was cut up: first by the editorial decision (of Samuel
Goodrich) that it was not suitably publishable as a book but might profita-
bly appear serially, in successive numbers of the *New-England Magazine;*
and then, according to the dictate of yet another editor (Park Benjamin),
that its various tales and sketches would have to appear independently,
without the connecting links of setting or narrative situation. One thing
thus became very many, each falling out of relation to the others and to
some idea of a literary whole. Moreover, each individual thing lost part of
its essential self-definition; for, even as Hawthorne's project was about to

demonstrate, literary meaning is never so inherent as to defy the rhetorical powers of speaker, occasion, and audience. And so it is not hard to believe the testimony of Hawthorne's sister-in-law (Elizabeth Peabody) that when they "tore up the book," Hawthorne "cared little for the stories afterward, which had in their original place . . . a great deal of significance."

Yet out they flooded, in the two or three years that followed, in the *New-England Magazine* and elsewhere; to be regrouped, sooner or later, in the various collections Hawthorne's improving luck and growing fame would authorize; but never as the composite cultural whole his all but inviolable historicity had first imagined. Whence our own largely ahistorical criticisms have had to take them up, one by one, each as some strangely dislocated or remarkably intense thing "in itself." Or else as fragments of some quaintly localized version of the romantic *bildungsroman*—as if the growth of the artist's own mind were the only available topic of interest.

In fact, however, the enabling cultural premise and even the initial framing construction of "The Story-Teller" have survived the original editorial deconstruction and the subsequent literary misprision: the premise alone, in a suggestive but probably superseded experiment called "The Seven Vagabonds" (not included in this volume); and both together, with clear and operative intention, in an intriguing four-part sketch which acquired the awkward and somewhat pitiful title of "Passages from a Relinquished Work." "Vagabonds" (1833) sets loose a "strolling gentleman," eager to become an "itinerant novelist," among a crowd of showmen, gypsies, and confidence men—idlers all, and all on their way to a Methodist camp meeting, there to divert the sober gentry as they rise up from the "anxious bench" of their sin and salvation; in the very next moment, however, the tale swiftly defeats the idle purpose of this hilarious little pilgrimage with the austere revelation, delivered by the lonely but imposing figure of the "circuit-riding" Methodist himself, that his revival meeting is quite "broke up." The ending has seemed a bit abrupt, yet the thematic implication is perfectly clear: according to somebody's dichotomy of spiritual culture, the literary career is being set over against the evangelical calling. And then, as if this obvious and painful dialectic could indeed have been missed, the "Fragments" (1834) puts it forth again.

A would-be storyteller elects to break free of the faithful watch of his ministerial foster parent, taking to the road with only his native wit for a saving grace. Instantly, however, he is joined by another would-be liver-off-the-word, an evangelical preacher named Eliakim Abbott. An odd couple, surely; yet henceforth the two will itinerate together, the one preaching salvation to all those who have ears to hear, the other seeking variously to amuse or mildly edify whoever happens to have the price of admission to some village theater. The dichotomy is too cruelly and humorously perfect to be anything but Hawthorne's satiric yet not quite self-pitying version of the problem of secular or "historical" literature in a puritanic or "typological" culture. It even sheds a little light on the tone and bearing of the famous "writer of story books!" passage in "The Custom-House."

What follows most immediately from this highly suggestive beginning is, clearly, the Story-Teller's first public performance: an impromptu recitation of a rather tall tale called "Mr. Higginbotham's Catastrophe" (1834), which used to be taken, in isolation, as evidence of Hawthorne's real gift for local color along with a spurious capacity for gratuitous overplotting, but which can yet be recovered as an outrageous parody of the philosophical problem of "testimony," particularly as it relates to the Christian story of a miraculous resurrection. The audience laughs uproariously, at nothing more than the name of the nominal protagonist, even as the Story-Teller deploys the schoolbook (but still potent) skepticism of David Hume; and even as Eliakim Abbott preaches that nearer-home crucifixion of Christian repentance, to a small congregation in the narrow confines of the local schoolhouse. Suddenly Hawthorne's talent for spiritual dilemma appears terribly up-to-date. Yet perhaps a present cultural situation is also history, whenever we choose to problematize it as such.

What was to follow along *after* this latter-day definition of the enduring "literary" hegemony of Puritanism will probably never become entirely clear. Evidently our fictional exponent (possibly to be named "Oberon") and his evangelical antagonist were to wander, in tandem and in tension, all around New England, observing what they found, philosophizing their radical differences, and situating, one way or another, a number of tales which opened the spiritual history of a country many observers declared barren of significance and hence of literary opportunity. Most of the tales and local sketches Hawthorne published between 1834 and 1837 have been more or less plausibly assigned to "The Story-Teller" but, as the significant connections have been impossible to reinvent, such ascriptions have seemed not so much speculative as empty. This collection includes only one compound example of "what might have been": "The Ambitious Guest" (1835), a moralized tale of what might be called the insecurity of nature, and which appears to echo Jonathan Edwards' infamous "Sinners in the Hands of an Angry God," is clearly (if partially) prepared for by the "aweful" speculations of a sketch called "The Notch," which was published as part of a larger unit called "Sketches from Memory by a Pedestrian" (1835). It is just possible that a few other such relationships may yet be discovered among the large assortment of tales and sketches which appeared separately in these years. But for the most part "The Story-Teller" comes down to us more as a cultural idea than as a literary reality.

Yet the idea remains full of critical significance. For one thing, the example of its elaborate narrative plan forces us to recognize the first collection Hawthorne *did* succeed in publishing as in fact a "miscellany." The cogently titled *Twice-told Tales* (1837)—which Horatio Bridge silently underwrote, even as his letters volubly tried to cheer up his badly discouraged college chum—really did end Hawthorne's long stint as nameless writer-of-supply for New England magazines and Christmas gift books; and clearly it did much, as the Preface to its third edition (1851) famously confesses, "to open an intercourse with the world." But it was, in the last analysis, a mere gathering together of a certain range or variety of individual literary productions, without the studied integrity of the earlier projects, and without the framing reminder of cultural origin and local reference which distinguishes the intention of "The Story-Teller." Its own being is remarkable enough to encourage investigation of its own looser sort of unity. Yet it strongly provokes the inference that Hawthorne had in some measure adjusted his more complex literary ambition to the terms in which his editors, rightly or wrongly, represented his audience. He simplified himself in order to survive.

More particularly, the entire dramatic form of "The Story-Teller" may prompt us to look for some narrator, lending distance and even a certain amount of irony to the most apparently personal of Hawthorne's sketches of the 1830s. Hawthorne's highly authoritative biographer, Arlin Turner, has detected farcical exaggeration in certain "Story-Teller" pieces which lament the bitter fate of "the artist," so that supposedly confessional pieces like the (excluded) "Devil in Manuscript" (1835) and "Fragments from the Journal of a Solitary Man" (1837) may exhibit more satire than self-pity. So may "The Haunted Mind" (1835), "Sunday at Home" (1837), and "Night Sketches" (1838)—all of which have been included as (ambiguous) examples of Hawthorne's treatment of the artistic (or otherwise "isolated") mentality and point of view. Any or all of these may once have been offered by the most fully characterized of Hawthorne's early narrators; certainly none can be read as unmediated autobiography. Evidently—the lesson of "The Story-Teller" suggests—Hawthorne's psychological sketches are far more likely to characterize than simply to confess.

It also appears that the narrator who reveals a bit of his literary biography even as he rehearses the rejected "Appeal" of the original "Alice Doane" is the very Story-Teller, who may as easily share a fact or two with "the real Hawthorne" as does, much later, the notoriously unreliable narrator of *The Blithedale Romance*. Certainly this would help to account for the repeated and otherwise problematic intrusion of the angry teller into the well-composed tale. It might even give us a way to understand why it seems so easy for that teller to end by blaming Cotton Mather for the witchcraft, in a way Hawthorne himself would elsewhere always resist.

This consideration may well bring us back to the most obviously historical, explicitly Puritan contents of "The Story-Teller." "Young Goodman Brown" does not by itself worry the conditions of its own telling; that, one suspects, has been part of its supposedly "timeless" power to fascinate and reveal. Yet we can easily imagine it as associated with the locale of Salem Village, which itself continues to stimulate the practice of psychohistory; and surely it is not amiss to wonder why the narrator raises only the problem of "dream," when the story itself retells the wondrous tale of "specter evidence" with assured historical authority. A similar and even more unsettling question attaches to "The Minister's Black Veil," which the alert reader may well associate with the decades (and the themes) of the "Great Awakening," but which the narrator offers as a somewhat more general—and sentimental—parable of painful solitude and pleasant society. More insistently still, "The Gray Champion" (1835) seems almost a case study in apparent narrative inconsistency, its oratorical conclusion broadly honoring the typological formula of Puritan politics the tale everywhere else portrays as paranoia. Most obviously, perhaps, "The May-Pole of Merry Mount" demands to be studied from the narrative perspective as firmly as from the historical: just whose authority is supposed to sponsor the tidy lesson in comparative colonization that is attached to the entirely fictional confrontation between a mythicized Governor Endicott and his misplaced "Priest of Baal"? And who wrote—to edit whose enthusiasm— the fey little footnote which exists to assure the decently empirical reader that, of course, nothing quite like the story's central symbolic event ever really took place? Perhaps the literary strategy of these tales is every bit as deep as their historical plot.

A simpler point remains cogent: from "The Story-Teller" as from the "Provincial Tales," Hawthorne's historical fictions survive *as historical,* just as they do survive. Full of explicit reminders of the events and personages of the past, they invite and reward the attempt to trace out their pattern of allusion. "Goodman Brown" implies the "spectral" theme of Cotton Mather almost as plainly as it pronounces his name. The "Black Veil" amply evokes a sunny but backslidden world that both demands and resists the power of some darkly conscientious awakening to the "true" sight of sin. The "Champion" draws the logic of providential vindication so tight it almost snaps—in the face of George Bancroft. And the "May-Pole" tries to force its honest reader to question the import and the power of an allegory that goes back to the very foundation of puritanic America. And when we put these tales beside Hawthorne's "provincial" histories, and add to them the half-dozen or so historical tales that appeared a year or two later, we are clearly in possession of the most authoritative and "survivable" achievement of Hawthorne's first period.

Yet evidently Hawthorne had meant there to be more. Not more tales of colonial and provincial history, necessarily, though here too some discoveries may yet be made; but more in the way of dramatic directive to cultural location. And with that a sense of what it might mean to retell the stories (if not quite the events) of the Puritan and Revolutionary past, in the midst of a bourgeois, democratic, and somewhat bumptious present, so that an available "Story-Teller" might fairly have prevented modern criticism from ever conceiving Hawthorne as a writer who fled from reality to imagination, or who treated the past as nothing more than fugitive fancy's temporal realm. Arguably he had begun that way, somewhere in his early and the century's middle twenties. But by 1835 he had fully mastered an art of history as subtle and self-aware as anything ever attempted in fiction.

The remainder of Hawthorne's career as "story-teller"—as opposed to his later appearance as our prime exemplar of the self-divided "romance-novel"—may be summarized much more briefly. Not because the tales and sketches of his second, "Old Manse," period are greatly inferior to those of his original, elongated, and still somewhat murky "Salem" phase. But because the outlines of his life and literary interests are much clearer at this later moment; and because his thematic relation to the "transcendental" concerns of his Emerson-inspired 1840s is altogether manifest and plausible. Hawthorne republished and added to his miscellaneous *Twice-told Tales* in 1842 and again in 1851; but the story of his next significant literary venture is well and strategically told by the fully public and suitably arranged contents of his *Mosses from an Old Manse* (1846).

Nothing could be clearer, biographically, than the "break" in Hawthorne's career just after the publication, finally, of a first collection. To be sure, many of his older interests continue through 1837 and 1838, with the latter year marked by the writing and publication of his four-part "Legends of the Province House," only one of which ("Edward Randolph's Portrait") can be included in this volume. Unfortunately, as together those tales subject the ideology of the American Revolution to a degree of rhetorical and psychic scrutiny it has seldom received since; and further so, as their unrelenting irony all but makes up for the uncensored sentiment let loose in a fair number of domestic tales published at this time. But then a whole new range of contemporaneous—and strenuously intellectual—interests begins to develop.

Much of the worldly "intercourse" opened up by the *Twice-told Tales* requires no arcane research to discover. The signature of that work identified Hawthorne, as an *author,* to the notably intellectual Peabody sisters of Salem. To the least assertive of these sisters, Sophia, Hawthorne soon became engaged, even as the far more aggressive Elizabeth was working to advance his (perilous) claim to political patronage from the Jacksonian Democratic Party. Though the years 1839 and 1840 seem most clearly marked by the outpouring of love letters Hawthorne wrote to his fiancée while he held the uncongenial post of Customs Inspector for the Port of Boston, it is worth remembering that the first of Hawthorne's extended works for children were also written at just this time; and that *The Whole History of Grandfather's Chair* (as this three-part history of Massachusetts was later to be entitled) offers a useful hint about the world Hawthorne had entered. Though the matter of the Puritans and of the Revolution was familiar and even backward-looking, the purpose was new, as Hawthorne clearly thought of his subtle but largely unironic re-retelling as a contribution to the reform of education, itself part of a larger "ferment" of protest which has seemed to define American social history in the 1840s. Evidently Hawthorne agreed with Horace Mann, the reformer about to marry yet another of the Peabody sisters, that it matters very much what children are given to read.

Other recognitions and agreements might not come so easily in Hawthorne's new environment. Boston, including its intellectual suburbs of Unitarian Cambridge and Transcendental Concord, was a vastly wider, more vibrant and fluid world than Salem had ever been. Having invested many of his summers traveling around New England, and having pressed one of his tours as far as Detroit, Hawthorne was of course no Robin Molineux; he had even spent six months in 1836 in New England's "metropolis," editing the *American Magazine of Useful and Entertaining Knowledge*. Such experiences could hardly fail to widen one's horizon. But this was different. For Hawthorne was now, in fact if not by personal preference, a part of the political machine; like it or not, he had to socialize with Bancroft. And though he tried to stand aside from the current of transcendental Lectures and feminist Conversations, his new relations inevitably drew him in: Sophia was herself an ardent enthusiast of Emersonian idealism; and Elizabeth Peabody, who had been secretary to William Ellery Channing (Emerson's Unitarian "bishop") and then assistant at the notoriously experimental school of Bronson Alcott (Emerson's Platonic "saint"), seemed to be at the center of everything connected with what people fell into calling "the Newness." She even wrote some of the public relations material for Brook Farm, George Ripley's transcendental commune at Roxbury, which she liked to describe as "Christ's idea of society."

Abruptly enough, therefore, a studious, somewhat reclusive, and intensely shy young man and writer—younger in social experience than his thirty-five years—was set down in close proximity to the center of a self-conscious "Renaissance," to which he would soon begin to make his own considerable contribution, but which was begun well before he arrived and would have been, even without his participation, one of the most significant intellectual and social awakenings in American history. Sooner or later our "moral historian" would have to estimate the mentality of his own generation of Transcendental Seekers, most of whom seemed more than a little puritanic still.

Yet it seems equally predictable that the *public* response did not come at once: over seventy tales and sketches had got themselves published by January 1839, but the new flood (of almost two dozen) does not begin until the middle of 1842. No doubt the unaccustomed routine of a Custom House was part of the reason for this long hiatus. So too the burden of physical labor Hawthorne exuberantly undertook when, unlike Emerson, he made himself a charter member of Brook Farm, in April 1841. Possibly

sharing Ripley's enthusiastic desire "to insure a more natural union between intellectual and manual labor than now exists," and certainly trying
to establish a style of life that would permit an ill-paid author to support a
wife, Hawthorne was nevertheless reporting by June that "this present life
gives me an antipathy to pen and ink, even more than my Custom House
experience did." And though he continued in residence through the end of
the year, his decision to leave is perfectly forecast in his observation that "a
man's soul may be buried and perish under a dungheap . . . as well as
under a pile of money." Equally relevant, however, is the available inference that it took Hawthorne a while to isolate his new center of thematic
interest, that he in fact required the intellectual experience of Brook Farm
to discover it.

Such is certainly the impression left by *The Blithedale Romance,* the most
obvious and direct literary outcome of Hawthorne's encounter with "the
community" of Brook Farm. Though most criticism now rightly treats Miles
Coverdale (the narrator of that later work) as an altogether ironic version of
Hawthorne himself, it remains true that Coverdale redundantly speaks the
sentiments of Hawthorne's letters and notebooks from this period. And a
significant stretch of intellectual biography seems plainly announced by
Coverdale's account of his initiation into the rhetoric of Newness:

I read interminably in Mr. Emerson's Essays, the Dial, Carlyle's works,
George Sand's romances, . . . and other books which one or another of the
brethren or sisterhood had brought with them. Agreeing in little else,
most of these utterances were like the cry of some solitary sentinel, whose
station was on the outposts of the advance-guard of human progres-
sion. . . . They were well adapted . . . to pilgrims like ourselves, whose
present bivouac was considerably farther into the waste of chaos than any
mortal army of crusaders had ever marched before.

Not that the stay at Brook Farm absolutely originated Hawthorne's experience of Emerson and his contemporaries, or that this brief list at all
exhausts the extent of his eventual familiarity. Yet some deep structure of
personal revelation seems abundantly clear: metaphorically, at least, it was
indeed "but well to be on friendly terms with all the inmates of the place
one lodges in." And further, if more literally, we should be surprised if
Hawthorne did not learn, from Ripley and others, the significant moral
and literary history of their decision to begin human life anew.

Once again, however, it is the allusive texture of the tales themselves which best indicates Hawthorne's newly updated thematic interest. Most challenging is the case of "Rappaccini's Daughter" (1844), which demands structural comparison with "Young Goodman Brown" (published just ahead of it in the *Mosses*) and yet insists on its own separate context and application. Its whimsical "Aubépine" introduction makes an only faintly disguised reference to Ripley's aggressively transcendental *Specimens of Modern Standard Literature* (1838), just before lamenting that, under one name or another, "the Transcendentalists have their share in all the current literature in the world." More internally still, the tale which follows—a painful faith-test for an elaborately misprepared Giovanni Guasconti—deploys Ripley's own logic of faith and evidence, in the very late-Renaissance world where modern skepticism and fideism were certifiably twin-born. The full import of the Paduan setting has required a rare mix of scholarly patience and readerly acumen fully to reconstruct; but the narrator's tendentious emphasis on Giovanni's failure to regard his intuitive "better evidence" plainly recalls the public battle over "miracles" which all the best and brightest young Transcendentalists had recently waged against the empiricism of their Unitarian mentors at Harvard.

Yet Ripley was scarcely the master spirit of America's Transcendental age, as most observers could recognize even then. It was, after all, Emerson who had delivered "The American Scholar" as Harvard's Phi Beta Kappa Address in 1837; and of course it was Emerson whom the divinity students asked to preach their graduation address in 1838. The studied but also uneasy ambivalences of that latter performance must certainly lie behind the problem which a "Giant Transcendentalist" creates for the latter-day pilgrims of Hawthorne's "Celestial Rail-road" (1843): they hardly know "whether to be encouraged or affrighted" by the wondrous mixture of ideal affirmation and historic denial. More centrally still, the insistent allusions of "The Hall of Fantasy" (1843) appear to identify the Emersonian philosophy as the most radical "apocalypse" of them all: the biblical speculations of a certain "Father Miller" may predict the immanent foreclosing of mankind's earthly career, but elsewhere—in Emerson's *Nature* (1836), for example—"the Idea" has already been declared to be "all in all." Emerson outgrew the arrogance, if not the idealism, of his early speculations, as every reader of his essay "Experience" (1844) is well aware. Still, Hawthorne's "Christmas Banquet" (1844) exists to notice that the psychological consequences of worldly denial are not so easy to unsay, as the puritanic self-absorption of "Egotism; or the Bosom Serpent" (1843) lapses to a positively schizophrenic sense of universal unreality. Possibly Emerson's philosophic cure was somehow worse than its correlative disease; perhaps a guilty identity *was* better than none.

For a more literal treatment of Emerson, the reader will have to turn (elsewhere) to "The Old Manse" (1846), a lengthy and revealing piece of fictionalized autobiography Hawthorne wrote to summarize his entire experience of Transcendental Concord, and to introduce the *Mosses*. Compressing several years of life into a single turning of the seasons, Hawthorne lovingly evokes the house and grounds, and also the historic associations, of the parsonage or "manse" to which he moved in the summer of 1842, just after his long delayed marriage to Sophia Peabody; and biographers have always used this work—along with another, less overtly personal sketch entitled "The New Adam and Eve" (1843)—to celebrate the bliss of Hawthorne's wedded life, and to elaborate his profound commitment to conservative values. Of equal significance is Hawthorne's strategic placement of himself, in the midst of a remarkable literary society that included, among many others, Bronson Alcott, Ellery Channing (the younger), and Henry David Thoreau, all swirling around the "great original thinker, who had his earthly abode at the opposite extremity of our village."

The formulation is literally accurate, as any visitor to present-day Concord may pleasantly discover. And it leads on to the personal confession that, "being happy," Hawthorne felt no need just then to ask "of this prophet the word that should solve . . . the riddle of the universe." Also suggested, however, is Hawthorne's own sense of his relation to Emerson and his various Transcendental disciples: he is among them, quite clearly, as Concord is but a village; and friendly, to the appearances of outward sociability; sharing, as F. O. Matthiessen well observed, a common aspiration for the democracy of American life and letters; yet he is opposite their metaphysical interest in a way he trusted only his fictions to express.

Most noticeably, perhaps, Hawthorne continued to uphold his classic principle that literature is a shared experience rather than a private or purely subjective concern. Utterly skeptical about the discoverability, perhaps even the existence, of some occult entity called "the Self," Hawthorne explicitly denies that he is "one of those supremely hospitable people who serve up their hearts, delicately fried, with brain sauce, as a tidbit for their beloved public." In fact, he resisted, as no other writer of his Romantic age, the temptation to make literature out of his own "soul." Appearing to answer the studied egotism of *Walden* in advance, "The Old Manse" invites its readers, at last, not to the personal intimacy of confession but to the dramatic interest of *some stories,* most of which turn out to suggest where the logic of the Newness might lead, if anyone dared follow its lead alone: to the "liberal" escape, in the "Rail-road," from the sense of sin and suffering; to the "apocalyptic" denial, in the "Hall," that the facts of life impose any final restraint on the autonomous life of the "fantasy"; and to the "idealist" and rather chilling discovery, in the "Banquet," that a self without relation is an empty philosophical construct and a deadly human end.

This last theme—of the ineluctable relationality of all personal exis-tence—may fairly be regarded as Hawthorne's own thematic "bottom line," everywhere, uniting works from all his later phases with earlier, puritanic manifestations such as "The Man of Adamant" (1837) and even "The Minister's Black Veil." Nor is it entirely misguided to regard the sobering tale of "Wakefield" as a sort of once-for-all abstraction of this variously adumbrated but repeatedly recurring psychological in-sight. Yet it is equally important to recognize that this one master idea lends structure to a significant variety of historical experiences; that in the "Old Manse" period it often mixes with and sometimes yields place to an altogether "timely" consideration only hinted at earlier, in his observations of the deadly hatred which the religious idealism of the Puritans regularly directed at all things merely "natural"; and that in fact some "death by idealism" emerges as the controlling theme of Hawthorne's anti-transcendental efforts of the 1840s.

The same spirit that unites Emerson with Father Miller—a sort of neopuritanical hatred of the merely existent—appears to motivate the pro-ject of radical reform as Hawthorne represents it in "Earth's Holocaust" (1844). An altogether unstable narrator ends by proposing, conservatively, that the notoriously American effort to purify the world will fail unless the human heart itself should undergo its own prior purgation. But the shape of the drama suggests the more radical possibility that some terrific lust for perfection will remain insatiate as long as any human trace remains; that the enthusiasm which had sponsored, in 1840, an entirely nonspecific "Convention of the Friends of Universal Reform" might be content with nothing less than the burning of the whole earth and all its heart-of-flesh inhabitants. And surely that dire hint is more than confirmed by "The Birth-mark" (1843), where the spiritual aspirations of contemporary "metascience" rise up to a monomania as dangerous to "the world's body" as the cosmic paranoia of Melville's Ahab.

Feminist critics may fairly notice that it is a hapless but worshipful wife who is elected to reveal the mark of fleshly imperfection and on whom, accordingly, the maddened Aylmer must perform his insane experiment. Yet as this gesture is itself problematized, it seems fair to suggest that it too is part of Hawthorne's historical *donnée,* especially as the tale appears to make more than a glancing reference to the "Ligeia" of Edgar Poe, whose Platonism repeatedly epitomized itself in the "most poetic" theme of the "death of a beautiful woman." Evidently Hawthorne wished to observe that certain Western, even Christian attitudes toward "Woman" are embedded in the language often used to express "Man's" more than Faustian desire for symbolic transcendence. Probably, if the truth were known, Aylmer's own body, born of woman, bore some small natal scar of its own; yet of this possibility we hear nothing. Nor would Hawthorne's idealist, and untrustworthy, narrator know what to make of an (untold) tale in which a wife, scientist or not, seeks perfection in neutralizing the flesh of a husband *almost* worthy of adoration.

The explicitly sexual implications of idealism are perfectly evident in "Rappaccini's Daughter," of course, where once again (in the memorable phrase of D. H. Lawrence) "Woman is the nemesis of doubting man"; but probably it is "The Artist of the Beautiful" (1844) which most directly extends Aylmer's treacherous logic of insatiable aspiration. No one dies, to be sure. And Owen's precious "Annie" seems happy enough bearing the babies of the local blacksmith. But Owen is left with the austere discovery that the platonizing artist achieves nothing beyond his own "spirit"; and his world is left without any credible figure of the service which celibates of "the beautiful" might render the rest of the endlessly prolific human community. Emerson's "The Transcendentalist" (1844) might venture to suggest, boldly or shrilly, the high religious benefit of watching the holy watchers; but evidently Hawthorne remained committed to an art which produced "objects" for popular consumption, even if we do tend to crush the butterfly.

Thus Hawthorne's historicism continued. Not only thematically, as in the self-embarrassed protests of the narrator of "The Hall of Fantasy" in favor of the endurability of the "great, round, solid self" of the world, themselves in echo of Hawthorne's own more private expressions of satisfaction (in his notebooks) with the swelling roundness of Sophia's pregnant belly; but formally as well, in his continuing concern to tell the tale of present-day attempts to nullify the world's material being. "The Old Manse" ends by regretting that the Concord years had produced "no profound treatise of ethics, no philosophic history, no novel even, that could stand on its own unsupported edges." We know, as Hawthorne could not, that the novels would come—even if the dazzling *Scarlet Letter* would require the quizzical "Custom-House" to stand without tipping. Even so, however, the rhetoric protests too much, as Hawthorne surely hoped his kindest readers would notice. For the art of telling America's "moral history" had gone right on, with undiminished seriousness: interrupted, no doubt, by an extended time out for worldly work; but augmented, as well, by the discovery that the Transcendentalist logic of "idea" had solved the problem of the world no better than the Puritan premise of "grace."

After 1846 Hawthorne published only a handful of new tales, and indeed "The Old Manse" explicitly promises that the *Mosses* will be the author's "last collection of this nature." Possibly Hawthorne was already meditating a second, more remunerative career, as novelist. Or perhaps he felt some more artistic sense of diminishing returns in the ironic short form he had both invented and perfected: "Unless I could do better, I have done enough in this kind." In any case, the promise was substantially kept.

The Scarlet Letter seems once to have been intended for inclusion in a collection to be titled "Old-Time Legends; together with sketches, experimental and ideal." But then, of course, "The Custom-House" came along to help it stand alone. Subsequently, *The Snow-Image* (1851) gathered up the four tales Hawthorne had produced in 1849 and 1850; but as the volume is filled out with a much larger number of earlier pieces hitherto uncollected, the whole seems more a publishing convenience than a literary project. And the second edition of the *Mosses* (1854) continues this same activity of universal self-collection—largely at the urging of now eager editors, and at some prejudice to the anti-transcendental unity of that remarkable work. By that date, of course, Hawthorne was the accomplished author of his "Three American Romances" and, searching in England for the theme of yet another extended romantic fiction, he was proportionately less concerned about the significance of his "obscure" years.

Of the post-1846 tales, several were solicited by friendly magazine editors. At least one, "The Snow-Image" (1850), was explicitly designated a "childish" performance; and it may be that "The Great Stone Face"

(1850) was also meant to reach Hawthorne's secondary audience of youthful readers. An extended sketch called "Main-Street" (1849) reveals once again the full wickedness of Hawthorne's mature historical irony, but it reads best as a self-conscious defense of the earlier career as "moral" (rather than "positivistic") historian of the Puritans; or else as a self-imposed review of the Puritan themes to be reactivated in *The Scarlet Letter*. And as it remains perfectly safe to regard "Ethan Brand" (1850) just as Hawthorne subtitled it, "A Chapter from an Abortive Romance," so it seems fair to accept the 1846 *Mosses* as a sort of formal conclusion to Hawthorne's career as writer and collector of tales and sketches. The novels were delayed, of course—in part, at least, by the second and more famous tour of custom-house service. But when they came, they came in a bunch. And in coming to constitute a sort of "Major Phase," they have fully overshadowed the last, scattered attempts at short fiction.

Yet no survey of Hawthorne's tales can afford to omit "Ethan Brand"— not only because it may signal Hawthorne's first, unsuccessful transition from tale to romance, but also, and more significantly, because it makes clear, one last time, that Hawthorne's most romantic imaginings are never quite free of historical source and local application. One powerful reason for believing "Ethan Brand" indeed survives as but a fragment of a longer work is that it draws on and virtually exausts the wealth of particular observation Hawthorne had set down in a 50,000-word notebook of his 1838 trip to western Massachusetts: bad policy, if one brief tale were all he had origi-nally intended. But the best reason for valuing the actual achievement of "Ethan Brand" is that in it all this "local color" is deployed in the career of an American Faust who has never ceased to be a Puritan, if only *malgré lui*.

When we ask, as we must, what it means for Ethan Brand to have begun his notorious search for the "unpardonable sin" in a spirit not of arrogance but of brotherhood, the answer keeps coming back that—like Melville's Ahab, whose creation he plainly helped to inspire—Brand has hoped to act as a sort of representative human hero, a kind of latter-day, backwoods New England Prometheus. Fire having already been snatched from the jealous gods, and long since harnessed to the civilized arts of environmental engineering, what daring task remained? Or else, more defiantly formu-lated, what secret remained, within the fire, to remind the brooding humanist of the awful uncertainty that still enshrouded human life? Not death, apparently, but only the knowledge of that one supposed sin which of its very nature defied the mercy of even a thoroughly encovenanted Jehova. Perhaps the secret was not entirely past finding out.

No doubt the question was, in itself, impious in the last degree, like Ahab's monomaniac inquisition into the mystery of universal iniquity. No doubt Brand looked "*too long* into the fire." So that the fiery conclusion—of suicide at the moment of cosmic blasphemy—may seem predictable enough. Yet the sense of triumph over all the world's "half-way" sinners is one that would have to develop. Himself, at last, a "Brand [Un]Plucked from the Burning," still this ultimate neopuritan rebel appears to have begun with a concern for the reason of human despair as plausible as that of Cotton Mather himself. Nor, as the insistent allusions to writers of the Enlightenment and of Romanticism make clear, had the matter of malignity been entirely settled or left behind; from which observation, we may infer, the author of *Moby-Dick* took considerable aid and comfort.

If Hawthorne's own effort proved "abortive," the explanation must surely lie in some temperamental inability to sustain a Melvillean protest against the enduring legacy of Calvinist orthodoxy. More historical than speculative, finally, Hawthorne's circumspect intelligence could see at once that the transcendence promised by perfect negation was as illusory as any other: one denied what one knew, then lapsed to the elements of universal process. Others endured, if not to tell the tale, at least to gather up the fragments.

Appropriately, therefore, *The Scarlet Letter*—the first and most compelling of the longer fictions—would return to the world whose moral shape Hawthorne knew best, the world of the Puritans as it functioned in the second decade of John Winthrop's model "City on a Hill." The laws of this would-be Utopia are strict, but they are known; and sinners must bear the burden of social cause and effect. No one need wish, as Hawthorne makes clear in "Main-Street," to repeat the *lives* of ancestors whom experience had taught so much "amiss": Winthrop's vaunted "liberty" seemed more "like an iron cage," and its "rigidity" appears to have generated even further "distortions of the moral nature." Yet the *tale* might still be retold, if only to illustrate the moral premise of historicism as such: even the most repressive ideologies had seemed like a good idea at the time; and no "self" entirely escapes the limits of its correlative world.

Not even the artist escapes. His domain might be divided between past and present, inner and outer. But gestures of ultimacy remained empty. His subject could be only his own world-in-process. And America was no exception.

A Note on the Text

All the texts printed here are those established by the Centenary Edition of Hawthorne's *Works* (Columbus: Ohio State University Press): *Twice-told Tales* (IX, 1974); *Mosses from an Old Manse* (X, 1974); *The Snow-Image and Uncollected Tales* (XI, 1974); and the forthcoming *Miscellany*. The sequence of printing, however, reflects the order of their first magazine or gift-book appearance. With two exceptions: "The Notch of the White Mountains" (Nov., 1835) appears as introductory to "The Ambitious Guest" (June, 1835); and "The Christmas Banquet" (Jan., 1844) is placed as immediate sequel to "Egotism; or, The Bosom-Serpent" (Mar., 1843).

SELECTED TALES
AND SKETCHES

The Hollow of the Three Hills

IN those strange old times, when fantastic dreams and mad-
men's reveries were realized among the actual circumstances of
life, two persons met together at an appointed hour and place.
One was a lady, graceful in form and fair of feature, though
pale and troubled, and smitten with an untimely blight in
what should have been the fullest bloom of her years; the other
was an ancient and meanly dressed woman, of ill-favored aspect, and so withered, shrunken and decrepit, that even the
space since she began to decay must have exceeded the ordinary
term of human existence. In the spot where they encountered,
no mortal could observe them. Three little hills stood near
each other, and down in the midst of them sunk a hollow basin, almost mathematically circular, two or three hundred feet
in breadth, and of such depth that a stately cedar might but
just be visible above the sides. Dwarf pines were numerous
upon the hills, and partly fringed the outer verge of the inter-
mediate hollow; within which there was nothing but the
brown grass of October, and here and there a tree-trunk, that
had fallen long ago, and lay mouldering with no green successor from its roots. One of these masses of decaying wood, formerly a majestic oak, rested close beside a pool of green and
sluggish water at the bottom of the basin. Such scenes as this
(so gray tradition tells) were once the resort of a Power of Evil
and his plighted subjects; and here, at midnight or on the dim
verge of evening, they were said to stand round the mantling

pool, disturbing its putrid waters in the performance of an impious baptismal rite. The chill beauty of an autumnal sunset was now gilding the three hill-tops, whence a paler tint stole down their sides into the hollow.

"Here is our pleasant meeting come to pass," said the aged crone, "according as thou hast desired. Say quickly what thou wouldst have of me, for there is but a short hour that we may tarry here."

As the old withered woman spoke, a smile glimmered on her countenance, like lamplight on the wall of a sepulchre. The lady trembled, and cast her eyes upward to the verge of the basin, as if meditating to return with her purpose unaccomplished. But it was not so ordained.

"I am stranger in this land, as you know," said she at length. "Whence I come it matters not;—but I have left those behind me with whom my fate was intimately bound, and from whom I am cut off forever. There is a weight in my bosom that I cannot away with, and I have come hither to inquire of their welfare."

"And who is there by this green pool, that can bring thee news from the ends of the Earth?" cried the old woman, peering into the lady's face. "Not from my lips mayst thou hear these tidings; yet, be thou bold, and the daylight shall not pass away from yonder hill-top, before thy wish be granted."

"I will do your bidding though I die," replied the lady desperately.

The old woman seated herself on the trunk of the fallen tree, threw aside the hood that shrouded her gray locks, and beckoned her companion to draw near.

"Kneel down," she said, "and lay your forehead on my knees."

She hesitated a moment, but the anxiety, that had long been kindling, burned fiercely up within her. As she knelt down, the border of her garment was dipped into the pool; she laid her forehead on the old woman's knees, and the latter drew a cloak about the lady's face, so that she was in darkness. Then she heard the muttered words of a prayer, in the midst of which she started, and would have arisen.

"Let me flee,—let me flee and hide myself, that they may not look upon me!" she cried. But, with returning recollection, she hushed herself, and was still as death.

For it seemed as if other voices—familiar in infancy, and unforgotten through many wanderings, and in all the vicissitudes of her heart and fortune—were mingling with the accents of the prayer. At first the words were faint and indistinct, not rendered so by distance, but rather resembling the dim pages of a book, which we strive to read by an imperfect and gradually brightening light. In such a manner, as the prayer proceeded, did those voices strengthen upon the ear; till at length the petition ended, and the conversation of an aged man, and of a woman broken and decayed like himself, became distinctly audible to the lady as she knelt. But those strangers appeared not to stand in the hollow depth between the three hills. Their voices were encompassed and re-echoed by the walls of a chamber, the windows of which were rattling in the breeze; the regular vibration of a clock, the crackling of a fire, and the tinkling of the embers as they fell among the ashes, rendered the scene almost as vivid as if painted to the eye. By a melancholy hearth sat these two old people, the man calmly despondent, the woman querulous and tearful, and their words were all of sorrow. They spoke of a daughter, a wanderer they knew not where, bearing dishonor along with her, and leaving shame and affliction to bring their gray heads to the grave. They alluded also to other and more recent woe, but in the midst of their talk, their voices seemed to melt into the sound of the wind sweeping mournfully among the autumn leaves; and when the lady lifted her eyes, there was she kneeling in the hollow between three hills.

"A weary and lonesome time yonder old couple have of it," remarked the old woman, smiling in the lady's face.

"And did you also hear them!" exclaimed she, a sense of intolerable humiliation triumphing over her agony and fear.

"Yea; and we have yet more to hear," replied the old woman. "Wherefore, cover thy face quickly."

Again the withered hag poured forth the monotonous words of a prayer that was not meant to be acceptable in Heaven; and soon, in the pauses of her breath, strange murmurings began to thicken, gradually increasing so as to drown and overpower the charm by which they grew. Shrieks pierced through the obscurity of sound, and were succeeded by the singing of sweet female voices, which in their turn gave way to a wild roar of laughter, broken suddenly by groanings and sobs, forming altogether a ghastly confusion of terror and mourning and mirth. Chains were rattling, fierce and stern voices uttered threats, and the scourge resounded at their command. All these noises deepened and became substantial to the listener's ear, till she could distinguish every soft and dreamy accent of the love songs, that died causelessly into funeral hymns. She shuddered at the unprovoked wrath which blazed up like the spontaneous kindling of flame, and she grew faint at the fearful merriment, raging miserably around her. In the midst of this wild scene, where unbound passions jostled each other in a drunken career, there was one solemn voice of a man, and a manly and melodious voice it might once have been. He went to-and-fro continually, and his feet sounded upon the floor. In each member of that frenzied company, whose own burning thoughts had become their exclusive world, he sought an auditor for the story of his individual wrong, and interpreted their laughter and tears as his reward of scorn or pity. He spoke of woman's perfidy, of a wife who had broken her holiest vows, of a home and heart made desolate. Even as he went on, the shout, the laugh, the shriek, the sob, rose up in unison, till they changed into the hollow, fitful, and uneven sound of the wind, as it fought among the pine-trees on those three lonely hills. The lady looked up, and there was the withered woman smiling in her face.

"Couldst thou háve thought there were such merry times in a Mad House?" inquired the latter.

"True, true," said the lady to herself; "there is mirth within its walls, but misery, misery without."

"Wouldst thou hear more?" demanded the old woman.

"There is one other voice I would fain listen to again," replied the lady faintly.

"Then lay down thy head speedily upon my knees, that thou may'st get thee hence before the hour be past."

The golden skirts of day were yet lingering upon the hills, but deep shades obscured the hollow and the pool, as if sombre night were rising thence to overspread the world. Again that evil woman began to weave her spell. Long did it proceed unanswered, till the knolling of a bell stole in among the intervals of her words, like a clang that had travelled far over valley and rising ground, and was just ready to die in the air. The lady shook upon her companion's knees, as she heard that boding sound. Stronger it grew and sadder, and deepened into the tone of a death-bell, knolling dolefully from some ivy-mantled tower, and bearing tidings of mortality and woe to the cottage, to the hall, and to the solitary wayfarer, that all might weep for the doom appointed in turn to them. Then came a measured tread, passing slowly, slowly on, as of mourners with a coffin, their garments trailing on the ground, so that the ear could measure the length of their melancholy array. Before them went the priest, reading the burial-service, while the leaves of his book were rustling in the breeze. And though no voice but his was heard to speak aloud, still there were revilings and anathemas, whispered but distinct, from women and from men, breathed against the daughter who had wrung the aged hearts of her parents,—the wife who had betrayed the trusting fondness of her husband,—the mother who had sinned against natural affection, and left her child to die. The sweeping sound of the funeral train faded away like a thin vapour, and the wind, that just before had seemed to shake the coffin-pall, moaned sadly round the verge of the Hollow between three Hills. But when the old woman stirred the kneeling lady, she lifted not her head.

"Here has been a sweet hour's sport!" said the withered crone, chuckling to herself.

Sir William Phips

Few of the personages of past times (except such as have gained renown in fire-side legends as well as in written history) are anything more than mere names to their successors. They seldom stand up in our Imaginations like men. The knowledge, communicated by the historian and biographer, is analogous to that which we acquire of a country by the map,—minute, perhaps, and accurate, and available for all necessary purposes,—but cold and naked, and wholly destitute of the mimic charm produced by landscape painting. These defects are partly remediable, and even without an absolute violation of literal truth, although by methods rightfully interdicted to professors of biographical exactness. A license must be assumed in brightening the materials which time has rusted, and in tracing out the half-obliterated inscriptions on the columns of antiquity; fancy must throw her reviving light on the faded incidents that indicate character, whence a ray will be reflected, more or less vividly, on the person to be described. The portrait of the ancient Governor, whose name stands at the head of this article, will owe any interest it may possess, not to his internal self, but to certain peculiarities of his fortune. These must be briefly noticed.

The birth and early life of Sir William Phips were rather an extraordinary prelude to his subsequent distinction. He was one of the twenty six children of a gun-smith, who exercised his trade—where hunting and war must have given it a full encouragement—in a small frontier settlement near the mouth of the river Keunebec. Within the boundaries of the Puritan provinces, and wherever those governments extended an effectual sway, no depth nor solitude of the wilderness could exclude youth from all the common opportunities of moral, and far more than common ones of religious education. Each settlement of the Pilgrims was a little piece of the old world, inserted into the new,—it was like Gideon's fleece, unwet with dew,—the desert wind, that breathed over it, left none of its wild influences there. But the first settlers of Maine and New-Hampshire were led thither entirely by carnal motives; their governments were feeble, uncertain, sometimes nominally annexed to their sister colonies, and sometimes asserting a troubled independence; their rulers might be deemed, in more than one instance, lawless adventurers, who found that security in the forest which they had forfeited in Europe. Their clergy (unlike that revered band who acquired so singular a fame elsewhere in New-England) were too often destitute of the religious fervor which should have kept them in the track of virtue, unaided by the restraints of human law and the dread of worldly dishonor; and there are records of lamentable lapses on the part of those holy men, which, if we may argue the disorder of the sheep from the unfitness of the shepherd, tell a sad tale as to the morality of the eastern provinces. In this state of society the future governor grew up, and many years after, sailing with a fleet and an army to make war upon the French, he pointed out the very hills where he had reached the age of manhood, unskilled even to read and write. The contrast between the commencement and close of his life was the effect of casual circumstances. During a considerable time, he was a mariner, at a period when there was much license on the high seas. After attaining to some rank in the English navy, he heard of an ancient Spanish wreck off the coast of Hispaniola, of such mighty value, that, according to the stories of the day, the sunken gold might be seen to glisten and the diamonds to flash, as the triumphant billows tossed about their spoil. These treasures of the deep (by the aid of certain noblemen, who claimed the lion's share) Sir William Phips sought for, and recovered, and was sufficiently enriched, even after an honest settlement with the partners of his adventure. That the land might give him honor, as the sea had given him wealth, he received knighthood from King James. Returning to New-England, he professed repentance of his sins, (of which, from the nature both of his early and more recent life, there could scarce fail to be some slight accumulation) was baptized, and, on the accession of the Prince of Orange to the throne, became the first governor under the second charter. And now, having arranged these preliminaries, we shall attempt to picture forth a day of Sir William's life, introducing no very remarkable events, because history supplies us with none such, convertible to our purpose.

It is the forenoon of a day in summer, shortly after the governor's arrival, and he stands upon his door-steps, preparatory to a walk through the metropolis. Sir William is a stout man, an inch or two below the middle size, and rather beyond the middle point of life; his dress is of velvet, a dark purple, broadly embroidered, and his sword-hilt, and the lion's head of his cane display specimens of the gold from the Spanish wreck; on his head, in the fashion of the court of Louis XIV, is a superb full-bottomed periwig, amid whose heap of ringlets his face shows like a rough pebble in the setting that befits a diamond. Just emerging from the door are two footmen, one an African slave of shining ebony, the other an English bond-servant, the property of the governor for a term of years. As Sir William comes down the steps, he is met by three elderly gentlemen in black, grave and solemn as three tombstones on a ramble from the burying ground. These are ministers of the town, among whom we recognize Dr. Increase Mather, the late provincial agent at the English court, the author of the present governor's appointment, and the right arm of his administration. Here follow many bows and a deal of angular politeness on both sides.

Sir William professes his anxiety to re-enter the house and give audience to the reverend gentlemen; they, on the other hand, cannot think of interrupting his walk; and the courteous dispute is concluded by a junction of the parties, Sir William and Dr. Mather setting forth side by side, the two other clergymen forming the centre of the column, and the black and white footmen bringing up the rear. The business in hand relates to the dealings of Satan in the town of Salem. Upon this subject the principal ministers of the province have been consulted, and these three eminent persons are their deputies, commissioned to express a doubtful opinion, implying upon the whole an exhortation to speedy and vigorous measures against the accused. To such councils, Sir William, bred in the forest and on the ocean, and tinctured with the superstitions of both, is well inclined to listen.

As the dignitaries of church and state make their way beneath the overhanging houses, the lattices are thrust ajar, and you may discern, just in the boundaries of light and shade, the prim faces of the little puritan damsels, eyeing the magnificent governor, and envious of the bolder curiosity of the men. Another object of almost equal interest, now appears in the middle of the way. It is a man clad in a hunting shirt and Indian stockings, and armed with a long gun; his feet have been wet with the waters of many an inland lake and stream, and the leaves and twigs of the tangled wilderness are intertwined with his garments; on his head he wears a trophy which we would not venture to record without good evidence of the fact,—a wig made of the long and straight black hair of his slain savage enemies. This grim old heathen stands bewildered in the midst of King-street. The governor regards him attentively, and recognizing a playmate of his youth, accosts him with a gracious smile, inquires as to the prosperity of their birth place and the life or death of their ancient neighbors, and makes appropriate remarks on the different stations allotted by fortune to two individuals, born and bred beside the same wild river. Finally, he puts into his hand, at parting, a shilling of the Massachusetts coinage, stamped with the figure of a stubbed pine tree, mistaken by King Charles for the oak which saved his royal life. Then all the people praise the humility and bountifulness of the good governor, who struts onward flourishing his gold-headed cane, while the gentleman in the straight black wig is left with a pretty accurate idea of the distance between himself and his old companion.

Meantime Sir William steers his course towards the town dock. A gallant figure is seen approaching on the opposite side of the street in a naval uniform profusely laced, and with a cutlass swinging by his side. This is Captain Short, the commander of a frigate in the service of the English King, now lying in the harbor. Sir William bristles up at sight of him, and crosses the street with a lowering front, unmindful of the hints of Dr. Mather, who is aware of an unsettled dispute between the captain and the governor, relative to the authority of the latter over a king's ship on the provincial station. Into this thorny subject Sir William plunges headlong; the captain makes answer with less deference than the dignity of the potentate requires; the affair grows hot, and the clergymen endeavor to interfere in the blessed capacity of peacemakers. The governor lifts his cane, and the captain lays his hand upon his sword, but is prevented from drawing by the zealous exertions of Doctor Mather; there is a furious stamping of feet, and a mighty uproar from every mouth, in the midst of which his Excellency inflicts several very sufficient whacks on the head of the unhappy Short. Having thus avenged himself by manual force, as befits a woodsman and a mariner, he vindicates the insulted majesty of the governor by committing his antagonist to prison. This done, Sir William removes his periwig, wipes away the sweat of the encounter, and gradually composes himself, giving vent to a few oaths, like the subsiding ebullitions of a pot that has boiled over.

It being now near twelve o'clock, the three ministers are bidden to dinner at the governor's table, where the party is completed by a few Old-Charter Senators, men reared at the feet of the pilgrims, and who remember the days when Cromwell was a nursing father to New England. Sir William presides with commendable decorum till grace is said, and the cloth removed. Then, as the grape-juice glides warm into the ventricles of his heart, it produces a change like that of a running stream upon enchanted shapes, and the rude man of the sea and wilderness appears in the very chair where the stately governor sat down. He overflows with jovial tales of the forecastle and of his father's hut, and stares to see the gravity of his guests become more and more portentous, in exact proportion as his own merriment increases. A noise of drum and fife fortunately breaks up the session.

The governor and his guests go forth, like men bound upon some grave business, to inspect the train-bands of the town. A great crowd of people is collected on the common, composed of whole families, from the hoary grandsire to the child of three years old; all ages and both sexes look with interest on the array of their defenders; and here and there stand a few dark Indians in their blankets, dull spectators of the strength that has swept away their race. The soldiers wear a proud and martial mien, conscious that beauty will reward them with her approving glances;—not to mention that there are a few less influential motives which contribute to keep up an heroic spirit, such as the dread of being made to 'ride the wooden horse,' (a very disagreeable mode of equestrian exercise,—hard riding, in the strictest sense,) or of being 'laid neck and heels,' in a position of more compendiousness than comfort. Sir William perceives some error in their tactics, and places himself with drawn sword at their head. After a variety of weary evolutions, evening begins to fall, like the veil of gray and misty years that have rolled betwixt that warlike band and us. They are drawn into a hollow square, the officers in the centre, and the governor (for John Dunton's authority will bear us out in this particular) leans his hands upon his sword-hilt, and closes the exercises of the day with a prayer.

Mrs. Hutchinson

THE character of this female suggests a train of thought which will form as natural an introduction to her story as most of the prefaces to Gay's Fables or the tales of Prior, besides that the general soundness of the moral may excuse any want of present applicability. We will not look for a living resemblance of Mrs. Hutchinson, though the search might not be altogether fruitless.—But there are portentous indications, changes gradually taking place in the habits and feelings of the gentle sex, which seem to threaten our posterity with many of those public women, whereof one was a burthen too grievous for our fathers. The press, however, is now the medium through which feminine ambition chiefly manifests itself, and we will not anticipate the period, (trusting to be gone hence ere it arrive,) when fair orators shall be as numerous as the fair authors of our own day. The hastiest glance may show, how much of the texture and body of cis-atlantic literature is the work of those slender fingers, from which only a light and fanciful embroidery has heretofore been required, that might sparkle upon the garment without enfeebling the web. Woman's intellect should never give the tone to that of man, and even her morality is not exactly the material for masculine virtue. A false liberality which mistakes the strong division lines of Nature for arbitrary distinctions, and a courtesy, which might polish criticism but should never soften it, have done their best to add a girlish feebleness to the tottering infancy of our literature. The evil is likely to be a growing one. As yet, the great body of American women are a domestic race; but when a continuance of ill-judged incitements shall have turned their hearts away from the fireside, there are obvious circumstances which will render female pens more numerous and more prolific than those of men, though but equally encouraged; and (limited of course by the scanty support of the public, but increasing indefinitely within those limits) the ink-stained Amazons will expel their rivals by actual pressure, and petticoats wave triumphant over all the field. But, allowing that such forebodings are slightly exaggerated, is it good for woman's self that the path of feverish hope, of tremulous success, of bitter and ignominious disappointment, should be left wide open to her? Is the prize worth her having if she win it? Fame does not increase the peculiar respect which men pay to female excellence, and there is a delicacy, (even in rude bosoms, where few would think to find it) that perceives, or fancies, a sort of impropriety in the display of woman's naked mind to the gaze of the world, with indications by which its inmost secrets may be searched out. In fine, criticism should examine with a stricter, instead of a more indulgent eye, the merits of females at its bar, because they are to justify themselves for an irregularity which men do not commit in appearing there; and woman, when she feels the impulse of genius like a command of Heaven within her, should be aware that she is relinquishing a part of the loveliness of her sex, and obey the inward voice with sorrowing reluctance, like the Arabian maid who bewailed the gift of Prophecy. Hinting thus imperfectly at sentiments which may be developed on a future occasion, we proceed to consider the celebrated subject of this sketch.

Mrs. Hutchinson was a woman of extraordinary talent and strong imagination, whom the latter quality, following the general direction taken by the enthusiasm of the times, prompted to stand forth as a reformer in religion. In her native country, she had shown symptoms of irregular and daring thought, but, chiefly by the influence of a favorite pastor, was restrained from open indiscretion. On the removal of this clergyman, becoming dissatisfied with the ministry under which she lived, she was drawn in by the great tide of Puritan emigration, and visited Massachusetts within a few years after its first settlement. But she bore trouble in her own bosom, and could find no peace in this chosen land.—She soon began to promulgate strange and dangerous opinions, tending, in the peculiar situation of the colony, and from the principles which were its basis and indispensable for its temporary support, to eat into its very existence. We shall endeavor to give a more practical idea of this part of her course.

It is a summer evening. The dusk has settled heavily upon the woods, the waves, and the Trimontane peninsula, increasing that dismal aspect of the embryo town which was said to have drawn tears of despondency from Mrs. Hutchinson, though she believed that her mission thither was divine. The houses, straw-thatched and lowly roofed, stand irregularly along streets that are yet roughened by the roots of the trees, as if the forest, departing at the approach of man, had left its reluctant foot prints behind. Most of the dwellings are lonely and silent; from a few we may hear the reading of some sacred text, or the quiet voice of prayer; but nearly all the sombre life of the scene is collected near the extremity of the village. A crowd of hooded women, and of men in steeple-hats and close cropt hair, are assembled at the door and open windows of a house newly built. An earnest expression glows in every face, and some press inward as if the bread of life were to be dealt forth, and they feared to lose their share, while others would fain hold them back, but enter with them since they may not be restrained. We also will go in, edging through the thronged doorway to an apartment which occupies the whole breadth of the house. At the upper end, behind a table on which are placed the Scriptures and two glimmering lamps, we see a woman, plainly attired as befits her ripened years; her hair, complexion, and eyes are dark, the latter somewhat dull and heavy, but kindling up with a gradual brightness. Let us look round upon the hearers. At her right hand, his countenance suiting well with the gloomy light which discovers it, stands Vane the youthful governor, preferred by a hasty judgment of the people over all the wise and hoary heads that had preceded him to New-England. In his mysterious eyes we may read a dark enthusiasm, akin to that of the woman whose cause he has espoused, combined with a shrewd worldly foresight, which tells him that her doctrines will be productive of change and tumult, the elements of his power and delight. On her left, yet slightly drawn back so as to evince a less decided support, is Cotton, no young and hot enthusiast, but a mild, grave man in the decline of life, deep in all the learning of the age, and sanctified in heart and made venerable in feature by the long exercise of his holy profession. He also is deceived by the strange fire now laid upon the altar, and he alone among his brethren is excepted in the denunciation of the new Apostle, as sealed and set apart by Heaven to the work of the ministry. Others of the priesthood stand full in front of the woman, striving to beat her down with brows of wrinkled iron, and whispering sternly and significantly among themselves, as she unfolds her seditious doctrines and grows warm in their support. Foremost is Hugh Peters, full of holy wrath, and scarce containing himself from rushing forward to convict her of damnable heresies; there also is Ward, meditating a reply of empty puns, and quaint antitheses, and tinkling jests that puzzle us with nothing but a sound. The audience are variously affected, but none indifferent. On the foreheads of the aged, the mature, and strong-minded, you may generally read steadfast disapprobation, though here and there is one, whose faith seems shaken in those whom he had trusted for years; the females, on the other hand, are shuddering and weeping, and at times they cast a desolate look of fear around them; while the young men lean forward, fiery and impatient, fit instruments for whatever rash deed may be suggested. And what is the eloquence that gives rise to all these passions? The woman tells them, (and cites texts from the Holy Book to prove her words,) that they have put their trust in unregenerated and uncommissioned men, and have followed them into the wilderness for naught. Therefore their hearts are turning from those whom they had chosen to lead them to Heaven, and they feel like children who have been enticed far from home, and see the features of their guides change all at once, assuming a fiendish shape in some frightful solitude.

These proceedings of Mrs. Hutchinson could not long be endured by the provincial government. The present was a most remarkable case, in which religious freedom was wholly inconsistent with public safety, and where the principles of an illiberal age indicated the very course which must have been pursued by worldly policy and enlightened wisdom. Unity of faith was the star that had guided these people over the deep, and a diversity of sects would either have scattered them from the land to which they had as yet so few attachments, or perhaps have excited a diminutive civil war among those who had come so far to worship together. The opposition to what may be termed the established church had now lost its chief support, by the removal of Vane from office and his departure for England, and Mr. Cotton began to have that light in regard to his errors, which will sometimes break in upon the wisest and most pious men, when their opinions are unhappily discordant with those of the Powers that be. A Synod, the first in New England, was speedily assembled, and pronounced its condemnation of the obnoxious doctrines. Mrs. Hutchinson was next summoned before the supreme civil tribunal, at which, however, the most eminent of the clergy were present, and appear to have taken a very active part as witnesses and advisers. We shall here resume the more picturesque style of narration.

It is a place of humble aspect where the Elders of the people are met, sitting in judgment upon the disturber of Israel. The floor of the low and narrow hall is laid with planks hewn by the axe,—the beams of the roof still wear the rugged bark with which they grew up in the forest, and the hearth is formed of one broad unhammered stone, heaped with logs that roll their blaze and smoke up a chimney of wood and clay. A sleety shower beats fitfully against the windows, driven by the November blast, which comes howling onward from the northern desert, the boisterous and unwelcome herald of a New England winter. Rude benches are arranged across the apartment and along its sides, occupied by men whose piety and learning might have entitled them to seats in those high Councils of the ancient Church, whence opinions were sent forth to confirm or supersede the Gospel in the belief of the whole world and of posterity.—Here are collected all those blessed Fathers of the land, who rank in our veneration next to the Evangelists of Holy Writ, and here also are many, unpurified from the fiercest errors of the age and ready to propagate the religion of peace by violence. In the highest place sits Winthrop, a man by whom the innocent and the guilty might alike desire to be judged, the first confiding in his integrity and wisdom, the latter hoping in his mildness. Next is Endicott, who would stand with his drawn sword at the gate of Heaven, and resist to the death all pilgrims thither, except they travelled his own path. The infant eyes of one in this assembly beheld the faggots blazing round the martyrs, in bloody Mary's time; in later life he dwelt long at Leyden, with the first who went from England for conscience sake; and now, in his weary age, it matters little where he lies down to die. There are others whose hearts were smitten in the high meridian of ambitious hope, and whose dreams still tempt them with the pomp of the old world and the din of its crowded cities, gleaming and echoing over the deep. In the midst, and in the centre of all eyes, we see the Woman. She stands loftily before her judges, with a determined brow, and, unknown to herself, there is a flash of carnal pride half hidden in her eye, as she surveys the many learned and famous men whom her doctrines have put in fear. They question her, and her answers are ready and acute; she reasons with them shrewdly, and brings scripture in support of every argument; the deepest controversialists of that scholastic day find here a woman, whom all their trained and sharpened intellects are inadequate to foil. But by the excitement of the contest, her heart is made to rise and swell within her, and she bursts forth into eloquence. She tells them of the long unquietness which she had endured in England, perceiving the corruption of the church, and yearning for a purer and more perfect light, and how, in a day of solitary prayer, that light was given; she claims for herself the peculiar power of distinguishing between the chosen of man and the Sealed of Heaven, and affirms that her gifted eye can see the glory round the foreheads of the Saints, sojourning in their mortal state. She declares herself commissioned to separate the true shepherds from the false, and denounces present and future judgments on the land, if she be disturbed in her celestial errand. Thus the accusations are proved from her own mouth. Her judges hesitate, and some speak faintly in her defence; but, with a few dissenting voices, sentence is pronounced, bidding her go out from among them, and trouble the land no more.

Mrs. Hutchinson's adherents throughout the colony were now disarmed, and she proceeded to Rhode Island, an accustomed refuge for the exiles of Massachusetts, in all seasons of persecution. Her enemies believed that the anger of Heaven was following her, of which Governor Winthrop does not disdain to record a notable instance, very interesting in a scientific point of view, but fitter for his old and homely narrative than for modern repetition. In a little time, also, she lost her husband, who is mentioned in history only as attending her footsteps, and whom we may conclude to have been (like most husbands of celebrated women) a mere insignificant appendage of his mightier wife. She now grew uneasy among the Rhode Island colonists, whose liberality towards her, at an era when liberality was not esteemed a christian virtue, probably arose from a comparative insolicitude on religious matters, more distasteful to Mrs. Hutchinson than even the uncompromising narrowness of the Puritans. Her final movement was to lead her family within the limits of the Dutch Jurisdiction, where, having felled the trees of a virgin soil, she became herself the virtual head, civil and ecclesiastical, of a little colony.

Perhaps here she found the repose, hitherto so vainly sought. Secluded from all whose faith she could not govern, surrounded by the dependents over whom she held an unlimited influence, agitated by none of the tumultuous billows which were left swelling behind her, we may suppose, that, in the stillness of Nature, her heart was stilled. But her impressive story was to have an awful close. Her last scene is as difficult to be portrayed as a shipwreck, where the shrieks of the victims die unheard along a desolate sea, and a shapeless mass of agony is all that can be brought home to the imagination. The savage foe was on the watch for blood. Sixteen persons assembled at the evening prayer; in the deep midnight, their cry rang through the forest; and daylight dawned upon the lifeless clay of all but one. It was a circumstance not to be unnoticed by our stern ancestors, in considering the fate of her who had so troubled their religion, that an infant daughter, the sole survivor amid the terrible destruction of her mother's household, was bred in a barbarous faith, and never learned the way to the Christian's Heaven. Yet we will hope, that there the mother and the child have met.

The Wives of the Dead

THE following story, the simple and domestic incidents of which may be deemed scarcely worth relating, after such a lapse of time, awakened some degree of interest, a hundred years ago, in a principal seaport of the Bay Province. The rainy twilight of an autumn day; a parlor on the second floor of a small house, plainly furnished, as beseemed the middling circumstances of its inhabitants, yet decorated with little curiosities from beyond the sea, and a few delicate specimens of Indian manufacture,—these are the only particulars to be premised in regard to scene and season. Two young and comely women sat together by the fireside, nursing their mutual and peculiar sorrows. They were the recent brides of two brothers, a sailor and a landsman, and two successive days had brought tidings of the death of each, by the chances of Canadian warfare, and the tempestuous Atlantic. The universal sympathy excited by this bereavement, drew numerous condoling guests to the habitation of the widowed sisters. Several, among whom was the minister, had remained till the verge of evening; when one by one, whispering many comfortable passages of Scripture, that were answered by more abundant tears, they took their leave and departed to their own happier homes. The mourners, though not insensible to the kindness of their friends, had yearned to be left alone. United, as they had been, by the relationship of the living, and now more closely so by that of the dead, each felt as if whatever consolation her grief admitted, were to be found in the bosom of the other. They joined their hearts, and wept together silently. But after an hour of such indulgence, one of the sisters, all of whose emotions were influenced by her mild, quiet, yet not feeble character, began to recollect the precepts of resignation and endurance, which piety had taught her, when she did not think to need them. Her misfortune, besides, as earliest known, should earliest cease to interfere with her regular course of duties; accordingly, having placed the table before the fire, and arranged a frugal meal, she took the hand of her companion.

'Come, dearest sister; you have eaten not a morsel to-day,' she said. 'Arise, I pray you, and let us ask a blessing on that which is provided for us.'

Her sister-in-law was of a lively and irritable temperament, and the first pangs of her sorrow had been expressed by shrieks and passionate lamentation. She now shrunk from Mary's words, like a wounded sufferer from a hand that revives the throb.

'There is no blessing left for me, neither will I ask it,' cried Margaret, with a fresh burst of tears. 'Would it were His will that I might never taste food more.'

Yet she trembled at these rebellious expressions, almost as soon as they were uttered, and, by degrees, Mary succeeded in bringing her sister's mind nearer to the situation of her own. Time went on, and their usual hour of repose arrived. The brothers and their brides, entering the married state with no more than the slender means which then sanctioned such a step, had confederated themselves in one household, with equal rights to the parlor, and claiming exclusive privileges in two sleeping rooms contiguous to it. Thither the widowed ones retired, after heaping ashes upon the dying embers of their fire, and placing a lighted lamp upon the hearth. The doors of both chambers were left open, so that a part of the interior of each, and the beds with their unclosed curtains, were reciprocally visible. Sleep did not steal upon the sisters at one

and the same time. Mary experienced the effect often consequent upon grief quietly borne, and soon sunk into temporary
forgetfulness, while Margaret became more disturbed and feverish, in proportion as the night advanced with its deepest and
stillest hours. She lay listening to the drops of rain, that came
down in monotonous succession, unswayed by a breath of
wind; and a nervous impulse continually caused her to lift her
head from the pillow, and gaze into Mary's chamber and the in-
termediate apartment. The cold light of the lamp threw the
shadows of the furniture up against the wall, stamping them
immoveably there, except when they were shaken by a sudden
flicker of the flame. Two vacant arm-chairs were in their old po-
sitions on opposite sides of the hearth, where the brothers had
been wont to sit in young and laughing dignity, as heads of
families; two humbler seats were near them, the true thrones of
that little empire, where Mary and herself had exercised in
love, a power that love had won. The cheerful radiance of the
fire had shone upon the happy circle, and the dead glimmer of
the lamp might have befitted their reunion now. While Margaret groaned in bitterness, she heard a knock at the street-door.

'How would my heart have leapt at that sound but yesterday!' thought she, remembering the anxiety with which she
had long awaited tidings from her husband. 'I care not for it
now; let them begone, for I will not arise.'

But even while a sort of childish fretfulness made her thus resolve, she was breathing hurriedly, and straining her ears to
catch a repetition of the summons. It is difficult to be convinced of the death of one whom we have deemed another self.
The knocking was now renewed in slow and regular strokes, apparently given with the soft end of a doubled fist, and was accompanied by words, faintly heard through several thicknesses
of wall. Margaret looked to her sister's chamber, and beheld
her still lying in the depths of sleep. She arose, placed her foot
upon the floor, and slightly arrayed herself, trembling between
fear and eagerness as she did so.

'Heaven help me!' sighed she. 'I have nothing left to fear, and methinks I am ten times more a coward than ever.'

Seizing the lamp from the hearth, she hastened to the window that overlooked the street-door. It was a lattice, turning upon hinges; and having thrown it back, she stretched her head a little way into the moist atmosphere. A lantern was reddening the front of the house, and melting its light in the neighboring puddles, while a deluge of darkness overwhelmed every other object. As the window grated on its hinges, a man in a broad brimmed hat and blanket-coat, stepped from under the shelter of the projecting story, and looked upward to discover whom his application had aroused. Margaret knew him as a friendly innkeeper of the town.

'What would you have, Goodman Parker?' cried the widow.

'Lack-a-day, is it you, Mistress Margaret?' replied the innkeeper. 'I was afraid it might be your sister Mary; for I hate to see a young woman in trouble, when I haven't a word of comfort to whisper her.'

'For Heaven's sake, what news do you bring?' screamed Margaret.

'Why, there has been an express through the town within this half hour,' said Goodman Parker, 'travelling from the eastern jurisdiction with letters from the governor and council. He tarried at my house to refresh himself with a drop and a morsel, and I asked him what tidings on the frontiers. He tells me we had the better in the skirmish you wot of, and that thirteen men reported slain are well and sound, and your husband among them. Besides, he is appointed of the escort to bring the captivated Frenchers and Indians home to the province jail. I judged you wouldn't mind being broke of your rest, and so I stept over to tell you. Good night.'

So saying, the honest man departed; and his lantern gleamed along the street, bringing to view indistinct shapes of things, and the fragments of a world, like order glimmering through chaos, or memory roaming over the past. But Marga-

ret staid not to watch these picturesque effects. Joy flashed into
her heart, and lighted it up at once, and breathless, and with
winged steps, she flew to the bedside of her sister. She paused,
however, at the door of the chamber, while a thought of pain
broke in upon her.

'Poor Mary!' said she to herself. 'Shall I waken her, to feel
her sorrow sharpened by my happiness? No; I will keep it
within my own bosom till the morrow.'

She approached the bed to discover if Mary's sleep were
peaceful. Her face was turned partly inward to the pillow, and
had been hidden there to weep; but a look of motionless con-
tentment was now visible upon it, as if her heart, like a deep
lake, had grown calm because its dead had sunk down so far
within. Happy is it, and strange, that the lighter sorrows are
those from which dreams are chiefly fabricated. Margaret
shrunk from disturbing her sister-in-law, and felt as if her own
better fortune, had rendered her involuntarily unfaithful, and
as if altered and diminished affection must be the consequence
of the disclosure she had to make. With a sudden step, she
turned away. But joy could not long be repressed, even by circumstances that would have excited heavy grief at another moment. Her mind was thronged with delightful thoughts, till
sleep stole on and transformed them to visions, more delightful and more wild, like the breath of winter, (but what a cold
comparison!) working fantastic tracery upon a window.

When the night was far advanced, Mary awoke with a sudden start. A vivid dream had latterly involved her in its unreal
life, of which, however, she could only remember that it had
been broken in upon at the most interesting point. For a little
time, slumber hung about her like a morning mist, hindering
her from perceiving the distinct outline of her situation. She listened with imperfect consciousness to two or three volleys of a
rapid and eager knocking; and first she deemed the noise a matter of course, like the breath she drew; next, it appeared a
thing in which she had no concern; and lastly, she became

aware that it was a summons necessary to be obeyed. At the same moment, the pang of recollection darted into her mind; the pall of sleep was thrown back from the face of grief; the dim light of the chamber, and the objects therein revealed, had retained all her suspended ideas, and restored them as soon as she unclosed her eyes. Again, there was a quick peal upon the street-door. Fearing that her sister would also be disturbed, Mary wrapped herself in a cloak and hood, took the lamp from the hearth, and hastened to the window. By some accident, it had been left unhasped, and yielded easily to her hand.

'Who's there?' asked Mary, trembling as she looked forth.

The storm was over, and the moon was up; it shone upon broken clouds above, and below upon houses black with moisture, and upon little lakes of the fallen rain, curling into silver beneath the quick enchantment of a breeze. A young man in a sailor's dress, wet as if he had come out of the depths of the sea, stood alone under the window. Mary recognized him as one whose livelihood was gained by short voyages along the coast; nor did she forget, that, previous to her marriage, he had been an unsuccessful wooer of her own.

'What do you seek here, Stephen?' said she.

'Cheer up, Mary, for I seek to comfort you,' answered the rejected lover. 'You must know I got home not ten minutes ago, and the first thing my good mother told me was the news about your husband. So, without saying a word to the old woman, I clapt on my hat, and ran out of the house. I couldn't have slept a wink before speaking to you, Mary, for the sake of old times.'

'Stephen, I thought better of you!' exclaimed the widow, with gushing tears, and preparing to close the lattice; for she was no whit inclined to imitate the first wife of Zadig.

'But stop, and hear my story out,' cried the young sailor. 'I tell you we spoke a brig yesterday afternoon, bound in from Old England. And who do you think I saw standing on deck, well and hearty, only a bit thinner than he was five months ago?'

Mary leaned from the window, but could not speak.

'Why, it was your husband himself,' continued the generous seaman. 'He and three others saved themselves on a spar, when the Blessing turned bottom upwards. The brig will beat into the bay by daylight, with this wind, and you'll see him here tomorrow. There's the comfort I bring you, Mary, and so good night.'

He hurried away, while Mary watched him with a doubt of waking reality, that seemed stronger or weaker as he alternately entered the shade of the houses, or emerged into the broad streaks of moonlight. Gradually, however, a blessed flood of conviction swelled into her heart, in strength enough to overwhelm her, had its increase been more abrupt. Her first impulse was to rouse her sister-in-law, and communicate the new-born gladness. She opened the chamber-door, which had been closed in the course of the night, though not latched, advanced to the bedside, and was about to lay her hand upon the slumberer's shoulder. But then she remembered that Margaret would awake to thoughts of death and woe, rendered not the less bitter by their contrast with her own felicity. She suffered the rays of the lamp to fall upon the unconscious form of the bereaved one. Margaret lay in unquiet sleep, and the drapery was displaced around her; her young cheek was rosy-tinted, and her lips half opened in a vivid smile; an expression of joy, debarred its passage by her sealed eyelids, struggled forth like incense from the whole countenance.

'My poor sister! you will waken too soon from that happy dream,' thought Mary.

Before retiring, she set down the lamp and endeavored to arrange the bed-clothes, so that the chill air might not do harm to the feverish slumberer. But her hand trembled against Margaret's neck, a tear also fell upon her cheek, and she suddenly awoke.

My Kinsman, Major Molineux

AFTER the kings of Great Britain had assumed the right of appointing the colonial governors, the measures of the latter seldom met with the ready and general approbation, which had been paid to those of their predecessors, under the original charters. The people looked with most jealous scrutiny to the exercise of power, which did not emanate from themselves, and they usually rewarded the rulers with slender gratitude, for the compliances, by which, in softening their instructions from beyond the sea, they had incurred the reprehension of those who gave them. The annals of Massachusetts Bay will inform us, that of six governors, in the space of about forty years from the surrender of the old charter, under James II., two were imprisoned by a popular insurrection; a third, as Hutchinson inclines to believe, was driven from the province by the whizzing of a musket ball; a fourth, in the opinion of the same historian, was hastened to his grave by continual bickerings with the House of Representatives; and the remaining two, as well as their successors, till the Revolution, were favored with few and brief intervals of peaceful sway. The inferior members of the court party, in times of high political excitement, led scarcely a more desirable life. These remarks may serve as preface to the following adventures, which chanced upon a summer night, not far from a hundred years ago. The reader, in order to avoid a long and dry detail of colonial affairs, is requested to dispense with an account of the train of circumstances, that had caused much temporary inflammation of the popular mind.

It was near nine o'clock of a moonlight evening, when a boat crossed the ferry with a single passenger, who had obtained his conveyance, at that unusual hour, by the promise of an extra fare. While he stood on the landing-place, searching in either pocket for the means of fulfilling his agreement, the ferryman lifted a lantern, by the aid of which, and the newly risen moon, he took a very accurate survey of the stranger's figure. He was a youth of barely eighteen years, evidently country-bred, and now, as it should seem, upon his first visit to town. He was clad in a coarse grey coat, well worn, but in excellent repair; his under garments were durably constructed of leather, and sat tight to a pair of serviceable and well-shaped limbs; his stockings of blue yarn, were the incontrovertible handiwork of a mother or a sister; and on his head was a three-cornered hat, which in its better days had perhaps sheltered the graver brow of the lad's father. Under his left arm was a heavy cudgel, formed of an oak sapling, and retaining a part of the hardened root; and his equipment was completed by a wallet, not so abundantly stocked as to incommode the vigorous shoulders on which it hung. Brown, curly hair, well-shaped features, and bright, cheerful eyes, were nature's gifts, and worth all that art could have done for his adornment.

The youth, one of whose names was Robin, finally drew from his pocket the half of a little province-bill of five shillings, which, in the depreciation of that sort of currency, did but satisfy the ferryman's demand, with the surplus of a sexangular piece of parchment valued at three pence. He then walked forward into the town, with as light a step, as if his day's journey had not already exceeded thirty miles, and with as eager an eye, as if he were entering London city, instead of the little metropolis of a New England colony. Before Robin had proceeded far, however, it occurred to him, that he knew not whither to direct his steps; so he paused, and looked up and down the narrow street, scrutinizing the small and mean wooden buildings, that were scattered on either side.

'This low hovel cannot be my kinsman's dwelling,' thought he, 'nor yonder old house, where the moonlight enters at the broken casement; and truly I see none hereabouts that might be worthy of him. It would have been wise to inquire my way of the ferryman, and doubtless he would have gone with me, and earned a shilling from the Major for his pains. But the next man I meet will do as well.'

He resumed his walk, and was glad to perceive that the street now became wider, and the houses more respectable in their appearance. He soon discerned a figure moving on moderately in advance, and hastened his steps to overtake it. As Robin drew nigh, he saw that the passenger was a man in years, with a full periwig of grey hair, a wide-skirted coat of dark cloth, and silk stockings rolled about his knees. He carried a long and polished cane, which he struck down perpendicularly before him, at every step; and at regular intervals he uttered two successive hems, of a peculiarly solemn and sepulchral intonation. Having made these observations, Robin laid hold of the skirt of the old man's coat, just when the light from the open door and windows of a barber's shop, fell upon both their figures.

'Good evening to you, honored Sir,' said he, making a low bow, and still retaining his hold of the skirt. 'I pray you to tell me whereabouts is the dwelling of my kinsman, Major Molineux?'

The youth's question was uttered very loudly; and one of the barbers, whose razor was descending on a well-soaped chin, and another who was dressing a Ramillies wig, left their occupations, and came to the door. The citizen, in the meantime, turned a long favored countenance upon Robin, and answered him in a tone of excessive anger and annoyance. His two sepulchral hems, however, broke into the very centre of his rebuke, with most singular effect, like a thought of the cold grave obtruding among wrathful passions.

'Let go my garment, fellow! I tell you, I know not the man you speak of. What! I have authority, I have—hem, hem—authority; and if this be the respect you show your betters, your feet shall be brought acquainted with the stocks, by daylight, tomorrow morning!'

Robin released the old man's skirt, and hastened away, pursued by an ill-mannered roar of laughter from the barber's shop. He was at first considerably surprised by the result of his question, but, being a shrewd youth, soon thought himself able to account for the mystery.

'This is some country representative,' was his conclusion, 'who has never seen the inside of my kinsman's door, and lacks the breeding to answer a stranger civilly. The man is old, or verily—I might be tempted to turn back and smite him on the nose. Ah, Robin, Robin! even the barber's boys laugh at you, for choosing such a guide! You will be wiser in time, friend Robin.'

He now became entangled in a succession of crooked and narrow streets, which crossed each other, and meandered at no great distance from the water-side. The smell of tar was obvious to his nostrils, the masts of vessels pierced the moonlight above the tops of the buildings, and the numerous signs, which Robin paused to read, informed him that he was near the centre of business. But the streets were empty, the shops were closed, and lights were visible only in the second stories of a few dwelling-houses. At length, on the corner of a narrow lane, through which he was passing, he beheld the broad countenance of a British hero swinging before the door of an inn, whence proceeded the voices of many guests. The casement of one of the lower windows was thrown back, and a very thin curtain permitted Robin to distinguish a party at supper, round a well-furnished table. The fragrance of the good cheer steamed forth into the outer air, and the youth could not fail to recollect, that the last remnant of his travelling stock of provision had yielded to his morning appetite, and that noon had found, and left him, dinnerless.

'Oh, that a parchment three-penny might give me a right to sit down at yonder table,' said Robin, with a sigh. 'But the Major will make me welcome to the best of his victuals; so I will even step boldly in, and inquire my way to his dwelling.'

He entered the tavern, and was guided by the murmur of voices, and fumes of tobacco, to the public room. It was a long and low apartment, with oaken walls, grown dark in the continual smoke, and a floor, which was thickly sanded, but of no immaculate purity. A number of persons, the larger part of whom appeared to be mariners, or in some way connected with the sea, occupied the wooden benches, or leather-bottomed chairs, conversing on various matters, and occasionally lending their attention to some topic of general interest. Three or four little groups were draining as many bowls of punch, which the great West India trade had long since made a familiar drink in the colony. Others, who had the aspect of men who lived by regular and laborious handicraft, preferred the insulated bliss of an unshared potation, and became more taciturn under its influence. Nearly all, in short, evinced a predilection for the Good Creature in some of its various shapes, for this is a vice, to which, as the Fast-day sermons of a hundred years ago will testify, we have a long hereditary claim. The only guests to whom Robin's sympathies inclined him, were two or three sheepish countrymen, who were using the inn somewhat after the fashion of a Turkish Caravansary; they had gotten themselves into the darkest corner of the room, and, heedless of the Nicotian atmosphere, were supping on the bread of their own ovens, and the bacon cured in their own chimney-smoke. But though Robin felt a sort of brotherhood with these strangers, his eyes were attracted from them, to a person who stood near the door, holding whispered conversation with a group of ill-dressed associates. His features were separately striking almost to grotesqueness, and the whole face left a deep impression in the memory. The forehead bulged out into a double prominence, with a vale between; the nose came boldly forth in an irregular curve, and its bridge was of more than a finger's breadth; the eyebrows were deep and shaggy, and the eyes glowed beneath them like fire in a cave.

While Robin deliberated of whom to inquire respecting his kinsman's dwelling, he was accosted by the innkeeper, a little man in a stained white apron, who had come to pay his professional welcome to the stranger. Being in the second generation from a French Protestant, he seemed to have inherited the courtesy of his parent nation; but no variety of circumstance was ever known to change his voice from the one shrill note in which he now addressed Robin.

'From the country, I presume, Sir?' said he, with a profound bow. 'Beg to congratulate you on your arrival, and trust you intend a long stay with us. Fine town here, Sir, beautiful buildings, and much that may interest a stranger. May I hope for the honor of your commands in respect to supper?'

'The man sees a family likeness! the rogue has guessed that I am related to the Major!' thought Robin, who had hitherto experienced little superfluous civility.

All eyes were now turned on the country lad, standing at the door, in his worn three-cornered hat, grey coat, leather breeches, and blue yarn stockings, leaning on an oaken cudgel, and bearing a wallet on his back.

Robin replied to the courteous innkeeper, with such an assumption of consequence, as befitted the Major's relative.

'My honest friend,' he said, 'I shall make it a point to patronize your house on some occasion, when—' here he could not help lowering his voice—'I may have more than a parchment three-pence in my pocket. My present business,' continued he, speaking with lofty confidence, 'is merely to inquire the way to the dwelling of my kinsman, Major Molineux.'

There was a sudden and general movement in the room, which Robin interpreted as expressing the eagerness of each individual to become his guide. But the innkeeper turned his eyes to a written paper on the wall, which he read, or seemed to read, with occasional recurrences to the young man's figure.

'What have we here?' said he, breaking his speech into little dry fragments. ' "Left the house of the subscriber, bounden servant, Hezekiah Mudge—had on, when he went away, grey coat, leather breeches, master's third best hat. One pound currency reward to whoever shall lodge him in any jail in the province." Better trudge, boy, better trudge!'

Robin had begun to draw his hand towards the lighter end of the oak cudgel, but a strange hostility in every countenance, induced him to relinquish his purpose of breaking the courteous innkeeper's head. As he turned to leave the room, he encountered a sneering glance from the bold-featured personage whom he had before noticed; and no sooner was he beyond the door, than he heard a general laugh, in which the innkeeper's voice might be distinguished, like the dropping of small stones into a kettle.

'Now is it not strange,' thought Robin, with his usual shrewdness, 'is it not strange, that the confession of an empty pocket, should outweigh the name of my kinsman, Major Molineux? Oh, if I had one of these grinning rascals in the woods, where I and my oak sapling grew up together, I would teach him that my arm is heavy, though my purse be light!'

On turning the corner of the narrow lane, Robin found himself in a spacious street, with an unbroken line of lofty houses on each side, and a steepled building at the upper end, whence the ringing of a bell announced the hour of nine. The light of the moon, and the lamps from numerous shop windows, discovered people promenading on the pavement, and amongst them, Robin hoped to recognize his hitherto inscrutable relative. The result of his former inquiries made him unwilling to hazard another, in a scene of such publicity, and he determined to walk slowly and silently up the street, thrusting his face close to that of every elderly gentleman, in search of the Major's lineaments. In his progress, Robin encountered many gay and gallant figures. Embroidered garments, of showy colors, enormous periwigs, gold-laced hats, and silver hilted swords, glided past him and dazzled his optics. Travelled youths, imitators of the European fine gentlemen of the period, trod jauntily along, half-dancing to the fashionable tunes which they hummed, and making poor Robin ashamed of his quiet and natural gait. At length, after many pauses to examine the gorgeous display of goods in the shop windows, and after suffering some rebukes for the impertinence of his scrutiny into people's faces, the Major's kinsman found himself near the steepled building, still unsuccessful in his search. As yet, however, he had seen only one side of the thronged street; so Robin crossed, and continued the same sort of inquisition down the opposite pavement, with stronger hopes than the philosopher seeking an honest man, but with no better fortune. He had arrived about midway towards the lower end, from which his course began, when he overheard the approach of some one, who struck down a cane on the flag-stones at every step, uttering, at regular intervals, two sepulchral hems.

'Mercy on us!' quoth Robin, recognizing the sound.

Turning a corner, which chanced to be close at his right hand, he hastened to pursue his researches, in some other part of the town. His patience was now wearing low, and he seemed to feel more fatigue from his rambles since he crossed the ferry, than from his journey of several days on the other side. Hunger also pleaded loudly within him, and Robin began to balance the propriety of demanding, violently and with lifted cudgel, the necessary guidance from the first solitary passenger, whom he should meet. While a resolution to this effect was gaining strength, he entered a street of mean appearance, on either side of which, a row of ill-built houses was straggling towards the harbor. The moonlight fell upon no passenger along the whole extent, but in the third domicile which Robin passed, there was a half-opened door, and his keen glance detected a woman's garment within.

'My luck may be better here,' said he to himself.

Accordingly, he approached the door, and beheld it shut closer as he did so; yet an open space remained, sufficing for the fair occupant to observe the stranger, without a corresponding display on her part. All that Robin could discern was a strip of scarlet petticoat, and the occasional sparkle of an eye, as if the moonbeams were trembling on some bright thing.

'Pretty mistress,'—for I may call her so with a good conscience, thought the shrewd youth, since I know nothing to the contrary—'my sweet pretty mistress, will you be kind enough to tell me whereabouts I must seek the dwelling of my kinsman, Major Molineux?'

Robin's voice was plaintive and winning, and the female, seeing nothing to be shunned in the handsome country youth, thrust open the door, and came forth into the moonlight. She was a dainty little figure, with a white neck, round arms, and a slender waist, at the extremity of which her scarlet petticoat jutted out over a hoop, as if she were standing in a balloon. Moreover, her face was oval and pretty, her hair dark beneath the little cap, and her bright eyes possessed a sly freedom, which triumphed over those of Robin.

'Major Molineux dwells here,' said this fair woman.

Now her voice was the sweetest Robin had heard that night, the airy counterpart of a stream of melted silver; yet he could not help doubting whether that sweet voice spoke Gospel truth. He looked up and down the mean street, and then surveyed the house before which they stood. It was a small, dark edifice of two stories, the second of which projected over the lower floor; and the front apartment had the aspect of a shop for petty commodities.

'Now truly I am in luck,' replied Robin, cunningly, 'and so indeed is my kinsman, the Major, in having so pretty a housekeeper. But I prithee trouble him to step to the door; I will deliver him a message from his friends in the country, and then go back to my lodgings at the inn.'

'Nay, the Major has been a-bed this hour or more,' said the lady of the scarlet petticoat; 'and it would be to little purpose to disturb him to-night, seeing his evening draught was of the strongest. But he is a kind-hearted man, and it would be as much as my life's worth, to let a kinsman of his turn away from the door. You are the good old gentleman's very picture, and I could swear that was his rainy-weather hat. Also, he has garments very much resembling those leather—But come in, I pray, for I bid you hearty welcome in his name.'

So saying, the fair and hospitable dame took our hero by the hand; and though the touch was light, and the force was gentleness, and though Robin read in her eyes what he did not hear in her words, yet the slender waisted woman, in the scarlet petticoat, proved stronger than the athletic country youth. She had drawn his half-willing footsteps nearly to the threshold, when the opening of a door in the neighborhood, startled the Major's housekeeper, and, leaving the Major's kinsman, she vanished speedily into her own domicile. A heavy yawn preceded the appearance of a man, who, like the Moonshine of Pyramus and Thisbe, carried a lantern, needlessly aiding his sister luminary in the heavens. As he walked sleepily up the street, he turned his broad, dull face on Robin, and displayed a long staff, spiked at the end.

'Home, vagabond, home!' said the watchman, in accents that seemed to fall asleep as soon as they were uttered. 'Home, or we'll set you in the stocks by peep of day!'

'This is the second hint of the kind,' thought Robin. 'I wish they would end my difficulties, by setting me there to-night.'

Nevertheless, the youth felt an instinctive antipathy towards the guardian of midnight order, which at first prevented him from asking his usual question. But just when the man was about to vanish behind the corner, Robin resolved not to lose the opportunity, and shouted lustily after him—

'I say, friend! will you guide me to the house of my kinsman, Major Molineux?'

The watchman made no reply, but turned the corner and was gone; yet Robin seemed to hear the sound of drowsy laughter stealing along the solitary street. At that moment, also, a pleasant titter saluted him from the open window above his head; he looked up, and caught the sparkle of a saucy eye; a round arm beckoned to him, and next he heard light footsteps descending the staircase within. But Robin, being of the household of a New England clergyman, was a good youth, as well as a shrewd one; so he resisted temptation, and fled away.

He now roamed desperately, and at random, through the town, almost ready to believe that a spell was on him, like that, by which a wizard of his country, had once kept three pursuers wandering, a whole winter night, within twenty paces of the cottage which they sought. The streets lay before him, strange and desolate, and the lights were extinguished in almost every house. Twice, however, little parties of men, among whom Robin distinguished individuals in outlandish attire, came hurrying along, but though on both occasions they paused to address him, such intercourse did not at all enlighten his perplexity. They did but utter a few words in some language of which Robin knew nothing, and perceiving his inability to answer, bestowed a curse upon him in plain English, and hastened away. Finally, the lad determined to knock at the door of every mansion that might appear worthy to be occupied by his kinsman, trusting that perseverance would overcome the fatality which had hitherto thwarted him. Firm in this resolve, he was passing beneath the walls of a church, which formed the corner of two streets, when, as he turned into the shade of its steeple, he encountered a bulky stranger, muffled in a cloak. The man was proceeding with the speed of earnest business, but Robin planted himself full before him, holding the oak cudgel with both hands across his body, as a bar to further passage.

'Halt, honest man, and answer me a question,' said he, very resolutely. 'Tell me, this instant, whereabouts is the dwelling of my kinsman, Major Molineux?'

'Keep your tongue between your teeth, fool, and let me pass,' said a deep, gruff voice, which Robin partly remembered. 'Let me pass, I say, or I'll strike you to the earth!'

'No, no, neighbor!' cried Robin, flourishing his cudgel, and then thrusting its larger end close to the man's muffled face. 'No, no, I'm not the fool you take me for, nor do you pass, till I have an answer to my question. Whereabouts is the dwelling of my kinsman, Major Molineux?'

The stranger, instead of attempting to force his passage, stept back into the moonlight, unmuffled his own face and stared full into that of Robin.

'Watch here an hour, and Major Molineux will pass by,' said he.

Robin gazed with dismay and astonishment, on the unprecedented physiognomy of the speaker. The forehead with its double prominence, the broad-hooked nose, the shaggy eyebrows, and fiery eyes, were those which he had noticed at the inn, but the man's complexion had undergone a singular, or, more properly, a two-fold change. One side of the face blazed of an intense red, while the other was black as midnight, the division line being in the broad bridge of the nose; and a mouth, which seemed to extend from ear to ear, was black or red, in contrast to the color of the cheek. The effect was as if two individual devils, a fiend of fire and a fiend of darkness, had united themselves to form this infernal visage. The stranger grinned in Robin's face, muffled his parti-colored features, and was out of sight in a moment.

'Strange things we travellers see!' ejaculated Robin.

He seated himself, however, upon the steps of the church-door, resolving to wait the appointed time for his kinsman's appearance. A few moments were consumed in philosophical speculations, upon the species of the *genus homo,* who had just left him, but having settled this point shrewdly, rationally, and satisfactorily, he was compelled to look elsewhere for amusement. And first he threw his eyes along the street; it was of more respectable appearance than most of those into which he had wandered, and the moon, 'creating, like the imaginative power, a beautiful strangeness in familiar objects,' gave something of romance to a scene, that might not have possessed it in the light of day. The irregular, and often quaint architecture of the houses, some of whose roofs were broken into numerous little peaks; while others ascended, steep and narrow, into a single point; and others again were square; the pure milk-white of some of their complexions, the aged darkness of others, and the thousand sparklings, reflected from bright substances in the plastered walls of many; these matters engaged Robin's attention for awhile, and then began to grow wearisome. Next he endeavored to define the forms of distant objects, starting away with almost ghostly indistinctness, just as his eye appeared to grasp them; and finally he took a minute survey of an edifice, which stood on the opposite side of the street, directly in front of the church-door, where he was stationed. It was a large square mansion, distinguished from its neighbors by a balcony, which rested on tall pillars, and by an elaborate Gothic window, communicating therewith.

'Perhaps this is the very house I have been seeking,' thought Robin.

Then he strove to speed away the time, by listening to a murmur, which swept continually along the street, yet was scarcely audible, except to an unaccustomed ear like his; it was a low, dull, dreamy sound, compounded of many noises, each of which was at too great a distance to be separately heard. Robin marvelled at this snore of a sleeping town, and marvelled more, whenever its continuity was broken, by now and then a distant shout, apparently loud where it originated. But altogether it was a sleep-inspiring sound, and to shake off its drowsy influence, Robin arose, and climbed a window-frame, that he might view the interior of the church. There the moonbeams came trembling in, and fell down upon the deserted pews, and extended along the quiet aisles. A fainter, yet more awful radiance, was hovering round the pulpit, and one solitary ray had dared to rest upon the opened page of the great Bible. Had Nature, in that deep hour, become a worshipper in the house, which man had builded? Or was that heavenly light the visible sanctity of the place, visible because no earthly and impure feet were within the walls? The scene made Robin's heart shiver with a sensation of loneliness, stronger than he had ever felt in the remotest depths of his native woods; so he turned away, and sat down again before the door. There were graves around the church, and now an uneasy thought obtruded into Robin's breast. What if the object of his search, which had been so often and so strangely thwarted, were all the time mouldering in his shroud? What if his kinsman should glide through yonder gate, and nod and smile to him in passing dimly by?

'Oh, that any breathing thing were here with me!' said Robin.

Recalling his thoughts from this uncomfortable track, he sent them over forest, hill, and stream, and attempted to imagine how that evening of ambiguity and weariness, had been spent by his father's household. He pictured them assembled at the door, beneath the tree, the great old tree, which had been spared for its huge twisted trunk, and venerable shade, when a thousand leafy brethren fell. There, at the going down of the summer sun, it was his father's custom to perform domestic worship, that the neighbors might come and join with him like brothers of the family, and that the wayfaring man might pause to drink at that fountain, and keep his heart pure by freshening the memory of home. Robin distinguished the seat of every individual of the little audience; he saw the good man in the midst, holding the Scriptures in the golden light that shone from the western clouds; he beheld him close the book, and all rise up to pray. He heard the old thanksgivings for daily mercies, the old supplications for their continuance, to which he had so often listened in weariness, but which were now among his dear remembrances. He perceived the slight inequality of his father's voice when he came to speak of the Absent One; he noted how his mother turned her face to the broad and knotted trunk; how his elder brother scorned, because the beard was rough upon his upper lip, to permit his features to be moved; how his younger sister drew down a low hanging branch before her eyes; and how the little one of all, whose sports had hitherto broken the decorum of the scene, understood the prayer for her playmate, and burst into clamorous grief. Then he saw them go in at the door; and when Robin would have entered also, the latch tinkled into its place, and he was excluded from his home.

'Am I here, or there?' cried Robin, starting; for all at once, when his thoughts had become visible and audible in a dream, the long, wide, solitary street shone out before him.

He aroused himself, and endeavored to fix his attention steadily upon the large edifice which he had surveyed before. But still his mind kept vibrating between fancy and reality; by turns, the pillars of the balcony lengthened into the tall, bare stems of pines, dwindled down to human figures, settled again in their true shape and size, and then commenced a new succession of changes. For a single moment, when he deemed himself awake, he could have sworn that a visage, one which he seemed to remember, yet could not absolutely name as his kinsman's, was looking towards him from the Gothic window. A deeper sleep wrestled with, and nearly overcame him, but fled at the sound of footsteps along the opposite pavement. Robin rubbed his eyes, discerned a man passing at the foot of the balcony, and addressed him in a loud, peevish, and lamentable cry.

'Halloo, friend! must I wait here all night for my kinsman, Major Molineux?'

The sleeping echoes awoke, and answered the voice; and the passenger, barely able to discern a figure sitting in the oblique shade of the steeple, traversed the street to obtain a nearer view. He was himself a gentleman in his prime, of open, intelligent, cheerful, and altogether prepossessing countenance. Perceiving a country youth, apparently homeless and without friends, he accosted him in a tone of real kindness, which had become strange to Robin's ears.

'Well, my good lad, why are you sitting here?' inquired he. 'Can I be of service to you in any way?'

'I am afraid not, Sir,' replied Robin, despondingly; 'yet I shall take it kindly, if you'll answer me a single question. I've been searching half the night for one Major Molineux; now, Sir, is there really such a person in these parts, or am I dreaming?'

'Major Molineux! The name is not altogether strange to me,' said the gentleman, smiling. 'Have you any objection to telling me the nature of your business with him?'

Then Robin briefly related that his father was a clergyman, settled on a small salary, at a long distance back in the country, and that he and Major Molineux were brothers' children. The Major, having inherited riches, and acquired civil and military rank, had visited his cousin in great pomp a year or two before; had manifested much interest in Robin and an elder brother, and, being childless himself, had thrown out hints respecting the future establishment of one of them in life. The elder brother was destined to succeed to the farm, which his father cultivated, in the interval of sacred duties; it was therefore determined that Robin should profit by his kinsman's generous intentions, especially as he had seemed to be rather the favorite, and was thought to possess other necessary endowments.

'For I have the name of being a shrewd youth,' observed Robin, in this part of his story.

'I doubt not you deserve it,' replied his new friend, good naturedly; 'but pray proceed.'

'Well, Sir, being nearly eighteen years old, and well-grown, as you see,' continued Robin, raising himself to his full height, 'I thought it high time to begin the world. So my mother and sister put me in handsome trim, and my father gave me half the remnant of his last year's salary, and five days ago I started for this place, to pay the Major a visit. But would you believe it, Sir? I crossed the ferry a little after dusk, and have yet found nobody that would show me the way to his dwelling; only an hour or two since, I was told to wait here, and Major Molineux would pass by.'

'Can you describe the man who told you this?' inquired the gentleman.

'Oh, he was a very ill-favored fellow, Sir,' replied Robin, 'with two great bumps on his forehead, a hook nose, fiery eyes, and, what struck me as the strangest, his face was of two different colors. Do you happen to know such a man, Sir?'

'Not intimately,' answered the stranger, 'but I chanced to meet him a little time previous to your stopping me. I believe you may trust his word, and that the Major will very shortly pass through this street. In the mean time, as I have a singular curiosity to witness your meeting, I will sit down here upon the steps, and bear you company.'

He seated himself accordingly, and soon engaged his companion in animated discourse. It was but of brief continuance, however, for a noise of shouting, which had long been remotely audible, drew so much nearer, that Robin inquired its cause.

'What may be the meaning of this uproar?' asked he. 'Truly, if your town be always as noisy, I shall find little sleep, while I am an inhabitant.'

'Why, indeed, friend Robin, there do appear to be three or four riotous fellows abroad to-night,' replied the gentleman. 'You must not expect all the stillness of your native woods, here in our streets. But the watch will shortly be at the heels of these lads, and—'

'Aye, and set them in the stocks by peep of day,' interrupted Robin, recollecting his own encounter with the drowsy lantern-bearer. 'But, dear Sir, if I may trust my ears, an army of watchmen would never make head against such a multitude of rioters. There were at least a thousand voices went to make up that one shout.'

'May not one man have several voices, Robin, as well as two complexions?' said his friend.

'Perhaps a man may; but Heaven forbid that a woman should!' responded the shrewd youth, thinking of the seductive tones of the Major's housekeeper.

The sounds of a trumpet in some neighboring street now became so evident and continual, that Robin's curiosity was strongly excited. In addition to the shouts, he heard frequent bursts from many instruments of discord, and a wild and confused laughter filled up the intervals. Robin rose from the steps, and looked wistfully towards a point, whither several people seemed to be hastening.

'Surely some prodigious merrymaking is going on,' exclaimed he. 'I have laughed very little since I left home, Sir, and should be sorry to lose an opportunity. Shall we just step round the corner by that darkish house, and take our share of the fun?'

'Sit down again, sit down, good Robin,' replied the gentleman, laying his hand on the skirt of the grey coat. 'You forget that we must wait here for your kinsman; and there is reason to believe that he will pass by, in the course of a very few moments.'

The near approach of the uproar had now disturbed the neighborhood; windows flew open on all sides; and many heads, in the attire of the pillow, and confused by sleep suddenly broken, were protruded to the gaze of whoever had leisure to observe them. Eager voices hailed each other from house to house, all demanding the explanation, which not a soul could give. Half-dressed men hurried towards the unknown commotion, stumbling as they went over the stone steps, that thrust themselves into the narrow foot-walk. The shouts, the laughter, and the tuneless bray, the antipodes of music, came onward with increasing din, till scattered individuals, and then denser bodies, began to appear round a corner, at the distance of a hundred yards.

'Will you recognize your kinsman, Robin, if he passes in this crowd?' inquired the gentleman.

'Indeed, I can't warrant it, Sir; but I'll take my stand here, and keep a bright look out,' answered Robin, descending to the outer edge of the pavement.

A mighty stream of people now emptied into the street, and came rolling slowly towards the church. A single horseman wheeled the corner in the midst of them, and close behind him came a band of fearful wind-instruments, sending forth a fresher discord, now that no intervening buildings kept it from the ear. Then a redder light disturbed the moonbeams, and a dense multitude of torches shone along the street, concealing by their glare whatever object they illuminated. The single horseman, clad in a military dress, and bearing a drawn sword, rode onward as the leader, and, by his fierce and variegated countenance, appeared like war personified; the red of one cheek was an emblem of fire and sword; the blackness of the other betokened the mourning which attends them. In his train, were wild figures in the Indian dress, and many fantastic shapes without a model, giving the whole march a visionary air, as if a dream had broken forth from some feverish brain, and were sweeping visibly through the midnight streets. A mass of people, inactive, except as applauding spectators, hemmed the procession in, and several women ran along the sidewalks, piercing the confusion of heavier sounds, with their shrill voices of mirth or terror.

'The double-faced fellow has his eye upon me,' muttered Robin, with an indefinite but uncomfortable idea, that he was himself to bear a part in the pageantry.

The leader turned himself in the saddle, and fixed his glance full upon the country youth, as the steed went slowly by. When Robin had freed his eyes from those fiery ones, the musicians were passing before him, and the torches were close at hand; but the unsteady brightness of the latter formed a veil which he could not penetrate. The rattling of wheels over the stones sometimes found its way to his ear, and confused traces of a human form appeared at intervals, and then melted into the vivid light. A moment more, and the leader thundered a command to halt; the trumpets vomited a horrid breath, and held their peace; the shouts and laughter of the people died away, and there remained only a universal hum, nearly allied to silence. Right before Robin's eyes was an uncovered cart. There the torches blazed the brightest, there the moon shone out like day, and there, in tar-and-feathery dignity, sate his kinsman, Major Molineux!

He was an elderly man, of large and majestic person, and strong, square features, betokening a steady soul; but steady as it was, his enemies had found the means to shake it. His face was pale as death, and far more ghastly; the broad forehead was contracted in his agony, so that his eyebrows formed one grizzled line; his eyes were red and wild, and the foam hung white upon his quivering lip. His whole frame was agitated by a quick, and continual tremor, which his pride strove to quell, even in those circumstances of overwhelming humiliation. But perhaps the bitterest pang of all was when his eyes met those of Robin; for he evidently knew him on the instant, as the youth stood witnessing the foul disgrace of a head that had grown grey in honor. They stared at each other in silence, and Robin's knees shook, and his hair bristled, with a mixture of pity and terror. Soon, however, a bewildering excitement began to seize upon his mind; the preceding adventures of the night, the unexpected appearance of the crowd, the torches, the confused din, and the hush that followed, the spectre of his kinsman reviled by that great multitude, all this, and more than all, a perception of tremendous ridicule in the whole scene, affected him with a sort of mental inebriety. At that moment a voice of sluggish merriment saluted Robin's ears; he turned instinctively, and just behind the corner of the church stood the lantern-bearer, rubbing his eyes, and drowsily enjoying the lad's amazement. Then he heard a peal of laughter like the ringing of silvery bells; a woman twitched his arm, a saucy eye met his, and he saw the lady of the scarlet petticoat. A sharp, dry cachinnation appealed to his memory, and, standing on tiptoe in the crowd, with his white apron over his head, he beheld the courteous little innkeeper. And lastly, there sailed over the heads of the multitude a great, broad laugh, broken in the midst by two sepulchral hems; thus—

'Haw, haw, haw—hem, hem—haw, haw, haw, haw!'

The sound proceeded from the balcony of the opposite edifice, and thither Robin turned his eyes. In front of the Gothic window stood the old citizen, wrapped in a wide gown, his grey periwig exchanged for a nightcap, which was thrust back from his forehead, and his silk stockings hanging down about his legs. He supported himself on his polished cane in a fit of convulsive merriment, which manifested itself on his solemn old features, like a funny inscription on a tomb-stone. Then Robin seemed to hear the voices of the barbers; of the guests of the inn; and of all who had made sport of him that night. The contagion was spreading among the multitude, when, all at once, it seized upon Robin, and he sent forth a shout of laughter that echoed through the street; every man shook his sides, every man emptied his lungs, but Robin's shout was the loudest there. The cloud-spirits peeped from their silvery islands, as the congregated mirth went roaring up the sky! The Man in the Moon heard the far bellow; 'Oho,' quoth he, 'the old Earth is frolicsome to-night!'

When there was a momentary calm in that tempestuous sea of sound, the leader gave the sign, the procession resumed its march. On they went, like fiends that throng in mockery round some dead potentate, mighty no more, but majestic still in his agony. On they went, in counterfeited pomp, in senseless uproar, in frenzied merriment, trampling all on an old man's heart. On swept the tumult, and left a silent street behind.

'Well, Robin, are you dreaming?' inquired the gentleman, laying his hand on the youth's shoulder.

Robin started, and withdrew his arm from the stone post, to which he had instinctively clung, while the living stream rolled by him. His cheek was somewhat pale, and his eye not quite so lively as in the earlier part of the evening.

'Will you be kind enough to show me the way to the ferry?' said he, after a moment's pause.

'You have then adopted a new subject of inquiry?' observed his companion, with a smile.

'Why, yes, Sir,' replied Robin, rather dryly. 'Thanks to you, and to my other friends, I have at last met my kinsman, and he will scarce desire to see my face again. I begin to grow weary of a town life, Sir. Will you show me the way to the ferry?'

'No, my good friend Robin, not to-night, at least,' said the gentleman. 'Some few days hence, if you continue to wish it, I will speed you on your journey. Or, if you prefer to remain with us, perhaps, as you are a shrewd youth, you may rise in the world, without the help of your kinsman, Major Molineux.'

Roger Malvin's Burial

ONE of the few incidents of Indian warfare, naturally susceptible of the moonlight of romance, was that expedition, under-
taken, for the defence of the frontiers, in the year 1725, which
resulted in the well-remembered 'Lovell's Fight.' Imagination,
by casting certain circumstances judiciously into the shade,
may see much to admire in the heroism of a little band, who
gave battle to twice their number in the heart of the enemy's
country. The open bravery displayed by both parties was in accordance with civilized ideas of valor, and chivalry itself might
not blush to record the deeds of one or two individuals. The
battle, though so fatal to those who fought, was not unfortunate in its consequences to the country; for it broke the
strength of a tribe, and conduced to the peace which subsisted
during several ensuing years. History and tradition are unusu-
ally minute in their memorials of this affair; and the captain of
a scouting party of frontier-men has acquired as actual a military renown, as many a victorious leader of thousands. Some of
the incidents contained in the following pages will be recognized, notwithstanding the substitution of fictitious names, by
such as have heard, from old men's lips, the fate of the few com-
batants who were in a condition to retreat, after 'Lovell's
Fight.'

The early sunbeams hovered cheerfully upon the tree-tops,
beneath which two weary and wounded men had stretched

their limbs the night before. Their bed of withered oak-leaves was strewn upon the small level space, at the foot of a rock, situated near the summit of one of the gentle swells, by which the face of the country is there diversified. The mass of granite, rearing its smooth, flat surface, fifteen or twenty feet above their heads, was not unlike a gigantic grave-stone, upon which the veins seemed to form an inscription in forgotten characters. On a tract of several acres around this rock, oaks and other hard-wood trees had supplied the place of the pines, which were the usual growth of the land; and a young and vigorous sapling stood close beside the travellers.

The severe wound of the elder man had probably deprived him of sleep; for, so soon as the first ray of sunshine rested on the top of the highest tree, he reared himself painfully from his recumbent posture, and sat erect. The deep lines of his countenance, and the scattered grey of his hair, marked him as past the middle age; but his muscular frame would, but for the effects of his wound, have been as capable of sustaining fatigue, as in the early vigor of life. Languor and exhaustion now sat upon his haggard features, and the despairing glance which he sent forward through the depths of the forest, proved his own conviction that his pilgrimage was at an end. He next turned his eyes to the companion, who reclined by his side. The youth, for he had scarcely attained the years of manhood, lay, with his head upon his arm, in the embrace of an unquiet sleep, which a thrill of pain from his wounds seemed each moment on the point of breaking. His right hand grasped a musket, and, to judge from the violent action of his features, his slumbers were bringing back a vision of the conflict, of which he was one of the few survivors. A shout,—deep and loud to his dreaming fancy,—found its way in an imperfect murmur to his lips, and, starting even at the slight sound of his own voice, he suddenly awoke. The first act of reviving recollection, was to make anxious inquiries respecting the condition of his wounded fellow traveller. The latter shook his head.

'Reuben, my boy,' said he, 'this rock, beneath which we sit, will serve for an old hunter's grave-stone. There is many and many a long mile of howling wilderness before us yet; nor would it avail me anything, if the smoke of my own chimney were but on the other side of that swell of land. The Indian bullet was deadlier than I thought.'

'You are weary with our three days' travel,' replied the youth, 'and a little longer rest will recruit you. Sit you here, while I search the woods for the herbs and roots, that must be our sustenance; and having eaten, you shall lean on me, and we will turn our faces homeward. I doubt not, that, with my help, you can attain to some one of the frontier garrisons.'

'There is not two days' life in me, Reuben,' said the other, calmly, 'and I will no longer burthen you with my useless body, when you can scarcely support your own. Your wounds are deep, and your strength is failing fast; yet, if you hasten onward alone, you may be preserved. For me there is no hope; and I will await death here.'

'If it must be so, I will remain and watch by you,' said Reuben, resolutely.

'No, my son, no,' rejoined his companion. 'Let the wish of a dying man have weight with you; give me one grasp of your hand, and get you hence. Think you that my last moments will be eased by the thought, that I leave you to die a more lingering death? I have loved you like a father, Reuben, and, at a time like this, I should have something of a father's authority. I charge you to be gone, that I may die in peace.'

'And because you have been a father to me, should I therefore leave you to perish, and to lie unburied in the wilderness?' exclaimed the youth. 'No; if your end be in truth approaching, I will watch by you, and receive your parting words. I will dig a grave here by the rock, in which, if my weakness overcome me, we will rest together; or, if Heaven gives me strength, I will seek my way home.'

'In the cities, and wherever men dwell,' replied the other,

'they bury their dead in the earth; they hide them from the sight of the living; but here, where no step may pass, perhaps for a hundred years, wherefore should I not rest beneath the open sky, covered only by the oak-leaves, when the autumn winds shall strew them? And for a monument, here is this grey rock, on which my dying hand shall carve the name of Roger Malvin; and the traveller in days to come will know, that here sleeps a hunter and a warrior. Tarry not, then, for a folly like this, but hasten away, if not for your own sake, for hers who will else be desolate.'

Malvin spoke the last few words in a faltering voice, and their effect upon his companion was strongly visible. They reminded him that there were other, and less questionable duties, than that of sharing the fate of a man whom his death could not benefit. Nor can it be affirmed that no selfish feeling strove to enter Reuben's heart, though the consciousness made him more earnestly resist his companion's entreaties.

'How terrible, to wait the slow approach of death, in this solitude!' exclaimed he. 'A brave man does not shrink in the battle, and, when friends stand round the bed, even women may die composedly; but here—'

'I shall not shrink, even here, Reuben Bourne,' interrupted Malvin. 'I am a man of no weak heart; and, if I were, there is a surer support than that of earthly friends. You are young, and life is dear to you. Your last moments will need comfort far more than mine; and when you have laid me in the earth, and are alone, and night is settling on the forest, you will feel all the bitterness of the death that may now be escaped. But I will urge no selfish motive to your generous nature. Leave me for my sake; that, having said a prayer for your safety, I may have space to settle my account, undisturbed by worldly sorrows.'

'And your daughter! How shall I dare to meet her eye?' exclaimed Reuben. 'She will ask the fate of her father, whose life I vowed to defend with my own. Must I tell her, that he travelled three days' march with me from the field of battle, and that then I left him to perish in the wilderness? Were it not better to lie down and die by your side, than to return safe, and say this to Dorcas?'

'Tell my daughter,' said Roger Malvin, 'that, though yourself sore wounded, and weak, and weary, you led my tottering footsteps many a mile, and left me only at my earnest entreaty, because I would not have your blood upon my soul. Tell her, that through pain and danger you were faithful, and that, if your life-blood could have saved me, it would have flowed to its last drop. And tell her, that you will be something dearer than a father, and that my blessing is with you both, and that my dying eyes can see a long and pleasant path, in which you will journey together.'

As Malvin spoke, he almost raised himself from the ground, and the energy of his concluding words seemed to fill the wild and lonely forest with a vision of happiness. But when he sank exhausted upon his bed of oak-leaves, the light, which had kindled in Reuben's eye, was quenched. He felt as if it were both sin and folly to think of happiness at such a moment. His companion watched his changing countenance, and sought, with generous art, to wile him to his own good.

'Perhaps I deceive myself in regard to the time I have to live,' he resumed. 'It may be, that, with speedy assistance, I might recover of my wound. The foremost fugitives must, ere this, have carried tidings of our fatal battle to the frontiers, and parties will be out to succour those in like condition with ourselves. Should you meet one of these, and guide them hither, who can tell but that I may sit by my own fireside again?'

A mournful smile strayed across the features of the dying man, as he insinuated that unfounded hope; which, however, was not without its effect on Reuben. No merely selfish motive, nor even the desolate condition of Dorcas, could have induced him to desert his companion, at such a moment. But his wishes seized upon the thought, that Malvin's life might be preserved, and his sanguine nature heightened, almost to certainty, the remote possibility of procuring human aid.

'Surely there is reason, weighty reason, to hope that friends are not far distant,' he said, half aloud. 'There fled one coward, unwounded, in the beginning of the fight, and most probably he made good speed. Every true man on the frontier would shoulder his musket, at the news; and though no party may range so far into the woods as this, I shall perhaps encounter them in one day's march. Counsel me faithfully,' he added, turning to Malvin, in distrust of his own motives. 'Were your situation mine, would you desert me while life remained?'

'It is now twenty years,' replied Roger Malvin, sighing, however, as he secretly acknowledged the wide dissimilarity between the two cases,—'it is now twenty years, since I escaped, with one dear friend, from Indian captivity, near Montreal. We journeyed many days through the woods, till at length, overcome with hunger and weariness, my friend lay down, and besought me to leave him; for he knew, that, if I remained, we both must perish. And, with but little hope of obtaining succour, I heaped a pillow of dry leaves beneath his head, and hastened on.'

'And did you return in time to save him?' asked Reuben, hanging on Malvin's words, as if they were to be prophetic of his own success.

'I did,' answered the other. 'I came upon the camp of a hunting party, before sunset of the same day. I guided them to the spot where my comrade was expecting death; and he is now a hale and hearty man, upon his own farm, far within the frontiers, while I lie wounded here, in the depths of the wilderness.'

This example, powerful in effecting Reuben's decision, was aided, unconsciously to himself, by the hidden strength of many another motive. Roger Malvin perceived that the victory was nearly won.

'Now go, my son, and Heaven prosper you!' he said. 'Turn

not back with our friends, when you meet them, lest your wounds and weariness overcome you; but send hitherward two or three, that may be spared, to search for me. And believe me, Reuben, my heart will be lighter with every step you take towards home.' Yet there was perhaps a change, both in his countenance and voice, as he spoke thus; for, after all, it was a ghastly fate, to be left expiring in the wilderness.

Reuben Bourne, but half convinced that he was acting rightly, at length raised himself from the ground, and prepared himself for his departure. And first, though contrary to Malvin's wishes, he collected a stock of roots and herbs, which had been their only food during the last two days. This useless supply he placed within reach of the dying man, for whom, also, he swept together a fresh bed of dry oak-leaves. Then, climbing to the summit of the rock, which on one side was rough and broken, he bent the oak-sapling downward, and bound his handkerchief to the topmost branch. This precaution was not unnecessary, to direct any who might come in search of Malvin; for every part of the rock, except its broad, smooth front, was concealed, at a little distance, by the dense undergrowth of the forest. The handkerchief had been the bandage of a wound upon Reuben's arm; and, as he bound it to the tree, he vowed, by the blood that stained it, that he would return, either to save his companion's life, or to lay his body in the grave. He then descended, and stood, with downcast eyes, to receive Roger Malvin's parting words.

The experience of the latter suggested much and minute advice, respecting the youth's journey through the trackless forest. Upon this subject he spoke with calm earnestness, as if he were sending Reuben to the battle or the chase, while he himself remained secure at home; and not as if the human countenance, that was about to leave him, were the last he would ever behold. But his firmness was shaken, before he concluded.

'Carry my blessing to Dorcas, and say that my last prayer shall be for her and you. Bid her have no hard thoughts because

you left me here'—Reuben's heart smote him—'for that your
life would not have weighed with you, if its sacrifice could
have done me good. She will marry you, after she has mourned
a little while for her father; and Heaven grant you long and
happy days! and may your children's children stand round your
death-bed! And, Reuben,' added he, as the weakness of mortality made its way at last, 'return, when your wounds are healed
and your weariness refreshed, return to this wild rock, and lay
my bones in the grave, and say a prayer over them.'

An almost superstitious regard, arising perhaps from the customs of the Indians, whose war was with the dead, as well as
the living, was paid by the frontier inhabitants to the rites of
sepulture; and there are many instances of the sacrifice of life,
in the attempt to bury those who had fallen by the 'sword of
the wilderness.' Reuben, therefore, felt the full importance of
the promise, which he most solemnly made, to return, and perform Roger Malvin's obsequies. It was remarkable, that the latter, speaking his whole heart in his parting words, no longer
endeavored to persuade the youth, that even the speediest
succour might avail to the preservation of his life. Reuben was
internally convinced, that he should see Malvin's living face no
more. His generous nature would fain have delayed him, at
whatever risk, till the dying scene were past; but the desire of
existence, and the hope of happiness had strengthened in his
heart, and he was unable to resist them.

'It is enough,' said Roger Malvin, having listened to Reuben's promise. 'Go, and God speed you!'

The youth pressed his hand in silence, turned, and was departing. His slow and faultering steps, however, had borne
him but a little way, before Malvin's voice recalled him.

'Reuben, Reuben,' said he, faintly; and Reuben returned
and knelt down by the dying man.

'Raise me, and let me lean against the rock,' was his last request. 'My face will be turned towards home, and I shall see
you a moment longer, as you pass among the trees.'

Reuben, having made the desired alteration in his companion's posture, again began his solitary pilgrimage. He walked more hastily at first, than was consistent with his strength; for a sort of guilty feeling, which sometimes torments men in their most justifiable acts, caused him to seek concealment from Malvin's eyes. But, after he had trodden far upon the rustling forest-leaves, he crept back, impelled by a wild and painful curiosity, and, sheltered by the earthy roots of an uptorn tree, gazed earnestly at the desolate man. The morning sun was unclouded, and the trees and shrubs imbibed the sweet air of the month of May; yet there seemed a gloom on Nature's face, as if she sympathized with mortal pain and sorrow. Roger Malvin's hands were uplifted in a fervent prayer, some of the words of which stole through the stillness of the woods, and entered Reuben's heart, torturing it with an unutterable pang. They were the broken accents of a petition for his own happiness and that of Dorcas; and, as the youth listened, conscience, or something in its similitude, pleaded strongly with him to return, and lie down again by the rock. He felt how hard was the doom of the kind and generous being whom he had deserted in his extremity. Death would come, like the slow approach of a corpse, stealing gradually towards him through the forest, and showing its ghastly and motionless features from behind a nearer, and yet a nearer tree. But such must have been Reuben's own fate, had he tarried another sunset; and who shall impute blame to him, if he shrank from so useless a sacrifice? As he gave a parting look, a breeze waved the little banner upon the sapling-oak, and reminded Reuben of his vow.

Many circumstances contributed to retard the wounded traveller, in his way to the frontiers. On the second day, the clouds, gathering densely over the sky, precluded the possibility of regulating his course by the position of the sun; and he knew not but that every effort of his almost exhausted strength, was removing him farther from the home he sought.

His scanty sustenance was supplied by the berries, and other spontaneous products of the forest. Herds of deer, it is true, sometimes bounded past him, and partridges frequently whirred up before his footsteps; but his ammunition had been expended in the fight, and he had no means of slaying them. His wounds, irritated by the constant exertion in which lay the only hope of life, wore away his strength, and at intervals confused his reason. But, even in the wanderings of intellect, Reuben's young heart clung strongly to existence, and it was only through absolute incapacity of motion, that he at last sank down beneath a tree, compelled there to await death. In this situation he was discovered by a party, who, upon the first intelligence of the fight, had been despatched to the relief of the survivors. They conveyed him to the nearest settlement, which chanced to be that of his own residence.

Dorcas, in the simplicity of the olden time, watched by the bed-side of her wounded lover, and administered all those comforts, that are in the sole gift of woman's heart and hand. During several days, Reuben's recollection strayed drowsily among the perils and hardships through which he had passed, and he was incapable of returning definite answers to the inquiries, with which many were eager to harass him. No authentic particulars of the battle had yet been circulated; nor could mothers, wives, and children tell, whether their loved ones were detained by captivity, or by the stronger chain of death. Dorcas nourished her apprehensions in silence, till one afternoon, when Reuben awoke from an unquiet sleep, and seemed to recognize her more perfectly than at any previous time. She saw that his intellect had become composed, and she could no longer restrain her filial anxiety.

'My father, Reuben?' she began; but the change in her lover's countenance made her pause.

The youth shrank, as if with a bitter pain, and the blood gushed vividly into his wan and hollow cheeks. His first impulse was to cover his face; but, apparently with a desperate effort, he half raised himself, and spoke vehemently, defending himself against an imaginary accusation.

'Your father was sore wounded in the battle, Dorcas, and he bade me not burthen myself with him, but only to lead him to the lake-side, that he might quench his thirst and die. But I would not desert the old man in his extremity, and, though bleeding myself, I supported him; I gave him half my strength, and led him away with me. For three days we journeyed on together, and your father was sustained beyond my hopes; but, awaking at sunrise on the fourth day, I found him faint and exhausted,—he was unable to proceed,—his life had ebbed away fast,—and—'

'He died!' exclaimed Dorcas, faintly.

Reuben felt it impossible to acknowledge, that his selfish love of life had hurried him away, before her father's fate was decided. He spoke not; he only bowed his head; and, between shame and exhaustion, sank back and hid his face in the pillow. Dorcas wept, when her fears were thus confirmed; but the shock, as it had been long anticipated, was on that account the less violent.

'You dug a grave for my poor father, in the wilderness, Reuben?' was the question by which her filial piety manifested itself.

'My hands were weak, but I did what I could,' replied the youth in a smothered tone. 'There stands a noble tomb-stone above his head, and I would to Heaven I slept as soundly as he!'

Dorcas, perceiving the wildness of his latter words, inquired no further at the time; but her heart found ease in the thought, that Roger Malvin had not lacked such funeral rites as it was possible to bestow. The tale of Reuben's courage and fidelity lost nothing, when she communicated it to her friends; and the poor youth, tottering from his sick chamber to breathe the sunny air, experienced from every tongue the miserable and humiliating torture of unmerited praise. All acknowledged that he might worthily demand the hand of the fair maiden, to whose father he had been 'faithful unto death'; and, as my tale is not of love, it shall suffice to say, that, in the space of a few months, Reuben became the husband of Dorcas Malvin. During the marriage ceremony, the bride was covered with blushes, but the bridegroom's face was pale.

There was now in the breast of Reuben Bourne an incommunicable thought; something which he was to conceal most heedfully from her whom he most loved and trusted. He regretted, deeply and bitterly, the moral cowardice that had restrained his words, when he was about to disclose the truth to Dorcas; but pride, the fear of losing her affection, the dread of universal scorn, forbade him to rectify this falsehood. He felt, that, for leaving Roger Malvin, he deserved no censure. His presence, the gratuitous sacrifice of his own life, would have added only another, and a needless agony to the last moments of the dying man. But concealment had imparted to a justifiable act, much of the secret effect of guilt; and Reuben, while reason told him that he had done right, experienced, in no small degree, the mental horrors, which punish the perpetrator of undiscovered crime. By a certain association of ideas, he at times almost imagined himself a murderer. For years, also, a thought would occasionally recur, which, though he perceived all its folly and extravagance, he had not power to banish from his mind; it was a haunting and torturing fancy, that his father-in-law was yet sitting at the foot of the rock, on the withered forest-leaves, alive, and awaiting his pledged assistance. These mental deceptions, however, came and went, nor did he ever mistake them for realities; but in the calmest and clearest moods of his mind, he was conscious that he had a deep vow unredeemed, and that an unburied corpse was calling to him, out of the wilderness. Yet, such was the consequence of his prevarication, that he could not obey the call. It was now too late to require the assistance of Roger Malvin's friends, in performing his long-deferred sepulture; and superstitious fears, of which none were more susceptible than the people of the outward settlements, forbade Reuben to go alone. Neither did he know where, in the pathless and illimitable forest, to seek that smooth and lettered rock, at the base of which the body lay; his remembrance of every portion of his travel thence was indistinct, and the latter part had left no impression upon his mind. There was, however, a continual impulse, a voice audible only to himself, commanding him to go forth and redeem his vow; and he had a strange impression, that, were he to make the trial, he would be led straight to Malvin's bones. But, year after year, that summons, unheard but felt, was disobeyed. His one secret thought, became like a chain, binding down his spirit, and, like a serpent, gnawing into his heart; and he was transformed into a sad and downcast, yet irritable man.

In the course of a few years after their marriage, changes began to be visible in the external prosperity of Reuben and Dorcas. The only riches of the former had been his stout heart and strong arm; but the latter, her father's sole heiress, had made her husband master of a farm, under older cultivation, larger, and better stocked than most of the frontier establishments. Reuben Bourne, however, was a neglectful husbandman; and while the lands of the other settlers became annually more fruitful, his deteriorated in the same proportion. The discouragements to agriculture were greatly lessened by the cessation of Indian war, during which men held the plough in one hand, and the musket in the other; and were fortunate if the products of their dangerous labor were not destroyed, either in the field or in the barn, by the savage enemy. But Reuben did not profit by the altered condition of the country; nor can it be denied, that his intervals of industrious attention to his affairs were but scantily rewarded with success. The irritability, by which he had recently become distinguished, was another cause of his declining prosperity, as it occasioned frequent quarrels, in his unavoidable intercourse with the neighboring settlers. The results of these were innumerable law-suits; for the people of New England, in the earliest stages and wildest circumstances of the country, adopted, whenever attainable, the legal mode of deciding their differences. To be brief, the world did not go well with Reuben Bourne, and, though not till many years after his marriage, he was finally a ruined man, with but one remaining expedient against the evil fate that had pursued him. He was to throw sunlight into some deep recess of the forest, and seek subsistence from the virgin bosom of the wilderness.

The only child of Reuben and Dorcas was a son, now arrived at the age of fifteen years, beautiful in youth, and giving promise of a glorious manhood. He was peculiarly qualified for, and already began to excel in, the wild accomplishments of frontier life. His foot was fleet, his aim true, his apprehension quick, his heart glad and high; and all, who anticipated the return of Indian war, spoke of Cyrus Bourne as a future leader in the land. The boy was loved by his father, with a deep and silent strength, as if whatever was good and happy in his own nature had been transferred to his child, carrying his affections with it. Even Dorcas, though loving and beloved, was far less dear to him; for Reuben's secret thoughts and insulated emotions had gradually made him a selfish man; and he could no longer love deeply, except where he saw, or imagined, some reflection or likeness of his own mind. In Cyrus he recognized what he had himself been in other days; and at intervals he seemed to partake of the boy's spirit, and to be revived with a fresh and happy life. Reuben was accompanied by his son in the expedition, for the purpose of selecting a tract of land, and felling and burning the timber, which necessarily preceded the removal of the household gods. Two months of autumn were thus occupied; after which Reuben Bourne and his young hunter returned, to spend their last winter in the settlements.

It was early in the month of May, that the little family snapped asunder whatever tendrils of affection had clung to inanimate objects, and bade farewell to the few, who, in the blight of fortune, called themselves their friends. The sadness of the parting moment had, to each of the pilgrims, its peculiar alleviations. Reuben, a moody man, and misanthropic because unhappy, strode onward, with his usual stern brow and downcast eye, feeling few regrets, and disdaining to acknowledge any. Dorcas, while she wept abundantly over the broken ties by which her simple and affectionate nature had bound itself to everything, felt that the inhabitants of her inmost heart moved on with her, and that all else would be supplied wherever she might go. And the boy dashed one tear-drop from his eye, and thought of the adventurous pleasures of the untrodden forest. Oh! who, in the enthusiasm of a day-dream, has not wished that he were a wanderer in a world of summer wilderness, with one fair and gentle being hanging lightly on his arm? In youth, his free and exulting step would know no barrier but the rolling ocean or the snow-topt mountains; calmer manhood would choose a home, where Nature had strewn a double wealth, in the vale of some transparent stream; and when hoary age, after long, long years of that pure life, stole on and found him there, it would find him the father of a race, the patriarch of a people, the founder of a mighty nation yet to be. When death, like the sweet sleep which we welcome after a day of happiness, came over him, his far descendants would mourn over the venerated dust. Enveloped by tradition in mysterious attributes, the men of future generations would call him godlike; and remote posterity would see him standing, dimly glorious, far up the valley of a hundred centuries!

The tangled and gloomy forest, through which the personages of my tale were wandering, differed widely from the dreamer's Land of Fantasie; yet there was something in their way of life that Nature asserted as her own; and the gnawing cares, which went with them from the world, were all that now obstructed their happiness. One stout and shaggy steed, the bearer of all their wealth, did not shrink from the added weight of Dorcas; although her hardy breeding sustained her, during the latter part of each day's journey, by her husband's side. Reuben and his son, their muskets on their shoulders, and their axes slung behind them, kept an unwearied pace, each watching with a hunter's eye for the game that supplied their food. When hunger bade, they halted and prepared their meal on the bank of some unpolluted forest-brook, which, as they knelt down with thirsty lips to drink, murmured a sweet unwillingness, like a maiden, at love's first kiss. They slept beneath a hut of branches, and awoke at peep of light, refreshed for the toils of another day. Dorcas and the boy went on joyously, and even Reuben's spirit shone at intervals with an outward gladness; but inwardly there was a cold, cold sorrow, which he compared to the snow-drifts, lying deep in the glens and hollows of the rivulets, while the leaves were brightly green above.

Cyrus Bourne was sufficiently skilled in the travel of the woods, to observe, that his father did not adhere to the course they had pursued, in their expedition of the preceding autumn. They were now keeping farther to the north, striking out more directly from the settlements, and into a region, of which savage beasts and savage men were as yet the sole possessors. The boy sometimes hinted his opinions upon the subject, and Reuben listened attentively, and once or twice altered the direction of their march in accordance with his son's counsel. But having so done, he seemed ill at ease. His quick and wandering glances were sent forward, apparently in search of enemies lurking behind the tree-trunks; and seeing nothing there, he would cast his eyes backward, as if in fear of some pursuer. Cyrus, perceiving that his father gradually resumed the old direction, forbore to interfere; nor, though something began to weigh upon his heart, did his adventurous nature permit him to regret the increased length and the mystery of their way.

On the afternoon of the fifth day, they halted and made their simple encampment, nearly an hour before sunset. The face of the country, for the last few miles, had been diversified by swells of land, resembling huge waves of a petrified sea; and in one of the corresponding hollows, a wild and romantic spot, had the family reared their hut, and kindled their fire. There is something chilling, and yet heart-warming, in the thought of these three, united by strong bands of love, and insulated from all that breathe beside. The dark and gloomy pines looked down upon them, and, as the wind swept through their tops, a pitying sound was heard in the forest; or did those old trees groan, in fear that men were come to lay the axe to their roots at last? Reuben and his son, while Dorcas made ready their meal, proposed to wander out in search of game, of which that day's march had afforded no supply. The boy, promising not to quit the vicinity of the encampment, bounded off with a step as light and elastic as that of the deer he hoped to slay; while his father, feeling a transient happiness as he gazed after him, was about to pursue an opposite direction. Dorcas, in the mean-while, had seated herself near their fire of fallen branches, upon the moss-grown and mouldering trunk of a tree, uprooted years before. Her employment, diversified by an occasional glance at the pot, now beginning to simmer over the blaze, was the perusal of the current year's Massachusetts Almanac, which, with the exception of an old black-letter Bible, comprised all the literary wealth of the family. None pay a greater regard to arbitrary divisions of time, than those who are excluded from society; and Dorcas mentioned, as if the information were of importance, that it was now the twelfth of May. Her husband started.

'The twelfth of May! I should remember it well,' muttered he, while many thoughts occasioned a momentary confusion in his mind. 'Where am I? Whither am I wandering? Where did I leave him?'

Dorcas, too well accustomed to her husband's wayward moods to note any peculiarity of demeanor, now laid aside the Almanac, and addressed him in that mournful tone, which the tender-hearted appropriate to griefs long cold and dead.

'It was near this time of the month, eighteen years ago, that my poor father left this world for a better. He had a kind arm to hold his head, and a kind voice to cheer him, Reuben, in his last moments; and the thought of the faithful care you took of him, has comforted me, many a time since. Oh! death would have been awful to a solitary man, in a wild place like this!'

'Pray Heaven, Dorcas,' said Reuben, in a broken voice, 'pray Heaven, that neither of us three die solitary, and lie unburied, in this howling wilderness!' And he hastened away, leaving her to watch the fire, beneath the gloomy pines.

Reuben Bourne's rapid pace gradually slackened, as the pang, unintentionally inflicted by the words of Dorcas, became less acute. Many strange reflections, however, thronged upon him; and, straying onward, rather like a sleep-walker than a hunter, it was attributable to no care of his own, that his devious course kept him in the vicinity of the encampment. His steps were imperceptibly led almost in a circle, nor did he observe that he was on the verge of a tract of land heavily timbered, but not with pine-trees. The place of the latter was here supplied by oaks, and other of the harder woods; and around their roots clustered a dense and bushy undergrowth, leaving, however, barren spaces between the trees, thick-strewn with withered leaves. Whenever the rustling of the branches, or the creaking of the trunks made a sound, as if the forest were waking from slumber, Reuben instinctively raised the musket that rested on his arm, and cast a quick, sharp glance on every side; but, convinced by a partial observation that no animal was near, he would again give himself up to his thoughts. He was musing on the strange influence, that had led him away from his premeditated course, and so far into the depths of the wilderness. Unable to penetrate to the secret place of his soul, where his motives lay hidden, he believed that a supernatural voice had called him onward, and that a supernatural power had obstructed his retreat. He trusted that it was Heaven's intent to afford him an opportunity of expiating his sin; he hoped that he might find the bones, so long unburied; and that, having laid the earth over them, peace would throw its sunlight into the sepulchre of his heart. From these thoughts he was aroused by a rustling in the forest, at some distance from the spot to which he had wandered. Perceiving the motion of some object behind a thick veil of undergrowth, he fired, with the instinct of a hunter, and the aim of a practised marksman. A low moan, which told his success, and by which even animals can express their dying agony, was unheeded by Reuben Bourne. What were the recollections now breaking upon him?

The thicket, into which Reuben had fired, was near the summit of a swell of land, and was clustered around the base of a rock, which, in the shape and smoothness of one of its surfaces, was not unlike a gigantic grave-stone. As if reflected in a mirror, its likeness was in Reuben's memory. He even recognized the veins which seemed to form an inscription in forgotten characters; everything remained the same, except that a thick covert of bushes shrouded the lower part of the rock, and would have hidden Roger Malvin, had he still been sitting there. Yet, in the next moment, Reuben's eye was caught by another change, that time had effected, since he last stood, where he was now standing again, behind the earthy roots of the uptorn tree. The sapling, to which he had bound the blood-stained symbol of his vow, had increased and strengthened into an oak, far indeed from its maturity, but with no mean spread of shadowy branches. There was one singularity, observable in this tree, which made Reuben tremble. The middle and lower branches were in luxuriant life, and an excess of vegetation had fringed the trunk, almost to the ground; but a blight had apparently stricken the upper part of the oak, and the very topmost bough was withered, sapless, and utterly dead. Reuben remembered how the little banner had fluttered on the topmost bough, when it was green and lovely, eighteen years before. Whose guilt had blasted it?

   Dorcas, after the departure of the two hunters, continued her preparations for their evening repast. Her sylvan table was the moss-covered trunk of a large fallen tree, on the broadest part of which she had spread a snow-white cloth, and arranged what were left of the bright pewter vessels, that had been her pride in the settlements. It had a strange aspect—that one little spot of homely comfort, in the desolate heart of Nature. The sunshine yet lingered upon the higher branches of the trees that grew on rising ground; but the shades of evening had deepened into the hollow, where the encampment was made; and the fire-light began to redden as it gleamed up the tall trunks of the pines, or hovered on the dense and obscure mass of foliage, that circled round the spot. The heart of Dorcas was not sad; for she felt that it was better to journey in the wilderness, with two whom she loved, than to be a lonely woman in a crowd that cared not for her. As she busied herself in arranging seats of mouldering wood, covered with leaves, for Reuben and her son, her voice danced through the gloomy forest, in the measure of a song that she had learned in youth. The rude melody, the production of a bard who won no name, was descriptive of a winter evening in a frontier-cottage, when, secured from savage inroad by the high-piled snow-drifts, the family rejoiced by their own fireside. The whole song possessed that nameless charm, peculiar to unborrowed thought; but four continually-recurring lines shone out from the rest, like the blaze of the hearth whose joys they celebrated. Into them, working magic with a few simple words, the poet had instilled the very essence of domestic love and household happiness, and they were poetry and picture joined in one. As Dorcas sang, the walls of her forsaken home seemed to encircle her; she no longer saw the gloomy pines, nor heard the wind, which still, as she began each verse, sent a heavy breath through the branches, and died away in a hollow moan, from the burthen of the song. She was aroused by the report of a gun, in the vicinity of the encampment; and either the sudden sound, or her loneliness by the glowing fire, caused her to tremble violently. The next moment, she laughed in the pride of a mother's heart.

'My beautiful young hunter! my boy has slain a deer!' she exclaimed, recollecting that, in the direction whence the shot proceeded, Cyrus had gone to the chase.

She waited a reasonable time, to hear her son's light step bounding over the rustling leaves, to tell of his success. But he did not immediately appear, and she sent her cheerful voice among the trees, in search of him.

'Cyrus! Cyrus!'

His coming was still delayed, and she determined, as the report had apparently been very near, to seek for him in person. Her assistance, also, might be necessary in bringing home the venison, which she flattered herself he had obtained. She therefore set forward, directing her steps by the long-past sound, and singing as she went, in order that the boy might be aware of her approach, and run to meet her. From behind the trunk of every tree, and from every hiding place in the thick foliage of the undergrowth, she hoped to discover the countenance of her son, laughing with the sportive mischief that is born of affection. The sun was now beneath the horizon, and the light that came down among the trees was sufficiently dim to create many illusions in her expecting fancy. Several times she seemed indistinctly to see his face gazing out from among the leaves; and once she imagined that he stood beckoning to her, at the base of a craggy rock. Keeping her eyes on this object, however, it proved to be no more than the trunk of an oak, fringed to the very ground with little branches, one of which, thrust out farther than the rest, was shaken by the breeze. Making her way round the foot of the rock, she suddenly found herself close to her husband, who had approached in another direction. Leaning upon the butt of his gun, the muzzle of which rested upon the withered leaves, he was apparently absorbed in the contemplation of some object at his feet.

'How is this, Reuben? Have you slain the deer, and fallen asleep over him?' exclaimed Dorcas, laughing cheerfully, on her first slight observation of his posture and appearance.

He stirred not, neither did he turn his eyes towards her; and a cold, shuddering fear, indefinite in its source and object, began to creep into her blood. She now perceived that her husband's face was ghastly pale, and his features were rigid, as if incapable of assuming any other expression than the strong despair which had hardened upon them. He gave not the slightest evidence that he was aware of her approach.

'For the love of Heaven, Reuben, speak to me!' cried Dorcas, and the strange sound of her own voice affrighted her even more than the dead silence.

Her husband started, stared into her face; drew her to the front of the rock, and pointed with his finger.

Oh! there lay the boy, asleep, but dreamless, upon the fallen forest-leaves! his cheek rested upon his arm, his curled locks were thrown back from his brow, his limbs were slightly relaxed. Had a sudden weariness overcome the youthful hunter? Would his mother's voice arouse him? She knew that it was death.

'This broad rock is the grave-stone of your near kindred, Dorcas,' said her husband. 'Your tears will fall at once over your father and your son.'

She heard him not. With one wild shriek, that seemed to force its way from the sufferer's inmost soul, she sank insensible by the side of her dead boy. At that moment, the withered topmost bough of the oak loosened itself, in the stilly air, and fell in soft, light fragments upon the rock, upon the leaves, upon Reuben, upon his wife and child, and upon Roger Malvin's bones. Then Reuben's heart was stricken, and the tears gushed out like water from a rock. The vow that the

wounded youth had made, the blighted man had come to redeem. His sin was expiated, the curse was gone from him; and,
in the hour, when he had shed blood dearer to him than his
own, a prayer, the first for years, went up to Heaven from the
lips of Reuben Bourne.

Passages from a Relinquished Work

At Home

FROM infancy, I was under the guardianship of a village parson, who made me the subject of daily prayer and the sufferer of innumerable stripes, using no distinction, as to these marks of paternal love, between myself and his own three boys. The result, it must be owned, has been very different in their cases and mine; they being all respectable men, and well settled in life, the eldest as the successor to his father's pulpit, the second as a physician, and the third as a partner in a wholesale shoe store; while I, with better prospects than either of them, have run the course, which this volume will describe. Yet there is room for doubt, whether I should have been any better contented with such success as theirs, than with my own misfortunes; at least, till after my experience of the latter had made it too late for another trial.

My guardian had a name of considerable eminence, and fitter for the place it occupies in ecclesiastical history, than for so frivolous a page as mine. In his own vicinity, among the lighter part of his hearers, he was called Parson Thumpcushion, from the very forcible gestures with which he illustrated his doctrines. Certainly, if his powers as a preacher were to be estimated by the damage done to his pulpit furniture, none of his living brethren, and but few dead ones, would have been worthy even to pronounce a benediction after him. Such pounding and expounding, the moment he began to grow warm, such slapping with his open palm, thumping with his closed fist, and banging with the whole weight of the great Bible, convinced me that he held, in imagination, either the Old Nick or some Unitarian infidel at bay, and belabored his unhappy cushion as proxy for those abominable adversaries. Nothing but this exercise of the body, while delivering his sermons, could have supported the good parson's health under the mental toil, which they cost him in composition.

Though Parson Thumpcushion had an upright heart, and some called it a warm one, he was invariably stern and severe, on principle, I suppose, to me. With late justice, though early enough, even now, to be tinctured with generosity, I acknowledge him to have been a good and a wise man, after his own fashion. If his management failed as to myself, it succeeded with his three sons; nor, I must frankly say, could any mode of education, with which it was possible for him to be acquainted, have made me much better than what I was, or led me to a happier fortune than the present. He could neither change the nature that God gave me, nor adapt his own inflexible mind to my peculiar character. Perhaps it was my chief misfortune that I had neither father nor mother alive; for parents have an instinctive sagacity, in regard to the welfare of their children; and the child feels a confidence both in the wisdom and affection of his parents, which he cannot transfer to any delegate of their duties, however conscientious. An orphan's fate is hard, be he rich or poor. As for Parson Thumpcushion, whenever I see the old gentleman in my dreams, he looks kindly and sorrowfully at me, holding out his hand, as if each had something to forgive. With such kindness, and such forgiveness, but without the sorrow, may our next meeting be!

I was a youth of gay and happy temperament, with an incorrigible levity of spirit, of no vicious propensities, sensible enough, but wayward and fanciful. What a character was this, to be brought in contact with the stern old Pilgrim spirit of my guardian! We were at variance on a thousand points; but our chief and final dispute arose from the pertinacity with which he insisted on my adopting a particular profession; while I, being heir to a moderate competence, had avowed my purpose of keeping aloof from the regular business of life. This would have been a dangerous resolution, any where in the world; it was fatal, in New-England. There is a grossness in the conceptions of my countrymen; they will not be convinced that any good thing may consist with what they call idleness; they can anticipate nothing but evil of a young man who neither studies physic, law, nor gospel, nor opens a store, nor takes to farming, but manifests an incomprehensible disposition to be satisfied with what his father left him. The principle is excellent, in its general influence, but most miserable in its effect on the few that violate it. I had a quick sensitiveness to public opinion, and felt as if it ranked me with the tavern-haunters and town-paupers,—with the drunken poet, who hawked his own fourth of July odes,—and the broken soldier, who had been good for nothing since last war. The consequence of all this, was a piece of lighthearted desperation.

I do not over-estimate my notoriety, when I take it for granted, that many of my readers must have heard of me, in the wild way of life which I adopted. The idea of becoming a wandering story teller had been suggested, a year or two before, by an encounter with several merry vagabonds in a showman's wagon, where they and I had sheltered ourselves during a summer shower. The project was not more extravagant than most which a young man forms. Stranger ones are executed every day; and not to mention my prototypes in the East, and the wandering orators and poets whom my own ears have heard, I had the example of one illustrious itinerant in the other hemisphere; of Goldsmith, who planned and performed his travels through France and Italy, on a less promising scheme than mine. I took credit to myself for various qualifications, mental and personal, suited to the undertaking. Besides, my mind had latterly tormented me for employment, keeping up an irregular activity even in sleep, and making me conscious that I must toil, if it were but in catching butter-flies. But my chief motives were discontent with home, and a bitter grudge against Parson Thumpcushion, who would rather have laid me in my father's tomb, than seen me either a novelist or an actor; two characters which I thus hit upon a method of uniting. After all, it was not half so foolish as if I had written romances, instead of reciting them.

The following pages will contain a picture of my vagrant life, intermixed with specimens, generally brief and slight, of that great mass of fiction to which I gave existence, and which has vanished like cloud-shapes. Besides the occasions when I sought a pecuniary reward, I was accustomed to exercise my narrative faculty, wherever chance had collected a little audience, idle enough to listen. These rehearsals were useful in testing the strong points of my stories; and, indeed, the flow of fancy soon came upon me so abundantly, that its indulgence was its own reward; though the hope of praise, also, became a powerful incitement. Since I shall never feel the warm gush of new thought, as I did then, let me beseech the reader to believe, that my tales were not always so cold as he may find them now. With each specimen will be given a sketch of the circumstances in which the story was told. Thus my air-drawn pictures will be set in frames, perhaps more valuable than the pictures them-selves, since they will be embossed with groups of characteristic figures, amid the lake and mountain scenery, the villages and fertile fields, of our native land. But I write the book for the sake of its moral, which many a dreaming youth may profit by, though it is the experience of a wandering story teller.

A Flight in the Fog

I set out on my rambles one morning in June, about sunrise. The day promised to be fair, though, at that early hour, a heavy mist lay along the earth, and settled, in minute globules, on the folds of my clothes, so that I looked precisely as if touched with a hoar-frost. The sky was quite obscured, and the trees and houses invisible, till they grew out of the fog as I came close upon them. There is a hill towards the west, whence the road goes abruptly down, holding a level course through the village, and ascending an eminence on the other side, behind which it disappears. The whole view comprises an extent of half a mile. Here I paused, and, while gazing through the misty veil, it partially rose and swept away, with so sudden an effect, that a gray cloud seemed to have taken the aspect of a small white town. A thin vapor being still diffused through the atmosphere, the wreaths and pillars of fog, whether hung in air or based on earth, appeared not less substantial than the edifices, and gave their own indistinctness to the whole. It was singular, that such an unromantic scene should look so visionary.

Half of the parson's dwelling was a dingy white house, and half of it was a cloud; but Squire Moody's mansion, the grandest in the village, was wholly visible, even the lattice-work of the balcony under the front window; while, in another place, only two red chimneys were seen above the mist, appertaining to my own paternal residence, then tenanted by strangers. I could not remember those with whom I had dwelt there, not even my mother. The brick edifice of the bank was in the clouds; the foundations of what was to be a great block of buildings had vanished, ominously, as it proved; the dry-good store of Mr. Nightingale seemed a doubtful concern; and Dominicus Pike's tobacco-manufactory an affair of smoke, except the splendid image of an Indian chief in front. The white spire of the meeting-house ascended out of the densest heap of vapor, as if that shadowy base were its only support; or, to give a truer interpretation, the steeple was the emblem of religion, enveloped in mystery below, yet pointing to a cloudless atmosphere, and catching the brightness of the east on its gilded vane.

As I beheld these objects, and the dewy street, with grassy intervals and a border of trees between the wheel-track and the side-walks, all so indistinct, and not to be traced without an effort, the whole seemed more like memory than reality. I would have imagined that years had already passed, and I was far away, contemplating that dim picture of my native place, which I should retain in my mind through the mist of time. No tears fell from my eyes among the dew-drops of the morning; nor does it occur to me that I heaved a sigh. In truth, I had never felt such a delicious excitement, nor known what freedom was till that moment, when I gave up my home, and took the whole world in exchange, fluttering the wings of my spirit, as if I would have flown from one star to another through the universe. I waved my hand towards the dusky village, bade it a joyous farewell, and turned away, to follow any path but that which might lead me back. Never was Childe Harold's sentiment adopted in a spirit more unlike his own.

Naturally enough, I thought of Don Quixote. Recollecting how the knight and Sancho had watched for auguries, when they took the road to Toboso, I began, between jest and earnest, to feel a similar anxiety. It was gratified, and by a more poetical phenomenon than the braying of the dappled ass, or the neigh of Rosinante. The sun, then just above the horizon, shone faintly through the fog, and formed a species of rainbow in the west, bestriding my intended road like a gigantic portal. I had never known, before, that a bow could be generated between the sunshine and the morning mist. It had no brilliancy, no perceptible hues; but was a mere unpainted framework, as white and ghost-like as the lunar rainbow, which is deemed ominous of evil. But, with a light heart, to which all omens were propitious, I advanced beneath the misty archway of futurity.

I had determined not to enter on my profession within a hundred miles of home, and then to cover myself with a fictitious name. The first precaution was reasonable enough, as other-

wise Parson Thumpcushion might have put an untimely catastrophe to my story; but as nobody would be much affected by
my disgrace, and all was to be suffered in my own person, I
know not why I cared about a name. For a week or two, I travelled almost at random, seeking hardly any guidance, except the
whirling of a leaf, at some turn of the road, or the green
bough, that beckoned me, or the naked branch, that pointed
its withered finger onward. All my care was to be farther from
home each night than the preceding morning.

A Fellow-Traveller

One day at noontide, when the sun had burst suddenly out
of a cloud and threatened to dissolve me, I looked round for
shelter, whether of tavern, cottage, barn, or shady tree. The
first which offered itself was a wood, not a forest, but a trim
plantation of young oaks, growing just thick enough to keep
the mass of sunshine out, while they admitted a few straggling
beams, and thus produced the most cheerful gloom imaginable. A brook, so small and clear, and apparently so cool, that
I wanted to drink it up, ran under the road through a little
arch of stone, without once meeting the sun, in its passage
from the shade on one side to the shade on the other. As there
was a stepping-place over the stone-wall, and a path along the
rivulet, I followed it and discovered its source,—a spring gushing out of an old barrel.

In this pleasant spot, I saw a light pack suspended from the
branch of a tree, a stick leaning against the trunk, and a person
seated on the grassy verge of the spring, with his back towards
me. He was a slender figure, dressed in black broadcloth,
which was none of the finest, nor very fashionably cut. On hearing my footsteps, he started up, rather nervously, and, turning
round, showed the face of a young man about my own age,
with his finger in a volume which he had been reading, till my

intrusion. His book was, evidently, a pocket-Bible. Though I piqued myself, at that period, on my great penetration into people's characters and pursuits, I could not decide whether this young man in black were an unfledged divine from Andover, a college-student, or preparing for college at some academy. In either case, I would quite as willingly have found a merrier companion; such, for instance, as the comedian with whom Gil Blas shared his dinner, beside a fountain in Spain.

After a nod, which was duly returned, I made a goblet of oak-leaves, filled and emptied it two or three times, and then remarked, to hit the stranger's classical associations, that this beautiful fountain ought to flow from an urn, instead of an old barrel. He did not show that he understood the allusion, and replied, very briefly, with a shyness that was quite out of place, between persons who met in such circumstances. Had he treated my next observation in the same way, we should have parted without another word.

"It is very singular," said I, "though, doubtless, there are good reasons for it, that Nature should provide drink so abundantly, and lavish it every where by the road-side, but so seldom any thing to eat. Why should not we find a loaf of bread on this tree, as well as a barrel of good liquor at the foot of it?"

"There is a loaf of bread on the tree," replied the stranger, without even smiling at a coincidence which made me laugh. "I have something to eat in my bundle, and if you can make a dinner with me, you shall be welcome."

"I accept your offer with pleasure," said I. "A pilgrim, such as I am, must not refuse a providential meal."

The young man had risen to take his bundle from the branch of the tree, but now turned round and regarded me with great earnestness, coloring deeply at the same time. However, he said nothing, and produced part of a loaf of bread, and some cheese, the former being, evidently, home-baked, though some days out of the oven. The fare was good enough, with a real welcome, such as his appeared to be. After spreading these articles on the stump of a tree, he proceeded to ask a blessing on our food; an unexpected ceremony, and quite an impressive one at our woodland table, with the fountain gushing beside us, and the bright sky glimmering through the boughs; nor did his brief petition affect me less, because his embarrassment made his voice tremble. At the end of the meal, he returned thanks with the same tremulous fervor.

He felt a natural kindness for me, after thus relieving my necessities, and showed it by becoming less reserved. On my part, I professed never to have relished a dinner better, and, in requital of the stranger's hospitality, solicited the pleasure of his company to supper.

"Where? At your home?" asked he.

"Yes," said I, smiling.

"Perhaps our roads are not the same," observed he.

"Oh, I can take any road but one, and yet not miss my way," answered I. "This morning I breakfasted at home; I shall sup at home to-night; and a moment ago, I dined at home. To be sure, there was a certain place which I called home; but I have resolved not to see it again, till I have been quite round the globe, and enter the street on the east, as I left it on the west. In the mean time, I have a home every where or no where, just as you please to take it."

"No where, then; for this transitory world is not our home," said the young man, with solemnity. "We are all pilgrims and wanderers; but it is strange that we two should meet."

I inquired the meaning of this remark, but could obtain no satisfactory reply. But we had eaten salt together, and it was right that we should form acquaintance after that ceremony, as the Arabs of the desert do; especially as he had learned something about myself, and the courtesy of the country entitled me to as much information in return. I asked whither he was travelling.

"I do not know," said he; "but God knows."

"That is strange!" exclaimed I; "not that God should know

it, but that you should not. And how is your road to be pointed out?"

"Perhaps by an inward conviction," he replied, looking sideways at me, to discover whether I smiled; "perhaps by an outward sign."

"Then believe me," said I, "the outward sign is already granted you, and the inward conviction ought to follow. We are told of pious men in old times, who committed themselves to the care of Providence, and saw the manifestation of its will in the slightest circumstances; as in the shooting of a star, the flight of a bird, or the course taken by some brute animal. Sometimes even a stupid ass was their guide. May not I be as good a one?"

"I do not know," said the pilgrim, with perfect simplicity.

We did, however, follow the same road, and were not overtaken, as I partly apprehended, by the keepers of any lunatic asylum in pursuit of a stray patient. Perhaps the stranger felt as much doubt of my sanity as I did of his, though certainly with less justice; since I was fully aware of my own extravagances, while he acted as wildly, and deemed it heavenly wisdom. We were a singular couple, strikingly contrasted, yet curiously assimilated, each of us remarkable enough by himself, and doubly so in the other's company. Without any formal compact, we kept together, day after day, till our union appeared permanent. Even had I seen nothing to love and admire in him, I could never have thought of deserting one who needed me continually; for I never knew a person, not even a woman, so unfit to roam the world in solitude, as he was—so painfully shy, so easily discouraged by slight obstacles, and so often depressed by a weight within himself.

I was now far from my native place, but had not yet stepped before the public. A slight tremor seized me, whenever I thought of relinquishing the immunities of a private character, and giving every man, and for money, too, the right, which no man yet possessed, of treating me with open scorn. But about a week after contracting the above alliance, I made my bow to an audience of nine persons, seven of whom hissed me in a very disagreeable manner, and not without good cause. Indeed, the failure was so signal, that it would have been mere swindling to retain the money which had been paid, on my implied contract to give its value of amusement; so I called in the door-keeper, bade him refund the whole receipts, a mighty sum, and was gratified with a round of applause, by way of offset to the hisses. This event would have looked most horrible in anticipation; a thing to make a man shoot himself, or run a muck, or hide himself in caverns, where he might not see his own burning blush; but the reality was not so very hard to bear. It is a fact, that I was more deeply grieved by an almost parallel misfortune, which happened to my companion on the same evening. In my own behalf, I was angry and excited, not depressed; my blood ran quick, my spirits rose buoyantly; and I had never felt such a confidence of future success, and determination to achieve it, as at that trying moment. I resolved to persevere, if it were only to wring the reluctant praise from my enemies.

Hitherto, I had immensely underrated the difficulties of my idle trade; now I recognized, that it demanded nothing short of my whole powers, cultivated to the utmost, and exerted with the same prodigality as if I were speaking for a great party, or for the nation at large, on the floor of the capitol. No talent or attainment could come amiss; every thing, indeed, was requisite; wide observation, varied knowledge, deep thoughts, and sparkling ones; pathos and levity, and a mixture of both, like sunshine in a rain-drop; lofty imagination, veiling itself in the garb of common life; and the practised art which alone could render these gifts, and more than these, available. Not that I ever hoped to be thus qualified. But my despair was no ignoble one; for, knowing the impossibility of satisfying myself, even should the world be satisfied, I did my best to overcome it, investigated the causes of every defect, and strove, with patient stubbornness, to remove them in the next attempt. It is one of my few sources of pride, that, ridiculous as the object was, I followed it up with the firmness and energy of a man.

I manufactured a great variety of plots and skeletons of tales, and kept them ready for use, leaving the filling up to the inspiration of the moment; though I cannot remember ever to have told a tale, which did not vary considerably from my pre-conceived idea, and acquire a novelty of aspect as often as I repeated it. Oddly enough, my success was generally in proportion to the difference between the conception and ac-complishment. I provided two or more commencements and catastrophes to many of the tales, a happy expedient, sug-gested by the double sets of sleeves and trimmings, which di-versified the suits in Sir Piercy Shafton's wardrobe. But my best efforts had a unity, a wholeness, and a separate character, that did not admit of this sort of mechanism.

The Village Theatre

About the first of September, my fellow-traveller and my-self arrived at a country town, where a small company of ac-tors, on their return from a summer's campaign in the British Provinces, were giving a series of dramatic exhibitions. A mod-erately sized hall of the tavern had been converted into a the-atre. The performances that evening were The Heir at Law, and No Song No Supper, with the recitation of Alexander's Feast between the play and farce. The house was thin and dull. But the next day, there appeared to be brighter prospects, the play-bills announcing, at every corner, on the town-pump, and, awful sacrilege! on the very door of the meeting-house, an Unprecedented Attraction!! After setting forth the ordinary entertainments of a theatre, the public were informed, in the hugest type that the printing-office could supply, that the

manager had been fortunate enough to accomplish an engage-
ment with the celebrated Story Teller. He would make his
first appearance that evening, and recite his famous tale of
"Mr. Higginbotham's Catastrophe!" which had been received
with rapturous applause, by audiences in all the principal cities. This outrageous flourish of trumpets, be it known, was
wholly unauthorized by me, who had merely made an engage-
ment for a single evening, without assuming any more celebrity than the little I possessed. As for the tale, it could hardly
have been applauded by rapturous audiences, being as yet an
unfilled plot; nor, even when I stepped upon the stage, was it
decided whether Mr. Higginbotham should live or die.

In two or three places, underneath the flaming bills which
announced the Story Teller, was pasted a small slip of paper,
giving notice, in tremulous characters, of a religious meeting,
to be held at the school-house, where, with Divine permission,
Eliakim Abbott would address sinners on the welfare of their
immortal souls.

In the evening, after the commencement of the tragedy of
Douglas, I took a ramble through the town, to quicken my
ideas by active motion. My spirits were good, with a certain
glow of mind, which I had already learned to depend upon as
the sure prognostic of success. Passing a small and solitary
school-house, where a light was burning dimly, and a few people were entering the door, I went in with them, and saw my
friend Eliakim at the desk. He had collected about fifteen hearers, mostly females. Just as I entered, he was beginning to
pray, in accents so low and interrupted, that he seemed to
doubt the reception of his efforts, both with God and man.
There was room for distrust, in regard to the latter. At the conclusion of the prayer, several of the little audience went out,
leaving him to begin his discourse under such discouraging circumstances, added to his natural and agonizing diffidence.
Knowing that my presence on these occasions increased his em-

barrassment, I had stationed myself in a dusky place near the door, and now stole softly out.

On my return to the tavern, the tragedy was already concluded, and being a feeble one in itself, and indifferently performed, it left so much the better chance for the Story Teller. The bar was thronged with customers, the toddy-stick keeping a continual tattoo, while in the hall there was a broad, deep, buzzing sound, with an occasional peal of impatient thunder, all symptoms of an overflowing house and an eager audience. I drank a glass of wine and water, and stood at the side-scene, conversing with a young person of doubtful sex. If a gentleman, how could he have performed the singing-girl, the night before, in No Song No Supper? Or if a lady, why did she enact Young Norval, and now wear a green coat and white pantaloons in the character of Little Pickle? In either case, the dress was pretty, and the wearer bewitching; so that, at the proper moment, I stepped forward, with a gay heart and a bold one; while the orchestra played a tune that had resounded at many a country ball, and the curtain, as it rose, discovered something like a country bar-room. Such a scene was well enough adapted to such a tale.

The orchestra of our little theatre consisted of two fiddles and a clarionet; but if the whole harmony of the Tremont had been there, it might have swelled in vain, beneath the tumult of applause that greeted me. The good people of the town, knowing that the world contained innumerable persons of celebrity, undreamt of by them, took it for granted that I was one, and that their roar of welcome was but a feeble echo of those which had thundered around me, in lofty theatres. Such an enthusiastic uproar was never heard; each person seemed a Briareus, clapping a hundred hands, besides keeping his feet and several cudgels in play, with stamping and thumping on the floor; while the ladies flourished their white cambric handkerchiefs, intermixed with yellow, and red bandanna, like the

flags of different nations. After such a salutation, the celebrated Story Teller felt almost ashamed to produce so humble
an affair as Mr. Higginbotham's Catastrophe.

This story was originally more dramatic, than as there presented, and afforded good scope for mimicry and buffoonry;
neither of which, to my shame, did I spare. I never knew the
"magic of a name," till I used that of Mr. Higginbotham; often
as I repeated it, there were louder bursts of merriment, than
those which responded to what, in my opinion, were more legitimate strokes of humor. The success of the piece was incalcu-
lably heightened by a stiff queue of horse-hair, which Little
Pickle, in the spirit of that mischief-loving character, had fastened to my collar, where, unknown to me, it kept making the
queerest gestures of its own, in correspondence with all mine.
The audience, supposing that some enormous joke was ap-
pended to this long tail behind, were ineffably delighted, and
gave way to such a tumult of approbation, that, just as the
story closed, the benches broke beneath them, and left one
whole row of my admirers on the floor. Even in that predicament, they continued their applause. In after times, when I
had grown a bitter moralizer, I took this scene for an example,
how much of fame is humbug; how much the meed of what
our better nature blushes at; how much an accident; how much
bestowed on mistaken principles; and how small and poor the
remnant. From pit and boxes there was now a universal call for
the Story Teller.

That celebrated personage came not, when they did call to
him. As I left the stage, the landlord, being also the postmas-
ter, had given me a letter, with the postmark of my native
village, and directed to my assumed name, in the stiff old
hand-writing of Parson Thumpcushion. Doubtless, he had
heard of the rising renown of the Story Teller, and conjectured
at once, that such a nondescript luminary could be no other
than his lost ward. His epistle, though I never read it, affected
me most painfully. I seemed to see the puritanic figure of my

guardian, standing among the fripperies of the theatre, and pointing to the players,—the fantastic and effeminate men, the painted women, the giddy girl in boy's clothes, merrier than modest,—pointing to these with solemn ridicule, and eyeing me with stern rebuke. His image was a type of the austere duty, and they of the vanities of life.

I hastened with the letter to my chamber, and held it unopened in my hand, while the applause of my buffoonry yet sounded through the theatre. Another train of thought came over me. The stern old man appeared again, but now with the gentleness of sorrow, softening his authority with love, as a father might, and even bending his venerable head, as if to say, that my errors had an apology in his own mistaken discipline. I strode twice across the chamber, then held the letter in the flame of the candle, and beheld it consume, unread. It is fixed in my mind, and was so at the time, that he had addressed me in a style of paternal wisdom, and love, and reconciliation, which I could not have resisted, had I but risked the trial. The thought still haunts me, that then I made my irrevocable choice between good and evil fate.

Meanwhile, as this occurrence had disturbed my mind, and indisposed me to the present exercise of my profession, I left the town, in spite of a laudatory critique in the newspaper, and untempted by the liberal offers of the manager. As we walked onward, following the same road, on two such different errands, Eliakim groaned in spirit, and labored, with tears, to convince me of the guilt and madness of my life.

Mr. Higginbotham's Catastrophe

A YOUNG fellow, a tobacco-pedler by trade, was on his way from Morristown, where he had dealt largely with the Deacon of the Shaker settlement, to the village of Parker's Falls on Salmon River. He had a neat little cart, painted green, with a box of cigars depicted on each side-pannel, and an Indian chief, holding a pipe and a golden tobacco-stalk, on the rear. The pedler drove a smart little mare, and was a young man of excellent character, keen at a bargain, but none the worse liked by the Yankees; who, as I have heard them say, would rather be shaved with a sharp razor than a dull one. Especially was he beloved by the pretty girls along the Connecticut, whose favor he used to court by presents of the best smoking-tobacco in his stock, knowing well that the country lasses of New England are generally great performers on pipes. Moreover, as will be seen in the course of my story, the pedler was inquisitive, and something of a tattler, always itching to hear the news, and anxious to tell it again.

After an early breakfast at Morristown, the tobacco-pedler, whose name was Dominicus Pike, had travelled seven miles through a solitary piece of woods, without speaking a word to any body but himself and his little gray mare. It being nearly seven o'clock, he was as eager to hold a morning gossip, as a city shopkeeper to read the morning paper. An opportunity seemed at hand, when, after lighting a cigar with a sun-glass, he looked up, and perceived a man coming over the brow of the hill, at the foot of which the pedler had stopped his green cart. Dominicus watched him as he descended, and noticed that he carried a bundle over his shoulder on the end of a stick, and travelled with a weary, yet determined pace. He did not look as if he had started in the freshness of the morning, but had footed it all night, and meant to do the same all day.

"Good morning, mister," said Dominicus, when within speaking distance. "You go a pretty good jog. What's the latest news at Parker's Falls?"

The man pulled the broad brim of a gray hat over his eyes, and answered, rather sullenly, that he did not come from Parker's Falls, which, as being the limit of his own day's journey, the pedler had naturally mentioned in his inquiry.

"Well, then," rejoined Dominicus Pike, "let's have the latest news where you did come from. I'm not particular about Parker's Falls. Any place will answer."

Being thus importuned, the traveller—who was as ill-looking a fellow as one would desire to meet, in a solitary piece of woods—appeared to hesitate a little, as if he were either searching his memory for news, or weighing the expediency of telling it. At last, mounting on the step of the cart, he whispered in the ear of Dominicus, though he might have shouted aloud, and no other mortal would have heard him.

"I do remember one little trifle of news," said he. "Old Mr. Higginbotham, of Kimballton, was murdered in his orchard, at eight o'clock last night, by an Irishman and a nigger. They strung him up to the branch of a St. Michael's pear-tree, where nobody would find him till the morning."

As soon as this horrible intelligence was communicated, the stranger betook himself to his journey again, with more speed than ever, not even turning his head when Dominicus invited him to smoke a Spanish cigar and relate all the particulars. The pedler whistled to his mare and went up the hill, pondering on the doleful fate of Mr. Higginbotham, whom he had known in the way of trade, having sold him many a bunch of long-nines, and a great deal of pig-tail, lady's twist, and fig tobacco. He was rather astonished at the rapidity, with which the news had spread. Kimballton was nearly sixty miles distant in a straight line; the murder had been perpetrated only at eight o'clock the preceding night; yet Dominicus had heard of it at seven in the morning, when, in all probability, poor Mr. Higginbotham's own family had but just discovered his corpse, hanging on the St. Michael's pear-tree. The stranger on foot must have worn seven-league boots, to travel at such a rate.

"Ill news flies fast, they say," thought Dominicus Pike; "but this beats rail-roads. The fellow ought to be hired to go express with the President's Message."

The difficulty was solved, by supposing that the narrator had made a mistake of one day, in the date of the occurrence; so that our friend did not hesitate to introduce the story at every tavern and country-store along the road, expending a whole bunch of Spanish-wrappers among at least twenty horrified audiences. He found himself invariably the first bearer of the intelligence, and was so pestered with questions, that he could not avoid filling up the outline, till it became quite a respectable narrative. He met with one piece of corroborative evidence. Mr. Higginbotham was a trader; and a former clerk of his, to whom Dominicus related the facts, testified that the old gentleman was accustomed to return home through the orchard, about night-fall, with the money and valuable papers of the store in his pocket. The clerk manifested but little grief at Mr. Higginbotham's catastrophe, hinting, what the pedler had discovered in his own dealings with him, that he was a crusty old fellow, as close as a vice. His property would descend to a pretty niece, who was now keeping school in Kimballton.

What with telling the news for the public good, and driving bargains for his own, Dominicus was so much delayed on the road, that he chose to put up at a tavern, about five miles short of Parker's Falls. After supper, lighting one of his prime cigars, he seated himself in the bar-room, and went through the story of the murder, which had grown so fast that it took him half an hour to tell. There were as many as twenty people in the room, nineteen of whom received it all for gospel. But the twentieth was an elderly farmer, who had arrived on horseback a short time before, and was now seated in a corner, smoking his pipe. When the story was concluded, he rose up very deliberately, brought his chair right in front of Dominicus, and stared him full in the face, puffing out the vilest tobacco smoke the pedler had ever smelt.

"Will you make affidavit," demanded he, in the tone of a country justice taking an examination, "that old Squire Higginbotham of Kimballton was murdered in his orchard, the night before last, and found hanging on his great pear-tree yesterday morning?"

"I tell the story as I heard it, mister," answered Dominicus, dropping his half-burnt cigar; "I don't say that I saw the thing done. So I can't take my oath that he was murdered exactly in that way."

"But I can take mine," said the farmer, "that if Squire Higginbotham was murdered night before last, I drank a glass of bitters with his ghost this morning. Being a neighbor of mine, he called me into his store, as I was riding by, and treated me, and then asked me to do a little business for him on the road. He didn't seem to know any more about his own murder than I did."

"Why, then it can't be a fact!" exclaimed Dominicus Pike.

"I guess he'd have mentioned, if it was," said the old farmer; and he removed his chair back to the corner, leaving Dominicus quite down in the mouth.

Here was a sad resurrection of old Mr. Higginbotham! The pedler had no heart to mingle in the conversation any more, but comforted himself with a glass of gin and water, and went to bed, where, all night long, he dreamt of hanging on the St. Michael's pear-tree. To avoid the old farmer, (whom he so detested, that his suspension would have pleased him better than Mr. Higginbotham's,) Dominicus rose in the gray of the morning, put the little mare into the green cart, and trotted swiftly away towards Parker's Falls. The fresh breeze, the dewy road, and the pleasant summer dawn, revived his spirits, and might have encouraged him to repeat the old story, had there been any body awake to hear it. But he met neither ox-team, light wagon, chaise, horseman, nor foot-traveller, till, just as he crossed Salmon River, a man came trudging down to the bridge, with a bundle over his shoulder, on the end of a stick.

"Good morning, mister," said the pedler, reining in his mare. "If you come from Kimballton or that neighborhood, may be you can tell me the real fact about this affair of old Mr. Higginbotham. Was the old fellow actually murdered, two or three nights ago, by an Irishman and a nigger?"

Dominicus had spoken in too great a hurry to observe, at first, that the stranger himself had a deep tinge of negro blood. On hearing this sudden question, the Ethiopian appeared to change his skin, its yellow hue becoming a ghastly white, while, shaking and stammering, he thus replied:—

"No! no! There was no colored man! It was an Irishman that hanged him last night, at eight o'clock. I came away at seven! His folks can't have looked for him in the orchard yet."

Scarcely had the yellow man spoken, when he interrupted himself, and, though he seemed weary enough before, continued his journey at a pace, which would have kept the pedler's mare on a smart trot. Dominicus stared after him in great perplexity. If the murder had not been committed till Tuesday night, who was the prophet that had foretold it, in all its circumstances, on Tuesday morning? If Mr. Higginbotham's corpse were not yet discovered by his own family, how came the mulatto, at above thirty miles distance, to know that he was hanging in the orchard, especially as he had left Kimballton before the unfortunate man was hanged at all? These ambiguous circumstances, with the stranger's surprise and terror, made Dominicus think of raising a hue and cry after him, as an accomplice in the murder; since a murder, it seemed, had really been perpetrated.

"But let the poor devil go," thought the pedler. "I don't want his black blood on my head; and hanging the nigger wouldn't unhang Mr. Higginbotham. Unhang the old gentleman! It's a sin, I know; but I should hate to have him come to life a second time, and give me the lie!"

With these meditations, Dominicus Pike drove into the street of Parker's Falls, which, as every body knows, is as thriving a village as three cotton-factories and a slitting-mill can make it. The machinery was not in motion, and but a few of the shop-doors unbarred, when he alighted in the stable-yard of the tavern, and made it his first business to order the mare four quarts of oats. His second duty, of course, was to impart Mr. Higginbotham's catastrophe to the ostler. He deemed it advisable, however, not to be too positive as to the date of the direful fact, and also to be uncertain whether it were perpetrated by an Irishman and a mulatto, or by the son of Erin alone. Neither did he profess to relate it on his own authority, or that of any one person; but mentioned it as a report generally diffused.

The story ran through the town like fire among girdled trees, and became so much the universal talk, that nobody could tell whence it had originated. Mr. Higginbotham was as well known at Parker's Falls as any citizen of the place, being part owner of the slitting-mill, and a considerable stockholder in the cotton-factories. The inhabitants felt their own prosperity interested in his fate. Such was the excitement, that the Parker's Falls Gazette anticipated its regular day of publication, and came out with half a form of blank paper, and a column of double pica, emphasized with capitals, and headed HORRID MURDER OF MR. HIGGINBOTHAM! Among other dreadful details, the printed account described the mark of the cord round the dead man's neck, and stated the number of thousand dollars of which he had been robbed; there was much pathos, also, about the affliction of his niece, who had gone from one fainting fit to another, ever since her uncle was found hanging on the St. Michael's pear-tree, with his pockets inside out. The village poet likewise commemorated the young lady's grief, in seventeen stanzas of a ballad. The selectmen held a meeting, and, in consideration of Mr. Higginbotham's claims on the town, determined to issue handbills, offering a reward of five hundred dollars for the apprehension of his murderers, and the recovery of the stolen property.

Meanwhile, the whole population of Parker's Falls, consisting of shopkeepers, mistresses of boarding-houses, factory-girls, mill-men, and school-boys, rushed into the street, and kept up such a terrible loquacity, as more than compensated for the silence of the cotton-machines, which refrained from their usual din out of respect to the deceased. Had Mr. Higginbotham cared about posthumous renown, his untimely ghost would have exulted in this tumult. Our friend Dominicus, in his vanity of heart, forgot his intended precautions, and, mounting on the town-pump, announced himself as the bearer of the authentic intelligence, which had caused so wonderful a sensation. He immediately became the great man of the moment, and had just begun a new edition of the narrative, with a voice like a field-preacher, when the mail stage drove into the village street. It had travelled all night, and must have shifted horses in Kimballton at three in the morning.

"Now we shall hear all the particulars," shouted the crowd.

The coach rumbled up to the piazza of the tavern, followed by a thousand people; for if any man had been minding his own business till then, he now left it at sixes and sevens, to hear the news. The pedler, foremost in the race, discovered two passengers, both of whom had been startled from a comfortable nap to find themselves in the centre of a mob. Every man assailing them with separate questions, all propounded at once, the couple were struck speechless, though one was a lawyer and the other a young lady.

"Mr. Higginbotham! Mr. Higginbotham! Tell us the particulars about old Mr. Higginbotham!" bawled the mob. "What is the coroner's verdict? Are the murderers apprehended? Is Mr. Higginbotham's niece come out of her fainting fits? Mr. Higginbotham! Mr. Higginbotham!!"

The coachman said not a word, except to swear awfully at the ostler for not bringing him a fresh team of horses. The lawyer inside had generally his wits about him, even when asleep; the first thing he did, after learning the cause of the excitement, was to produce a large red pocket-book. Meantime, Dominicus Pike, being an extremely polite young man, and also suspecting that a female tongue would tell the story as glibly as a lawyer's, had handed the lady out of the coach. She was a fine smart girl, now wide awake and bright as a button, and had such a sweet pretty mouth, that Dominicus would almost as lieves have heard a love-tale from it, as a tale of murder.

"Gentlemen and ladies," said the lawyer, to the shopkeepers, the mill-men, and the factory-girls, "I can assure you that some unaccountable mistake, or, more probably, a wilful falsehood, maliciously contrived to injure Mr. Higginbotham's credit, has excited this singular uproar. We passed through Kimballton at three o'clock this morning, and most certainly should have been informed of the murder, had any been perpetrated. But I have proof nearly as strong as Mr. Higginbotham's own oral testimony, in the negative. Here is a note, relating to a suit of his in the Connecticut courts, which was delivered me from that gentleman himself. I find it dated at ten o'clock last evening."

So saying, the lawyer exhibited the date and signature of the note, which irrefragably proved, either that this perverse Mr. Higginbotham was alive when he wrote it, or,—as some deemed the more probable case, of two doubtful ones,—that he was so absorbed in worldly business as to continue to transact it, even after his death. But unexpected evidence was forthcoming. The young lady, after listening to the pedler's explanation, merely seized a moment to smooth her gown and put her curls in order, and then appeared at the tavern-door, making a modest signal to be heard.

"Good people," said she, "I am Mr. Higginbotham's niece."

A wondering murmur passed through the crowd, on beholding her so rosy and bright; that same unhappy niece whom they had supposed, on the authority of the Parker's Falls Gazette, to be lying at death's door in a fainting fit. But some shrewd fellows had doubted, all along, whether a young lady would be quite so desperate at the hanging of a rich old uncle.

"You see," continued Miss Higginbotham, with a smile, "that this strange story is quite unfounded, as to myself; and I believe I may affirm it to be equally so, in regard to my dear uncle Higginbotham. He has the kindness to give me a home in his house, though I contribute to my own support by teaching a school. I left Kimballton this morning, to spend the vacation of commencement-week with a friend, about five miles from Parker's Falls. My generous uncle, when he heard me on the stairs, called me to his bed-side, and gave me two dollars and fifty cents to pay my stage-fare, and another dollar for my extra expenses. He then laid his pocket-book under his pillow, shook hands with me, and advised me to take some biscuits in my bag, instead of breakfasting on the road. I feel confident, therefore, that I left my beloved relative alive, and trust that I shall find him so on my return."

The young lady courtesied at the close of her speech, which was so sensible and well-worded, and delivered with such grace and propriety, that every body thought her fit to be Preceptress of the best Academy in the State. But a stranger would have supposed that Mr. Higginbotham was an object of abhorrence at Parker's Falls, and that a thanksgiving had been proclaimed for his murder; so excessive was the wrath of the inhabitants, on learning their mistake. The mill-men resolved to bestow public honors on Dominicus Pike, only hesitating whether to tar and feather him, ride him on a rail, or refresh him with an ablution at the town-pump, on the top of which he had declared himself the bearer of the news. The selectmen, by advice of the lawyer, spoke of prosecuting him for a misdemeanor, in circulating unfounded reports, to the great disturbance of the peace of the commonwealth. Nothing saved Dominicus, either from mob-law or a court of justice, but an eloquent appeal made by the young lady in his behalf. Addressing a few words of heartfelt gratitude to his benefactress, he mounted the green cart and rode out of town, under a discharge of artillery from the school-boys, who found plenty of ammunition in the neighboring clay-pits and mud-holes. As he turned his head, to exchange a fare-well glance with Mr. Higginbotham's niece, a ball, of the consistence of hasty-pudding, hit him slap in the mouth, giving him a most grim aspect. His whole person was so bespattered with the like filthy missiles, that he had almost a mind to ride back, and supplicate for the threatened ablution at the town-pump; for, though not meant in kindness, it would now have been a deed of charity.

However, the sun shone bright on poor Dominicus, and the mud, an emblem of all stains of undeserved opprobrium, was easily brushed off when dry. Being a funny rogue, his heart soon cheered up; nor could he refrain from a hearty laugh at the uproar which his story had excited. The handbills of the select-men would cause the commitment of all the vagabonds in the State; the paragraph in the Parker's Falls Gazette would be reprinted from Maine to Florida, and perhaps form an item in the London newspapers; and many a miser would tremble for his money-bags and life, on learning the catastrophe of Mr. Higginbotham. The pedler meditated with much fervor on the charms of the young school-mistress, and swore that Daniel Webster never spoke nor looked so like an angel as Miss Higginbotham, while defending him from the wrathful populace at Parker's Falls.

Dominicus was now on the Kimballton turnpike, having all along determined to visit that place, though business had drawn him out of the most direct road from Morristown. As he approached the scene of the supposed murder, he continued to revolve the circumstances in his mind, and was astonished at the aspect which the whole case assumed. Had nothing occurred to corroborate the story of the first traveller, it might now have been considered as a hoax; but the yellow man was evidently acquainted either with the report or the fact; and there was a mystery in his dismayed and guilty look, on being abruptly questioned. When, to this singular combination of incidents, it was added that the rumour tallied exactly with Mr. Higginbotham's character and habits of life; and that he had an orchard, and a St. Michael's pear-tree, near which he always passed at night-fall; the circumstantial evidence appeared so strong, that Dominicus doubted whether the autograph produced by the lawyer, or even the niece's direct testimony, ought to be equivalent. Making cautious inquiries along the road, the pedler further learned that Mr. Higginbotham had in his service an Irishman of doubtful character, whom he had hired without a recommendation, on the score of economy.

"May I be hanged myself," exclaimed Dominicus Pike aloud, on reaching the top of a lonely hill, "if I'll believe old Higginbotham is unhanged, till I see him with my own eyes, and hear it from his own mouth! And, as he's a real shaver, I'll have the minister, or some other responsible man, for an endorser."

It was growing dusk when he reached the toll-house on Kimballton turnpike, about a quarter of a mile from the village of this name. His little mare was fast bringing him up with a man on horseback, who trotted through the gate a few rods in advance of him, nodded to the toll-gatherer, and kept on towards the village. Dominicus was acquainted with the toll-man, and while making change, the usual remarks on the weather passed between them.

"I suppose," said the pedler, throwing back his whip-lash, to bring it down like a feather on the mare's flank, "you have not seen any thing of old Mr. Higginbotham within a day or two?"

"Yes," answered the toll-gatherer. "He passed the gate just before you drove up; and yonder he rides now, if you can see him through the dusk. He's been to Woodfield this afternoon, attending a sheriff's sale there. The old man generally shakes hands and has a little chat with me; but to-night, he nodded,—as if to say, 'charge my toll,'—and jogged on; for wherever he goes, he must always be at home by eight o'clock."

"So they tell me," said Dominicus.

"I never saw a man look so yellow and thin as the squire does," continued the toll-gatherer. "Says I to myself, to-night, he's more like a ghost or an old mummy than good flesh and blood."

The pedler strained his eyes through the twilight, and could just discern the horseman, now far ahead on the village-road. He seemed to recognize the rear of Mr. Higginbotham; but through the evening shadows, and amid the dust from the horse's feet, the figure appeared dim and unsubstantial; as if the shape of the mysterious old man were faintly moulded of darkness and gray light. Dominicus shivered.

"Mr. Higginbotham has come back from the other world, by way of the Kimballton turnpike," thought he.

He shook the reins and rode forward, keeping about the same distance in the rear of the gray old shadow, till the latter was concealed by a bend of the road. On reaching this point, the pedler no longer saw the man on horseback, but found himself at the head of the village street, not far from a number of stores and two taverns, clustered round the meeting-house steeple. On his left was a stone-wall and a gate, the boundary of a wood-lot, beyond which lay an orchard, further still, a mow-

ing-field, and last of all, a house. These were the premises of
Mr. Higginbotham, whose dwelling stood beside the old highway, but had been left in the back-ground by the Kimballton
turnpike. Dominicus knew the place; and the little mare
stopped short by instinct; for he was not conscious of tighten-
ing the reins.

"For the soul of me, I cannot get by this gate!" said he, trembling. "I never shall be my own man again, till I see whether
Mr. Higginbotham is hanging on the St. Michael's pear-tree!"

He leaped from the cart, gave the rein a turn round the gate-
post, and ran along the green path of the wood-lot, as if Old
Nick were chasing behind. Just then the village clock tolled
eight, and as each deep stroke fell, Dominicus gave a fresh
bound and flew faster than before, till, dim in the solitary centre
of the orchard, he saw the fated pear-tree. One great branch
stretched from the old contorted trunk across the path, and
threw the darkest shadow on that one spot. But something
seemed to struggle beneath the branch!

The pedler had never pretended to more courage than befits
a man of peaceable occupation, nor could he account for his
valor on this awful emergency. Certain it is, however, that he
rushed forward, prostrated a sturdy Irishman with the butt-
end of his whip, and found—not, indeed, hanging on the St.
Michael's pear-tree, but trembling beneath it, with a halter
round his neck—the old identical Mr. Higginbotham!

"Mr. Higginbotham," said Dominicus, tremulously,
"you're an honest man, and I'll take your word for it. Have you
been hanged or not?"

If the riddle be not already guessed, a few words will explain
the simple machinery, by which this "coming event" was made
to "cast its shadow before." Three men had plotted the robbery
and murder of Mr. Higginbotham; two of them, successively,
lost courage and fled, each delaying the crime one night, by
their disappearance; the third was in the act of perpetration,
when a champion, blindly obeying the call of fate, like the he-

roes of old romance, appeared in the person of Dominicus Pike.

It only remains to say, that Mr. Higginbotham took the pedler into high favor, sanctioned his addresses to the pretty school-mistress, and settled his whole property on their children, allowing themselves the interest. In due time, the old gentleman capped the climax of his favors, by dying a Christian death, in bed; since which melancholy event, Dominicus Pike has removed from Kimballton, and established a large tobacco manufactory in my native village.

The Haunted Mind

WHAT a singular moment is the first one, when you have hardly begun to recollect yourself, after starting from midnight slumber! By unclosing your eyes so suddenly, you seem to have surprised the personages of your dream in full convocation round your bed, and catch one broad glance at them before they can flit into obscurity. Or, to vary the metaphor, you find yourself, for a single instant, wide awake in that realm of illusions, whither sleep has been the passport, and behold its ghostly inhabitants and wondrous scenery, with a perception of their strangeness, such as you never attain while the dream is undisturbed. The distant sound of a church clock is borne faintly on the wind. You question with yourself, half seriously, whether it has stolen to your waking ear from some gray tower, that stood within the precincts of your dream. While yet in suspense, another clock flings its heavy clang over the slumbering town, with so full and distinct a sound, and such a long murmur in the neighboring air, that you are certain it must proceed from the steeple at the nearest corner. You count the strokes—one—two—and there they cease, with a booming sound, like the gathering of a third stroke within the bell.

If you could choose an hour of wakefulness out of the whole night, it would be this. Since your sober bedtime, at eleven, you have had rest enough to take off the pressure of yesterday's fatigue; while before you, till the sun comes from 'far Cathay' to brighten your window, there is almost the space of a summer night; one hour to be spent in thought, with the mind's eye half shut, and two in pleasant dreams, and two in that strangest of enjoyments, the forgetfulness alike of joy and woe. The moment of rising belongs to another period of time, and appears so distant, that the plunge out of a warm bed into the frosty air cannot yet be anticipated with dismay. Yesterday has already vanished among the shadows of the past; to-morrow has not yet emerged from the future. You have found an inter-mediate space, where the business of life does not intrude; where the passing moment lingers, and becomes truly the pres-ent; a spot where Father Time, when he thinks nobody is watching him, sits down by the way side to take breath. Oh, that he would fall asleep, and let mortals live on without grow-ing older!

Hitherto you have lain perfectly still, because the slightest motion would dissipate the fragments of your slumber. Now, being irrevocably awake, you peep through the half drawn win-dow curtain, and observe that the glass is ornamented with fan-ciful devices in frost work, and that each pane presents some-thing like a frozen dream. There will be time enough to trace out the analogy, while waiting the summons to breakfast. Seen through the clear portion of the glass, where the silvery moun-tain peaks of the frost scenery do not ascend, the most conspicu-ous object is the steeple; the white spire of which directs you to the wintry lustre of the firmament. You may almost distin-guish the figures on the clock that has just told the hour. Such a frosty sky, and the snow covered roofs, and the long vista of the frozen street, all white, and the distant water hardened into rock, might make you shiver, even under four blankets and a woolen comforter. Yet look at that one glorious star! Its beams are distinguishable from all the rest, and actually cast the shadow of the casement on the bed, with a radiance of deeper hue than moonlight, though not so accurate an outline.

You sink down and muffle your head in the clothes, shiver-ing all the while, but less from bodily chill, than the bare idea of a polar atmosphere. It is too cold even for the thoughts to venture abroad. You speculate on the luxury of wearing out a whole existence in bed, like an oyster in its shell, content with the sluggish ecstasy of inaction, and drowsily conscious of nothing but delicious warmth, such as you now feel again. Ah! that idea has brought a hideous one in its train. You think how the dead are lying in their cold shrouds and narrow coffins, through the drear winter of the grave, and cannot persuade your fancy that they neither shrink nor shiver, when the snow is drifting over their little hillocks, and the bitter blast howls against the door of the tomb. That gloomy thought will collect a gloomy multitude, and throw its complexion over your wakeful hour.

In the depths of every heart, there is a tomb and a dungeon, though the lights, the music, and revelry above may cause us to forget their existence, and the buried ones, or prisoners whom they hide. But sometimes, and oftenest at midnight, those dark receptacles are flung wide open. In an hour like this, when the mind has a passive sensibility, but no active strength; when the imagination is a mirror, imparting vividness to all ideas, without the power of selecting or controlling them; then pray that your griefs may slumber, and the brotherhood of remorse not break their chain. It is too late! A funeral train comes gliding by your bed, in which Passion and Feeling assume bodily shape, and things of the mind become dim spectres to the eye. There is your earliest Sorrow, a pale young mourner, wearing a sister's likeness to first love, sadly beautiful, with a hallowed sweetness in her melancholy features, and grace in the flow of her sable robe. Next appears a shade of ruined loveliness, with dust among her golden hair, and her bright garments all faded and defaced, stealing from your glance with drooping head, as fearful of reproach; she was your fondest Hope, but a delusive one; so call her Disappointment now. A sterner form succeeds, with a brow of wrinkles, a look and gesture of iron authority; there is no name for him unless it be Fatality, an emblem of the evil influence that rules your fortunes; a demon to whom you subjected yourself by some error at the outset of life, and were bound his slave forever, by once obeying him. See! those fiendish lineaments graven on the darkness, the writhed lip of scorn, the mockery of that living eye, the pointed finger, touching the sore place in your heart! Do you remember any act of enormous folly, at which you would blush, even in the remotest cavern of the earth? Then recognize your Shame.

Pass, wretched band! Well for the wakeful one, if, riotously miserable, a fiercer tribe do not surround him, the devils of a guilty heart, that holds its hell within itself. What if Remorse should assume the features of an injured friend? What if the fiend should come in woman's garments, with a pale beauty amid sin and desolation, and lie down by your side? What if he should stand at your bed's foot, in the likeness of a corpse, with a bloody stain upon the shroud? Sufficient without such guilt, is this nightmare of the soul; this heavy, heavy sinking of the spirits; this wintry gloom about the heart; this indistinct horror of the mind, blending itself with the darkness of the chamber.

By a desperate effort, you start upright, breaking from a sort of conscious sleep, and gazing wildly round the bed, as if the fiends were any where but in your haunted mind. At the same moment, the slumbering embers on the hearth send forth a gleam which palely illuminates the whole outer room, and flickers through the door of the bed-chamber, but cannot quite dispel its obscurity. Your eye searches for whatever may remind you of the living world. With eager minuteness, you take note of the table near the fire-place, the book with an ivory knife between its leaves, the unfolded letter, the hat and the fallen glove. Soon the flame vanishes, and with it the whole scene is gone, though its image remains an instant in your mind's eye, when darkness has swallowed the reality. Throughout the chamber, there is the same obscurity as before, but not the same gloom within your breast. As your head falls back upon the pillow, you think—in a whisper be it spoken—how pleasant in these night solitudes, would be the rise and fall of a softer breathing than your own, the slight pressure of a tenderer bosom, the quiet throb of a purer heart, imparting its peacefulness to your troubled one, as if the fond sleeper were involving you in her dream.

Her influence is over you, though she have no existence but in that momentary image. You sink down in a flowery spot, on the borders of sleep and wakefulness, while your thoughts rise before you in pictures, all disconnected, yet all assimilated by a pervading gladsomeness and beauty. The wheeling of gorgeous squadrons, that glitter in the sun, is succeeded by the merriment of children round the door of a school-house, beneath the glimmering shadow of old trees, at the corner of a rustic lane. You stand in the sunny rain of a summer shower, and wander among the sunny trees of an autumnal wood, and look upward at the brightest of all rainbows, over-arching the unbroken sheet of snow, on the American side of Niagara. Your mind struggles pleasantly between the dancing radiance round the hearth of a young man and his recent bride, and the twittering flight of birds in spring, about their new-made nest. You feel the merry bounding of a ship before the breeze; and watch the tuneful feet of rosy girls, as they twine their last and merriest dance, in a splendid ball room; and find yourself in the brilliant circle of a crowded theatre, as the curtain falls over a light and airy scene.

With an involuntary start, you seize hold on consciousness, and prove yourself but half awake, by running a doubtful parallel between human life and the hour which has now elapsed. In both you emerge from mystery, pass through a vicissitude that you can but imperfectly control, and are borne onward to another mystery. Now comes the peal of the distant clock, with fainter and fainter strokes as you plunge farther into the wilderness of sleep. It is the knell of a temporary death. Your spirit has departed, and strays like a free citizen, among the people of a shadowy world, beholding strange sights, yet without wonder or dismay. So calm, perhaps, will be the final change; so undisturbed, as if among familiar things, the entrance of the soul to its Eternal home!

Alice Doane's Appeal

ON a pleasant afternoon of June, it was my good fortune to be the companion of two young ladies in a walk. The direction of our course being left to me, I led them neither to Legge's Hill, nor to the Cold Spring, nor to the rude shores and old batteries of the Neck, nor yet to Paradise; though if the latter place were rightly named, my fair friends would have been at home there. We reached the outskirts of the town, and turning aside from a street of tanners and curriers, began to ascend a hill, which at a distance, by its dark slope and the even line of its summit, resembled a green rampart along the road. It was less steep than its aspect threatened. The eminence formed part of an extensive tract of pasture land, and was traversed by cow paths in various directions; but, strange to tell, though the whole slope and summit were of a peculiarly deep green, scarce a blade of grass was visible from the base upward. This deceitful verdure was occasioned by a plentiful crop of 'wood-wax,' which wears the same dark and glossy green throughout the summer, except at one short period, when it puts forth a profusion of yellow blossoms. At that season to a distant spectator, the hill appears absolutely overlaid with gold, or covered with a glory of sunshine, even beneath a clouded sky. But the curious wanderer on the hill will perceive that all the grass, and every thing that should nourish man or beast, has been destroyed by this vile and ineradicable weed: its tufted roots make the soil their own, and permit nothing else to vegetate among them; so that a physical curse may be said to have blasted the spot, where guilt and phrenzy consummated the most execrable scene, that our history blushes to record. For this was the field where superstition won her darkest triumph; the high place where our fathers set up their shame, to the mournful gaze of generations far remote. The dust of martyrs was beneath our feet. We stood on Gallows Hill.

For my own part, I have often courted the historic influence of the spot. But it is singular, how few come on pilgrimage to this famous hill; how many spend their lives almost at its base, and never once obey the summons of the shadowy past, as it beckons them to the summit. Till a year or two since, this portion of our history had been very imperfectly written, and, as we are not a people of legend or tradition, it was not every citizen of our ancient town that could tell, within half a century, so much as the date of the witchcraft delusion. Recently, indeed, an historian has treated the subject in a manner that will keep his name alive, in the only desirable connection with the errors of our ancestry, by converting the hill of their disgrace into an honorable monument of his own antiquarian lore, and of that better wisdom, which draws the moral while it tells the tale. But we are a people of the present and have no heartfelt interest in the olden time. Every fifth of November, in commemoration of they know not what, or rather without an idea beyond the momentary blaze, the young men scare the town with bonfires on this haunted height, but never dream of paying funeral honors to those who died so wrongfully, and without a coffin or a prayer, were buried here.

Though with feminine susceptibility, my companions caught all the melancholy associations of the scene, yet these could but imperfectly overcome the gayety of girlish spirits. Their emotions came and went with quick vicissitude, and sometimes combined to form a peculiar and delicious excitement, the mirth brightening the gloom into a sunny shower of feeling, and a rainbow in the mind. My own more sombre mood was tinged by theirs. With now a merry word and next a sad one, we trod among the tangled weeds, and almost hoped that our feet would sink into the hollow of a witch's grave. Such vestiges were to be found within the memory of man, but have vanished now, and with them, I believe, all traces of the precise spot of the executions. On the long and broad ridge of the eminence, there is no very decided elevation of any one point, nor other prominent marks, except the decayed stumps of two trees, standing near each other, and here and there the rocky substance of the hill, peeping just above the wood-wax.

There are few such prospects of town and village, woodland and cultivated field, steeples and country seats, as we beheld from this unhappy spot. No blight had fallen on old Essex; all was prosperity and riches, healthfully distributed. Before us lay our native town, extending from the foot of the hill to the harbor, level as a chess board, embraced by two arms of the sea, and filling the whole peninsula with a close assemblage of wooden roofs, overtopt by many a spire, and intermixed with frequent heaps of verdure, where trees threw up their shade from unseen trunks. Beyond, was the bay and its islands, almost the only objects, in a country unmarked by strong natural features, on which time and human toil had produced no change. Retaining these portions of the scene, and also the peaceful glory and tender gloom of the declining sun, we threw, in imagination, a veil of deep forest over the land, and pictured a few scattered villages, and this old town itself a village, as when the prince of hell bore sway there. The idea thus gained, of its former aspect, its quaint edifices standing far apart, with peaked roofs and projecting stories, and its single meeting house pointing up a tall spire in the midst; the vision, in short, of the town in 1692, served to introduce a wondrous tale of those old times.

I had brought the manuscript in my pocket. It was one of a series written years ago, when my pen, now sluggish and perhaps feeble, because I have not much to hope or fear, was driven by stronger external motives, and a more passionate impulse within, than I am fated to feel again. Three or four of these tales had appeared in the Token, after a long time and various adventures, but had incumbered me with no troublesome notoriety, even in my birth place. One great heap had met a brighter destiny: they had fed the flames; thoughts meant to delight the world and endure for ages, had perished in a moment, and stirred not a single heart but mine. The story now to be introduced, and another, chanced to be in kinder custody at the time, and thus by no conspicuous merits of their own, escaped destruction.

The ladies, in consideration that I had never before intruded my performances on them, by any but the legitimate medium, through the press, consented to hear me read. I made them sit down on a moss-grown rock, close by the spot where we chose to believe that the death-tree had stood. After a little hesitation on my part, caused by a dread of renewing my acquaintance with fantasies that had lost their charm, in the ceaseless flux of mind, I began the tale, which opened darkly with the discovery of a murder.

A hundred years, and nearly half that time, have elapsed since the body of a murdered man was found, at about the distance of three miles, on the old road to Boston. He lay in a solitary spot, on the bank of a small lake, which the severe frost of December had covered with a sheet of ice. Beneath this, it seemed to have been the intention of the murderer to conceal his victim in a chill and watery grave, the ice being deeply hacked, perhaps with the weapon that had slain him, though its solidity was too stubborn for the patience of a man with blood upon his hand. The corpse therefore reclined on the earth, but was separated from the road by a thick growth of dwarf pines. There had been a slight fall of snow during the night, and as if Nature were shocked at the deed, and strove to hide it with her frozen tears, a little drifted heap had partly buried the body, and lay deepest over the pale dead face. An early traveller, whose dog had led him to the spot, ventured to uncover the features, but was affrighted by their expression. A look of evil and scornful triumph had hardened on them, and made death so life-like and so terrible, that the beholder at once took flight, as swiftly as if the stiffened corpse would rise up and follow.

I read on, and identified the body as that of a young man, a stranger in the country, but resident during several preceding months in the town which lay at our feet. The story described, at some length, the excitement caused by the murder, the unavailing quest after the perpetrator, the funeral ceremonies, and other common place matters, in the course of which, I brought forward the personages who were to move among the succeeding events. They were but three. A young man and his sister; the former characterized by a diseased imagination and morbid feelings; the latter, beautiful and virtuous, and instilling something of her own excellence into the wild heart of her brother, but not enough to cure the deep taint of his nature. The third person was a wizard; a small, gray, withered man, with fiendish ingenuity in devising evil, and superhuman power to execute it, but senseless as an idiot and feebler than a child, to all better purposes. The central scene of the story was an interview between this wretch and Leonard Doane, in the wizard's hut, situated beneath a range of rocks at some distance from the town. They sat beside a mouldering fire, while a tempest of wintry rain was beating on the roof. The young man spoke of the closeness of the tie which united him and Alice, the concentrated fervor of their affection from childhood upwards, their sense of lonely sufficiency to each other, because they only of their race had escaped death, in a night attack by the Indians. He related his discovery, or suspicion of a secret sympathy between his sister and Walter Brome, and told how a distempered jealousy had maddened him. In the following passage, I threw a glimmering light on the mystery of the tale.

'Searching,' continued Leonard, 'into the breast of Walter Brome, I at length found a cause why Alice must inevitably love him. For he was my very counterpart! I compared his mind by each individual portion, and as a whole, with mine. There was a resemblance from which I shrank with sickness, and loathing, and horror, as if my own features had come and stared upon me in a solitary place, or had met me in struggling through a crowd. Nay! the very same thoughts would often express themselves in the same words from our lips, proving a hateful sympathy in our secret souls. His education, indeed, in the cities of the old world, and mine in this rude wilderness, had wrought a superficial difference. The evil of his character, also, had been strengthened and rendered prominent by a reckless and ungoverned life, while mine had been softened and purified by the gentle and holy nature of Alice. But my soul had been conscious of the germ of all the fierce and deep passions, and of all the many varieties of wickedness, which accident had brought to their full maturity in him. Nor will I deny, that in the accursed one, I could see the withered blossom of every virtue, which by a happier culture, had been made to bring forth fruit in me. Now, here was a man, whom Alice might love with all the strength of sisterly affection, added to that impure passion which alone engrosses all the heart. The stranger would have more than the love which had been gathered to me from the many graves of our household—and I be desolate!'

Leonard Doane went on to describe the insane hatred that had kindled his heart into a volume of hellish flame. It appeared, indeed, that his jealousy had grounds, so far as that Walter Brome had actually sought the love of Alice, who also had betrayed an undefinable, but powerful interest in the unknown youth. The latter, in spite of his passion for Alice, seemed to return the loathful antipathy of her brother; the similarity of their dispositions made them like joint possessors of an individual nature, which could not become wholly the property of one, unless by the extinction of the other. At last, with the same devil in each bosom, they chanced to meet, they two on a lonely road. While Leonard spoke, the wizard had sat listening to what he already knew, yet with tokens of pleasurable interest, manifested by flashes of expression across his vacant features, by grisly smiles and by a word here and there, mysteriously filling up some void in the narrative. But when the young man told, how Walter Brome had taunted him with indubitable proofs of the shame of Alice, and before the triumphant sneer could vanish from his face, had died by her brother's hand, the wizard laughed aloud. Leonard started, but just then a gust of wind came down the chimney, forming itself into a close resemblance of the slow, unvaried laughter, by which he had been interrupted. 'I was deceived,' thought he; and thus pursued his fearful story.

'I trod out his accursed soul, and knew that he was dead; for my spirit bounded as if a chain had fallen from it and left me free. But the burst of exulting certainty soon fled, and was succeeded by a torpor over my brain and a dimness before my eyes, with the sensation of one who struggles through a dream. So I bent down over the body of Walter Brome, gazing into his face, and striving to make my soul glad with the thought, that he, in very truth, lay dead before me. I know not what space of time I had thus stood, nor how the vision came. But it seemed to me that the irrevocable years, since childhood had rolled back, and a scene, that had long been confused and broken in my memory, arrayed itself with all its first distinctness. Methought I stood a weeping infant by my father's hearth; by the cold and blood-stained hearth where he lay dead. I heard the childish wail of Alice, and my own cry arose with hers, as we beheld the features of our parent, fierce with the strife and distorted with the pain, in which his spirit had passed away. As I gazed, a cold wind whistled by, and waved my father's hair. Immediately, I stood again in the lonesome road, no more a sinless child, but a man of blood, whose tears were falling fast over the face of his dead enemy. But the delusion was not wholly gone; that face still wore a likeness of my father; and because my soul shrank from the fixed glare of the eyes, I bore the body to the lake, and would have buried it there. But before his icy sepulchre was hewn, I heard the voices of two travellers and fled.'

Such was the dreadful confession of Leonard Doane. And now tortured by the idea of his sister's guilt, yet sometimes yielding to a conviction of her purity; stung with remorse for the death of Walter Brome, and shuddering with a deeper sense of some unutterable crime, perpetrated, as he imagined, in madness or a dream; moved also by dark impulses, as if a fiend were whispering him to meditate violence against the life of Alice; he had sought this interview with the wizard, who, on certain conditions, had no power to withhold his aid in unravelling the mystery. The tale drew near its close.

The moon was bright on high; the blue firmament appeared to glow with an inherent brightness; the greater stars were burning in their spheres; the northern lights threw their mysterious glare far over the horizon; the few small clouds aloft were burthened with radiance; but the sky with all its variety of light, was scarcely so brilliant as the earth. The rain of the preceding night had frozen as it fell, and, by that simple magic, had wrought wonders. The trees were hung with diamonds and many-colored gems; the houses were overlaid with silver, and the streets paved with slippery brightness; a frigid glory was flung over all familiar things, from the cottage chimney to the steeple of the meeting house, that gleamed upward to the sky.

This living world, where we sit by our firesides, or go forth to meet beings like ourselves, seemed rather the creation of wizard power, with so much of resemblance to known objects, that a man might shudder at the ghostly shape of his old beloved dwelling, and the shadow of a ghostly tree before his door. One looked to behold inhabitants suited to such a town, glittering in icy garments, with motionless features, cold, sparkling eyes, and just sensation enough in their frozen hearts to shiver at each other's presence.

By this fantastic piece of description, and more in the same style, I intended to throw a ghostly glimmer round the reader, so that his imagination might view the town through a medium that should take off its every day aspect, and make it a proper theatre for so wild a scene as the final one. Amid this unearthly show, the wretched brother and sister were represented as setting forth, at midnight, through the gleaming streets, and directing their steps to a grave yard, where all the dead had been laid, from the first corpse in that ancient town, to the murdered man who was buried three days before. As they went, they seemed to see the wizard gliding by their sides, or walking dimly on the path before them. But here I paused, and gazed into the faces of my two fair auditors, to judge whether, even on the hill where so many had been brought to death by wilder tales than this, I might venture to proceed. Their bright eyes were fixed on me; their lips apart. I took courage, and led the fated pair to a new made grave, where for a few moments, in the bright and silent midnight, they stood alone. But suddenly, there was a multitude of people among the graves.

Each family tomb had given up its inhabitants, who, one by one, through distant years, had been borne to its dark chamber, but now came forth and stood in a pale group together. There was the gray ancestor, the aged mother, and all their descendants, some withered and full of years, like themselves, and others in their prime; there, too, were the children who went prattling to the tomb, and there the maiden who yielded her early beauty to death's embrace, before passion had polluted it. Husbands and wives arose, who had lain many years side by side, and young mothers who had forgotten to kiss their first babes, though pillowed so long on their bosoms. Many had been buried in the habiliments of life, and still wore their ancient garb; some were old defenders of the infant colony, and gleamed forth in their steel caps and bright breastplates, as if starting up at an Indian war-cry; other venerable shapes had been pastors of the church, famous among the New England clergy, and now leaned with hands clasped over their grave stones, ready to call the congregation to prayer. There stood the early settlers, those old illustrious ones, the heroes of tradition and fireside legends, the men of history whose features had been so long beneath the sod, that few alive could have remembered them. There, too, were faces of former townspeople, dimly recollected from childhood, and others, whom Leonard and Alice had wept in later years, but who now were most terrible of all, by their ghastly smile of recognition. All, in short, were there; the dead of other generations, whose moss-grown names could scarce be read upon their tomb stones, and their successors, whose graves were not yet green; all whom black funerals had followed slowly thither, now re-appeared where the mourners left them. Yet none but souls accursed were there, and fiends counterfeiting the likeness of departed saints.

The countenances of those venerable men, whose very features had been hallowed by lives of piety, were contorted now by intolerable pain or hellish passion, and now by an unearthly and derisive merriment. Had the pastors prayed, all saintlike as they seemed, it had been blasphemy. The chaste matrons, too, and the maidens with untasted lips, who had slept in their virgin graves apart from all other dust, now wore a look from which the two trembling mortals shrank, as if the unimaginable sin of twenty worlds were collected there. The faces of fond lovers, even of such as had pined into the tomb, because there their treasure was, were bent on one another with glances of hatred and smiles of bitter scorn, passions that are to devils, what love is to the blest. At times, the features of those, who had passed from a holy life to heaven, would vary to and fro, between their assumed aspect and the fiendish lineaments whence they had been transformed. The whole miserable multitude, both sinful souls and false spectres of good men, groaned horribly and gnashed their teeth, as they looked upward to the calm loveliness of the midnight sky, and beheld those homes of bliss where they must never dwell. Such was the apparition, though too shadowy for language to portray; for here would be the moonbeams on the ice, glittering through a warrior's breastplate, and there the letters of a tomb stone, on the form that stood before it; and whenever a breeze went by, it swept the old men's hoary heads, the women's fearful beauty, and all the unreal throng, into one indistinguishable cloud together.

I dare not give the remainder of the scene, except in a very brief epitome. This company of devils and condemned souls had come on a holiday, to revel in the discovery of a complicated crime; as foul a one as ever was imagined in their dreadful abode. In the course of the tale, the reader had been permitted to discover, that all the incidents were results of the machinations of the wizard, who had cunningly devised that Walter Brome should tempt his unknown sister to guilt and shame, and himself perish by the hand of his twin-brother. I described the glee of the fiends, at this hideous conception, and their eagerness to know if it were consummated. The story concluded with the Appeal of Alice to the spectre of Walter Brome; his reply, absolving her from every stain; and the trembling awe with which ghost and devil fled, as from the sinless presence of an angel.

The sun had gone down. While I held my page of wonders in the fading light, and read how Alice and her brother were left alone among the graves, my voice mingled with the sigh of a summer wind, which passed over the hill top with the broad and hollow sound, as of the flight of unseen spirits. Not a word was spoken, till I added, that the wizard's grave was close beside us, and that the wood-wax had sprouted originally from his unhallowed bones. The ladies started; perhaps their cheeks might have grown pale, had not the crimson west been blushing on them; but after a moment they began to laugh, while the breeze took a livelier motion, as if responsive to their mirth. I kept an awful solemnity of visage, being indeed a little piqued, that a narrative which had good authority in our ancient superstitions, and would have brought even a church deacon to Gallows Hill, in old witch times, should now be considered too grotesque and extravagant, for timid maids to tremble at. Though it was past supper time, I detained them a while longer on the hill, and made a trial whether truth were more powerful than fiction.

We looked again towards the town, no longer arrayed in that icy splendor of earth, tree and edifice, beneath the glow of a wintry midnight, which, shining afar through the gloom of a century, had made it appear the very home of visions in visionary streets. An indistinctness had begun to creep over the mass of buildings and blend them with the intermingled tree tops, except where the roof of a statelier mansion, and the steeples and brick towers of churches, caught the brightness of some cloud that yet floated in the sunshine. Twilight over the landscape was congenial to the obscurity of time. With such eloquence as my share of feeling and fancy could supply, I called back hoar antiquity, and bade my companions imagine an ancient multitude of people, congregated on the hill side, spreading far below, clustering on the steep old roofs, and climbing the adjacent heights, wherever a glimpse of this spot might be obtained. I strove to realize and faintly communi-

cate, the deep, unutterable loathing and horror, the indignation, the affrighted wonder, that wrinkled on every brow, and
filled the universal heart. See! the whole crowd turns pale and
shrinks within itself, as the virtuous emerge from yonder
street. Keeping pace with that devoted company, I described
them one by one; here tottered a woman in her dotage, knowing neither the crime imputed her, nor its punishment; there
another, distracted by the universal madness, till feverish
dreams were remembered as realities, and she almost believed
her guilt. One, a proud man once, was so broken down by the
intolerable hatred heaped upon him, that he seemed to hasten
his steps, eager to hide himself in the grave hastily dug, at the
foot of the gallows. As they went slowly on, a mother looked
behind, and beheld her peaceful dwelling; she cast her eyes
elsewhere, and groaned inwardly, yet with bitterest anguish;
for there was her little son among the accusers. I watched the
face of an ordained pastor, who walked onward to the same
death; his lips moved in prayer, no narrow petition for himself
alone, but embracing all, his fellow sufferers and the frenzied
multitude; he looked to heaven and trod lightly up the hill.

Behind their victims came the afflicted, a guilty and miserable band; villains who had thus avenged themselves on their
enemies, and viler wretches, whose cowardice had destroyed
their friends; lunatics, whose ravings had chimed in with the
madness of the land; and children, who had played a game that
the imps of darkness might have envied them, since it dis-
graced an age, and dipped a people's hands in blood. In the rear
of the procession rode a figure on horseback, so darkly conspicuous, so sternly triumphant, that my hearers mistook him for
the visible presence of the fiend himself; but it was only his
good friend, Cotton Mather, proud of his well won dignity, as
the representative of all the hateful features of his time; the one
blood-thirsty man, in whom were concentrated those vices of
spirit and errors of opinion, that sufficed to madden the whole
surrounding multitude. And thus I marshalled them onward,

the innocent who were to die, and the guilty who were to grow old in long remorse—tracing their every step, by rock, and shrub, and broken track, till their shadowy visages had circled round the hill-top, where we stood. I plunged into my imagination for a blacker horror, and a deeper woe, and pictured the scaffold——

But here my companions seized an arm on each side; their nerves were trembling; and sweeter victory still, I had reached the seldom trodden places of their hearts, and found the well-spring of their tears. And now the past had done all it could. We slowly descended, watching the lights as they twinkled gradually through the town, and listening to the distant mirth of boys at play, and to the voice of a young girl, warbling somewhere in the dusk, a pleasant sound to wanderers from old witch times. Yet ere we left the hill, we could not but regret, that there is nothing on its barren summit, no relic of old, nor lettered stone of later days, to assist the imagination in appealing to the heart. We build the memorial column on the height which our fathers made sacred with their blood, poured out in a holy cause. And here in dark, funereal stone, should rise another monument, sadly commemorative of the errors of an earlier race, and not to be cast down, while the human heart has one infirmity that may result in crime.

The Gray Champion

THERE was once a time, when New-England groaned under the actual pressure of heavier wrongs, than those threatened ones which brought on the Revolution. James II., the bigoted successor of Charles the Voluptuous, had annulled the charters of all the colonies, and sent a harsh and unprincipled soldier to take away our liberties and endanger our religion. The administration of Sir Edmund Andros lacked scarcely a single characteristic of tyranny: a Governor and Council, holding office from the King, and wholly independent of the country; laws made and taxes levied without concurrence of the people, immediate or by their representatives; the rights of private citizens violated, and the titles of all landed property declared void; the voice of complaint stifled by restrictions on the press; and, finally, disaffection overawed by the first band of mercenary troops that ever marched on our free soil. For two years, our ancestors were kept in sullen submission, by that filial love which had invariably secured their allegiance to the mother country, whether its head chanced to be a Parliament, Protector, or popish Monarch. Till these evil times, however, such allegiance had been merely nominal, and the colonists had ruled themselves, enjoying far more freedom, than is even yet the privilege of the native subjects of Great Britain.

At length, a rumor reached our shores, that the Prince of Orange had ventured on an enterprise, the success of which would be the triumph of civil and religious rights and the salvation of New-England. It was but a doubtful whisper; it might be false, or the attempt might fail; and, in either case, the man, that stirred against King James, would lose his head. Still the intelligence produced a marked effect. The people smiled mysteriously in the streets, and threw bold glances at their oppressors; while, far and wide, there was a subdued and silent agitation, as if the slightest signal would rouse the whole land from its sluggish despondency. Aware of their danger, the rulers resolved to avert it by an imposing display of strength, and perhaps to confirm their despotism by yet harsher measures. One afternoon in April, 1689, Sir Edmund Andros and his favorite councillors, being warm with wine, assembled the red-coats of the Governor's Guard, and made their appearance in the streets of Boston. The sun was near setting when the march commenced.

The roll of the drum, at that unquiet crisis, seemed to go through the streets, less as the martial music of the soldiers, than as a muster-call to the inhabitants themselves. A multitude, by various avenues, assembled in King-street, which was destined to be the scene, nearly a century afterwards, of another encounter between the troops of Britain, and a people struggling against her tyranny. Though more than sixty years had elapsed, since the Pilgrims came, this crowd of their descendants still showed the strong and sombre features of their character, perhaps more strikingly in such a stern emergency than on happier occasions. There was the sober garb, the general severity of mien, the gloomy but undismayed expression, the scriptural forms of speech, and the confidence in Heaven's blessing on a righteous cause, which would have marked a band of the original Puritans, when threatened by some peril of the wilderness. Indeed, it was not yet time for the old spirit to be extinct; since there were men in the street, that day, who had worshipped there beneath the trees, before a house was reared to the God, for whom they had become exiles. Old soldiers of the Parliament were here too, smiling grimly at the thought, that their aged arms might strike another blow against the house of Stuart. Here also, were the veterans of King Philip's war, who had burnt villages and slaughtered young and old, with pious fierceness, while the godly souls throughout the land were helping them with prayer. Several ministers were scattered among the crowd, which, unlike all other mobs, regarded them with such reverence, as if there were sanctity in their very garments. These holy men exerted their influence to quiet the people, but not to disperse them. Meantime, the purpose of the Governor, in disturbing the peace of the town, at a period when the slightest commotion might throw the country into a ferment, was almost the universal subject of inquiry, and variously explained.

'Satan will strike his master-stroke presently,' cried some, 'because he knoweth that his time is short. All our godly pastors are to be dragged to prison! We shall see them at a Smithfield fire in King-street!'

Hereupon, the people of each parish gathered closer round their minister, who looked calmly upwards and assumed a more apostolic dignity, as well befitted a candidate for the highest honor of his profession, the crown of martyrdom. It was actually fancied, at that period, that New-England might have a John Rogers of her own, to take the place of that worthy in the Primer.

'The Pope of Rome has given orders for a new St. Bartholomew!' cried others. 'We are to be massacred, man and male child!'

Neither was this rumor wholly discredited, although the wiser class believed the Governor's object somewhat less atrocious. His predecessor under the old charter, Bradstreet, a venerable companion of the first settlers, was known to be in town. There were grounds for conjecturing, that Sir Edmund Andros intended, at once, to strike terror, by a parade of military force, and to confound the opposite faction, by possessing himself of their chief.

'Stand firm for the old charter Governor!' shouted the crowd, seizing upon the idea. 'The good old Governor Bradstreet!'

While this cry was at the loudest, the people were surprised by the well known figure of Governor Bradstreet himself, a patriarch of nearly ninety, who appeared on the elevated steps of a door, and, with characteristic mildness, besought them to submit to the constituted authorities.

'My children,' concluded this venerable person, 'do nothing rashly. Cry not aloud, but pray for the welfare of New-England, and expect patiently what the Lord will do in this matter!'

The event was soon to be decided. All this time, the roll of the drum had been approaching through Cornhill, louder and deeper, till, with reverberations from house to house, and the regular tramp of martial footsteps, it burst into the street. A double rank of soldiers made their appearance, occupying the whole breadth of the passage, with shouldered matchlocks, and matches burning, so as to present a row of fires in the dusk. Their steady march was like the progress of a machine, that would roll irresistibly over every thing in its way. Next, moving slowly, with a confused clatter of hoofs on the pavement, rode a party of mounted gentlemen, the central figure being Sir Edmund Andros, elderly, but erect and soldier-like. Those around him were his favorite councillors, and the bitterest foes of New-England. At his right hand rode Edward Randolph, our arch enemy, that 'blasted wretch,' as Cotton Mather calls him, who achieved the downfall of our ancient government, and was followed with a sensible curse, through life and to his grave. On the other side was Bullivant, scattering jests and mockery as he rode along. Dudley came behind, with a downcast look, dreading, as well he might, to meet the indignant gaze of the people, who beheld him, their only countryman by birth, among the oppressors of his native land. The captain of a frigate in the harbor, and two or three civil officers

under the Crown, were also there. But the figure which most
attracted the public eye, and stirred up the deepest feeling,
was the Episcopal clergyman of King's Chapel, riding haughtily among the magistrates in his priestly vestments, the fitting representative of prelacy and persecution, the union of
church and state, and all those abominations which had driven
the Puritans to the wilderness. Another guard of soldiers, in
double rank, brought up the rear.

The whole scene was a picture of the condition of New-England, and its moral, the deformity of any government that
does not grow out of the nature of things and the character of
the people. On one side the religious multitude, with their sad
visages and dark attire, and on the other, the group of despotic
rulers, with the high churchman in the midst, and here and
there a crucifix at their bosoms, all magnificently clad, flushed
with wine, proud of unjust authority, and scoffing at the universal groan. And the mercenary soldiers, waiting but the
word to deluge the street with blood, shewed the only means
by which obedience could be secured.

'Oh! Lord of Hosts,' cried a voice among the crowd, 'provide
a Champion for thy people!'

This ejaculation was loudly uttered, and served as a herald's
cry, to introduce a remarkable personage. The crowd had
rolled back, and were now huddled together nearly at the extremity of the street, while the soldiers had advanced no more
than a third of its length. The intervening space was empty—a
paved solitude, between lofty edifices, which threw almost a
twilight shadow over it. Suddenly, there was seen the figure of
an ancient man, who seemed to have emerged from among the
people, and was walking by himself along the centre of the
street, to confront the armed band. He wore the old Puritan
dress, a dark cloak and a steeple-crowned hat, in the fashion of
at least fifty years before, with a heavy sword upon his thigh,
but a staff in his hand, to assist the tremulous gait of age.

When at some distance from the multitude, the old man

turned slowly round, displaying a face of antique majesty, rendered doubly venerable by the hoary beard that descended on his breast. He made a gesture at once of encouragement and warning, then turned again, and resumed his way.

'Who is this gray patriarch?' asked the young men of their sires.

'Who is this venerable brother?' asked the old men among themselves.

But none could make reply. The fathers of the people, those of four-score years and upwards, were disturbed, deeming it strange that they should forget one of such evident authority, whom they must have known in their early days, the associate of Winthrop and all the old Councillors, giving laws, and making prayers, and leading them against the savage. The elderly men ought to have remembered him, too, with locks as gray in their youth, as their own were now. And the young! How could he have passed so utterly from their memories—that hoary sire, the relic of long departed times, whose awful benediction had surely been bestowed on their uncovered heads, in childhood?

'Whence did he come? What is his purpose? Who can this old man be?' whispered the wondering crowd.

Meanwhile, the venerable stranger, staff in hand, was pursuing his solitary walk along the centre of the street. As he drew near the advancing soldiers, and as the roll of their drum came full upon his ear, the old man raised himself to a loftier mien, while the decrepitude of age seemed to fall from his shoulders, leaving him in gray, but unbroken dignity. Now, he marched onward with a warrior's step, keeping time to the military music. Thus the aged form advanced on one side, and the whole parade of soldiers and magistrates on the other, till, when scarcely twenty yards remained between, the old man grasped his staff by the middle, and held it before him like a leader's truncheon.

'Stand!' cried he.

The eye, the face, and attitude of command; the solemn, yet warlike peal of that voice, fit either to rule a host in the battle-field or be raised to God in prayer, were irresistible. At the old man's word and outstretched arm, the roll of the drum was hushed at once, and the advancing line stood still. A tremulous enthusiasm seized upon the multitude. That stately form, combining the leader and the saint, so gray, so dimly seen, in such an ancient garb, could only belong to some old champion of the righteous cause, whom the oppressor's drum had summoned from his grave. They raised a shout of awe and exultation, and looked for the deliverance of New-England.

The Governor, and the gentlemen of his party, perceiving themselves brought to an unexpected stand, rode hastily forward, as if they would have pressed their snorting and affrighted horses right against the hoary apparition. He, however, blenched not a step, but glancing his severe eye round the group, which half encompassed him, at last bent it sternly on Sir Edmund Andros. One would have thought that the dark old man was chief ruler there, and that the Governor and Council, with soldiers at their back, representing the whole power and authority of the Crown, had no alternative but obedience.

'What does this old fellow here?' cried Edward Randolph, fiercely. 'On, Sir Edmund! Bid the soldiers forward, and give the dotard the same choice that you give all his countrymen—to stand aside or be trampled on!'

'Nay, nay, let us show respect to the good grandsire,' said Bullivant, laughing. 'See you not, he is some old round-headed dignitary, who hath lain asleep these thirty years, and knows nothing of the change of times? Doubtless, he thinks to put us down with a proclamation in Old Noll's name!'

'Are you mad, old man?' demanded Sir Edmund Andros, in loud and harsh tones. 'How dare you stay the march of King James's Governor?'

'I have staid the march of a King himself, ere now,' replied the gray figure, with stern composure. 'I am here, Sir Governor, because the cry of an oppressed people hath disturbed me in my secret place; and beseeching this favor earnestly of the Lord, it was vouchsafed me to appear once again on earth, in the good old cause of his Saints. And what speak ye of James? There is no longer a popish tyrant on the throne of England, and by to-morrow noon, his name shall be a by-word in this very street, where ye would make it a word of terror. Back, thou that wast a Governor, back! With this night, thy power is ended—to-morrow, the prison!—back, lest I foretell the scaffold!'

The people had been drawing nearer and nearer, and drinking in the words of their champion, who spoke in accents long disused, like one unaccustomed to converse, except with the dead of many years ago. But his voice stirred their souls. They confronted the soldiers, not wholly without arms, and ready to convert the very stones of the street into deadly weapons. Sir Edmund Andros looked at the old man; then he cast his hard and cruel eye over the multitude, and beheld them burning with that lurid wrath, so difficult to kindle or to quench; and again he fixed his gaze on the aged form, which stood obscurely in an open space, where neither friend nor foe had thrust himself. What were his thoughts, he uttered no word which might discover. But whether the oppressor were over-awed by the Gray Champion's look, or perceived his peril in the threatening attitude of the people, it is certain that he gave back, and ordered his soldiers to commence a slow and guarded retreat. Before another sunset, the Governor, and all that rode so proudly with him, were prisoners, and long ere it was known that James had abdicated, King William was proclaimed throughout New-England.

But where was the Gray Champion? Some reported, that when the troops had gone from King-street, and the people were thronging tumultuously in their rear, Bradstreet, the aged Governor, was seen to embrace a form more aged than his own. Others soberly affirmed, that while they marvelled at the venerable grandeur of his aspect, the old man had faded from their eyes, melting slowly into the hues of twilight, till, where he stood, there was an empty space. But all agreed, that the hoary shape was gone. The men of that generation watched for his re-appearance, in sunshine and in twilight, but never saw him more, nor knew when his funeral passed, nor where his grave-stone was.

And who was the Gray Champion? Perhaps his name might be found in the records of that stern Court of Justice, which passed a sentence, too mighty for the age, but glorious in all after times, for its humbling lesson to the monarch and its high example to the subject. I have heard, that, whenever the descendants of the Puritans are to show the spirit of their sires, the old man appears again. When eighty years had passed, he walked once more in King-street. Five years later, in the twilight of an April morning, he stood on the green, beside the meeting-house, at Lexington, where now the obelisk of granite, with a slab of slate inlaid, commemorates the first fallen of the Revolution. And when our fathers were toiling at the breast-work on Bunker's Hill, all through that night, the old warrior walked his rounds. Long, long may it be, ere he comes again! His hour is one of darkness, and adversity, and peril. But should domestic tyranny oppress us, or the invader's step pollute our soil, still may the Gray Champion come; for he is the type of New-England's hereditary spirit; and his shadowy march, on the eve of danger, must ever be the pledge, that New-England's sons will vindicate their ancestry.

Young Goodman Brown

YOUNG Goodman Brown came forth, at sunset, into the street of Salem village, but put his head back, after crossing the threshold, to exchange a parting kiss with his young wife. And Faith, as the wife was aptly named, thrust her own pretty head into the street, letting the wind play with the pink ribbons of her cap, while she called to Goodman Brown.

'Dearest heart,' whispered she, softly and rather sadly, when her lips were close to his ear, 'pr'y thee, put off your journey until sunrise, and sleep in your own bed to-night. A lone woman is troubled with such dreams and such thoughts, that she's afeard of herself, sometimes. Pray, tarry with me this night, dear husband, of all nights in the year!'

'My love and my Faith,' replied young Goodman Brown, 'of all nights in the year, this one night must I tarry away from thee. My journey, as thou callest it, forth and back again, must needs be done 'twixt now and sunrise. What, my sweet, pretty wife, dost thou doubt me already, and we but three months married!'

'Then, God bless you!' said Faith, with the pink ribbons, 'and may you find all well, when you come back.'

'Amen!' cried Goodman Brown. 'Say thy prayers, dear Faith, and go to bed at dusk, and no harm will come to thee.'

So they parted; and the young man pursued his way, until, being about to turn the corner by the meeting-house, he looked back, and saw the head of Faith still peeping after him, with a melancholy air, in spite of her pink ribbons.

'Poor little Faith!' thought he, for his heart smote him. 'What a wretch am I, to leave her on such an errand! She talks of dreams, too. Methought, as she spoke, there was trouble in her face, as if a dream had warned her what work is to be done to-night. But, no, no! 'twould kill her to think it. Well; she's a blessed angel on earth; and after this one night, I'll cling to her skirts and follow her to Heaven.'

With this excellent resolve for the future, Goodman Brown felt himself justified in making more haste on his present evil purpose. He had taken a dreary road, darkened by all the gloomiest trees of the forest, which barely stood aside to let the narrow path creep through, and closed immediately behind. It was all as lonely as could be; and there is this peculiarity in such a solitude, that the traveller knows not who may be concealed by the innumerable trunks and the thick boughs overhead; so that, with lonely footsteps, he may yet be passing through an unseen multitude.

'There may be a devilish Indian behind every tree,' said Goodman Brown, to himself; and he glanced fearfully behind him, as he added, 'What if the devil himself should be at my very elbow!'

His head being turned back, he passed a crook of the road, and looking forward again, beheld the figure of a man, in grave and decent attire, seated at the foot of an old tree. He arose, at Goodman Brown's approach, and walked onward, side by side with him.

'You are late, Goodman Brown,' said he. 'The clock of the Old South was striking as I came through Boston; and that is full fifteen minutes agone.'

'Faith kept me back awhile,' replied the young man, with a tremor in his voice, caused by the sudden appearance of his companion, though not wholly unexpected.

It was now deep dusk in the forest, and deepest in that part of it where these two were journeying. As nearly as could be discerned, the second traveller was about fifty years old, apparently in the same rank of life as Goodman Brown, and bearing a considerable resemblance to him, though perhaps more in expression than features. Still, they might have been taken for father and son. And yet, though the elder person was as simply clad as the younger, and as simple in manner too, he had an indescribable air of one who knew the world, and would not have felt abashed at the governor's dinner-table, or in King William's court, were it possible that his affairs should call him thither. But the only thing about him, that could be fixed upon as remarkable, was his staff, which bore the likeness of a great black snake, so curiously wrought, that it might almost be seen to twist and wriggle itself, like a living serpent. This, of course, must have been an ocular deception, assisted by the uncertain light.

'Come, Goodman Brown!' cried his fellow-traveller, 'this is a dull pace for the beginning of a journey. Take my staff, if you are so soon weary.'

'Friend,' said the other, exchanging his slow pace for a full stop, 'having kept covenant by meeting thee here, it is my purpose now to return whence I came. I have scruples, touching the matter thou wot'st of.'

'Sayest thou so?' replied he of the serpent, smiling apart. 'Let us walk on, nevertheless, reasoning as we go, and if I convince thee not, thou shalt turn back. We are but a little way in the forest, yet.'

'Too far, too far!' exclaimed the goodman, unconsciously resuming his walk. 'My father never went into the woods on such an errand, nor his father before him. We have been a race of honest men and good Christians, since the days of the martyrs. And shall I be the first of the name of Brown, that ever took this path, and kept—'

'Such company, thou wouldst say,' observed the elder person, interpreting his pause. 'Well said, Goodman Brown! I have been as well acquainted with your family as with ever a one among the Puritans; and that's no trifle to say. I helped your grandfather, the constable, when he lashed the Quaker woman so smartly through the streets of Salem. And it was I that brought your father a pitch-pine knot, kindled at my own hearth, to set fire to an Indian village, in King Philip's war. They were my good friends, both; and many a pleasant walk have we had along this path, and returned merrily after midnight. I would fain be friends with you, for their sake.'

'If it be as thou sayest,' replied Goodman Brown, 'I marvel they never spoke of these matters. Or, verily, I marvel not, seeing that the least rumor of the sort would have driven them from New-England. We are a people of prayer, and good works, to boot, and abide no such wickedness.'

'Wickedness or not,' said the traveller with the twisted staff, 'I have a very general acquaintance here in New-England. The deacons of many a church have drunk the communion wine with me; the selectmen, of divers towns, make me their chairman; and a majority of the Great and General Court are firm supporters of my interest. The governor and I, too—but these are state-secrets.'

'Can this be so!' cried Goodman Brown, with a stare of amazement at his undisturbed companion. 'Howbeit, I have nothing to do with the governor and council; they have their own ways, and are no rule for a simple husbandman, like me. But, were I to go on with thee, how should I meet the eye of that good old man, our minister, at Salem village? Oh, his voice would make me tremble, both Sabbath-day and lecture-day!'

Thus far, the elder traveller had listened with due gravity, but now burst into a fit of irrepressible mirth, shaking himself so violently, that his snake-like staff actually seemed to wriggle in sympathy.

'Ha! ha! ha!' shouted he, again and again; then composing

himself, 'Well, go on, Goodman Brown, go on; but pr'y thee, don't kill me with laughing!'

'Well, then, to end the matter at once,' said Goodman Brown, considerably nettled, 'there is my wife, Faith. It would break her dear little heart; and I'd rather break my own!'

'Nay, if that be the case,' answered the other, 'e'en go thy ways, Goodman Brown. I would not, for twenty old women like the one hobbling before us, that Faith should come to any harm.'

As he spoke, he pointed his staff at a female figure on the path, in whom Goodman Brown recognized a very pious and exemplary dame, who had taught him his catechism, in youth, and was still his moral and spiritual adviser, jointly with the minister and Deacon Gookin.

'A marvel, truly, that Goody Cloyse should be so far in the wilderness, at night-fall!' said he. 'But, with your leave, friend, I shall take a cut through the woods, until we have left this Christian woman behind. Being a stranger to you, she might ask whom I was consorting with, and whither I was going.'

'Be it so,' said his fellow-traveller. 'Betake you to the woods, and let me keep the path.'

Accordingly, the young man turned aside, but took care to watch his companion, who advanced softly along the road, until he had come within a staff's length of the old dame. She, meanwhile, was making the best of her way, with singular speed for so aged a woman, and mumbling some indistinct words, a prayer, doubtless, as she went. The traveller put forth his staff, and touched her withered neck with what seemed the serpent's tail.

'The devil!' screamed the pious old lady.

'Then Goody Cloyse knows her old friend?' observed the traveller, confronting her, and leaning on his writhing stick.

'Ah, forsooth, and is it your worship, indeed?' cried the

good dame. 'Yea, truly is it, and in the very image of my old gossip, Goodman Brown, the grandfather of the silly fellow that now is. But—would your worship believe it?—my broomstick hath strangely disappeared, stolen, as I suspect, by that unhanged witch, Goody Cory, and that, too, when I was all anointed with the juice of smallage and cinque-foil and wolf's-bane—'

'Mingled with fine wheat and the fat of a new-born babe,' said the shape of old Goodman Brown.

'Ah, your worship knows the receipt,' cried the old lady, cackling aloud. 'So, as I was saying, being all ready for the meeting, and no horse to ride on, I made up my mind to foot it; for they tell me, there is a nice young man to be taken into communion to-night. But now your good worship will lend me your arm, and we shall be there in a twinkling.'

'That can hardly be,' answered her friend. 'I may not spare you my arm, Goody Cloyse, but here is my staff, if you will.'

So saying, he threw it down at her feet, where, perhaps, it assumed life, being one of the rods which its owner had formerly lent to the Egyptian Magi. Of this fact, however, Goodman Brown could not take cognizance. He had cast up his eyes in astonishment, and looking down again, beheld neither Goody Cloyse nor the serpentine staff, but his fellow-traveller alone, who waited for him as calmly as if nothing had happened.

'That old woman taught me my catechism!' said the young man; and there was a world of meaning in this simple comment.

They continued to walk onward, while the elder traveller exhorted his companion to make good speed and persevere in the path, discoursing so aptly, that his arguments seemed rather to spring up in the bosom of his auditor, than to be suggested by himself. As they went, he plucked a branch of maple, to serve for a walking-stick, and began to strip it of the twigs and little boughs, which were wet with evening dew. The moment his fingers touched them, they became strangely withered and dried up, as with a week's sunshine. Thus the pair proceeded, at a good free pace, until suddenly, in a gloomy hollow of the road, Goodman Brown sat himself down on the stump of a tree, and refused to go any farther.

'Friend,' said he, stubbornly, 'my mind is made up. Not another step will I budge on this errand. What if a wretched old woman do choose to go to the devil, when I thought she was going to Heaven! Is that any reason why I should quit my dear Faith, and go after her?'

'You will think better of this, by-and-by,' said his acquaintance, composedly. 'Sit here and rest yourself awhile; and when you feel like moving again, there is my staff to help you along.'

Without more words, he threw his companion the maple stick, and was as speedily out of sight, as if he had vanished into the deepening gloom. The young man sat a few moments, by the road-side, applauding himself greatly, and thinking with how clear a conscience he should meet the minister, in his morning-walk, nor shrink from the eye of good old Deacon Gookin. And what calm sleep would be his, that very night, which was to have been spent so wickedly, but purely and sweetly now, in the arms of Faith! Amidst these pleasant and praiseworthy meditations, Goodman Brown heard the tramp of horses along the road, and deemed it advisable to conceal himself within the verge of the forest, conscious of the guilty purpose that had brought him thither, though now so happily turned from it.

On came the hoof-tramps and the voices of the riders, two grave old voices, conversing soberly as they drew near. These mingled sounds appeared to pass along the road, within a few yards of the young man's hiding-place; but owing, doubtless, to the depth of the gloom, at that particular spot, neither the travellers nor their steeds were visible. Though their figures brushed the small boughs by the way-side, it could not be seen that they intercepted, even for a moment, the faint gleam from the strip of bright sky, athwart which they must have passed.

Goodman Brown alternately crouched and stood on tip-toe, pulling aside the branches, and thrusting forth his head as far as he durst, without discerning so much as a shadow. It vexed him the more, because he could have sworn, were such a thing possible, that he recognized the voices of the minister and Deacon Gookin, jogging along quietly, as they were wont to do, when bound to some ordination or ecclesiastical council. While yet within hearing, one of the riders stopped to pluck a switch.

'Of the two, reverend Sir,' said the voice like the deacon's, 'I had rather miss an ordination-dinner than to-night's meeting. They tell me that some of our community are to be here from Falmouth and beyond, and others from Connecticut and Rhode-Island; besides several of the Indian powows, who, after their fashion, know almost as much deviltry as the best of us. Moreover, there is a goodly young woman to be taken into communion.'

'Mighty well, Deacon Gookin!' replied the solemn old tones of the minister. 'Spur up, or we shall be late. Nothing can be done, you know, until I get on the ground.'

The hoofs clattered again, and the voices, talking so strangely in the empty air, passed on through the forest, where no church had ever been gathered, nor solitary Christian prayed. Whither, then, could these holy men be journeying, so deep into the heathen wilderness? Young Goodman Brown caught hold of a tree, for support, being ready to sink down on the ground, faint and overburthened with the heavy sickness of his heart. He looked up to the sky, doubting whether there really was a Heaven above him. Yet, there was the blue arch, and the stars brightening in it.

'With Heaven above, and Faith below, I will yet stand firm against the devil!' cried Goodman Brown.

While he still gazed upward, into the deep arch of the firmament, and had lifted his hands to pray, a cloud, though no wind was stirring, hurried across the zenith, and hid the brightening stars. The blue sky was still visible, except directly overhead, where this black mass of cloud was sweeping swiftly northward. Aloft in the air, as if from the depths of the cloud, came a confused and doubtful sound of voices. Once, the listener fancied that he could distinguish the accents of town's-people of his own, men and women, both pious and ungodly, many of whom he had met at the communion-table, and had seen others rioting at the tavern. The next moment, so indistinct were the sounds, he doubted whether he had heard aught but the murmur of the old forest, whispering without a wind. Then came a stronger swell of those familiar tones, heard daily in the sunshine, at Salem village, but never, until now, from a cloud of night. There was one voice, of a young woman, uttering lamentations, yet with an uncertain sorrow, and entreating for some favor, which, perhaps, it would grieve her to obtain. And all the unseen multitude, both saints and sinners, seemed to encourage her onward.

'Faith!' shouted Goodman Brown, in a voice of agony and desperation; and the echoes of the forest mocked him, crying—'Faith! Faith!' as if bewildered wretches were seeking her, all through the wilderness.

The cry of grief, rage, and terror, was yet piercing the night, when the unhappy husband held his breath for a response. There was a scream, drowned immediately in a louder murmur of voices, fading into far-off laughter, as the dark cloud swept away, leaving the clear and silent sky above Goodman Brown. But something fluttered lightly down through the air, and caught on the branch of a tree. The young man seized it, and beheld a pink ribbon.

'My Faith is gone!' cried he, after one stupefied moment. 'There is no good on earth; and sin is but a name. Come, devil! for to thee is this world given.'

And maddened with despair, so that he laughed loud and long, did Goodman Brown grasp his staff and set forth again, at such a rate, that he seemed to fly along the forest-path, rather than to walk or run. The road grew wilder and drearier, and more faintly traced, and vanished at length, leaving him in the heart of the dark wilderness, still rushing onward, with the instinct that guides mortal man to evil. The whole forest was peopled with frightful sounds; the creaking of the trees, the howling of wild beasts, and the yell of Indians; while, sometimes, the wind tolled like a distant church-bell, and sometimes gave a broad roar around the traveller, as if all Nature were laughing him to scorn. But he was himself the chief horror of the scene, and shrank not from its other horrors.

'Ha! ha! ha!' roared Goodman Brown, when the wind laughed at him. 'Let us hear which will laugh loudest! Think not to frighten me with your deviltry! Come witch, come wizard, come Indian powow, come devil himself! and here comes Goodman Brown. You may as well fear him as he fear you!'

In truth, all through the haunted forest, there could be nothing more frightful than the figure of Goodman Brown. On he flew, among the black pines, brandishing his staff with frenzied gestures, now giving vent to an inspiration of horrid blasphemy, and now shouting forth such laughter, as set all the echoes of the forest laughing like demons around him. The fiend in his own shape is less hideous, than when he rages in the breast of man. Thus sped the demoniac on his course, until, quivering among the trees, he saw a red light before him, as when the felled trunks and branches of a clearing have been set on fire, and throw up their lurid blaze against the sky, at the hour of midnight. He paused, in a lull of the tempest that had driven him onward, and heard the swell of what seemed a hymn, rolling solemnly from a distance, with the weight of many voices. He knew the tune; it was a familiar one in the choir of the village meeting-house. The verse died heavily away, and was lengthened by a chorus, not of human voices, but of all the sounds of the benighted wilderness, pealing in awful harmony together. Goodman Brown cried out; and his cry was lost to his own ear, by its unison with the cry of the desert.

In the interval of silence, he stole forward, until the light glared full upon his eyes. At one extremity of an open space, hemmed in by the dark wall of the forest, arose a rock, bearing some rude, natural resemblance either to an altar or a pulpit, and surrounded by four blazing pines, their tops aflame, their stems untouched, like candles at an evening meeting. The mass of foliage, that had overgrown the summit of the rock, was all on fire, blazing high into the night, and fitfully illuminating the whole field. Each pendent twig and leafy festoon was in a blaze. As the red light arose and fell, a numerous congregation alternately shone forth, then disappeared in shadow, and again grew, as it were, out of the darkness, peopling the heart of the solitary woods at once.

'A grave and dark-clad company!' quoth Goodman Brown.

In truth, they were such. Among them, quivering to-and-fro, between gloom and splendor, appeared faces that would be seen, next day, at the council-board of the province, and others which, Sabbath after Sabbath, looked devoutly heavenward, and benignantly over the crowded pews, from the holiest pulpits in the land. Some affirm, that the lady of the governor was there. At least, there were high dames well known to her, and wives of honored husbands, and widows, a great multitude, and ancient maidens, all of excellent repute, and fair young girls, who trembled, lest their mothers should espy them. Either the sudden gleams of light, flashing over the obscure field, bedazzled Goodman Brown, or he recognized a score of the church-members of Salem village, famous for their especial sanctity. Good old Deacon Gookin had arrived, and waited at the skirts of that venerable saint, his revered pastor. But, irreverently consorting with these grave, reputable, and pious people, these elders of the church, these chaste dames and dewy virgins, there were men of dissolute lives and women of spotted fame, wretches given over to all mean and filthy vice, and suspected even of horrid crimes. It was strange to see, that the good shrank not from the wicked, nor were the sinners abashed by the saints. Scattered, also, among their pale-faced enemies, were the Indian priests, or powows, who had often scared their native forest with more hideous incantations than any known to English witchcraft.

'But, where is Faith?' thought Goodman Brown; and, as hope came into his heart, he trembled.

Another verse of the hymn arose, a slow and mournful strain, such as the pious love, but joined to words which expressed all that our nature can conceive of sin, and darkly hinted at far more. Unfathomable to mere mortals is the lore of fiends. Verse after verse was sung, and still the chorus of the desert swelled between, like the deepest tone of a mighty organ. And, with the final peal of that dreadful anthem, there came a sound, as if the roaring wind, the rushing streams, the howling beasts, and every other voice of the unconverted wilderness, were mingling and according with the voice of guilty man, in homage to the prince of all. The four blazing pines threw up a loftier flame, and obscurely discovered shapes and visages of horror on the smoke-wreaths, above the impious assembly. At the same moment, the fire on the rock shot redly forth, and formed a glowing arch above its base, where now appeared a figure. With reverence be it spoken, the figure bore no slight similitude, both in garb and manner, to some grave divine of the New-England churches.

'Bring forth the converts!' cried a voice, that echoed through the field and rolled into the forest.

At the word, Goodman Brown stept forth from the shadow of the trees, and approached the congregation, with whom he felt a loathful brotherhood, by the sympathy of all that was wicked in his heart. He could have well nigh sworn, that the shape of his own dead father beckoned him to advance, looking downward from a smoke-wreath, while a woman, with dim features of despair, threw out her hand to warn him back. Was it his mother? But he had no power to retreat one step, nor to resist, even in thought, when the minister and good old Deacon Gookin seized his arms, and led him to the blazing rock. Thither came also the slender form of a veiled female, led between Goody Cloyse, that pious teacher of the catechism, and Martha Carrier, who had received the devil's promise to be queen of hell. A rampant hag was she! And there stood the proselytes, beneath the canopy of fire.

'Welcome, my children,' said the dark figure, 'to the communion of your race! Ye have found, thus young, your nature and your destiny. My children, look behind you!'

They turned; and flashing forth, as it were, in a sheet of flame, the fiend-worshippers were seen; the smile of welcome gleamed darkly on every visage.

'There,' resumed the sable form, 'are all whom ye have reverenced from youth. Ye deemed them holier than yourselves, and shrank from your own sin, contrasting it with their lives of righteousness, and prayerful aspirations heavenward. Yet, here are they all, in my worshipping assembly! This night it shall be granted you to know their secret deeds; how hoary-bearded elders of the church have whispered wanton words to the young maids of their households; how many a woman, eager for widow's weeds, has given her husband a drink at bedtime, and let him sleep his last sleep in her bosom; how beardless youths have made haste to inherit their fathers' wealth; and how fair damsels—blush not, sweet ones!—have dug little graves in the garden, and bidden me, the sole guest, to an infant's funeral. By the sympathy of your human hearts for sin, ye shall scent out all the places—whether in church, bed-chamber, street, field, or forest—where crime has been committed, and shall exult to behold the whole earth one stain of guilt, one mighty blood-spot. Far more than this! It shall be yours to penetrate, in every bosom, the deep mystery of sin, the fountain of all wicked arts, and which inexhaustibly supplies more evil impulses than human power—than my power, at its utmost!—can make manifest in deeds. And now, my children, look upon each other.'

They did so; and, by the blaze of the hell-kindled torches, the wretched man beheld his Faith, and the wife her husband, trembling before that unhallowed altar.

'Lo! there ye stand, my children,' said the figure, in a deep and solemn tone, almost sad, with its despairing awfulness, as if his once angelic nature could yet mourn for our miserable race. 'Depending upon one another's hearts, ye had still hoped, that virtue were not all a dream. Now are ye undeceived! Evil is the nature of mankind. Evil must be your only happiness. Welcome, again, my children, to the communion of your race!'

'Welcome!' repeated the fiend-worshippers, in one cry of despair and triumph.

And there they stood, the only pair, as it seemed, who were yet hesitating on the verge of wickedness, in this dark world. A basin was hollowed, naturally, in the rock. Did it contain water, reddened by the lurid light? or was it blood? or, perchance, a liquid flame? Herein did the Shape of Evil dip his hand, and prepare to lay the mark of baptism upon their foreheads, that they might be partakers of the mystery of sin, more conscious of the secret guilt of others, both in deed and thought, than they could now be of their own. The husband cast one look at his pale wife, and Faith at him. What polluted wretches would the next glance shew them to each other, shuddering alike at what they disclosed and what they saw!

'Faith! Faith!' cried the husband. 'Look up to Heaven, and resist the Wicked One!'

Whether Faith obeyed, he knew not. Hardly had he spoken, when he found himself amid calm night and solitude, listening to a roar of the wind, which died heavily away through the forest. He staggered against the rock and felt it chill and damp, while a hanging twig, that had been all on fire, besprinkled his cheek with the coldest dew.

The next morning, young Goodman Brown came slowly into the street of Salem village, staring around him like a bewildered man. The good old minister was taking a walk along the grave-yard, to get an appetite for breakfast and meditate his sermon, and bestowed a blessing, as he passed, on Goodman Brown. He shrank from the venerable saint, as if to avoid an anathema. Old Deacon Gookin was at domestic worship, and the holy words of his prayer were heard through the open window. 'What God doth the wizard pray to?' quoth Goodman Brown. Goody Cloyse, that excellent old Christian, stood in the early sunshine, at her own lattice, catechising a little girl, who had brought her a pint of morning's milk. Goodman Brown snatched away the child, as from the grasp of the fiend himself. Turning the corner by the meeting-house, he spied the head of Faith, with the pink ribbons, gazing anxiously forth, and bursting into such joy at sight of him, that she skipt along the street, and almost kissed her husband before the whole village. But, Goodman Brown looked sternly and sadly into her face, and passed on without a greeting.

Had Goodman Brown fallen asleep in the forest, and only dreamed a wild dream of a witch-meeting?

Be it so, if you will. But, alas! it was a dream of evil omen for young Goodman Brown. A stern, a sad, a darkly meditative, a distrustful, if not a desperate man, did he become, from the night of that fearful dream. On the Sabbath-day, when the congregation were singing a holy psalm, he could not listen, because an anthem of sin rushed loudly upon his ear, and drowned all the blessed strain. When the minister spoke from the pulpit, with power and fervid eloquence, and, with his hand on the open Bible, of the sacred truths of our religion, and of saint-like lives and triumphant deaths, and of future bliss or misery unutterable, then did Goodman Brown turn pale, dreading, lest the roof should thunder down upon the gray blasphemer and his hearers. Often, awakening suddenly at midnight, he shrank from the bosom of Faith, and at morning or eventide, when the family knelt down at prayer, he scowled, and muttered to himself, and gazed sternly at his wife, and turned away. And when he had lived long, and was borne to his grave, a hoary corpse, followed by Faith, an aged woman, and children and grand-children, a goodly procession, besides neighbors, not a few, they carved no hopeful verse upon his tomb-stone; for his dying hour was gloom.

Wakefield

In some old magazine or newspaper, I recollect a story, told as truth, of a man—let us call him Wakefield—who absented himself for a long time, from his wife. The fact, thus abstractedly stated, is not very uncommon, nor—without a proper distinction of circumstances—to be condemned either as naughty or nonsensical. Howbeit, this, though far from the most aggravated, is perhaps the strangest instance, on record, of marital delinquency; and, moreover, as remarkable a freak as may be found in the whole list of human oddities. The wedded couple lived in London. The man, under pretence of going a journey, took lodgings in the next street to his own house, and there, unheard of by his wife or friends, and without the shadow of a reason for such self-banishment, dwelt upwards of twenty years. During that period, he beheld his home every day, and frequently the forlorn Mrs. Wakefield. And after so great a gap in his matrimonial felicity—when his death was reckoned certain, his estate settled, his name dismissed from memory, and his wife, long, long ago, resigned to her autumnal widowhood—he entered the door one evening, quietly, as from a day's absence, and became a loving spouse till death.

This outline is all that I remember. But the incident, though of the purest originality, unexampled, and probably never to be repeated, is one, I think, which appeals to the general sympathies of mankind. We know, each for himself, that none of us would perpetrate such a folly, yet feel as if some other might. To my own contemplations, at least, it has often recurred, always exciting wonder, but with a sense that the story must be true, and a conception of its hero's character. Whenever any subject so forcibly affects the mind, time is well spent in thinking of it. If the reader choose, let him do his own meditation; or if he prefer to ramble with me through the twenty years of Wakefield's vagary, I bid him welcome; trusting that there will be a pervading spirit and a moral, even should we fail to find them, done up neatly, and condensed into the final sentence. Thought has always its efficacy, and every striking incident its moral.

What sort of a man was Wakefield? We are free to shape out our own idea, and call it by his name. He was now in the meridian of life; his matrimonial affections, never violent, were sobered into a calm, habitual sentiment; of all husbands, he was likely to be the most constant, because a certain sluggishness would keep his heart at rest, wherever it might be placed. He was intellectual, but not actively so; his mind occupied itself in long and lazy musings, that tended to no purpose, or had not vigor to attain it; his thoughts were seldom so energetic as to seize hold of words. Imagination, in the proper meaning of the term, made no part of Wakefield's gifts. With a cold, but not depraved nor wandering heart, and a mind never feverish with riotous thoughts, nor perplexed with originality, who could have anticipated, that our friend would entitle himself to a foremost place among the doers of eccentric deeds? Had his acquaintances been asked, who was the man in London, the surest to perform nothing to-day which should be remembered on the morrow, they would have thought of Wakefield. Only the wife of his bosom might have hesitated. She, without having analyzed his character, was partly aware of a quiet selfishness, that had rusted into his inactive mind—of a peculiar sort of vanity, the most uneasy attribute about him—of a disposition to craft, which had seldom produced more positive effects than the keeping of petty secrets, hardly worth revealing—and, lastly, of what she called a little strangeness, sometimes, in the good man. This latter quality is indefinable, and perhaps non-existent.

Let us now imagine Wakefield bidding adieu to his wife. It is the dusk of an October evening. His equipment is a drab great-coat, a hat covered with an oil-cloth, top-boots, an umbrella in one hand and a small portmanteau in the other. He has informed Mrs. Wakefield that he is to take the night-coach into the country. She would fain inquire the length of his journey, its object, and the probable time of his return; but, indulgent to his harmless love of mystery, interrogates him only by a look. He tells her not to expect him positively by the return coach, nor to be alarmed should he tarry three or four days; but, at all events, to look for him at supper on Friday evening. Wakefield himself, be it considered, has no suspicion of what is before him. He holds out his hand; she gives her own, and meets his parting kiss, in the matter-of-course way of a ten years' matrimony; and forth goes the middle-aged Mr. Wakefield, almost resolved to perplex his good lady by a whole week's absence. After the door has closed behind him, she perceives it thrust partly open, and a vision of her husband's face, through the aperture, smiling on her, and gone in a moment. For the time, this little incident is dismissed without a thought. But, long afterwards, when she has been more years a widow than a wife, that smile recurs, and flickers across all her reminiscences of Wakefield's visage. In her many musings, she surrounds the original smile with a multitude of fantasies, which make it strange and awful; as, for instance, if she imagines him in a coffin, that parting look is frozen on his pale features; or, if she dreams of him in Heaven, still his blessed spirit wears a quiet and crafty smile. Yet, for its sake, when all others have given him up for dead, she sometimes doubts whether she is a widow.

But, our business is with the husband. We must hurry after him, along the street, ere he lose his individuality, and melt into the great mass of London life. It would be vain searching for him there. Let us follow close at his heels, therefore, until, after several superfluous turns and doublings, we find him comfortably established by the fireside of a small apartment, previously bespoken. He is in the next street to his own, and at his journey's end. He can scarcely trust his good fortune, in having got thither unperceived—recollecting that, at one time, he was delayed by the throng, in the very focus of a lighted lantern; and, again, there were footsteps, that seemed to tread behind his own, distinct from the multitudinous tramp around him; and, anon, he heard a voice shouting afar, and fancied that it called his name. Doubtless, a dozen busy-bodies had been watching him, and told his wife the whole affair. Poor Wakefield! Little knowest thou thine own insignificance in this great world! No mortal eye but mine has traced thee. Go quietly to thy bed, foolish man; and, on the morrow, if thou wilt be wise, get thee home to good Mrs. Wakefield, and tell her the truth. Remove not thyself, even for a little week, from thy place in her chaste bosom. Were she, for a single moment, to deem thee dead, or lost, or lastingly divided from her, thou wouldst be woefully conscious of a change in thy true wife, forever after. It is perilous to make a chasm in human affections; not that they gape so long and wide—but so quickly close again!

Almost repenting of his frolic, or whatever it may be termed, Wakefield lies down betimes, and starting from his first nap, spreads forth his arms into the wide and solitary waste of the unaccustomed bed. 'No'—thinks he, gathering the bed-clothes about him—'I will not sleep alone another night.'

In the morning, he rises earlier than usual, and sets himself to consider what he really means to do. Such are his loose and rambling modes of thought, that he has taken this very singular step, with the consciousness of a purpose, indeed, but without being able to define it sufficiently for his own contemplation.

The vagueness of the project, and the convulsive effort with which he plunges into the execution of it, are equally characteristic of a feeble-minded man. Wakefield sifts his ideas, however, as minutely as he may, and finds himself curious to know the progress of matters at home—how his exemplary wife will endure her widowhood, of a week; and, briefly, how the little sphere of creatures and circumstances, in which he was a central object, will be affected by his removal. A morbid vanity, therefore, lies nearest the bottom of the affair. But, how is he to attain his ends? Not, certainly, by keeping close in this comfortable lodging, where, though he slept and awoke in the next street to his home, he is as effectually abroad, as if the stage-coach had been whirling him away all night. Yet, should he reappear, the whole project is knocked in the head. His poor brains being hopelessly puzzled with this dilemma, he at length ventures out, partly resolving to cross the head of the street, and send one hasty glance towards his forsaken domicile. Habit—for he is a man of habits—takes him by the hand, and guides him, wholly unaware, to his own door, where, just at the critical moment, he is aroused by the scraping of his foot upon the step. Wakefield! whither are you going?

At that instant, his fate was turning on the pivot. Little dreaming of the doom to which his first backward step devotes him, he hurries away, breathless with agitation hitherto unfelt, and hardly dares turn his head, at the distant corner. Can it be, that nobody caught sight of him? Will not the whole household—the decent Mrs. Wakefield, the smart maid-servant, and the dirty little foot-boy—raise a hue-and-cry, through London streets, in pursuit of their fugitive lord and master? Wonderful escape! He gathers courage to pause and look homeward, but is perplexed with a sense of change about the familiar edifice, such as affects us all, when, after a separation of months or years, we again see some hill or lake, or work of art, with which we were friends, of old. In ordinary cases, this indescribable impression is caused by the comparison and contrast between our imperfect reminiscences and the reality. In Wakefield, the magic of a single night has wrought a similar transformation, because, in that brief period, a great moral change has been effected. But this is a secret from himself. Before leaving the spot, he catches a far and momentary glimpse of his wife, passing athwart the front window, with her face turned towards the head of the street. The crafty nincompoop takes to his heels, scared with the idea, that, among a thousand such atoms of mortality, her eye must have detected him. Right glad is his heart, though his brain be somewhat dizzy, when he finds himself by the coal-fire of his lodgings.

So much for the commencement of this long whim-wham. After the initial conception, and the stirring up of the man's sluggish temperament to put it in practice, the whole matter evolves itself in a natural train. We may suppose him, as the result of deep deliberation, buying a new wig, of reddish hair, and selecting sundry garments, in a fashion unlike his customary suit of brown, from a Jew's old-clothes bag. It is accomplished. Wakefield is another man. The new system being now established, a retrograde movement to the old would be almost as difficult as the step that placed him in his unparalleled position. Furthermore, he is rendered obstinate by a sulkiness, occasionally incident to his temper, and brought on, at present, by the inadequate sensation which he conceives to have been produced in the bosom of Mrs. Wakefield. He will not go back until she be frightened half to death. Well, twice or thrice has she passed before his sight, each time with a heavier step, a paler cheek, and more anxious brow; and, in the third week of his non-appearance, he detects a portent of evil entering the house, in the guise of an apothecary. Next day, the knocker is muffled. Towards night-fall, comes the chariot of a physician, and deposits its big-wigged and solemn burthen at Wakefield's door, whence, after a quarter of an hour's visit, he emerges, perchance the herald of a funeral. Dear woman! Will she die? By this time, Wakefield is excited to something like energy of feeling, but still lingers away from his wife's bedside, pleading with his conscience, that she must not be disturbed at such a juncture. If aught else restrains him, he does not know it. In the course of a few weeks, she gradually recovers; the crisis is over; her heart is sad, perhaps, but quiet; and, let him return soon or late, it will never be feverish for him again. Such ideas glimmer through the mist of Wakefield's mind, and render him indistinctly conscious, that an almost impassable gulf divides his hired apartment from his former home. 'It is but in the next street!' he sometimes says. Fool! it is in another world. Hitherto, he has put off his return from one particular day to another; henceforward, he leaves the precise time undetermined. Not to-morrow—probably next week—pretty soon. Poor man! The dead have nearly as much chance of re-visiting their earthly homes, as the self-banished Wakefield.

Would that I had a folio to write, instead of an article of a dozen pages! Then might I exemplify how an influence, beyond our control, lays its strong hand on every deed which we do, and weaves its consequences into an iron tissue of necessity. Wakefield is spell-bound. We must leave him, for ten years or so, to haunt around his house, without once crossing the threshold, and to be faithful to his wife, with all the affection of which his heart is capable, while he is slowly fading out of hers. Long since, it must be remarked, he has lost the perception of singularity in his conduct.

Now for a scene! Amid the throng of a London street, we distinguish a man, now waxing elderly, with few characteristics to attract careless observers, yet bearing, in his whole aspect, the hand-writing of no common fate, for such as have the skill to read it. He is meagre; his low and narrow forehead is deeply wrinkled; his eyes, small and lustreless, sometimes wander apprehensively about him, but oftener seem to look inward. He bends his head, but moves with an indescribable obliquity of gait, as if unwilling to display his full front to the world. Watch him, long enough to see what we have described, and you will allow, that circumstances—which often produce remarkable men from nature's ordinary handiwork—have produced one such here. Next, leaving him to sidle along the foot-walk, cast your eyes in the opposite direction, where a portly female, considerably in the wane of life, with a prayer-book in her hand, is proceeding to yonder church. She has the placid mien of settled widowhood. Her regrets have either died away, or have become so essential to her heart, that they would be poorly exchanged for joy. Just as the lean man and well conditioned woman are passing, a slight obstruction occurs, and brings these two figures directly in contact. Their hands touch; the pressure of the crowd forces her bosom against his shoulder; they stand, face to face, staring into each other's eyes. After a ten years' separation, thus Wakefield meets his wife!

The throng eddies away, and carries them asunder. The sober widow, resuming her former pace, proceeds to church; but pauses in the portal, and throws a perplexed glance along the street. She passes in, however, opening her prayer-book as she goes. And the man? With so wild a face, that busy and selfish London stands to gaze after him, he hurries to his lodgings, bolts the door, and throws himself upon the bed. The latent feelings of years break out; his feeble mind acquires a brief energy from their strength; all the miserable strangeness of his life is revealed to him at a glance; and he cries out, passionately—'Wakefield! Wakefield! You are mad!'

Perhaps he was so. The singularity of his situation must have so moulded him to itself, that, considered in regard to his fellow-creatures and the business of life, he could not be said to possess his right mind. He had contrived, or rather he had happened, to dissever himself from the world—to vanish—to give up his place and privileges with living men, without being admitted among the dead. The life of a hermit is nowise parallel to his. He was in the bustle of the city, as of old; but the crowd swept by, and saw him not; he was, we may figuratively say, always beside his wife, and at his hearth, yet must never feel the warmth of the one, nor the affection of the other. It was Wakefield's unprecedented fate, to retain his original share of human sympathies, and to be still involved in human interests, while he had lost his reciprocal influence on them. It would be a most curious speculation, to trace out the effect of such circumstances on his heart and intellect, separately, and in unison. Yet, changed as he was, he would seldom be conscious of it, but deem himself the same man as ever; glimpses of the truth, indeed, would come, but only for the moment; and still he would keep saying—'I shall soon go back!'—nor reflect, that he had been saying so for twenty years.

I conceive, also, that these twenty years would appear, in the retrospect, scarcely longer than the week to which Wakefield had at first limited his absence. He would look on the affair as no more than an interlude in the main business of his life. When, after a little while more, he should deem it time to re-enter his parlor, his wife would clap her hands for joy, on beholding the middle-aged Mr. Wakefield. Alas, what a mistake! Would Time but await the close of our favorite follies, we should be young men, all of us, and till Doom's Day.

One evening, in the twentieth year since he vanished, Wakefield is taking his customary walk towards the dwelling which he still calls his own. It is a gusty night of autumn, with frequent showers, that patter down upon the pavement, and are gone, before a man can put up his umbrella. Pausing near the house, Wakefield discerns, through the parlor-windows of the second floor, the red glow, and the glimmer and fitful flash, of a comfortable fire. On the ceiling, appears a grotesque shadow of good Mrs. Wakefield. The cap, the nose and chin, and the broad waist, form an admirable caricature, which dances, moreover, with the up-flickering and down-sinking blaze, almost too merrily for the shade of an elderly widow. At this instant, a shower chances to fall, and is driven, by the unmannerly gust, full into Wakefield's face and bosom. He is quite penetrated with its autumnal chill. Shall he stand, wet and shivering here, when his own hearth has a good fire to warm him, and his own wife will run to fetch the gray coat and small-clothes, which, doubtless, she has kept carefully in the closet of their bed-chamber? No! Wakefield is no such fool. He ascends the steps—heavily!—for twenty years have stiffened his legs, since he came down—but he knows it not. Stay, Wakefield! Would you go to the sole home that is left you? Then step into your grave! The door opens. As he passes in, we have a parting glimpse of his visage, and recognize the crafty smile, which was the precursor of the little joke, that he has ever since been playing off at his wife's expense. How unmercifully has he quizzed the poor woman! Well; a good night's rest to Wakefield!

This happy event—supposing it to be such—could only have occurred at an unpremeditated moment. We will not follow our friend across the threshold. He has left us much food for thought, a portion of which shall lend its wisdom to a moral; and be shaped into a figure. Amid the seeming confusion of our mysterious world, individuals are so nicely adjusted to a system, and systems to one another, and to a whole, that, by stepping aside for a moment, a man exposes himself to a fearful risk of losing his place forever. Like Wakefield, he may become, as it were, the Outcast of the Universe.

The Notch of the White Mountains

It was now the middle of September. We had come since sunrise from Bartlett, passing up through the valley of the Saco, which extends between mountainous walls, sometimes with a steep ascent, but often as level as a church-aisle. All that day and two preceding ones, we had been loitering towards the heart of the White Mountains—those old crystal hills, whose mysterious brilliancy had gleamed upon our distant wanderings before we thought of visiting them. Height after height had risen and towered one above another, till the clouds began to hang below the peaks. Down their slopes were the red path-ways of the Slides, those avalanches of earth, stones and trees, which descend into the hollows, leaving vestiges of their track, hardly to be effaced by the vegetation of ages. We had mountains behind us and mountains on each side, and a group of mightier ones ahead. Still our road went up along the Saco, right towards the centre of that group, as if to climb above the clouds, in its passage to the farther region.

In old times, the settlers used to be astounded by the inroads of the northern Indians, coming down upon them from this mountain rampart, through some defile known only to themselves. It is indeed a wondrous path. A demon, it might be fancied, or one of the Titans, was travelling up the valley, elbowing the heights carelessly aside as he passed, till at length a great mountain took its stand directly across his intended road. He tarries not for such an obstacle, but rending it asunder, a thousand feet from peak to base, discloses its treasures of hidden minerals, its sunless waters, all the secrets of the mountain's inmost heart, with a mighty fracture of rugged precipices on each side. This is the Notch of the White Hills. Shame on me, that I have attempted to describe it by so mean an image—feeling, as I do, that it is one of those symbolic scenes, which lead the mind to the sentiment, though not to the conception, of Omnipotence.

We had now reached a narrow passage, which showed almost the appearance of having been cut by human strength and artifice in the solid rock. There was a wall of granite on each side, high and precipitous, especially on our right, and so smooth that a few evergreens could hardly find foothold enough to grow there. This is the entrance, or, in the direction we were going, the extremity of the romantic defile of the Notch. Before emerging from it, the rattling of wheels approached behind us, and a stage-coach rumbled out of the mountain, with seats on top and trunks behind, and a smart driver, in a drab great-coat, touching the wheel horses with the whip-stock, and reining in the leaders. To my mind, there was a sort of poetry in such an incident, hardly inferior to what would have accompanied the painted array of an Indian war-party, gliding forth from the same wild chasm. All the passengers, except a very fat lady on the back seat, had alighted. One was a mineralogist, a scientific, green-spectacled figure in black, bearing a heavy hammer, with which he did great damage to the precipices, and put the fragments in his pocket. Another was a well-dressed young man, who carried an opera glass set in gold, and seemed to be making a quotation from some of Byron's rhapsodies on mountain scenery. There was also a trader, returning from Portland to the upper part of Vermont; and a fair young girl, with a very faint bloom, like one of those pale and delicate flowers, which sometimes occur among Alpine cliffs.

They disappeared, and we followed them, passing through a

deep pine forest, which, for some miles, allowed us to see nothing but its own dismal shade. Towards night-fall, we reached a level amphitheatre, surrounded by a great rampart of hills, which shut out the sunshine long before it left the external world. It was here that we obtained our first view, except at a distance, of the principal group of mountains. They are majestic, and even awful, when contemplated in a proper mood; yet, by their breadth of base, and the long ridges which support them, give the idea of immense bulk, rather than of towering height. Mount Washington, indeed, looked near to Heaven; he was white with snow a mile downward, and had caught the only cloud that was sailing through the atmosphere, to veil his head. Let us forget the other names of American statesmen, that have been stamped upon these hills, but still call the loftiest—WASHINGTON. Mountains are Earth's undecaying monuments. They must stand while she endures, and never should be consecrated to the mere great men of their own age and country, but to the mighty ones alone, whose glory is universal, and whom all time will render illustrious.

The air, not often sultry in this elevated region, nearly two thousand feet above the sea, was now sharp and cold, like that of a clear November evening in the low-lands. By morning, probably, there would be a frost, if not a snow-fall, on the grass and rye, and an icy surface over the standing water. I was glad to perceive a prospect of comfortable quarters, in a house which we were approaching, and of pleasant company in the guests who were assembled at the door.

The Ambitious Guest

ONE September night, a family had gathered round their hearth, and piled it high with the drift-wood of mountain-streams, the dry cones of the pine, and the splintered ruins of great trees, that had come crashing down the precipice. Up the chimney roared the fire, and brightened the room with its broad blaze. The faces of the father and mother had a sober gladness; the children laughed; the eldest daughter was the image of Happiness at seventeen; and the aged grandmother, who sat knitting in the warmest place, was the image of Happiness grown old. They had found the 'herb, heart's ease,' in the bleakest spot of all New-England. This family were situated in the Notch of the White Hills, where the wind was sharp throughout the year, and pitilessly cold in the winter—giving their cottage all its fresh inclemency, before it descended on the valley of the Saco. They dwelt in a cold spot and a danger-ous one; for a mountain towered above their heads, so steep, that the stones would often rumble down its sides, and startle them at midnight.

The daughter had just uttered some simple jest, that filled them all with mirth, when the wind came through the Notch and seemed to pause before their cottage—rattling the door, with a sound of wailing and lamentation, before it passed into the valley. For a moment, it saddened them, though there was nothing unusual in the tones. But the family were glad again, when they perceived that the latch was lifted by some traveller, whose footsteps had been unheard amid the dreary blast, which heralded his approach, and wailed as he was entering, and went moaning away from the door.

Though they dwelt in such a solitude, these people held daily converse with the world. The romantic pass of the Notch is a great artery, through which the life-blood of internal commerce is continually throbbing, between Maine, on one side, and the Green Mountains and the shores of the St. Lawrence on the other. The stage-coach always drew up before the door of the cottage. The wayfarer, with no companion but his staff, paused here to exchange a word, that the sense of loneliness might not utterly overcome him, ere he could pass through the cleft of the mountain, or reach the first house in the valley. And here the teamster, on his way to Portland market, would put up for the night—and, if a bachelor, might sit an hour beyond the usual bed-time, and steal a kiss from the mountain-maid, at parting. It was one of those primitive taverns, where the traveller pays only for food and lodging, but meets with a homely kindness, beyond all price. When the footsteps were heard, therefore, between the outer door and the inner one, the whole family rose up, grandmother, children, and all, as if about to welcome some one who belonged to them, and whose fate was linked with theirs.

The door was opened by a young man. His face at first wore the melancholy expression, almost despondency, of one who travels a wild and bleak road, at night-fall and alone, but soon brightened up, when he saw the kindly warmth of his reception. He felt his heart spring forward to meet them all, from the old woman, who wiped a chair with her apron, to the little child that held out its arms to him. One glance and smile placed the stranger on a footing of innocent familiarity with the eldest daughter.

'Ah, this fire is the right thing!' cried he; 'especially when there is such a pleasant circle round it. I am quite benumbed; for the Notch is just like the pipe of a great pair of bellows; it has blown a terrible blast in my face, all the way from Bart-lett.'

'Then you are going towards Vermont?' said the master of the house, as he helped to take a light knapsack off the young man's shoulders.

'Yes; to Burlington, and far enough beyond,' replied he. 'I meant to have been at Ethan Crawford's, to-night; but a pedestrian lingers along such a road as this. It is no matter; for, when I saw this good fire, and all your cheerful faces, I felt as if you had kindled it on purpose for me, and were waiting my arrival. So I shall sit down among you, and make myself at home.'

The frank-hearted stranger had just drawn his chair to the fire, when something like a heavy footstep was heard without, rushing down the steep side of the mountain, as with long and rapid strides, and taking such a leap, in passing the cottage, as to strike the opposite precipice. The family held their breath, because they knew the sound, and their guest held his, by instinct.

'The old Mountain has thrown a stone at us, for fear we should forget him,' said the landlord, recovering himself. 'He sometimes nods his head, and threatens to come down; but we are old neighbors, and agree together pretty well, upon the whole. Besides, we have a sure place of refuge, hard by, if he should be coming in good earnest.'

Let us now suppose the stranger to have finished his supper of bear's meat; and, by his natural felicity of manner, to have placed himself on a footing of kindness with the whole family—so that they talked as freely together, as if he belonged to their mountain brood. He was of a proud, yet gentle spirit—haughty and reserved among the rich and great; but ever ready to stoop his head to the lowly cottage door, and be like a brother or a son at the poor man's fireside. In the household of the Notch, he found warmth and simplicity of feeling, the pervading intelligence of New-England, and a poetry, of native growth, which they had gathered, when they little thought of it, from the mountain-peaks and chasms, and at the very threshold of their romantic and dangerous abode. He had travelled far and alone; his whole life, indeed, had been a solitary path; for, with the lofty caution of his nature, he had kept himself apart from those who might otherwise have been his companions. The family, too, though so kind and hospitable, had that consciousness of unity among themselves, and separation from the world at large, which, in every domestic circle, should still keep a holy place, where no stranger may intrude. But, this evening, a prophetic sympathy impelled the refined and educated youth to pour out his heart before the simple mountaineers, and constrained them to answer him with the same free confidence. And thus it should have been. Is not the kindred of a common fate a closer tie than that of birth?

The secret of the young man's character was, a high and abstracted ambition. He could have borne to live an undistinguished life, but not to be forgotten in the grave. Yearning desire had been transformed to hope; and hope, long cherished, had become like certainty, that, obscurely as he journeyed now, a glory was to beam on all his path-way—though not, perhaps, while he was treading it. But, when posterity should gaze back into the gloom of what was now the present, they would trace the brightness of his footsteps, brightening as meaner glories faded, and confess, that a gifted one had passed from his cradle to his tomb, with none to recognize him.

'As yet,' cried the stranger—his cheek glowing and his eye flashing with enthusiasm—'as yet, I have done nothing. Were I to vanish from the earth to-morrow, none would know so much of me as you; that a nameless youth came up, at nightfall, from the valley of the Saco, and opened his heart to you in the evening, and passed through the Notch, by sunrise, and was seen no more. Not a soul would ask—"Who was he?—

Whither did the wanderer go?" But, I cannot die till I have achieved my destiny. Then, let Death come! I shall have built my monument!'

There was a continual flow of natural emotion, gushing forth amid abstracted reverie, which enabled the family to understand this young man's sentiments, though so foreign from their own. With quick sensibility of the ludicrous, he blushed at the ardor into which he had been betrayed.

'You laugh at me,' said he, taking the eldest daughter's hand, and laughing himself. 'You think my ambition as nonsensical as if I were to freeze myself to death on the top of Mount Washington, only that people might spy at me from the country roundabout. And truly, that would be a noble pedestal for a man's statue!'

'It is better to sit here, by this fire,' answered the girl, blushing, 'and be comfortable and contented, though nobody thinks about us.'

'I suppose,' said her father, after a fit of musing, 'there is something natural in what the young man says; and if my mind had been turned that way, I might have felt just the same. It is strange, wife, how his talk has set my head running on things, that are pretty certain never to come to pass.'

'Perhaps they may,' observed the wife. 'Is the man thinking what he will do when he is a widower?'

'No, no!' cried he, repelling the idea with reproachful kindness. 'When I think of your death, Esther, I think of mine, too. But I was wishing we had a good farm, in Bartlett, or Bethlehem, or Littleton, or some other township round the White Mountains; but not where they could tumble on our heads. I should want to stand well with my neighbors, and be called 'Squire, and sent to General Court, for a term or two; for a plain, honest man may do as much good there as a lawyer. And when I should be grown quite an old man, and you an old woman, so as not to be long apart, I might die happy enough in my bed, and leave you all crying around me. A slate grave-stone would suit me as well as a marble one—with just my name and age, and a verse of a hymn, and something to let people know, that I lived an honest man and died a Christian.'

'There now!' exclaimed the stranger; 'it is our nature to desire a monument, be it slate, or marble, or a pillar of granite, or a glorious memory in the universal heart of man.'

'We're in a strange way, to-night,' said the wife, with tears in her eyes. 'They say it's a sign of something, when folks' minds go a wandering so. Hark to the children!'

They listened accordingly. The younger children had been put to bed in another room, but with an open door between, so that they could be heard talking busily among themselves. One and all seemed to have caught the infection from the fireside circle, and were outvying each other, in wild wishes, and childish projects of what they would do, when they came to be men and women. At length, a little boy, instead of addressing his brothers and sisters, called out to his mother.

'I'll tell you what I wish, mother,' cried he. 'I want you and father and grandma'm, and all of us, and the stranger too, to start right away, and go and take a drink out of the basin of the Flume!'

Nobody could help laughing at the child's notion of leaving a warm bed, and dragging them from a cheerful fire, to visit the basin of the Flume—a brook, which tumbles over the precipice, deep within the Notch. The boy had hardly spoken, when a wagon rattled along the road, and stopped a moment before the door. It appeared to contain two or three men, who were cheering their hearts with the rough chorus of a song, which resounded, in broken notes, between the cliffs, while the singers hesitated whether to continue their journey, or put up here for the night.

'Father,' said the girl, 'they are calling you by name.'

But the good man doubted whether they had really called him, and was unwilling to show himself too solicitous of gain, by inviting people to patronize his house. He therefore did not hurry to the door; and the lash being soon applied, the travellers plunged into the Notch, still singing and laughing, though their music and mirth came back drearily from the heart of the mountain.

'There, mother!' cried the boy, again. 'They'd have given us a ride to the Flume.'

Again they laughed at the child's pertinacious fancy for a night-ramble. But it happened, that a light cloud passed over the daughter's spirit; she looked gravely into the fire, and drew a breath that was almost a sigh. It forced its way, in spite of a little struggle to repress it. Then starting and blushing, she looked quickly round the circle, as if they had caught a glimpse into her bosom. The stranger asked what she had been thinking of.

'Nothing,' answered she, with a downcast smile. 'Only I felt lonesome just then.'

'Oh, I have always had a gift of feeling what is in other people's hearts,' said he, half seriously. 'Shall I tell the secrets of yours? For I know what to think, when a young girl shivers by a warm hearth, and complains of lonesomeness at her mother's side. Shall I put these feelings into words?'

'They would not be a girl's feelings any longer, if they could be put into words,' replied the mountain-nymph, laughing, but avoiding his eye.

All this was said apart. Perhaps a germ of love was springing in their hearts, so pure that it might blossom in Paradise, since it could not be matured on earth; for women worship such gentle dignity as his; and the proud, contemplative, yet kindly soul is oftenest captivated by simplicity like hers. But, while they spoke softly, and he was watching the happy sadness, the lightsome shadows, the shy yearnings of a maiden's nature, the wind, through the Notch, took a deeper and drearier sound. It seemed, as the fanciful stranger said, like the choral strain of the spirits of the blast, who, in old Indian times, had their dwelling among these mountains, and made their heights and recesses a sacred region. There was a wail, along the road, as if a funeral were passing. To chase away the gloom, the family threw pine branches on their fire, till the dry leaves crackled and the flame arose, discovering once again a scene of peace and humble happiness. The light hovered about them fondly, and caressed them all. There were the little faces of the children, peeping from their bed apart, and here the father's frame of strength, the mother's subdued and careful mien, the high-browed youth, the budding girl, and the good old grandam, still knitting in the warmest place. The aged woman looked up from her task, and, with fingers ever busy, was the next to speak.

'Old folks have their notions,' said she, 'as well as young ones. You've been wishing and planning; and letting your heads run on one thing and another, till you've set my mind a wandering too. Now what should an old woman wish for, when she can go but a step or two before she comes to her grave? Children, it will haunt me night and day, till I tell you.'

'What is it, mother?' cried the husband and wife, at once.

Then the old woman, with an air of mystery, which drew the circle closer round the fire, informed them that she had provided her grave-clothes some years before—a nice linen shroud, a cap with a muslin ruff, and everything of a finer sort than she had worn since her wedding-day. But, this evening, an old superstition had strangely recurred to her. It used to be said, in her younger days, that, if anything were amiss with a corpse, if only the ruff were not smooth, or the cap did not set right, the corpse, in the coffin and beneath the clods, would strive to put up its cold hands and arrange it. The bare thought made her nervous.

'Don't talk so, grandmother!' said the girl, shuddering.

'Now,'—continued the old woman, with singular earnestness, yet smiling strangely at her own folly,—'I want one of you, my children—when your mother is drest, and in the coffin—I want one of you to hold a looking-glass over my face. Who knows but I may take a glimpse at myself, and see whether all's right?'

'Old and young, we dream of graves and monuments,' murmured the stranger-youth. 'I wonder how mariners feel, when the ship is sinking, and they, unknown and undistinguished, are to be buried together in the ocean—that wide and nameless sepulchre!'

For a moment, the old woman's ghastly conception so engrossed the minds of her hearers, that a sound, abroad in the night, rising like the roar of a blast, had grown broad, deep, and terrible, before the fated group were conscious of it. The house, and all within it, trembled; the foundations of the earth seemed to be shaken, as if this awful sound were the peal of the last trump. Young and old exchanged one wild glance, and remained an instant, pale, affrighted, without utterance, or power to move. Then the same shriek burst simultaneously from all their lips.

'The Slide! The Slide!'

The simplest words must intimate, but not portray, the unutterable horror of the catastrophe. The victims rushed from their cottage, and sought refuge in what they deemed a safer spot—where, in contemplation of such an emergency, a sort of barrier had been reared. Alas! they had quitted their security, and fled right into the pathway of destruction. Down came the whole side of the mountain, in a cataract of ruin. Just before it reached the house, the stream broke into two branches—shivered not a window there, but overwhelmed the whole vicinity, blocked up the road, and annihilated everything in its dreadful course. Long ere the thunder of that great Slide had ceased to roar among the mountains, the mortal agony had been endured, and the victims were at peace. Their bodies were never found.

The next morning, the light smoke was seen stealing from the cottage-chimney, up the mountain-side. Within, the fire was yet smouldering on the hearth, and the chairs in a circle round it, as if the inhabitants had but gone forth to view the devastation of the Slide, and would shortly return, to thank Heaven for their miraculous escape. All had left separate tokens, by which those, who had known the family, were made to shed a tear for each. Who has not heard their name? The story had been told far and wide, and will forever be a legend of these mountains. Poets have sung their fate.

There were circumstances, which led some to suppose that a stranger had been received into the cottage on this awful night, and had shared the catastrophe of all its inmates. Others denied that there were sufficient grounds for such a conjecture. Wo, for the high-souled youth, with his dream of Earthly Immortality! His name and person utterly unknown; his history, his way of life, his plans, a mystery never to be solved; his death and his existence, equally a doubt! Whose was the agony of that death-moment?

The May-Pole of Merry Mount

There is an admirable foundation for a philosophic romance, in the curious history of the early settlement of Mount Wollaston, or Merry Mount. In the slight sketch here attempted, the facts, recorded on the grave pages of our New England annalists, have wrought themselves, almost spontaneously, into a sort of allegory. The masques, mummeries, and festive customs, described in the text, are in accordance with the manners of the age. Authority on these points may be found in Strutt's Book of English Sports and Pastimes.

BRIGHT were the days at Merry Mount, when the May-Pole was the banner-staff of that gay colony! They who reared it, should their banner be triumphant, were to pour sunshine over New England's rugged hills, and scatter flower-seeds throughout the soil. Jollity and gloom were contending for an empire. Midsummer eve had come, bringing deep verdure to the forest, and roses in her lap, of a more vivid hue than the tender buds of Spring. But May, or her mirthful spirit, dwelt all the year round at Merry Mount, sporting with the Summer months, and revelling with Autumn, and basking in the glow of Winter's fireside. Through a world of toil and care, she flitted with a dreamlike smile, and came hither to find a home among the lightsome hearts of Merry Mount.

Never had the May-Pole been so gaily decked as at sunset on midsummer eve. This venerated emblem was a pine tree, which had preserved the slender grace of youth, while it equalled the loftiest height of the old wood monarchs. From its top streamed a silken banner, colored like the rainbow. Down nearly to the ground, the pole was dressed with birchen boughs, and others of the liveliest green, and some with silvery leaves, fastened by ribbons that fluttered in fantastic knots of twenty different colors, but no sad ones. Garden flowers, and blossoms of the wilderness, laughed gladly forth amid the verdure, so fresh and dewy, that they must have grown by magic

on that happy pine tree. Where this green and flowery splendor terminated, the shaft of the May-Pole was stained with the
seven brilliant hues of the banner at its top. On the lowest
green bough hung an abundant wreath of roses, some that had
been gathered in the sunniest spots of the forest, and others, of
still richer blush, which the colonists had reared from English
seed. Oh, people of the Golden Age, the chief of your hus-
bandry, was to raise flowers!

But what was the wild throng that stood hand in hand about
the May-Pole? It could not be, that the Fauns and Nymphs,
when driven from their classic groves and homes of ancient fable, had sought refuge, as all the persecuted did, in the fresh
woods of the West. These were Gothic monsters, though perhaps of Grecian ancestry. On the shoulders of a comely youth,
uprose the head and branching antlers of a stag; a second, human in all other points, had the grim visage of a wolf; a third,
still with the trunk and limbs of a mortal man, showed the
beard and horns of a venerable he-goat. There was the likeness
of a bear erect, brute in all but his hind legs, which were
adorned with pink silk stockings. And here again, almost as
wondrous, stood a real bear of the dark forest, lending each of
his fore paws to the grasp of a human hand, and as ready for the
dance as any in that circle. His inferior nature rose half-way, to
meet his companions as they stooped. Other faces wore the similitude of man or woman, but distorted or extravagant, with
red noses pendulous before their mouths, which seemed of awful depth, and stretched from ear to ear in an eternal fit of
laughter. Here might be seen the Salvage Man, well known in
heraldry, hairy as a baboon, and girdled with green leaves. By
his side, a nobler figure, but still a counterfeit, appeared an Indian hunter, with feathery crest and wampum belt. Many of
this strange company wore fools-caps, and had little bells ap-
pended to their garments, tinkling with a silvery sound, responsive to the inaudible music of their gleesome spirits. Some

youths and maidens were of soberer garb, yet well maintained their places in the irregular throng, by the expression of wild revelry upon their features. Such were the colonists of Merry Mount, as they stood in the broad smile of sunset, round their venerated May-Pole.

Had a wanderer, bewildered in the melancholy forest, heard their mirth, and stolen a half-affrighted glance, he might have fancied them the crew of Comus, some already transformed to brutes, some midway between man and beast, and the others rioting in the flow of tipsey jollity that foreran the change. But a band of Puritans, who watched the scene, invisible themselves, compared the masques to those devils and ruined souls, with whom their supersitition peopled the black wilderness.

Within the ring of monsters, appeared the two airiest forms, that had ever trodden on any more solid footing than a purple and golden cloud. One was a youth, in glistening apparel, with a scarf of the rainbow pattern crosswise on his breast. His right hand held a gilded staff, the ensign of high dignity among the revellers, and his left grasped the slender fingers of a fair maiden, not less gaily decorated than himself. Bright roses glowed in contrast with the dark and glossy curls of each, and were scattered round their feet, or had sprung up spontaneously there. Behind this lightsome couple, so close to the May-Pole that its boughs shaded his jovial face, stood the figure of an English priest, canonically dressed, yet decked with flowers, in heathen fashion, and wearing a chaplet of the native vine leaves. By the riot of his rolling eye, and the pagan decorations of his holy garb, he seemed the wildest monster there, and the very Comus of the crew.

'Votaries of the May-Pole,' cried the flower-decked priest, 'merrily, all day long, have the woods echoed to your mirth. But be this your merriest hour, my hearts! Lo, here stand the Lord and Lady of the May, whom I, a clerk of Oxford, and high priest of Merry Mount, am presently to join in holy matrimony. Up with your nimble spirits, ye morrice-dancers, green-men, and glee-maidens, bears and wolves, and horned gentlemen! Come; a chorus now, rich with the old mirth of Merry England, and the wilder glee of this fresh forest; and then a dance, to show the youthful pair what life is made of, and how airily they should go through it! All ye that love the May-Pole, lend your voices to the nuptial song of the Lord and Lady of the May!'

This wedlock was more serious than most affairs of Merry Mount, where jest and delusion, trick and fantasy, kept up a continued carnival. The Lord and Lady of the May, though their titles must be laid down at sunset, were really and truly to be partners for the dance of life, beginning the measure that same bright eve. The wreath of roses, that hung from the lowest green bough of the May-Pole, had been twined for them, and would be thrown over both their heads, in symbol of their flowery union. When the priest had spoken, therefore, a riotous uproar burst from the rout of monstrous figures.

'Begin you the stave, reverend Sir,' cried they all; 'and never did the woods ring to such a merry peal, as we of the May-Pole shall send up!'

Immediately a prelude of pipe, cittern, and viol, touched with practised minstrelsy, began to play from a neighboring thicket, in such a mirthful cadence, that the boughs of the May-Pole quivered to the sound. But the May Lord, he of the gilded staff, chancing to look into his Lady's eyes, was wonderstruck at the almost pensive glance that met his own.

'Edith, sweet Lady of the May,' whispered he, reproachfully, 'is yon wreath of roses a garland to hang above our graves, that you look so sad? Oh, Edith, this is our golden time! Tarnish it not by any pensive shadow of the mind; for it may be, that nothing of futurity will be brighter than the mere remembrance of what is now passing.'

'That was the very thought that saddened me! How came it in your mind too?' said Edith, in a still lower tone than he; for it was high treason to be sad at Merry Mount. 'Therefore do I

sigh amid this festive music. And besides, dear Edgar, I struggle as with a dream, and fancy that these shapes of our jovial
friends are visionary, and their mirth unreal, and that we are
no true Lord and Lady of the May. What is the mystery in my
heart?'

Just then, as if a spell had loosened them, down came a little
shower of withering rose leaves from the May-Pole. Alas, for
the young lovers! No sooner had their hearts glowed with real
passion, than they were sensible of something vague and unsubstantial in their former pleasures, and felt a dreary presenti-
ment of inevitable change. From the moment that they truly
loved, they had subjected themselves to earth's doom of care,
and sorrow, and troubled joy, and had no more a home at
Merry Mount. That was Edith's mystery. Now leave we the
priest to marry them, and the masquers to sport round the
May-Pole, till the last sunbeam be withdrawn from its summit, and the shadows of the forest mingle gloomily in the
dance. Meanwhile, we may discover who these gay people
were.

Two hundred years ago, and more, the old world and its inhabitants became mutually weary of each other. Men voyaged
by thousands to the West; some to barter glass beads, and such
like jewels, for the furs of the Indian hunter; some to conquer
virgin empires; and one stern band to pray. But none of these
motives had much weight with the colonists of Merry Mount.
Their leaders were men who had sported so long with life, that
when Thought and Wisdom came, even these unwelcome
guests were led astray, by the crowd of vanities which they
should have put to flight. Erring Thought and perverted Wisdom were made to put on masques, and play the fool. The men
of whom we speak, after losing the heart's fresh gaiety, imagined a wild philosophy of pleasure, and came hither to act out
their latest day-dream. They gathered followers from all that
giddy tribe, whose whole life is like the festal days of soberer
men. In their train were minstrels, not unknown in London

streets; wandering players, whose theatres had been the halls of noblemen; mummers, rope-dancers, and mountebanks, who would long be missed at wakes, church-ales, and fairs; in a word, mirth-makers of every sort, such as abounded in that age, but now began to be discountenanced by the rapid growth of Puritanism. Light had their footsteps been on land, and as lightly they came across the sea. Many had been maddened by their previous troubles into a gay despair; others were as madly gay in the flush of youth, like the May Lord and his Lady; but whatever might be the quality of their mirth, old and young were gay at Merry Mount. The young deemed themselves happy. The elder spirits, if they knew that mirth was but the counterfeit of happiness, yet followed the false shadow wilfully, because at least her garments glittered brightest. Sworn triflers of a lifetime, they would not venture among the sober truths of life, not even to be truly blest.

All the hereditary pastimes of Old England were transplanted hither. The King of Christmas was duly crowned, and the Lord of Misrule bore potent sway. On the eve of Saint John, they felled whole acres of the forest to make bonfires, and danced by the blaze all night, crowned with garlands, and throwing flowers into the flame. At harvest time, though their crop was of the smallest, they made an image with the sheaves of Indian corn, and wreathed it with autumnal garlands, and bore it home triumphantly. But what chiefly characterized the colonists of Merry Mount, was their veneration for the May-Pole. It has made their true history a poet's tale. Spring decked the hallowed emblem with young blossoms and fresh green boughs; Summer brought roses of the deepest blush, and the perfected foliage of the forest; Autumn enriched it with that red and yellow gorgeousness, which converts each wild-wood leaf into a painted flower; and Winter silvered it with sleet, and hung it round with icicles, till it flashed in the cold sunshine, itself a frozen sunbeam. Thus each alternate season did homage to the May-Pole, and paid it a tribute of its own richest splendor. Its votaries danced round it, once, at least, in every month; sometimes they called it their religion, or their altar; but always, it was the banner-staff of Merry Mount.

Unfortunately, there were men in the new world, of a sterner faith than these May-Pole worshippers. Not far from Merry Mount was a settlement of Puritans, most dismal wretches, who said their prayers before daylight, and then wrought in the forest or the cornfield, till evening made it prayer time again. Their weapons were always at hand, to shoot down the straggling savage. When they met in conclave, it was never to keep up the old English mirth, but to hear sermons three hours long, or to proclaim bounties on the heads of wolves and the scalps of Indians. Their festivals were fast-days, and their chief pastime the singing of psalms. Woe to the youth or maiden, who did but dream of a dance! The selectman nodded to the constable; and there sat the light-heeled reprobate in the stocks; or if he danced, it was round the whipping-post, which might be termed the Puritan May-Pole.

A party of these grim Puritans, toiling through the difficult woods, each with a horse-load of iron armor to burthen his footsteps, would sometimes draw near the sunny precincts of Merry Mount. There were the silken colonists, sporting round their May-Pole; perhaps teaching a bear to dance, or striving to communicate their mirth to the grave Indian; or masquerading in the skins of deer and wolves, which they had hunted for that especial purpose. Often, the whole colony were playing at blindman's buff, magistrates and all with their eyes bandaged, except a single scape-goat, whom the blinded sinners pursued by the tinkling of the bells at his garments. Once, it is said, they were seen following a flower-decked corpse, with merriment and festive music, to his grave. But did the dead man laugh? In their quietest times, they sang ballads and told tales, for the edification of their pious visiters; or perplexed them with juggling tricks; or grinned at them through horse-collars; and when sport itself grew wearisome, they made game of their own stupidity, and began a yawning match. At the very least of these enormities, the men of iron shook their heads and frowned so darkly, that the revellers looked up, imagining that a momentary cloud had overcast the sunshine, which was to be perpetual there. On the other hand, the Puritans affirmed, that, when a psalm was pealing from their place of worship, the echo, which the forest sent them back, seemed often like the chorus of a jolly catch, closing with a roar of laughter. Who but the fiend, and his bond-slaves, the crew of Merry Mount, had thus disturbed them! In due time, a feud arose, stern and bitter on one side, and as serious on the other as any thing could be, among such light spirits as had sworn allegiance to the May-Pole. The future complexion of New England was involved in this important quarrel. Should the grisly saints establish their jurisdiction over the gay sinners, then would their spirits darken all the clime, and make it a land of clouded visages, of hard toil, of sermon and psalm, forever. But should the banner-staff of Merry Mount be fortunate, sunshine would break upon the hills, and flowers would beautify the forest, and late posterity do homage to the May-Pole!

After these authentic passages from history, we return to the nuptials of the Lord and Lady of the May. Alas! we have delayed too long, and must darken our tale too suddenly. As we glance again at the May-Pole, a solitary sunbeam is fading from the summit, and leaves only a faint golden tinge, blended with the hues of the rainbow banner. Even that dim light is now withdrawn, relinquishing the whole domain of Merry Mount to the evening gloom, which has rushed so instantaneously from the black surrounding woods. But some of these black shadows have rushed forth in human shape.

Yes: with the setting sun, the last day of mirth had passed from Merry Mount. The ring of gay masquers was disordered and broken; the stag lowered his antlers in dismay; the wolf grew weaker than a lamb; the bells of the morrice-dancers tinkled with tremulous affright. The Puritans had played a characteristic part in the May-Pole mummeries. Their darksome figures were intermixed with the wild shapes of their foes, and made the scene a picture of the moment, when waking thoughts start up amid the scattered fantasies of a dream. The leader of the hostile party stood in the centre of the circle, while the rout of monsters cowered around him, like evil spirits in the presence of a dread magician. No fantastic foolery could look him in the face. So stern was the energy of his aspect, that the whole man, visage, frame, and soul, seemed wrought of iron, gifted with life and thought, yet all of one substance with his head-piece and breast-plate. It was the Puritan of Puritans; it was Endicott himself!

'Stand off, priest of Baal!' said he, with a grim frown, and laying no reverent hand upon the surplice. 'I know thee, Blackstone!* Thou art the man, who couldst not abide the rule even of thine own corrupted church, and hast come hither to preach iniquity, and to give example of it in thy life. But now shall it be seen that the Lord hath sanctified this wilderness for his peculiar people. Woe unto them that would defile it! And first for this flower-decked abomination, the altar of thy worship!'

And with his keen sword, Endicott assaulted the hallowed May-Pole. Nor long did it resist his arm. It groaned with a dismal sound; it showered leaves and rose-buds upon the remorseless enthusiast; and finally, with all its green boughs, and ribbons, and flowers, symbolic of departed pleasures, down fell the banner-staff of Merry Mount. As it sank, tradition says, the evening sky grew darker, and the woods threw forth a more sombre shadow.

---

*Did Governor Endicott speak less positively, we should suspect a mistake here. The Rev. Mr. Blackstone, though an eccentric, is not known to have been an immoral man. We rather doubt his identity with the priest of Merry Mount.

'There,' cried Endicott, looking triumphantly on his work, 'there lies the only May-Pole in New England! The thought is strong within me, that, by its fall, is shadowed forth the fate of light and idle mirth-makers, amongst us and our posterity. Amen, saith John Endicott!'

'Amen!' echoed his followers.

But the votaries of the May-Pole gave one groan for their idol. At the sound, the Puritan leader glanced at the crew of Comus, each a figure of broad mirth, yet, at this moment, strangely expressive of sorrow and dismay.

'Valiant captain,' quoth Peter Palfrey, the Ancient of the band, 'what order shall be taken with the prisoners?'

'I thought not to repent me of cutting down a May-Pole,' replied Endicott, 'yet now I could find in my heart to plant it again, and give each of these bestial pagans one other dance round their idol. It would have served rarely for a whipping-post!'

'But there are pine trees enow,' suggested the lieutenant.

'True, good Ancient,' said the leader. 'Wherefore, bind the heathen crew, and bestow on them a small matter of stripes apiece, as earnest of our future justice. Set some of the rogues in the stocks to rest themselves, so soon as Providence shall bring us to one of our own well-ordered settlements, where such accommodations may be found. Further penalties, such as branding and cropping of ears, shall be thought of hereafter.'

'How many stripes for the priest?' inquired Ancient Palfrey.

'None as yet,' answered Endicott, bending his iron frown upon the culprit. 'It must be for the Great and General Court to determine, whether stripes and long imprisonment, and other grievous penalty, may atone for his transgressions. Let him look to himself! For such as violate our civil order, it may be permitted us to show mercy. But woe to the wretch that troubleth our religion!'

'And this dancing bear,' resumed the officer. 'Must he share the stripes of his fellows?'

'Shoot him through the head!' said the energetic Puritan. 'I suspect witchcraft in the beast.'

'Here be a couple of shining ones,' continued Peter Palfrey, pointing his weapon at the Lord and Lady of the May. 'They seem to be of high station among these mis-doers. Methinks their dignity will not be fitted with less than a double share of stripes.'

Endicott rested on his sword, and closely surveyed the dress and aspect of the hapless pair. There they stood, pale, down-cast, and apprehensive. Yet there was an air of mutual support, and of pure affection, seeking aid and giving it, that showed them to be man and wife, with the sanction of a priest upon their love. The youth, in the peril of the moment, had dropped his gilded staff, and thrown his arm about the Lady of the May, who leaned against his breast, too lightly to burthen him, but with weight enough to express that their destinies were linked together, for good or evil. They looked first at each other, and then into the grim captain's face. There they stood, in the first hour of wedlock, while the idle pleasures, of which their companions were the emblems, had given place to the sternest cares of life, personified by the dark Puritans. But never had their youthful beauty seemed so pure and high, as when its glow was chastened by adversity.

'Youth,' said Endicott, 'ye stand in an evil case, thou and thy maiden wife. Make ready presently; for I am minded that ye shall both have a token to remember your wedding-day!'

'Stern man,' cried the May Lord, 'how can I move thee? Were the means at hand, I would resist to the death. Being powerless, I entreat! Do with me as thou wilt; but let Edith go untouched!'

'Not so,' replied the immitigable zealot. 'We are not wont to show an idle courtesy to that sex, which requireth the stricter discipline. What sayest thou, maid? Shall thy silken bridegroom suffer thy share of the penalty, besides his own?'

'Be it death,' said Edith, 'and lay it all on me!'

Truly, as Endicott had said, the poor lovers stood in a woeful case. Their foes were triumphant, their friends captive and abased, their home desolate, the benighted wilderness around them, and a rigorous destiny, in the shape of the Puritan leader, their only guide. Yet the deepening twilight could not altogether conceal, that the iron man was softened; he smiled, at the fair spectacle of early love; he almost sighed, for the inevitable blight of early hopes.

'The troubles of life have come hastily on this young couple,' observed Endicott. 'We will see how they comport themselves under their present trials, ere we burthen them with greater. If, among the spoil, there be any garments of a more decent fashion, let them be put upon this May Lord and his Lady, instead of their glistening vanities. Look to it, some of you.'

'And shall not the youth's hair be cut?' asked Peter Palfrey, looking with abhorrence at the love-lock and long glossy curls of the young man.

'Crop it forthwith, and that in the true pumpkin-shell fashion,' answered the captain. 'Then bring them along with us, but more gently than their fellows. There be qualities in the youth, which may make him valiant to fight, and sober to toil, and pious to pray; and in the maiden, that may fit her to become a mother in our Israel, bringing up babes in better nurture than her own hath been. Nor think ye, young ones, that they are the happiest, even in our lifetime of a moment, who misspend it in dancing round a May-Pole!'

And Endicott, the severest Puritan of all who laid the rock-foundation of New England, lifted the wreath of roses from the ruin of the May-Pole, and threw it, with his own gauntleted hand, over the heads of the Lord and Lady of the May. It was a deed of prophecy. As the moral gloom of the world overpowers all systematic gaiety, even so was their home of wild mirth made desolate amid the sad forest. They returned to it no more. But, as their flowery garland was wreathed of the brightest roses that had grown there, so, in the tie that united them, were intertwined all the purest and best of their early joys. They went heavenward, supporting each other along the difficult path which it was their lot to tread, and never wasted one regretful thought on the vanities of Merry Mount.

The Minister's Black Veil

A PARABLE*

THE sexton stood in the porch of Milford meeting-house, pulling lustily at the bell-rope. The old people of the village came stooping along the street. Children, with bright faces, tript merrily beside their parents, or mimicked a graver gait, in the conscious dignity of their Sunday clothes. Spruce bachelors looked sidelong at the pretty maidens, and fancied that the Sabbath sunshine made them prettier than on week-days. When the throng had mostly streamed into the porch, the sexton began to toll the bell, keeping his eye on the Reverend Mr. Hooper's door. The first glimpse of the clergyman's figure was the signal for the bell to cease its summons.

'But what has good Parson Hooper got upon his face?' cried the sexton in astonishment.

All within hearing immediately turned about, and beheld the semblance of Mr. Hooper, pacing slowly his meditative way towards the meeting-house. With one accord they started, expressing more wonder than if some strange minister were coming to dust the cushions of Mr. Hooper's pulpit.

'Are you sure it is our parson?' inquired Goodman Gray of the sexton.

*Another clergyman in New England, Mr. Joseph Moody, of York, Maine, who died about eighty years since, made himself remarkable by the same eccentricity that is here related of the Reverend Mr. Hooper. In his case, however, the symbol had a different import. In early life he had accidentally killed a beloved friend; and from that day till the hour of his own death, he hid his face from men.

'Of a certainty it is good Mr. Hooper,' replied the sexton. 'He was to have exchanged pulpits with Parson Shute of Westbury; but Parson Shute sent to excuse himself yesterday, being to preach a funeral sermon.'

The cause of so much amazement may appear sufficiently slight. Mr. Hooper, a gentlemanly person of about thirty, though still a bachelor, was dressed with due clerical neatness, as if a careful wife had starched his band, and brushed the weekly dust from his Sunday's garb. There was but one thing remarkable in his appearance. Swathed about his forehead, and hanging down over his face, so low as to be shaken by his breath, Mr. Hooper had on a black veil. On a nearer view, it seemed to consist of two folds of crape, which entirely concealed his features, except the mouth and chin, but probably did not intercept his sight, farther than to give a darkened aspect to all living and inanimate things. With this gloomy shade before him, good Mr. Hooper walked onward, at a slow and quiet pace, stooping somewhat and looking on the ground, as is customary with abstracted men, yet nodding kindly to those of his parishioners who still waited on the meeting-house steps. But so wonder-struck were they, that his greeting hardly met with a return.

'I can't really feel as if good Mr. Hooper's face was behind that piece of crape,' said the sexton.

'I don't like it,' muttered an old woman, as she hobbled into the meeting-house. 'He has changed himself into something awful, only by hiding his face.'

'Our parson has gone mad!' cried Goodman Gray, following him across the threshold.

A rumor of some unaccountable phenomenon had preceded Mr. Hooper into the meeting-house, and set all the congregation astir. Few could refrain from twisting their heads towards the door; many stood upright, and turned directly about; while several little boys clambered upon the seats, and came down again with a terrible racket. There was a general bustle, a rustling of the women's gowns and shuffling of the men's feet, greatly at variance with that hushed repose which should attend the entrance of the minister. But Mr. Hooper appeared not to notice the perturbation of his people. He entered with an almost noiseless step, bent his head mildly to the pews on each side, and bowed as he passed his oldest parishioner, a white-haired great-grandsire, who occupied an arm-chair in the centre of the aisle. It was strange to observe, how slowly this venerable man became conscious of something singular in the appearance of his pastor. He seemed not fully to partake of the prevailing wonder, till Mr. Hooper had ascended the stairs, and showed himself in the pulpit, face to face with his congregation, except for the black veil. That mysterious emblem was never once withdrawn. It shook with his measured breath as he gave out the psalm; it threw its obscurity between him and the holy page, as he read the Scriptures; and while he prayed, the veil lay heavily on his uplifted countenance. Did he seek to hide it from the dread Being whom he was addressing?

Such was the effect of this simple piece of crape, that more than one woman of delicate nerves was forced to leave the meeting-house. Yet perhaps the pale-faced congregation was almost as fearful a sight to the minister, as his black veil to them.

Mr. Hooper had the reputation of a good preacher, but not an energetic one: he strove to win his people heavenward, by mild persuasive influences, rather than to drive them thither, by the thunders of the Word. The sermon which he now delivered, was marked by the same characteristics of style and manner, as the general series of his pulpit oratory. But there was something, either in the sentiment of the discourse itself, or in the imagination of the auditors, which made it greatly the most powerful effort that they had ever heard from their pastor's lips. It was tinged, rather more darkly than usual, with the gentle gloom of Mr. Hooper's temperament. The subject had reference to secret sin, and those sad mysteries which we hide from our nearest and dearest, and would fain conceal from our own consciousness, even forgetting that the Omniscient can detect them. A subtle power was breathed into his words. Each member of the congregation, the most innocent girl, and the man of hardened breast, felt as if the preacher had crept upon them, behind his awful veil, and discovered their hoarded iniquity of deed or thought. Many spread their clasped hands on their bosoms. There was nothing terrible in what Mr. Hooper said; at least, no violence; and yet, with every tremor of his melancholy voice, the hearers quaked. An unsought pathos came hand in hand with awe. So sensible were the audience of some unwonted attribute in their minister, that they longed for a breath of wind to blow aside the veil, almost believing that a stranger's visage would be discovered, though the form, gesture, and voice were those of Mr. Hooper.

At the close of the services, the people hurried out with indecorous confusion, eager to communicate their pent-up amazement, and conscious of lighter spirits, the moment they lost sight of the black veil. Some gathered in little circles, huddled closely together, with their mouths all whispering in the centre; some went homeward alone, wrapt in silent meditation; some talked loudly, and profaned the Sabbath-day with ostentatious laughter. A few shook their sagacious heads, intimating that they could penetrate the mystery; while one or two affirmed that there was no mystery at all, but only that Mr. Hooper's eyes were so weakened by the midnight lamp, as to require a shade. After a brief interval, forth came good Mr. Hooper also, in the rear of his flock. Turning his veiled face from one group to another, he paid due reverence to the hoary heads, saluted the middle-aged with kind dignity, as their friend and spiritual guide, greeted the young with mingled authority and love, and laid his hands on the little children's heads to bless them. Such was always his custom on the Sabbath-day. Strange and bewildered looks repaid him for his courtesy. None, as on former occasions, aspired to the honor of walking by their pastor's side. Old Squire Saunders, doubtless by an accidental lapse of memory, neglected to invite Mr. Hooper to his table, where the good clergyman had been wont to bless the food, almost every Sunday since his settlement. He returned, therefore, to the parsonage, and, at the moment of closing the door, was observed to look back upon the people, all of whom had their eyes fixed upon the minister. A sad smile gleamed faintly from beneath the black veil, and flickered about his mouth, glimmering as he disappeared.

'How strange,' said a lady, 'that a simple black veil, such as any woman might wear on her bonnet, should become such a terrible thing on Mr. Hooper's face!'

'Something must surely be amiss with Mr. Hooper's intellects,' observed her husband, the physician of the village. 'But the strangest part of the affair is the effect of this vagary, even on a sober-minded man like myself. The black veil, though it covers only our pastor's face, throws its influence over his whole person, and makes him ghost-like from head to foot. Do you not feel it so?'

'Truly do I,' replied the lady; 'and I would not be alone with him for the world. I wonder he is not afraid to be alone with himself!'

'Men sometimes are so,' said her husband.

The afternoon service was attended with similar circumstances. At its conclusion, the bell tolled for the funeral of a young lady. The relatives and friends were assembled in the house, and the more distant acquaintances stood about the door, speaking of the good qualities of the deceased, when their talk was interrupted by the appearance of Mr. Hooper, still covered with his black veil. It was now an appropriate emblem. The clergyman stepped into the room where the corpse was laid, and bent over the coffin, to take a last farewell of his deceased parishioner. As he stooped, the veil hung straight down from his forehead, so that, if her eye-lids had not been closed for ever, the dead maiden might have seen his face. Could Mr. Hooper be fearful of her glance, that he so hastily

caught back the black veil? A person, who watched the interview between the dead and living, scrupled not to affirm, that,
at the instant when the clergyman's features were disclosed,
the corpse had slightly shuddered, rustling the shroud and
muslin cap, though the countenance retained the composure of
death. A superstitious old woman was the only witness of this
prodigy. From the coffin, Mr. Hooper passed into the chamber
of the mourners, and thence to the head of the staircase, to
make the funeral prayer. It was a tender and heart-dissolving
prayer, full of sorrow, yet so imbued with celestial hopes, that
the music of a heavenly harp, swept by the fingers of the dead,
seemed faintly to be heard among the saddest accents of the
minister. The people trembled, though they but darkly understood him, when he prayed that they, and himself, and all of
mortal race, might be ready, as he trusted this young maiden
had been, for the dreadful hour that should snatch the veil
from their faces. The bearers went heavily forth, and the
mourners followed, saddening all the street, with the dead before them, and Mr. Hooper in his black veil behind.

'Why do you look back?' said one in the procession to his
partner.

'I had a fancy,' replied she, 'that the minister and the maid-
en's spirit were walking hand in hand.'

'And so had I, at the same moment,' said the other.

That night, the handsomest couple in Milford village were to
be joined in wedlock. Though reckoned a melancholy man, Mr.
Hooper had a placid cheerfulness for such occasions, which often excited a sympathetic smile, where livelier merriment
would have been thrown away. There was no quality of his disposition which made him more beloved than this. The company
at the wedding awaited his arrival with impatience, trusting
that the strange awe, which had gathered over him throughout
the day, would now be dispelled. But such was not the result.
When Mr. Hooper came, the first thing that their eyes rested
on was the same horrible black veil, which had added deeper

gloom to the funeral, and could portend nothing but evil to the wedding. Such was its immediate effect on the guests, that a cloud seemed to have rolled duskily from beneath the black crape, and dimmed the light of the candles. The bridal pair stood up before the minister. But the bride's cold fingers quivered in the tremulous hand of the bridegroom, and her death-like paleness caused a whisper, that the maiden who had been buried a few hours before, was come from her grave to be married. If ever another wedding were so dismal, it was that famous one, where they tolled the wedding-knell. After performing the ceremony, Mr. Hooper raised a glass of wine to his lips, wishing happiness to the new-married couple, in a strain of mild pleasantry that ought to have brightened the features of the guests, like a cheerful gleam from the hearth. At that instant, catching a glimpse of his figure in the looking-glass, the black veil involved his own spirit in the horror with which it overwhelmed all others. His frame shuddered—his lips grew white—he spilt the untasted wine upon the carpet—and rushed forth into the darkness. For the Earth, too, had on her Black Veil.

The next day, the whole village of Milford talked of little else than Parson Hooper's black veil. That, and the mystery concealed behind it, supplied a topic for discussion between acquaintances meeting in the street, and good women gossiping at their open windows. It was the first item of news that the tavern-keeper told to his guests. The children babbled of it on their way to school. One imitative little imp covered his face with an old black handkerchief, thereby so affrighting his playmates, that the panic seized himself, and he well nigh lost his wits by his own waggery.

It was remarkable, that, of all the busy-bodies and impertinent people in the parish, not one ventured to put the plain question to Mr. Hooper, wherefore he did this thing. Hitherto, whenever there appeared the slightest call for such interference, he had never lacked advisers, nor shown himself averse to be guided by their judgment. If he erred at all, it was by so painful a degree of self-distrust, that even the mildest censure would lead him to consider an indifferent action as a crime. Yet, though so well acquainted with this amiable weakness, no individual among his parishioners chose to make the black veil a subject of friendly remonstrance. There was a feeling of dread, neither plainly confessed nor carefully concealed, which caused each to shift the responsibility upon another, till at length it was found expedient to send a deputation of the church, in order to deal with Mr. Hooper about the mystery, before it should grow into a scandal. Never did an embassy so ill discharge its duties. The minister received them with friendly courtesy, but became silent, after they were seated, leaving to his visiters the whole burthen of introducing their important business. The topic, it might be supposed, was obvious enough. There was the black veil, swathed round Mr. Hooper's forehead, and concealing every feature above his placid mouth, on which, at times, they could perceive the glimmering of a melancholy smile. But that piece of crape, to their imagination, seemed to hang down before his heart, the symbol of a fearful secret between him and them. Were the veil but cast aside, they might speak freely of it, but not till then. Thus they sat a considerable time, speechless, confused, and shrinking uneasily from Mr. Hooper's eye, which they felt to be fixed upon them with an invisible glance. Finally, the deputies returned abashed to their constituents, pronouncing the matter too weighty to be handled, except by a council of the churches, if, indeed, it might not require a general synod.

But there was one person in the village, unappalled by the awe with which the black veil had impressed all beside herself. When the deputies returned without an explanation, or even venturing to demand one, she, with the calm energy of her character, determined to chase away the strange cloud that appeared to be settling round Mr. Hooper, every moment more darkly than before. As his plighted wife, it should be her privilege to know what the black veil concealed. At the minister's first visit, therefore, she entered upon the subject, with a direct simplicity, which made the task easier both for him and her. After he had seated himself, she fixed her eyes steadfastly upon the veil, but could discern nothing of the dreadful gloom that had so overawed the multitude: it was but a double fold of crape, hanging down from his forehead to his mouth, and slightly stirring with his breath.

'No,' said she aloud, and smiling, 'there is nothing terrible in this piece of crape, except that it hides a face which I am always glad to look upon. Come, good sir, let the sun shine from behind the cloud. First lay aside your black veil: then tell me why you put it on.'

Mr. Hooper's smile glimmered faintly.

'There is an hour to come,' said he, 'when all of us shall cast aside our veils. Take it not amiss, beloved friend, if I wear this piece of crape till then.'

'Your words are a mystery too,' returned the young lady. 'Take away the veil from them, at least.'

'Elizabeth, I will,' said he, 'so far as my vow may suffer me. Know, then, this veil is a type and a symbol, and I am bound to wear it ever, both in light and darkness, in solitude and before the gaze of multitudes, and as with strangers, so with my familiar friends. No mortal eye will see it withdrawn. This dismal shade must separate me from the world: even you, Elizabeth, can never come behind it!'

'What grievous affliction hath befallen you,' she earnestly inquired, 'that you should thus darken your eyes for ever?'

'If it be a sign of mourning,' replied Mr. Hooper, 'I, perhaps, like most other mortals, have sorrows dark enough to be typified by a black veil.'

'But what if the world will not believe that it is the type of an innocent sorrow?' urged Elizabeth. 'Beloved and respected as you are, there may be whispers, that you hide your face under the consciousness of secret sin. For the sake of your holy office, do away this scandal!'

The color rose into her cheeks, as she intimated the nature of the rumors that were already abroad in the village. But Mr. Hooper's mildness did not forsake him. He even smiled again—that same sad smile, which always appeared like a faint glimmering of light, proceeding from the obscurity beneath the veil.

'If I hide my face for sorrow, there is cause enough,' he merely replied; 'and if I cover it for secret sin, what mortal might not do the same?'

And with this gentle, but unconquerable obstinacy, did he resist all her entreaties. At length Elizabeth sat silent. For a few moments she appeared lost in thought, considering, probably, what new methods might be tried, to withdraw her lover from so dark a fantasy, which, if it had no other meaning, was perhaps a symptom of mental disease. Though of a firmer character than his own, the tears rolled down her cheeks. But, in an instant, as it were, a new feeling took the place of sorrow: her eyes were fixed insensibly on the black veil, when, like a sudden twilight in the air, its terrors fell around her. She arose, and stood trembling before him.

'And do you feel it then at last?' said he mournfully.

She made no reply, but covered her eyes with her hand, and turned to leave the room. He rushed forward and caught her arm.

'Have patience with me, Elizabeth!' cried he passionately. 'Do not desert me, though this veil must be between us here on earth. Be mine, and hereafter there shall be no veil over my face, no darkness between our souls! It is but a mortal veil—it is not for eternity! Oh! you know not how lonely I am, and how frightened to be alone behind my black veil. Do not leave me in this miserable obscurity for ever!'

'Lift the veil but once, and look me in the face,' said she.

'Never! It cannot be!' replied Mr. Hooper.

'Then, farewell!' said Elizabeth.

She withdrew her arm from his grasp, and slowly departed,

pausing at the door, to give one long, shuddering gaze, that seemed almost to penetrate the mystery of the black veil. But, even amid his grief, Mr. Hooper smiled to think that only a material emblem had separated him from happiness, though the horrors which it shadowed forth, must be drawn darkly between the fondest of lovers.

From that time no attempts were made to remove Mr. Hooper's black veil, or, by a direct appeal, to discover the secret which it was supposed to hide. By persons who claimed a superiority to popular prejudice, it was reckoned merely an eccentric whim, such as often mingles with the sober actions of men otherwise rational, and tinges them all with its own semblance of insanity. But with the multitude, good Mr. Hooper was irreparably a bugbear. He could not walk the streets with any peace of mind, so conscious was he that the gentle and timid would turn aside to avoid him, and that others would make it a point of hardihood to throw themselves in his way. The impertinence of the latter class compelled him to give up his customary walk, at sunset, to the burial ground; for when he leaned pensively over the gate, there would always be faces behind the grave-stones, peeping at his black veil. A fable went the rounds, that the stare of the dead people drove him thence. It grieved him, to the very depth of his kind heart, to observe how the children fled from his approach, breaking up their merriest sports, while his melancholy figure was yet afar off. Their instinctive dread caused him to feel, more strongly than aught else, that a preternatural horror was interwoven with the threads of the black crape. In truth, his own antipathy to the veil was known to be so great, that he never willingly passed before a mirror, nor stooped to drink at a still fountain, lest, in its peaceful bosom, he should be affrighted by himself. This was what gave plausibility to the whispers, that Mr. Hooper's conscience tortured him for some great crime, too horrible to be entirely concealed, or otherwise than so obscurely intimated. Thus, from beneath the black veil, there rolled a cloud into the sunshine, an ambiguity of sin or sorrow, which enveloped the poor minister, so that love or sympathy could never reach him. It was said, that ghost and fiend consorted with him there. With self-shudderings and outward terrors, he walked continually in its shadow, groping darkly within his own soul, or gazing through a medium that saddened the whole world. Even the lawless wind, it was believed, respected his dreadful secret, and never blew aside the veil. But still good Mr. Hooper sadly smiled, at the pale visages of the worldly throng as he passed by.

Among all its bad influences, the black veil had the one desirable effect, of making its wearer a very efficient clergyman. By the aid of his mysterious emblem—for there was no other apparent cause—he became a man of awful power, over souls that were in agony for sin. His converts always regarded him with a dread peculiar to themselves, affirming, though but figuratively, that, before he brought them to celestial light, they had been with him behind the black veil. Its gloom, indeed, enabled him to sympathize with all dark affections. Dying sinners cried aloud for Mr. Hooper, and would not yield their breath till he appeared; though ever, as he stooped to whisper consolation, they shuddered at the veiled face so near their own. Such were the terrors of the black veil, even when Death had bared his visage! Strangers came long distances to attend service at his church, with the mere idle purpose of gazing at his figure, because it was forbidden them to behold his face. But many were made to quake ere they departed! Once, during Governor Belcher's administration, Mr. Hooper was appointed to preach the election sermon. Covered with his black veil, he stood before the chief magistrate, the council, and the representatives, and wrought so deep an impression, that the legislative measures of that year, were characterized by all the gloom and piety of our earliest ancestral sway.

In this manner Mr. Hooper spent a long life, irreproachable in outward act, yet shrouded in dismal suspicions; kind and loving, though unloved, and dimly feared; a man apart from men, shunned in their health and joy, but ever summoned to their aid in mortal anguish. As years wore on, shedding their snows above his sable veil, he acquired a name throughout the New-England churches, and they called him Father Hooper. Nearly all his parishioners, who were of mature age when he was settled, had been borne away by many a funeral: he had one congregation in the church, and a more crowded one in the church-yard; and having wrought so late into the evening, and done his work so well, it was now good Father Hooper's turn to rest.

Several persons were visible by the shaded candlelight, in the death-chamber of the old clergyman. Natural connections he had none. But there was the decorously grave, though unmoved physician, seeking only to mitigate the last pangs of the patient whom he could not save. There were the deacons, and other eminently pious members of his church. There, also, was the Reverend Mr. Clark, of Westbury, a young and zealous divine, who had ridden in haste to pray by the bed-side of the expiring minister. There was the nurse, no hired handmaiden of death, but one whose calm affection had endured thus long, in secrecy, in solitude, amid the chill of age, and would not perish, even at the dying hour. Who, but Elizabeth! And there lay the hoary head of good Father Hooper upon the death-pillow, with the black veil still swathed about his brow and reaching down over his face, so that each more difficult gasp of his faint breath caused it to stir. All through life that piece of crape had hung between him and the world: it had separated him from cheerful brotherhood and woman's love, and kept him in that saddest of all prisons, his own heart; and still it lay upon his face, as if to deepen the gloom of his darksome chamber, and shade him from the sunshine of eternity.

For some time previous, his mind had been confused, wavering doubtfully between the past and the present, and hovering forward, as it were, at intervals, into the indistinctness of the world to come. There had been feverish turns, which tossed him from side to side, and wore away what little strength he had. But in his most convulsive struggles, and in the wildest vagaries of his intellect, when no other thought retained its sober influence, he still showed an awful solicitude lest the black veil should slip aside. Even if his bewildered soul could have forgotten, there was a faithful woman at his pillow, who, with averted eyes, would have covered that aged face, which she had last beheld in the comeliness of manhood. At length the death-stricken old man lay quietly in the torpor of mental and bodily exhaustion, with an imperceptible pulse, and breath that grew fainter and fainter, except when a long, deep, and irregular inspiration seemed to prelude the flight of his spirit.

The minister of Westbury approached the bedside.

'Venerable Father Hooper,' said he, 'the moment of your release is at hand. Are you ready for the lifting of the veil, that shuts in time from eternity?'

Father Hooper at first replied merely by a feeble motion of his head; then, apprehensive, perhaps, that his meaning might be doubtful, he exerted himself to speak.

'Yea,' said he, in faint accents, 'my soul hath a patient weariness until that veil be lifted.'

'And is it fitting,' resumed the Reverend Mr. Clark, 'that a man so given to prayer, of such a blameless example, holy in deed and thought, so far as mortal judgment may pronounce; is it fitting that a father in the church should leave a shadow on his memory, that may seem to blacken a life so pure? I pray you, my venerable brother, let not this thing be! Suffer us to be gladdened by your triumphant aspect, as you go to your reward. Before the veil of eternity be lifted, let me cast aside this black veil from your face!'

And thus speaking, the Reverend Mr. Clark bent forward to reveal the mystery of so many years. But, exerting a sudden energy, that made all the beholders stand aghast, Father Hooper snatched both his hands from beneath the bed-clothes, and pressed them strongly on the black veil, resolute to struggle, if the minister of Westbury would contend with a dying man.

'Never!' cried the veiled clergyman. 'On earth, never!'

'Dark old man!' exclaimed the affrighted minister, 'with what horrible crime upon your soul are you now passing to the judgment?'

Father Hooper's breath heaved; it rattled in his throat; but, with a mighty effort, grasping forward with his hands, he caught hold of life, and held it back till he should speak. He even raised himself in bed; and there he sat, shivering with the arms of death around him, while the black veil hung down, aw-ful, at that last moment, in the gathered terrors of a life-time. And yet the faint, sad smile, so often there, now seemed to glim-mer from its obscurity, and linger on Father Hooper's lips.

'Why do you tremble at me alone?' cried he, turning his veiled face round the circle of pale spectators. 'Tremble also at each other! Have men avoided me, and women shown no pity, and children screamed and fled, only for my black veil? What, but the mystery which it obscurely typifies, has made this piece of crape so awful? When the friend shows his inmost heart to his friend; the lover to his best-beloved; when man does not vainly shrink from the eye of his Creator, loathsomely treasuring up the secret of his sin; then deem me a monster, for the symbol beneath which I have lived, and die! I look around me, and, lo! on every visage a Black Veil!'

While his auditors shrank from one another, in mutual af-fright, Father Hooper fell back upon his pillow, a veiled corpse, with a faint smile lingering on the lips. Still veiled, they laid him in his coffin, and a veiled corpse they bore him to the grave. The grass of many years has sprung up and withered on that grave, the burial-stone is moss-grown, and good Mr. Hooper's face is dust; but awful is still the thought, that it mouldered beneath the Black Veil!

Sunday at Home

EVERY Sabbath morning, in the summer time, I thrust back the curtain, to watch the sunrise stealing down a steeple, which stands opposite my chamber window. First, the weather-cock begins to flash; then, a fainter lustre gives the spire an airy aspect; next it encroaches on the tower, and causes the index of the dial to glisten like gold, as it points to the gilded figure of the hour. Now, the loftiest window gleams, and now the lower. The carved frame-work of the portal is marked strongly out. At length, the morning glory, in its descent from Heaven, comes down the stone steps, one by one; and there stands the steeple, glowing with fresh radiance, while the shades of twilight still hide themselves among the nooks of the adjacent buildings. Methinks, though the same sun brightens it, every fair morning, yet the steeple has a peculiar robe of brightness for the Sabbath.

By dwelling near a church, a person soon contracts an attachment for the edifice. We naturally personify it, and conceive its massy walls, and its dim emptiness, to be instinct with a calm, and meditative, and somewhat melancholy spirit. But the steeple stands foremost, in our thoughts, as well as locally. It impresses us as a giant, with a mind comprehensive and discriminating enough to care for the great and small concerns of all the town. Hourly, while it speaks a moral to the few that think, it reminds thousands of busy individuals of their separate and most secret affairs. It is the steeple, too, that flings

abroad the hurried and irregular accents of general alarm; neither have gladness and festivity found a better utterance, than
by its tongue; and when the dead are slowly passing to their
home, the steeple has a melancholy voice to bid them welcome. Yet, in spite of this connection with human interests,
what a moral loneliness, on week-days, broods round about its
stately height! It has no kindred with the houses above which
it towers; it looks down into the narrow thoroughfare, the lonelier, because the crowd are elbowing their passage at its base.
A glance at the body of the church deepens this impression.
Within, by the light of distant windows, amid refracted shadows, we discern the vacant pews and empty galleries, the silent
organ, the voiceless pulpit, and the clock, which tells to solitude how time is passing. Time—where man lives not—what
is it but eternity? And in the church, we might suppose, are
garnered up, throughout the week, all thoughts and feelings
that have reference to eternity, until the holy day comes round
again, to let them forth. Might not, then, its more appropriate
site be in the outskirts of the town, with space for old trees to
wave around it, and throw their solemn shadows over a quiet
green? We will say more of this, hereafter.

But, on the Sabbath, I watch the earliest sunshine, and
fancy that a holier brightness marks the day, when there shall
be no buzz of voices on the Exchange, nor traffic in the shops,
nor crowd, nor business, anywhere but at church. Many have
fancied so. For my own part, whether I see it scattered down
among tangled woods, or beaming broad across the fields, or
hemmed in between brick buildings, or tracing out the figure
of the casement on my chamber floor, still I recognize the Sabbath sunshine.—And ever let me recognize it! Some illusions,
and this among them, are the shadows of great truths. Doubts
may flit around me, or seem to close their evil wings, and settle down; but, so long as I imagine that the earth is hallowed,
and the light of heaven retains its sanctity, on the Sabbath—
while that blessed sunshine lives within me—never can my

soul have lost the instinct of its faith. If it have gone astray, it will return again.

I love to spend such pleasant Sabbaths, from morning till night, behind the curtain of my open window. Are they spent amiss? Every spot, so near the church as to be visited by the circling shadow of the steeple, should be deemed consecrated ground, to-day. With stronger truth be it said, that a devout heart may consecrate a den of thieves, as an evil one may convert a temple to the same. My heart, perhaps, has not such holy, nor, I would fain trust, such impious potency. It must suffice, that, though my form be absent, my inner man goes constantly to church, while many, whose bodily presence fills the accustomed seats, have left their souls at home. But I am there, even before my friend, the sexton. At length, he comes—a man of kindly, but sombre aspect, in dark gray clothes, and hair of the same mixture—he comes, and applies his key to the wide portal. Now, my thoughts may go in among the dusty pews, or ascend the pulpit without sacrilege, but soon come forth again, to enjoy the music of the bell. How glad, yet solemn too! All the steeples in town are talking together, aloft in the sunny air, and rejoicing among themselves, while their spires point heavenward. Meantime, here are the children assembling to the Sabbath-school, which is kept somewhere within the church. Often, while looking at the arched portal, I have been gladdened by the sight of a score of these little girls and boys, in pink, blue, yellow, and crimson frocks, bursting suddenly forth into the sunshine, like a swarm of gay butterflies that had been shut up in the solemn gloom. Or I might compare them to cherubs, haunting that holy place.

About a quarter of an hour before the second ringing of the bell, individuals of the congregation begin to appear. The earliest is invariably an old woman in black, whose bent frame and rounded shoulders are evidently laden with some heavy affliction, which she is eager to rest upon the altar. Would that the

Sabbath came twice as often, for the sake of that sorrowful old soul! There is an elderly man, also, who arrives in good season, and leans against the corner of the tower, just within the line of its shadow, looking downward with a darksome brow. I sometimes fancy that the old woman is the happier of the two. After these, others drop in singly, and by twos and threes, either disappearing through the door-way, or taking their stand in its vicinity. At last, and always with an unexpected sensation, the bell turns in the steeple overhead, and throws out an irregular clangor, jarring the tower to its foundation. As if there were magic in the sound, the sidewalks of the street, both up and down along, are immediately thronged with two long lines of people, all converging hitherward, and streaming into the church. Perhaps the far-off roar of a coach draws nearer—a deeper thunder by its contrast with the surrounding stillness—until it sets down the wealthy worshippers at the portal, among their humblest brethren. Beyond that entrance, in theory at least, there are no distinctions of earthly rank; nor, indeed, by the goodly apparel which is flaunting in the sun, would there seem to be such, on the hither side. Those pretty girls! Why will they disturb my pious meditations! Of all days in the week, they should strive to look least fascinating on the Sabbath, instead of heightening their mortal loveliness, as if to rival the blessed angels, and keep our thoughts from heaven. Were I the minister himself, I must needs look. One girl is white muslin from the waist upward, and black silk downward to her slippers; a second blushes from top-knot to shoe-tie, one universal scarlet; another shines of a pervading yellow, as if she had made a garment of the sunshine. The greater part, however, have adopted a milder cheerfulness of hue. Their veils, especially when the wind raises them, give a lightness to the general effect, and make them appear like airy phantoms, as they flit up the steps, and vanish into the sombre door-way. Nearly all—though it is very strange that I should know it—wear white stockings, white as snow, and neat slippers, laced cross-wise with black ribbon, pretty high above the ankles. A white stocking is infinitely more effective than a black one.

Here comes the clergyman, slow and solemn, in severe simplicity, needing no black silk gown to denote his office. His aspect claims my reverence, but cannot win my love. Were I to picture Saint Peter, keeping fast the gate of Heaven, and frowning, more stern than pitiful, on the wretched applicants, that face should be my study. By middle age, or sooner, the creed has generally wrought upon the heart, or been attempered by it. As the minister passes into the church, the bell holds its iron tongue, and all the low murmur of the congregation dies away. The gray sexton looks up and down the street, and then at my window curtain, where, through the small peep-hole, I half fancy that he has caught my eye. Now, every loiterer has gone in, and the street lies asleep in the quiet sun, while a feeling of loneliness comes over me, and brings also an uneasy sense of neglected privileges and duties. Oh, I ought to have gone to church! The bustle of the rising congregation reaches my ears. They are standing up to pray. Could I bring my heart into unison with those who are praying in yonder church, and lift it heavenward, with a fervor of supplication, but no distinct request, would not that be the safest kind of prayer? 'Lord, look down upon me in mercy!' With that sentiment gushing from my soul, might I not leave all the rest to Him?

Hark! the hymn. This, at least, is a portion of the service which I can enjoy better than if I sat within the walls, where the full choir, and the massive melody of the organ, would fall with a weight upon me. At this distance, it thrills through my frame, and plays upon my heart-strings, with a pleasure both of the sense and spirit. Heaven be praised, I know nothing of music, as a science; and the most elaborate harmonies, if they please me, please as simply as a nurse's lullaby. The strain has ceased, but prolongs itself in my mind, with fanciful echoes, till I start from my reverie, and find that the sermon has commenced. It is my misfortune seldom to fructify, in a regular way, by any but printed sermons. The first strong idea, which the preacher utters, gives birth to a train of thought, and leads me onward, step by step, quite out of hearing of the good man's voice, unless he be indeed a son of thunder. At my open window, catching now and then a sentence of the 'parson's saw,' I am as well situated as at the foot of the pulpit stairs. The broken and scattered fragments of this one discourse will be the texts of many sermons, preached by those colleague pastors—colleagues, but often disputants—my Mind and Heart. The former pretends to be a scholar, and perplexes me with doctrinal points; the latter takes me on the score of feeling; and both, like several other preachers, spend their strength to very little purpose. I, their sole auditor, cannot always understand them.

Suppose that a few hours have passed, and behold me still behind my curtain, just before the close of the afternoon service. The hour hand on the dial has passed beyond four o'clock. The declining sun is hidden behind the steeple, and throws its shadow straight across the street, so that my chamber is darkened, as with a cloud. Around the church door, all is solitude, and an impenetrable obscurity, beyond the threshold. A commotion is heard. The seats are slammed down, and the pew doors thrown back—a multitude of feet are trampling along the unseen aisles—and the congregation bursts suddenly through the portal. Foremost, scampers a rabble of boys, behind whom moves a dense and dark phalanx of grown men, and lastly, a crowd of females, with young children, and a few scattered husbands. This instantaneous outbreak of life into loneliness is one of the pleasantest scenes of the day. Some of the good people are rubbing their eyes, thereby intimating that they have been wrapt, as it were, in a sort of holy trance, by the fervor of their devotion. There is a young man, a third-rate coxcomb, whose first care is always to flourish a white handkerchief, and brush the seat of a tight pair of black silk pantaloons, which shine as if varnished. They must have been made of the stuff called 'everlasting,' or perhaps of the same piece as Christian's garments, in the Pilgrim's Progress, for he put them on two summers ago, and has not yet worn the gloss off. I have taken a great liking to those black silk pantaloons. But, now, with nods and greetings among friends, each matron takes her husband's arm, and paces gravely homeward, while the girls also flutter away, after arranging sunset walks with their favored bachelors. The Sabbath eve is the eve of love. At length, the whole congregation is dispersed. No; here, with faces as glossy as black satin, come two sable ladies and a sable gentleman, and close in their rear, the minister, who softens his severe visage, and bestows a kind word on each. Poor souls! To them, the most captivating picture of bliss in Heaven, is—'There we shall be white!'

All is solitude again. But, hark!—a broken warbling of voices, and now, attuning its grandeur to their sweetness, a stately peal of the organ. Who are the choristers? Let me dream, that the angels, who came down from Heaven, this blessed morn, to blend themselves with the worship of the truly good, are playing and singing their farewell to the earth.—On the wings of that rich melody, they were borne upward.

This, gentle reader, is merely a flight of poetry. A few of the singing men and singing women had lingered behind their fellows, and raised their voices fitfully, and blew a careless note upon the organ. Yet, it lifted my soul higher than all their former strains. They are gone—the sons and daughters of music—and the gray sexton is just closing the portal. For six days more, there will be no face of man in the pews, and aisles, and galleries, nor a voice in the pulpit, nor music in the choir. Was it worth while to rear this massive edifice, to be a desert in the heart of the town, and populous only for a few hours of each seventh day? Oh! but the church is a symbol of religion. May its site, which was consecrated on the day when the first tree was felled, be kept holy forever, a spot of solitude and peace, amid the trouble and vanity of our week-day world! There is a moral, and a religion too, even in the silent walls. And, may the steeple still point heavenward, and be decked with the hallowed sunshine of the Sabbath morn!

The Man of Adamant

AN APOLOGUE

In the old times of religious gloom and intolerance, lived Richard Digby, the gloomiest and most intolerant of a stern brotherhood. His plan of salvation was so narrow, that, like a plank in a tempestuous sea, it could avail no sinner but himself, who bestrode it triumphantly, and hurled anathemas against the wretches whom he saw struggling with the billows of eternal death. In his view of the matter, it was a most abominable crime—as, indeed, it is a great folly—for men to trust to their own strength, or even to grapple to any other fragment of the wreck, save this narrow plank, which, moreover, he took special care to keep out of their reach. In other words, as his creed was like no man's else, and being well pleased that Providence had entrusted him, alone of mortals, with the treasure of a true faith, Richard Digby determined to seclude himself to the sole and constant enjoyment of his happy fortune.

'And verily,' thought he, 'I deem it a chief condition of Heaven's mercy to myself, that I hold no communion with those abominable myriads which it hath cast off to perish. Peradventure, were I to tarry longer in the tents of Kedar, the gracious boon would be revoked, and I also be swallowed up in the deluge of wrath, or consumed in the storm of fire and brimstone, or involved in whatever new kind of ruin is ordained for the horrible perversity of this generation.'

So Richard Digby took an axe, to hew space enough for a tabernacle in the wilderness, and some few other necessaries, especially a sword and gun, to smite and slay any intruder upon his hallowed seclusion; and plunged into the dreariest depths of the forest. On its verge, however, he paused a moment, to shake off the dust of his feet against the village where he had dwelt, and to invoke a curse on the meeting-house, which he regarded as a temple of heathen idolatry. He felt a curiosity, also, to see whether the fire and brimstone would not rush down from Heaven at once, now that the one righteous man had provided for his own safety. But, as the sunshine continued to fall peacefully on the cottages and fields, and the husbandmen labored and children played, and as there were many tokens of present happiness, and nothing ominous of a speedy judgment, he turned away, somewhat disappointed. The further he went, however, and the lonelier he felt himself, and the thicker the trees stood along his path, and the darker the shadow overhead, so much the more did Richard Digby exult. He talked to himself, as he strode onward; he read his Bible to himself, as he sat beneath the trees; and, as the gloom of the forest hid the blessed sky, I had almost added, that, at morning, noon, and eventide, he prayed to himself. So congenial was this mode of life to his disposition, that he often laughed to himself, but was displeased when an echo tossed him back the long, loud roar.

In this manner, he journeyed onward three days and two nights, and came, on the third evening, to the mouth of a cave, which, at first sight, reminded him of Elijah's cave at Horeb, though perhaps it more resembled Abraham's sepulchral cave, at Machpelah. It entered into the heart of a rocky hill. There was so dense a veil of tangled foliage about it, that none but a sworn lover of gloomy recesses would have discovered the low arch of its entrance, or have dared to step within its vaulted chamber, where the burning eyes of a panther might encounter him. If Nature meant this remote and dismal cavern for the use of man, it could only be, to bury in its gloom the victims of a pestilence, and then to block up its mouth with stones, and avoid the spot forever after. There was nothing bright nor cheerful near it, except a bubbling fountain, some twenty paces off, at which Richard Digby hardly threw away a glance. But he thrust his head into the cave, shivered, and congratulated himself.

'The finger of Providence hath pointed my way!' cried he, aloud, while the tomb-like den returned a strange echo, as if some one within were mocking him. 'Here my soul will be at peace; for the wicked will not find me. Here I can read the Scriptures, and be no more provoked with lying interpretations. Here I can offer up acceptable prayers, because my voice will not be mingled with the sinful supplications of the multitude. Of a truth, the only way to Heaven leadeth through the narrow entrance of this cave—and I alone have found it!'

In regard to this cave, it was observable that the roof, so far as the imperfect light permitted it to be seen, was hung with substances resembling opaque icicles; for the damps of unknown centuries, dripping down continually, had become as hard as adamant; and wherever that moisture fell, it seemed to possess the power of converting what it bathed to stone. The fallen leaves and sprigs of foliage, which the wind had swept into the cave, and the little feathery shrubs, rooted near the threshold, were not wet with a natural dew, but had been embalmed by this wondrous process. And here I am put in mind, that Richard Digby, before he withdrew himself from the world, was supposed by skilful physicians to have contracted a disease, for which no remedy was written in their medical books. It was a deposition of calculous particles within his heart, caused by an obstructed circulation of the blood, and unless a miracle should be wrought for him, there was danger that the malady might act on the entire substance of the organ, and change his fleshly heart to stone. Many, indeed, affirmed that the process was already near its consummation. Richard Digby, however, could never be convinced that any such direful work was going on within him; nor when he saw the sprigs of marble foliage, did his heart even throb the quicker, at the similitude suggested by these once tender herbs. It may be, that this same insensibility was a symptom of the disease.

Be that as it might, Richard Digby was well contented with his sepulchral cave. So dearly did he love this congenial spot, that, instead of going a few paces to the bubbling spring for water, he allayed his thirst with now and then a drop of moisture from the roof, which, had it fallen any where but on his tongue, would have been congealed into a pebble. For a man predisposed to stoniness of the heart, this surely was unwholesome liquor. But there he dwelt, for three days more, eating herbs and roots, drinking his own destruction, sleeping, as it were, in a tomb, and awaking to the solitude of death, yet esteeming this horrible mode of life as hardly inferior to celestial bliss. Perhaps superior; for, above the sky, there would be angels to disturb him. At the close of the third day, he sat in the portal of his mansion, reading the Bible aloud, because no other ear could profit by it, and reading it amiss, because the rays of the setting sun did not penetrate the dismal depth of shadow roundabout him, nor fall upon the sacred page. Suddenly, however, a faint gleam of light was thrown over the volume, and raising his eyes, Richard Digby saw that a young woman stood before the mouth of the cave, and that the sunbeams bathed her white garment, which thus seemed to possess a radiance of its own.

'Good evening, Richard,' said the girl, 'I have come from afar to find thee.'

The slender grace and gentle loveliness of this young woman were at once recognized by Richard Digby. Her name was Mary Goffe. She had been a convert to his preaching of the word in England, before he yielded himself to that exclusive bigotry, which now enfolded him with such an iron grasp, that no other sentiment could reach his bosom. When he came a pilgrim to America, she had remained in her father's hall, but now, as it appeared, had crossed the ocean after him, impelled by the same faith that led other exiles hither, and perhaps by love almost as holy. What else but faith and love united could have sustained so delicate a creature, wandering thus far into the forest, with her golden hair dishevelled by the boughs, and her feet wounded by the thorns! Yet, weary and faint though she must have been, and affrighted at the dreariness of the cave, she looked on the lonely man with a mild and pitying expression, such as might beam from an angel's eyes, towards an afflicted mortal. But the recluse, frowning sternly upon her, and keeping his finger between the leaves of his half closed Bible, motioned her away with his hand.

'Off!' cried he. 'I am sanctified, and thou art sinful. Away!'

'Oh, Richard,' said she, earnestly, 'I have come this weary way, because I heard that a grievous distemper had seized upon thy heart; and a great Physician hath given me the skill to cure it. There is no other remedy than this which I have brought thee. Turn me not away, therefore, nor refuse my medicine; for then must this dismal cave be thy sepulchre.'

'Away!' replied Richard Digby, still with a dark frown. 'My heart is in better condition than thine own. Leave me, earthly one; for the sun is almost set; and when no light reaches the door of the cave, then is my prayer time!'

Now, great as was her need, Mary Goffe did not plead with this stony hearted man for shelter and protection, nor ask any thing whatever for her own sake. All her zeal was for his welfare.

'Come back with me!' she exclaimed, clasping her hands— 'Come back to thy fellow men; for they need thee, Richard; and thou hast tenfold need of them. Stay not in this evil den; for the air is chill, and the damps are fatal; nor will any, that perish within it, ever find the path to Heaven. Hasten hence, I entreat thee, for thine own soul's sake; for either the roof will fall upon thy head, or some other speedy destruction is at hand.'

'Perverse woman!' answered Richard Digby, laughing

aloud; for he was moved to bitter mirth by her foolish vehemence. 'I tell thee that the path to Heaven leadeth straight through this narrow portal, where I sit. And, moreover, the destruction thou speakest of, is ordained, not for this blessed cave, but for all other habitations of mankind, throughout the earth. Get thee hence speedily, that thou may'st have thy share!'

So saying, he opened his Bible again, and fixed his eyes intently on the page, being resolved to withdraw his thoughts from this child of sin and wrath, and to waste no more of his holy breath upon her. The shadow had now grown so deep, where he was sitting, that he made continual mistakes in what he read, converting all that was gracious and merciful, to denunciations of vengeance and unutterable woe, on every created being but himself. Mary Goffe, meanwhile, was leaning against a tree, beside the sepulchral cave, very sad, yet with something heavenly and ethereal in her unselfish sorrow. The light from the setting sun still glorified her form, and was reflected a little way within the darksome den, discovering so terrible a gloom, that the maiden shuddered for its self-doomed inhabitant. Espying the bright fountain near at hand, she hastened thither, and scooped up a portion of its water, in a cup of birchen bark. A few tears mingled with the draught, and perhaps gave it all its efficacy. She then returned to the mouth of the cave, and knelt down at Richard Digby's feet.

'Richard,' she said, with passionate fervor, yet a gentleness in all her passion, 'I pray thee, by thy hope of Heaven, and as thou wouldst not dwell in this tomb forever, drink of this hallowed water, be it but a single drop! Then, make room for me by thy side, and let us read together one page of that blessed volume—and, lastly, kneel down with me and pray! Do this; and thy stony heart shall become softer than a babe's, and all be well.'

But Richard Digby, in utter abhorrence of the proposal, cast the Bible at his feet, and eyed her with such a fixed and evil frown, that he looked less like a living man than a marble statue, wrought by some dark imagined sculptor to express the most repulsive mood that human features could assume. And, as his look grew even devilish, so, with an equal change, did Mary Goffe become more sad, more mild, more pitiful, more like a sorrowing angel. But, the more heavenly she was, the more hateful did she seem to Richard Digby, who at length raised his hand, and smote down the cup of hallowed water upon the threshold of the cave, thus rejecting the only medicine that could have cured his stony heart. A sweet perfume lingered in the air for a moment, and then was gone.

'Tempt me no more, accursed woman,' exclaimed he, still with his marble frown, 'lest I smite thee down also! What hast thou to do with my Bible?—what with my prayers?—what with my Heaven?'

No sooner had he spoken these dreadful words, than Richard Digby's heart ceased to beat; while—so the legend says—the form of Mary Goffe melted into the last sunbeams, and returned from the sepulchral cave to Heaven. For Mary Goffe had been buried in an English churchyard, months before; and either it was her ghost that haunted the wild forest, or else a dreamlike spirit, typifying pure Religion.

Above a century afterwards, when the trackless forest of Richard Digby's day had long been interspersed with settlements, the children of a neighbouring farmer were playing at the foot of a hill. The trees, on account of the rude and broken surface of this acclivity, had never been felled, and were crowded so densely together, as to hide all but a few rocky prominences, wherever their roots could grapple with the soil. A little boy and girl, to conceal themselves from their playmates, had crept into the deepest shade, where not only the darksome pines, but a thick veil of creeping plants suspended from an overhanging rock, combined to make a twilight at noonday, and almost a midnight at all other seasons. There the children hid themselves, and shouted, repeating the cry at intervals, till the whole party of pursuers were drawn thither, and pulling aside the matted foliage, let in a doubtful glimpse of daylight. But scarcely was this accomplished, when the little group uttered a simultaneous shriek and tumbled headlong down the hill, making the best of their way homeward, without a second glance into the gloomy recess. Their father, unable to comprehend what had so startled them, took his axe, and by felling one or two trees, and tearing away the creeping plants, laid the mystery open to the day. He had discovered the entrance of a cave, closely resembling the mouth of a sepulchre, within which sat the figure of a man, whose gesture and attitude warned the father and children to stand back, while his visage wore a most forbidding frown. This repulsive personage seemed to have been carved in the same gray stone that formed the walls and portal of the cave. On minuter inspection, indeed, such blemishes were observed, as made it doubtful whether the figure were really a statue, chiselled by human art, and somewhat worn and defaced by the lapse of ages, or a freak of Nature, who might have chosen to imitate, in stone, her usual handiwork of flesh. Perhaps it was the least unreasonable idea, suggested by this strange spectacle, that the moisture of the cave possessed a petrifying quality, which had thus awfully embalmed a human corpse.

There was something so frightful in the aspect of this Man of Adamant, that the farmer, the moment that he recovered from the fascination of his first gaze, began to heap stones into the mouth of the cavern. His wife, who had followed him to the hill, assisted her husband's efforts. The children, also, approached as near as they durst, with their little hands full of pebbles, and cast them on the pile. Earth was then thrown into the crevices, and the whole fabric overlaid with sods. Thus all traces of the discovery were obliterated, leaving only a marvellous legend, which grew wilder from one generation to another, as the children told it to their grandchildren, and they to their posterity, till few believed that there had ever been a cavern or a statue, where now they saw but a grassy patch on the shadowy hill-side. Yet, grown people avoid the spot, nor do children play there. Friendship, and Love, and Piety, all human and celestial sympathies, should keep aloof from that hidden cave; for there still sits, and, unless an earthquake crumble down the roof upon his head, shall sit forever, the shape of Richard Digby, in the attitude of repelling the whole race of mortals—not from Heaven—but from the horrible loneliness of his dark, cold sepulchre.

Endicott and the Red Cross

Aᴛ noon of an autumnal day, more than two centuries ago, the English colors were displayed by the standard-bearer of the Salem trainband, which had mustered for martial exercise under the orders of John Endicott. It was a period, when the religious exiles were accustomed often to buckle on their armour, and practise the handling of their weapons of war. Since the first settlement of New England, its prospects had never been so dismal. The dissensions between Charles the First and his subjects were then, and for several years afterwards, confined to the floor of Parliament. The measures of the King and ministry were rendered more tyrannically violent by an opposition, which had not yet acquired sufficient confidence in its own strength, to resist royal injustice with the sword. The bigoted and haughty primate, Laud, Archbishop of Canterbury, controlled the religious affairs of the realm, and was consequently invested with powers which might have wrought the utter ruin of the two Puritan colonies, Plymouth and Massachusetts. There is evidence on record, that our forefathers perceived their danger, but were resolved that their infant country should not fall without a struggle, even beneath the giant strength of the King's right arm.

Such was the aspect of the times, when the folds of the English banner, with the Red Cross in its field, were flung out over a company of Puritans. Their leader, the famous Endicott, was a man of stern and resolute countenance, the effect of

which was heightened by a grizzled beard that swept the upper
portion of his breastplate. This piece of armour was so highly
polished, that the whole surrounding scene had its image in
the glittering steel. The central object, in the mirrored picture, was an edifice of humble architecture, with neither steeple nor bell to proclaim it,—what nevertheless it was,—the
house of prayer. A token of the perils of the wilderness was
seen in the grim head of a wolf, which had just been slain
within the precincts of the town, and, according to the regular
mode of claiming the bounty, was nailed on the porch of the
meetinghouse. The blood was still plashing on the door-step.
There happened to be visible, at the same noontide hour, so
many other characteristics of the times and manners of the Puritans, that we must endeavour to represent them in a sketch,
though far less vividly than they were reflected in the polished
breastplate of John Endicott.

In close vicinity to the sacred edifice appeared that important engine of Puritanic authority, the whipping-post,—with
the soil around it well trodden by the feet of evil-doers, who
had there been disciplined. At one corner of the meetinghouse
was the pillory, and at the other the stocks; and, by a singular
good fortune for our sketch, the head of an Episcopalian and
suspected Catholic was grotesquely encased in the former machine; while a fellow-criminal, who had boisterously quaffed a
health to the King, was confined by the legs in the latter. Side
by side, on the meetinghouse steps, stood a male and a female
figure. The man was a tall, lean, haggard personification of fa-
naticism, bearing on his breast this label,—A WANTON GOS-
PELLER,—which betokened that he had dared to give interpretations of Holy Writ, unsanctioned by the infallible judgment
of the civil and religious rulers. His aspect showed no lack of
zeal to maintain his heterodoxies, even at the stake. The
woman wore a cleft stick on her tongue, in appropriate retribution for having wagged that unruly member against the elders
of the church; and her countenance and gestures gave much

cause to apprehend, that, the moment the stick should be removed, a repetition of the offence would demand new ingenuity in chastising it.

The abovementioned individuals had been sentenced to undergo their various modes of ignominy, for the space of one hour at noonday. But among the crowd were several, whose punishment would be life-long; some, whose ears had been cropt, like those of puppy-dogs; others, whose cheeks had been branded with the initials of their misdemeanors; one, with his nostrils slit and seared; and another, with a halter about his neck, which he was forbidden ever to take off, or to conceal beneath his garments. Methinks he must have been grievously tempted to affix the other end of the rope to some convenient beam or bough. There was likewise a young woman, with no mean share of beauty, whose doom it was to wear the letter A on the breast of her gown, in the eyes of all the world and her own children. And even her own children knew what that initial signified. Sporting with her infamy, the lost and desperate creature had embroidered the fatal token in scarlet cloth, with golden thread, and the nicest art of needle-work; so that the capital A might have been thought to mean Admirable, or any thing rather than Adulteress.

Let not the reader argue, from any of these evidences of iniquity, that the times of the Puritans were more vicious than our own, when, as we pass along the very street of this sketch, we discern no badge of infamy on man or woman. It was the policy of our ancestors to search out even the most secret sins, and expose them to shame, without fear or favor, in the broadest light of the noonday sun. Were such the custom now, perchance we might find materials for a no less piquant sketch than the above.

Except the malefactors whom we have described, and the diseased or infirm persons, the whole male population of the town, between sixteen years and sixty, were seen in the ranks of the trainband. A few stately savages, in all the pomp and dignity of the primeval Indian, stood gazing at the spectacle. Their flint-headed arrows were but childish weapons, compared with the matchlocks of the Puritans, and would have rattled harmlessly against the steel caps and hammered iron breastplates, which enclosed each soldier in an individual fortress. The valiant John Endicott glanced with an eye of pride at his sturdy followers, and prepared to renew the martial toils of the day.

"Come, my stout hearts!" quoth he, drawing his sword. "Let us show these poor heathen that we can handle our weapons like men of might. Well for them, if they put us not to prove it in earnest!"

The iron-breasted company straightened their line, and each man drew the heavy butt of his matchlock close to his left foot, thus awaiting the orders of the captain. But, as Endicott glanced right and left along the front, he discovered a personage at some little distance, with whom it behoved him to hold a parley. It was an elderly gentleman, wearing a black cloak and band, and a high-crowned hat, beneath which was a velvet skull-cap, the whole being the garb of a Puritan minister. This reverend person bore a staff, which seemed to have been recently cut in the forest, and his shoes were bemired, as if he had been travelling on foot through the swamps of the wilderness. His aspect was perfectly that of a pilgrim, heightened also by an apostolic dignity. Just as Endicott perceived him, he laid aside his staff, and stooped to drink at a bubbling fountain, which gushed into the sunshine about a score of yards from the corner of the meetinghouse. But, ere the good man drank, he turned his face heavenward in thankfulness, and then, holding back his gray beard with one hand, he scooped up his simple draught in the hollow of the other.

"What, ho! good Mr. Williams," shouted Endicott. "You are welcome back again to our town of peace. How does our worthy Governor Winthrop? And what news from Boston?"

"The Governor hath his health, worshipful Sir," answered

Roger Williams, now resuming his staff, and drawing near. "And, for the news, here is a letter, which, knowing I was to travel hitherward to-day, his Excellency committed to my charge. Belike it contains tidings of much import; for a ship arrived yesterday from England."

Mr. Williams, the minister of Salem, and of course known to all the spectators, had now reached the spot where Endicott was standing under the banner of his company, and put the Governor's epistle into his hand. The broad seal was impressed with Winthrop's coat of arms. Endicott hastily unclosed the letter, and began to read; while, as his eye passed down the page, a wrathful change came over his manly countenance. The blood glowed through it, till it seemed to be kindling with an internal heat; nor was it unnatural to suppose that his breastplate would likewise become red-hot, with the angry fire of the bosom which it covered. Arriving at the conclusion, he shook the letter fiercely in his hand, so that it rustled as loud as the flag above his head.

"Black tidings these, Mr. Williams," said he; "blacker never came to New England. Doubtless you know their purport?"

"Yea, truly," replied Roger Williams; "for the Governor consulted, respecting this matter, with my brethren in the ministry at Boston; and my opinion was likewise asked. And his Excellency entreats you by me, that the news be not suddenly noised abroad, lest the people be stirred up unto some outbreak, and thereby give the King and the Archbishop a handle against us."

"The Governor is a wise man,—a wise man, and a meek and moderate," said Endicott, setting his teeth grimly. "Nevertheless, I must do according to my own best judgment. There is neither man, woman, nor child in New England, but has a concern as dear as life in these tidings; and, if John Endicott's voice be loud enough, man, woman, and child shall hear them. Soldiers, wheel into a hollow square! Ho, good people! Here are news for one and all of you."

The soldiers closed in around their captain; and he and Roger Williams stood together under the banner of the Red Cross; while the women and the aged men pressed forward, and the mothers held up their children to look Endicott in the face. A few taps of the drum gave signal for silence and attention.

"Fellow-soldiers,—fellow-exiles," began Endicott, speaking under strong excitement, yet powerfully restraining it, "wherefore did ye leave your native country? Wherefore, I say, have we left the green and fertile fields, the cottages, or, perchance, the old gray halls, where we were born and bred, the churchyards where our forefathers lie buried? Wherefore have we come hither to set up our own tombstones in a wilderness? A howling wilderness it is! The wolf and the bear meet us within halloo of our dwellings. The savage lieth in wait for us in the dismal shadow of the woods. The stubborn roots of the trees break our ploughshares, when we would till the earth. Our children cry for bread, and we must dig in the sands of the sea-shore to satisfy them. Wherefore, I say again, have we sought this country of a rugged soil and wintry sky? Was it not for the enjoyment of our civil rights? Was it not for liberty to worship God according to our conscience?"

"Call you this liberty of conscience?" interrupted a voice on the steps of the meetinghouse.

It was the Wanton Gospeller. A sad and quiet smile flitted across the mild visage of Roger Williams. But Endicott, in the excitement of the moment, shook his sword wrathfully at the culprit,—an ominous gesture from a man like him.

"What hast thou to do with conscience, thou knave?" cried he. "I said, liberty to worship God, not license to profane and ridicule him. Break not in upon my speech; or I will lay thee neck and heels till this time to-morrow! Hearken to me, friends, nor heed that accursed rhapsodist. As I was saying, we have sacrificed all things, and have come to a land whereof the old world hath scarcely heard, that we might make a new world unto ourselves, and painfully seek a path from hence to Heaven. But what think ye now? This son of a Scotch tyrant,—this grandson of a papistical and adulterous Scotch woman, whose death proved that a golden crown doth not always save an anointed head from the block—"

"Nay, brother, nay," interposed Mr. Williams; "thy words are not meet for a secret chamber, far less for a public street."

"Hold thy peace, Roger Williams!" answered Endicott, imperiously. "My spirit is wiser than thine, for the business now in hand. I tell ye, fellow-exiles, that Charles of England, and Laud, our bitterest persecutor, arch-priest of Canterbury, are resolute to pursue us even hither. They are taking counsel, saith this letter, to send over a governor-general, in whose breast shall be deposited all the law and equity of the land. They are minded, also, to establish the idolatrous forms of English Episcopacy; so that, when Laud shall kiss the Pope's toe, as cardinal of Rome, he may deliver New England, bound hand and foot, into the power of his master!"

A deep groan from the auditors,—a sound of wrath, as well as fear and sorrow,—responded to this intelligence.

"Look ye to it, brethren," resumed Endicott, with increasing energy. "If this king and this arch-prelate have their will, we shall briefly behold a cross on the spire of this tabernacle which we have builded, and a high altar within its walls, with wax tapers burning round it at noonday. We shall hear the sacring-bell, and the voices of the Romish priests saying the mass. But think ye, Christian men, that these abominations may be suffered without a sword drawn? without a shot fired? without blood spilt, yea, on the very stairs of the pulpit? No,—be ye strong of hand, and stout of heart! Here we stand on our own soil, which we have bought with our goods, which we have won with our swords, which we have cleared with our axes, which we have tilled with the sweat of our brows, which we have sanctified with our prayers to the God that brought us hither! Who shall enslave us here? What have we to do with this mitred prelate,—with this crowned king? What have we to do with England?"

Endicott gazed round at the excited countenances of the people, now full of his own spirit, and then turned suddenly to the standard-bearer, who stood close behind him.

"Officer, lower your banner!" said he.

The officer obeyed; and, brandishing his sword, Endicott thrust it through the cloth, and, with his left hand, rent the Red Cross completely out of the banner. He then waved the tattered ensign above his head.

"Sacrilegious wretch!" cried the high-churchman in the pillory, unable longer to restrain himself; "thou hast rejected the symbol of our holy religion!"

"Treason, treason!" roared the royalist in the stocks. "He hath defaced the King's banner!"

"Before God and man, I will avouch the deed," answered Endicott. "Beat a flourish, drummer!—shout, soldiers and people!—in honor of the ensign of New England. Neither Pope nor Tyrant hath part in it now!"

With a cry of triumph, the people gave their sanction to one of the boldest exploits which our history records. And, for ever honored be the name of Endicott! We look back through the mist of ages, and recognize, in the rending of the Red Cross from New England's banner, the first omen of that deliverance which our fathers consummated, after the bones of the stern Puritan had lain more than a century in the dust.

Night Sketches

Beneath an Umbrella

PLEASANT is a rainy winter's day, within doors! The best study for such a day, or the best amusement,—call it which you will,—is a book of travels, describing scenes the most unlike that sombre one, which is mistily presented through the windows. I have experienced, that fancy is then most successful in imparting distinct shapes and vivid colors to the objects which the author has spread upon his page, and that his words become magic spells to summon up a thousand varied pictures. Strange landscapes glimmer through the familiar walls of the room, and outlandish figures thrust themselves almost within the sacred precincts of the hearth. Small as my chamber is, it has space enough to contain the ocean-like circumference of an Arabian desert, its parched sands tracked by the long line of a caravan, with the camels patiently journeying through the heavy sunshine. Though my ceiling be not lofty, yet I can pile up the mountains of Central Asia beneath it, till their summits shine far above the clouds of the middle atmosphere. And, with my humble means, a wealth that is not taxable, I can transport hither the magnificent merchandise of an Oriental bazaar, and call a crowd of purchasers from distant countries, to pay a fair profit for the precious articles which are displayed on all sides. True it is, however, that, amid the bustle of traffic, or whatever else may seem to be going on around me, the rain-drops will occasionally be heard to patter against my window-panes, which look forth upon one of the quietest streets in a

New England town. After a time, too, the visions vanish, and will not appear again at my bidding. Then, it being nightfall, a gloomy sense of unreality depresses my spirits, and impels me to venture out, before the clock shall strike bedtime, to satisfy myself that the world is not entirely made up of such shadowy materials, as have busied me throughout the day. A dreamer may dwell so long among fantasies, that the things without him will seem as unreal as those within.

When eve has fairly set in, therefore, I sally forth, tightly buttoning my shaggy over-coat, and hoisting my umbrella, the silken dome of which immediately resounds with the heavy drumming of the invisible rain-drops. Pausing on the lowest door-step, I contrast the warmth and cheerfulness of my deserted fireside, with the drear obscurity and chill discomfort, into which I am about to plunge. Now come fearful auguries, innumerable as the drops of rain. Did not my manhood cry shame upon me, I should turn back within doors, resume my elbow-chair, my slippers, and my book, pass such an evening of sluggish enjoyment as the day has been, and go to bed inglorious. The same shivering reluctance, no doubt, has quelled, for a moment, the adventurous spirit of many a traveller, when his feet, which were destined to measure the earth around, were leaving their last tracks in the home-paths.

In my own case, poor human nature may be allowed a few misgivings. I look upward, and discern no sky, not even an unfathomable void, but only a black, impenetrable nothingness, as though heaven and all its lights were blotted from the system of the universe. It is as if Nature were dead, and the world had put on black, and the clouds were weeping for her. With their tears upon my cheek, I turn my eyes earthward, but find little consolation here below. A lamp is burning dimly at the distant corner, and throws just enough of light along the street, to show, and exaggerate by so faintly showing, the perils and difficulties which beset my path. Yonder dingily white remnant of a huge snowbank,—which will yet cumber the sidewalk till the latter days of March,—over or through that wintry waste must I stride onward. Beyond, lies a certain Slough of Despond, a concoction of mud and liquid filth, ankle-deep, leg-deep, neck-deep,—in a word, of unknown bottom,—on which the lamp-light does not even glimmer, but which I have occasionally watched, in the gradual growth of its horrors, from morn till nightfall. Should I flounder into its depths, farewell to upper earth! And hark! how roughly resounds the roaring of a stream, the turbulent career of which is partially reddened by the gleam of the lamp, but elsewhere brawls noisily through the densest gloom. Oh, should I be swept away in fording that impetuous and unclean torrent, the coroner will have a job with an unfortunate gentleman, who would fain end his troubles anywhere but in a mud-puddle!

Pshaw! I will linger not another instant at arm's length from these dim terrors, which grow more obscurely formidable, the longer I delay to grapple with them. Now for the onset! And lo! with little damage, save a dash of rain in the face and breast, a splash of mud high up the pantaloons, and the left boot full of ice-cold water, behold me at the corner of the street. The lamp throws down a circle of red light around me; and, twinkling onward from corner to corner, I discern other beacons, marshalling my way to a brighter scene. But this is a lonesome and dreary spot. The tall edifices bid gloomy defiance to the storm, with their blinds all closed, even as a man winks when he faces a spattering gust. How loudly tinkles the collected rain down the tin spouts! The puffs of wind are boisterous, and seem to assail me from various quarters at once. I have often observed that this corner is a haunt and loitering-place for those winds which have no work to do upon the deep, dashing ships against our iron-bound shores; nor in the forest, tearing up the sylvan giants with half a rood of soil at their vast roots. Here they amuse themselves with lesser freaks of mischief. See, at this moment, how they assail yonder poor woman, who is passing just within the verge of the lamp-light!

One blast struggles for her umbrella, and turns it wrong side outward; another whisks the cape of her cloak across her eyes; while a third takes most unwarrantable liberties with the lower part of her attire. Happily, the good dame is no gossamer, but a figure of rotundity and fleshly substance; else would these aërial tormentors whirl her aloft, like a witch upon a broomstick, and set her down, doubtless, in the filthiest kennel hereabout.

From hence I tread upon firm pavements into the centre of the town. Here there is almost as brilliant an illumination as when some great victory has been won, either on the battle-field or at the polls. Two rows of shops, with windows down nearly to the ground, cast a glow from side to side, while the black night hangs overhead like a canopy, and thus keeps the splendor from diffusing itself away. The wet sidewalks gleam with a broad sheet of red light. The rain-drops glitter, as if the sky were pouring down rubies. The spouts gush with fire. Methinks the scene is an emblem of the deceptive glare, which mortals throw around their footsteps in the moral world, thus bedazzling themselves, till they forget the impenetrable obscurity that hems them in, and that can be dispelled only by radiance from above. And, after all, it is a cheerless scene, and cheerless are the wanderers in it. Here comes one who has so long been familiar with tempestuous weather, that he takes the bluster of the storm for a friendly greeting, as if it should say, "How fare ye, brother?" He is a retired sea-captain, wrapped in some nameless garment of the pea-jacket order, and is now laying his course towards the Marine Insurance Office, there to spin yarns of gale and ship-wreck, with a crew of old sea-dogs like himself. The blast will put in its word among their hoarse voices, and be understood by all of them. Next I meet an unhappy slip-shod gentleman, with a cloak flung hastily over his shoulders, running a race with boisterous winds, and striving to glide between the drops of rain. Some domestic emergency or other has blown this miserable man from his warm fireside, in quest of a doctor! See that little vagabond,—how carelessly he has taken his stand right underneath a spout, while staring at some object of curiosity in a shop-window! Surely the rain is his native element; he must have fallen with it from the clouds, as frogs are supposed to do.

Here is a picture, and a pretty one. A young man and a girl, both enveloped in cloaks, and huddled beneath the scanty protection of a cotton umbrella. She wears rubber over-shoes; but he is in his dancing-pumps; and they are on their way, no doubt, to some cotillon-party, or subscription-ball at a dollar a head, refreshments included. Thus they struggle against the gloomy tempest, lured onward by a vision of festal splendor. But, ah! a most lamentable disaster. Bewildered by the red, blue, and yellow meteors in an apothecary's window, they have stepped upon a slippery remnant of ice, and are precipitated into a confluence of swollen floods, at the corner of two streets. Luckless lovers! Were it my nature to be other than a looker-on in life, I would attempt your rescue. Since that may not be, I vow, should you be drowned, to weave such a pathetic story of your fate, as shall call forth tears enough to drown you both anew. Do ye touch bottom, my young friends? Yes; they emerge like a water-nymph and a river-deity, and paddle hand-in-hand out of the depths of the dark pool. They hurry homeward, dripping, disconsolate, abashed, but with love too warm to be chilled by the cold water. They have stood a test which proves too strong for many. Faithful, though over head and ears in trouble!

Onward I go, deriving a sympathetic joy or sorrow from the varied aspect of mortal affairs, even as my figure catches a gleam from the lighted windows, or is blackened by an interval of darkness. Not that mine is altogether a chameleon spirit, with no hue of its own. Now I pass into a more retired street, where the dwellings of wealth and poverty are intermingled, presenting a range of strongly contrasted pictures. Here, too, may be found the golden mean. Through yonder casement I discern a family circle,—the grandmother, the parents, and the children,—all flickering, shadow-like, in the glow of a wood-fire. Bluster, fierce blast, and beat, thou wintry rain, against the window-panes! Ye cannot damp the enjoyment of that fire-side. Surely my fate is hard, that I should be wandering home-less here, taking to my bosom night, and storm, and solitude, instead of wife and children. Peace, murmurer! Doubt not that darker guests are sitting round the hearth, though the warm blaze hides all but blissful images. Well; here is still a brighter scene. A stately mansion, illuminated for a ball, with cut-glass chandeliers and alabaster lamps in every room, and sunny land-scapes hanging round the walls. See! a coach has stopped, whence emerges a slender beauty, who, canopied by two umbrellas, glides within the portal, and vanishes amid light-some thrills of music. Will she ever feel the night-wind and the rain? Perhaps,—perhaps! And will Death and Sorrow ever en-ter that proud mansion? As surely as the dancers will be gay within its halls to-night. Such thoughts sadden, yet satisfy my heart; for they teach me that the poor man, in this mean, weather-beaten hovel, without a fire to cheer him, may call the rich his brother,—brethren by Sorrow, who must be an inmate of both their households,—brethren by Death, who will lead them both to other homes.

Onward, still onward, I plunge into the night. Now have I reached the utmost limits of the town, where the last lamp struggles feebly with the darkness, like the farthest star that stands sentinel on the borders of uncreated space. It is strange what sensations of sublimity may spring from a very humble source. Such are suggested by this hollow roar of a subterra-nean cataract, where the mighty stream of a kennel precipitates itself beneath an iron grate, and is seen no more on earth. Lis-ten awhile to its voice of mystery; and fancy will magnify it, till you start, and smile at the illusion. And now another sound,—the rumbling of wheels,—as the mail-coach, outward bound, rolls heavily off the pavements, and splashes through the mud and water of the road. All night long, the poor passengers will be tossed to and fro between drowsy watch and troubled sleep, and will dream of their own quiet beds, and awake to find themselves still jolting onward. Happier my lot, who will straightway hie me to my familiar room, and toast myself comfortably before the fire, musing, and fitfully dozing, and fancying a strangeness in such sights as all may see. But first let me gaze at this solitary figure, who comes hitherward with a tin lantern, which throws the circular pattern of its punched holes on the ground about him. He passes fearlessly into the unknown gloom, whither I will not follow him.

This figure shall supply me with a moral, wherewith, for lack of a more appropriate one, I may wind up my sketch. He fears not to tread the dreary path before him, because his lantern, which was kindled at the fireside of his home, will light him back to that same fireside again. And thus we, night-wanderers through a stormy and dismal world, if we bear the lamp of Faith, enkindled at a celestial fire, it will surely lead us home to that Heaven whence its radiance was borrowed.

Edward Randolph's Portrait

FROM LEGENDS OF THE PROVINCE-HOUSE

THE old legendary guest of the Province-House abode in my remembrance from mid-summer till January. One idle evening, last winter, confident that he would be found in the snuggest corner of the bar-room, I resolved to pay him another visit, hoping to deserve well of my country by snatching from oblivion some else unheard-of fact of history. The night was chill and raw, and rendered boisterous by almost a gale of wind, which whistled along Washington street, causing the gas-lights to flare and flicker within the lamps. As I hurried onward, my fancy was busy with a comparison between the present aspect of the street, and that which it probably wore when the British Governors inhabited the mansion whither I was now going. Brick edifices in those times were few, till a succession of destructive fires had swept, and swept again, the wooden dwellings and ware-houses from the most populous quarters of the town. The buildings stood insulated and independent, not, as now, merging their separate existences into connected ranges, with a front of tiresome identity,—but each possessing features of its own, as if the owner's individual taste had shaped it,—and the whole presenting a picturesque irregularity, the absence of which is hardly compensated by any beauties of our modern architecture. Such a scene, dimly vanishing from the eye by the ray of here and there a tallow candle, glimmering through the small panes of scattered windows, would form a sombre contrast to the street, as I beheld it, with the gas-lights blazing from corner to corner, flaming within the shops, and throwing a noon-day brightness through the huge plates of glass.

But the black, lowering sky, as I turned my eyes upward, wore, doubtless, the same visage as when it frowned upon the ante-revolutionary New Englanders. The wintry blast had the same shriek that was familiar to their ears. The Old South Church, too, still pointed its antique spire into the darkness, and was lost between earth and heaven; and as I passed, its clock, which had warned so many generations how transitory was their life-time, spoke heavily and slow the same unregarded moral to myself. "Only seven o'clock," thought I. "My old friend's legends will scarcely kill the hours 'twixt this and bed-time."

Passing through the narrow arch, I crossed the court-yard, the confined precincts of which were made visible by a lanthern over the portal of the Province-House. On entering the bar-room, I found, as I expected, the old tradition-monger seated by a special good fire of anthracite, compelling clouds of smoke from a corpulent cigar. He recognized me with evident pleasure; for my rare properties as a patient listener invariably make me a favorite with elderly gentlemen and ladies, of narrative propensities. Drawing a chair to the fire, I desired mine host to favor us with a glass a-piece of whiskey punch, which was speedily prepared, steaming hot, with a slice of lemon at the bottom, a dark-red stratum of port wine upon the surface, and a sprinkling of nutmeg strewn over all. As we touched our glasses together, my legendary friend made himself known to me as Mr. Bela Tiffany; and I rejoiced at the oddity of the name, because it gave his image and character a sort of individuality in my conception. The old gentleman's draught acted as a solvent upon his memory, so that it overflowed with tales, traditions, anecdotes of famous dead people, and traits of ancient manners, some of which were childish as a nurse's lullaby, while others might have been worth the notice of the grave historian. Nothing impressed me more than a story of a black, mysterious picture, which used to hang in one of the chambers of the Province-House, directly above the room where we were now sitting. The following is as correct a version of the fact as the reader would be likely to obtain from any other source; although, assuredly, it has a tinge of romance approaching to the marvellous:

In one of the apartments of the Province-House there was long preserved an ancient picture, the frame of which was as black as ebony, and the canvass itself so dark with age, damp, and smoke, that not a touch of the painter's art could be discerned. Time had thrown an impenetrable veil over it, and left to tradition, and fable, and conjecture, to say what had once been there portrayed. During the rule of many successive governors, it had hung, by prescriptive and undisputed right, over the mantel-piece of the same chamber; and it still kept its place when Lieutenant-Governor Hutchinson assumed the administration of the province, on the departure of Sir Francis Bernard.

The Lieutenant-Governor sat, one afternoon, resting his head against the carved back of his stately arm chair, and gazing up thoughtfully at the void blackness of the picture. It was scarcely a time for such inactive musing, when affairs of the deepest moment required the ruler's decision; for, within that very hour, Hutchinson had received intelligence of the arrival of a British fleet, bringing three regiments from Halifax to overawe the insubordination of the people. These troops awaited his permission to occupy the fortress of Castle William, and the town itself. Yet, instead of affixing his signature to an official order, there sat the Lieutenant-Governor, so carefully scrutinizing the black waste of canvass, that his demeanour attracted the notice of two young persons who attended him. One, wearing a military dress of buff, was his kinsman, Francis Lincoln, the

Provincial Captain of Castle William; the other, who sat on a low stool beside his chair, was Alice Vane, his favorite niece.

She was clad entirely in white, a pale, ethereal creature, who, though a native of New England, had been educated abroad, and seemed not merely a stranger from another clime, but almost a being from another world. For several years, until left an orphan, she had dwelt with her father in sunny Italy, and there had acquired a taste and enthusiasm for sculpture and painting, which she found few opportunities of gratifying in the undecorated dwellings of the colonial gentry. It was said that the early productions of her own pencil exhibited no inferior genius, though, perhaps, the rude atmosphere of New England had cramped her hand, and dimmed the glowing colors of her fancy. But observing her uncle's steadfast gaze, which appeared to search through the mist of years to discover the subject of the picture, her curiosity was excited.

"Is it known, my dear uncle," inquired she, "what this old picture once represented? Possibly, could it be made visible, it might prove a masterpiece of some great artist—else why has it so long held such a conspicuous place?"

As her uncle, contrary to his usual custom, (for he was as attentive to all the humors and caprices of Alice as if she had been his own best beloved child,) did not immediately reply, the young Captain of Castle William took that office upon himself.

"This dark old square of canvass, my fair cousin," said he, "has been an heir-loom in the Province-House from time immemorial. As to the painter, I can tell you nothing; but, if half the stories told of it be true, not one of the great Italian masters has ever produced so marvellous a piece of work, as that before you."

Captain Lincoln proceeded to relate some of the strange fables and fantasies, which, as it was impossible to refute them by ocular demonstration, had grown to be articles of popular belief, in reference to this old picture. One of the wildest, and at the same time the best accredited accounts, stated it to be an original and authentic portrait of the Evil One, taken at a witch meeting near Salem; and that its strong and terrible resemblance had been confirmed by several of the confessing wizards and witches, at their trial, in open court. It was likewise affirmed that a familiar spirit, or demon, abode behind the blackness of the picture, and had shown himself, at seasons of public calamity, to more than one of the royal governors. Shirley, for instance, had beheld this ominous apparition, on the even of General Abercrombie's shameful and bloody defeat under the walls of Ticonderoga. Many of the servants of the Province-House had caught glimpses of a visage frowning down upon them, at morning or evening twilight,—or in the depths of night, while raking up the fire that glimmered on the hearth beneath; although, if any were bold enough to hold a torch before the picture, it would appear as black and undistinguishable as ever. The oldest inhabitant of Boston recollected that his father, in whose days the portrait had not wholly faded out of sight, had once looked upon it, but would never suffer himself to be questioned as to the face which was there represented. In connection with such stories, it was remarkable that over the top of the frame there were some ragged remnants of black silk, indicating that a veil had formerly hung down before the picture, until the duskiness of time had so effectually concealed it. But, after all, it was the most singular part of the affair, that so many of the pompous governors of Massachusetts had allowed the obliterated picture to remain in the state-chamber of the Province-House.

"Some of these fables are really awful," observed Alice Vane, who had occasionally shuddered, as well as smiled, while her cousin spoke. "It would be almost worth while to wipe away the black surface of the canvass, since the original picture can hardly be so formidable as those which fancy paints instead of it."

"But would it be possible," inquired her cousin, "to restore this dark picture to its pristine hues?"

"Such arts are known in Italy," said Alice.

The Lieutenant-Governor had roused himself from his abstracted mood, and listened with a smile to the conversation of his young relatives. Yet his voice had something peculiar in its tones, when he undertook the explanation of the mystery.

"I am sorry, Alice, to destroy your faith in the legends of which you are so fond," remarked he; "but my antiquarian researches have long since made me acquainted with the subject of this picture—if picture it can be called—which is no more visible, nor ever will be, than the face of the long buried man whom it once represented. It was the portrait of Edward Randolph, the founder of this house, a person famous in the history of New England."

"Of that Edward Randolph," exclaimed Captain Lincoln, "who obtained the repeal of the first provincial charter, under which our forefathers had enjoyed almost democratic privileges! He that was styled the arch enemy of New England, and whose memory is still held in detestation, as the destroyer of our liberties!"

"It was the same Randolph," answered Hutchinson, moving uneasily in his chair. "It was his lot to taste the bitterness of popular odium."

"Our annals tell us," continued the Captain of Castle William, "that the curse of the people followed this Randolph wherever he went, and wrought evil in all the subsequent events of his life, and that its effect was seen likewise in the manner of his death. They say, too, that the inward misery of that curse worked itself outward, and was visible on the wretched man's countenance, making it too horrible to be looked upon. If so, and if this picture truly represented his aspect, it was in mercy that the cloud of blackness has gathered over it."

"These traditions are folly, to one who has proved, as I have, how little of historic truth lies at the bottom," said the Lieutenant-Governor. "As regards the life and character of Edward Randolph, too implicit credence has been given to Dr. Cotton Mather, who—I must say it, though some of his blood runs in my veins—has filled our early history with old women's tales, as fanciful and extravagant as those of Greece or Rome."

"And yet," whispered Alice Vane, "may not such fables have a moral? And methinks, if the visage of this portrait be so dreadful, it is not without a cause that it has hung so long in a chamber of the Province-House. When the rulers feel themselves irresponsible, it were well that they should be reminded of the awful weight of a People's curse."

The Lieutenant-Governor started, and gazed for a moment at his niece, as if her girlish fantasies had struck upon some feeling in his own breast, which all his policy or principles could not entirely subdue. He knew, indeed, that Alice, in spite of her foreign education, retained the native sympathies of a New England girl.

"Peace, silly child," cried he, at last, more harshly than he had ever before addressed the gentle Alice. "The rebuke of a king is more to be dreaded than the clamor of a wild, misguided multitude. Captain Lincoln, it is decided. The fortress of Castle William must be occupied by the Royal troops. The two remaining regiments shall be billeted in the town, or encamped upon the Common. It is time, after years of tumult, and almost rebellion, that his majesty's government should have a wall of strength about it."

"Trust, sir—trust yet awhile to the loyalty of the people," said Captain Lincoln; "nor teach them that they can ever be on other terms with British soldiers than those of brotherhood, as when they fought side by side through the French war. Do not convert the streets of your native town into a camp. Think twice before you give up old Castle William, the key of the province, into other keeping than that of true born New Englanders."

"Young man, it is decided," repeated Hutchinson, rising from his chair. "A British officer will be in attendance this evening, to receive the necessary instructions for the disposal of the troops. Your presence also will be required. Till then, farewell."

With these words the Lieutenant-Governor hastily left the room, while Alice and her cousin more slowly followed, whispering together, and once pausing to glance back at the mysterious picture. The Captain of Castle William fancied that the girl's air and mien were such as might have belonged to one of those spirits of fable—fairies, or creatures of a more antique mythology, who sometimes mingled their agency with mortal affairs, half in caprice, yet with a sensibility to human weal or wo. As he held the door for her to pass, Alice beckoned to the picture and smiled.

"Come forth, dark and evil Shape!" cried she. "It is thine hour!"

In the evening, Lieutenant-Governor Hutchinson sat in the same chamber where the foregoing scene had occurred, surrounded by several persons whose various interests had summoned them together. There were the Selectmen of Boston, plain, patriarchal fathers of the people, excellent representives of the old puritanical founders, whose sombre strength had stamped so deep an impress upon the New England character. Contrasting with these were one or two members of the Council, richly dressed in the white wigs, the embroidered waistcoats and other magnificence of the time, and making a somewhat ostentatious display of courtier-like ceremonial. In attendance, likewise, was a major of the British army, awaiting the Lieutenant-Governor's orders for the landing of the troops, which still remained on board the transports. The Captain of Castle William stood beside Hutchinson's chair, with folded arms, glancing rather haughtily at the British officer, by whom he was soon to be superseded in his command. On a table, in the centre of the chamber, stood a branched silver candlestick, throwing down the glow of half a dozen wax lights upon a paper apparently ready for the Lieutenant-Governor's signature.

Partly shrouded in the voluminous folds of one of the window-curtains, which fell from the ceiling to the floor, was seen the white drapery of a lady's robe. It may appear strange that Alice Vane should have been there, at such a time; but there was something so child-like, so wayward, in her singular character, so apart from ordinary rules, that her presence did not surprise the few who noticed it. Meantime, the chairman of the Selectmen was addressing to the Lieutenant-Governor a long and solemn protest against the reception of the British troops into the town.

"And if your Honor," concluded this excellent, but somewhat prosy old gentleman, "shall see fit to persist in bringing these mercenary sworders and musketeers into our quiet streets, not on our heads be the responsibility. Think, sir, while there is yet time, that if one drop of blood be shed, that blood shall be an eternal stain upon your Honor's memory. You, sir, have written, with an able pen, the deeds of our forefathers. The more to be desired is it, therefore, that yourself should deserve honorable mention, as a true patriot and upright ruler, when your own doings shall be written down in history."

"I am not insensible, my good sir, to the natural desire to stand well in the annals of my country," replied Hutchinson, controlling his impatience into courtesy, "nor know I any better method of attaining that end than by withstanding the merely temporary spirit of mischief, which, with your pardon, seems to have infected elder men than myself. Would you have me wait till the mob shall sack the Province-House, as they did my private mansion? Trust me, sir, the time may come when you will be glad to flee for protection to the King's banner, the raising of which is now so distasteful to you."

"Yes," said the British major, who was impatiently expecting the Lieutenant-Governor's orders. "The demagogues of this Province have raised the devil, and cannot lay him again. We will exorcise him, in God's name and the King's."

"If you meddle with the devil, take care of his claws!" answered the Captain of Castle William, stirred by the taunt against his countrymen.

"Craving your pardon, young sir," said the venerable Selectman, "let not an evil spirit enter into your words. We will strive against the oppressor with prayer and fasting, as our forefathers would have done. Like them, moreover, we will submit to whatever lot a wise Providence may send us,—always, after our own best exertions to amend it."

"And there peep forth the devil's claws!" muttered Hutchinson, who well understood the nature of Puritan submission. "This matter shall be expedited forthwith. When there shall be a sentinel at every corner, and a court of guard before the town-house, a loyal gentleman may venture to walk abroad. What to me is the outcry of a mob, in this remote province of the realm? The King is my master, and England is my country! Upheld by their armed strength, I set my foot upon the rabble, and defy them!"

He snatched a pen, and was about to affix his signature to the paper that lay on the table, when the Captain of Castle William placed his hand upon his shoulder. The freedom of the action, so contrary to the ceremonious respect which was then considered due to rank and dignity, awakened general surprise, and in none more than in the Lieutenant-Governor himself. Looking angrily up, he perceived that his young relative was pointing his finger to the opposite wall. Hutchinson's eye followed the signal; and he saw, what had hitherto been unobserved, that a black silk curtain was suspended before the mysterious picture, so as completely to conceal it. His thoughts immediately recurred to the scene of the preceding afternoon; and, in his surprise, confused by indistinct emotions, yet sensible that his niece must have had an agency in this phenomenon, he called loudly upon her.

"Alice!—Come hither, Alice!"

No sooner had he spoken than Alice Vane glided from her station, and pressing one hand across her eyes, with the other snatched away the sable curtain that concealed the portrait. An exclamation of surprise burst from every beholder; but the Lieutenant-Governor's voice had a tone of horror.

"By Heaven," said he, in a low, inward murmur, speaking rather to himself than to those around him, "if the spirit of Edward Randolph were to appear among us from the place of torment, he could not wear more of the terrors of hell upon his face!"

"For some wise end," said the aged Selectman, solemnly, "hath Providence scattered away the mist of years that had so long hid this dreadful effigy. Until this hour no living man hath seen what we behold!"

Within the antique frame, which so recently had enclosed a sable waste of canvass, now appeared a visible picture, still dark, indeed, in its hues and shadings, but thrown forward in strong relief. It was a half-length figure of a gentleman in a rich, but very old-fashioned dress of embroidered velvet, with a broad ruff and a beard, and wearing a hat, the brim of which overshadowed his forehead. Beneath this cloud the eyes had a peculiar glare, which was almost life-like. The whole portrait started so distinctly out of the back-ground, that it had the effect of a person looking down from the wall at the astonished and awe-stricken spectators. The expression of the face, if any words can convey an idea of it, was that of a wretch detected in some hideous guilt, and exposed to the bitter hatred, and laughter, and withering scorn, of a vast surrounding multitude. There was the struggle of defiance, beaten down and overwhelmed by the crushing weight of ignominy. The torture of the soul had come forth upon the countenance. It seemed as if the picture, while hidden behind the cloud of immemorial years, had been all the time acquiring an intenser depth and darkness of expression, till now it gloomed forth again, and threw its evil omen over the present hour. Such, if the wild legend may be credited, was the portrait of Edward Randolph, as he appeared when a people's curse had wrought its influence upon his nature.

" 'Twould drive me mad—that awful face!" said Hutchinson, who seemed fascinated by the contemplation of it.

"Be warned, then!" whispered Alice. "He trampled on a people's rights. Behold his punishment—and avoid a crime like his!"

The Lieutenant-Governor actually trembled for an instant; but, exerting his energy—which was not, however, his most characteristic feature—he strove to shake off the spell of Randolph's countenance.

"Girl!" cried he, laughing bitterly, as he turned to Alice, "have you brought hither your painter's art—your Italian spirit of intrigue—your tricks of stage-effect—and think to influence the councils of rulers and the affairs of nations, by such shallow contrivances? See here!"

"Stay yet awhile," said the Selectman, as Hutchinson again snatched the pen; "for if ever mortal man received a warning from a tormented soul, your Honor is that man!"

"Away!" answered Hutchinson fiercely. "Though yonder senseless picture cried 'Forbear!'—it should not move me!"

Casting a scowl of defiance at the pictured face, (which seemed, at that moment, to intensify the horror of its miserable and wicked look,) he scrawled on the paper, in characters that betokened it a deed of desperation, the name of Thomas Hutchinson. Then, it is said, he shuddered, as if that signature had granted away his salvation.

"It is done," said he; and placed his hand upon his brow.

"May Heaven forgive the deed," said the soft, sad accents of Alice Vane, like the voice of a good spirit flitting away.

When morning came there was a stifled whisper through the household, and spreading thence about the town, that the dark, mysterious picture had started from the wall, and spoken face to face with Lieutenant-Governor Hutchinson. If such a miracle had been wrought, however, no traces of it remained behind; for within the antique frame, nothing could be discerned, save the impenetrable cloud, which had covered the canvass since the memory of man. If the figure had, indeed, stepped forth, it had fled back, spirit-like, at the day-dawn, and hidden itself behind a century's obscurity. The truth probably was, that Alice Vane's secret for restoring the hues of the picture had merely effected a temporary renovation. But those who, in that brief interval, had beheld the awful visage of Edward Randolph, desired no second glance, and ever afterwards trembled at the recollection of the scene, as if an evil spirit had appeared visibly among them. And as for Hutchinson, when, far over the ocean, his dying hour drew on, he gasped for breath, and complained that he was choking with the blood of the Boston Massacre; and Francis Lincoln, the former Captain of Castle William, who was standing at his bedside, perceived a likeness in his frenzied look to that of Edward Randolph. Did his broken spirit feel, at that dread hour, the tremendous burthen of a People's curse?

At the conclusion of this miraculous legend I inquired of mine host whether the picture still remained in the chamber over our heads, but Mr. Tiffany informed me that it had long since been removed, and was supposed to be hidden in some out-of-the-way corner of the New England Museum. Perchance some curious antiquary may light upon it there, and, with the assistance of Mr. Howorth, the picture-cleaner, may supply a not unnecessary proof of the authenticity of the facts here set down. During the progress of the story a storm had been gathering abroad, and raging and rattling so loudly in the upper regions of the Province-House, that it seemed as if all the old Governors and great men were running riot above stairs, while Mr. Bela Tiffany babbled of them below. In the course of generations, when many people have lived and died in an ancient house, the whistling of the wind through its crannies, and the creaking of its beams and rafters, become strangely like the tones of the human voice, or thundering laughter, or heavy footsteps treading the deserted chambers. It is as if the echoes of half a century were revived. Such were the ghostly sounds that roared and murmured in our ears, when I took leave of the circle round the fireside of the Province-House, and plunging down the door-steps, fought my way homeward against a drifting snow-storm.

The Hall of Fantasy

I⊤ has happened to me, on various occasions, to find myself in a certain edifice, which would appear to have some of the characteristics of a public Exchange. Its interior is a spacious hall, with a pavement of white marble. Overhead is a lofty dome, supported by long rows of pillars, of fantastic architecture, the idea of which was probably taken from the Moorish ruins of the Alhambra, or perhaps from some enchanted edifice in the Arabian Tales. The windows of this hall have a breadth and grandeur of design, and an elaborateness of workmanship, that have nowhere been equalled, except in the Gothic cathedrals of the old world. Like their prototypes, too, they admit the light of heaven only through stained and pictured glass, thus filling the hall with many-colored radiance, and painting its marble floor with beautiful or grotesque designs; so that its inmates breathe, as it were, a visionary atmosphere, and tread upon the fantasies of poetic minds. These peculiarities, combining a wilder mixture of styles than even an American architect usually recognizes as allowable—Grecian, Gothic, Oriental, and nondescript—cause the whole edifice to give the impression of a dream, which might be dissipated and shattered to fragments, by merely stamping the foot upon the pavement. Yet, with such modifications and repairs as successive ages demand, the Hall of Fantasy is likely to endure longer than the most substantial structure that ever cumbered the earth.

It is not at all times that one can gain admittance into this edifice; although most persons enter it at some period or other of their lives—if not in their waking moments, then by the universal passport of a dream. At my last visit, I wandered thither unawares, while my mind was busy with an idle tale, and was startled by the throng of people who seemed suddenly to rise up around me.

"Bless me! Where am I?" cried I, with but a dim recognition of the place.

"You are in a spot," said a friend, who chanced to be near at hand, "which occupies, in the world of fancy, the same position which the Bourse, the Rialto, and the Exchange, do in the commercial world. All who have affairs in that mystic region, which lies above, below, or beyond the Actual, may here meet, and talk over the business of their dreams."

"It is a noble hall," observed I.

"Yes," he replied. "Yet we see but a small portion of the edifice. In its upper stories are said to be apartments, where the inhabitants of earth may hold converse with those of the moon. And beneath our feet are gloomy cells, which communicate with the infernal regions, and where monsters and chimeras are kept in confinement, and fed with all unwholesomeness."

In niches and on pedestals, around about the hall, stood the statues or busts of men, who, in every age, have been rulers and demi-gods in the realms of imagination, and its kindred regions. The grand old countenance of Homer; the shrunken and decrepit form, but vivid face of Æsop; the dark presence of Dante; the wild Ariosto; Rabelais's smile of deep-wrought mirth; the profound, pathetic humor of Cervantes; the all-glorious Shakespeare; Spenser, meet guest for an allegoric structure; the severe divinity of Milton; and Bunyan, moulded of homeliest clay, but instinct with celestial fire—were those that chiefly attracted my eye. Fielding, Richardson, and Scott, occupied conspicuous pedestals. In an obscure and shadowy niche was reposited the bust of our countryman, the author of Arthur Mervyn.

"Besides these indestructible memorials of real genius," remarked my companion, "each century has erected statues of its own ephemeral favorites, in wood."

"I observe a few crumbling relics of such," said I. "But ever and anon, I suppose, Oblivion comes with her huge broom, and sweeps them all from the marble floor. But such will never be the fate of this fine statue of Goethe."

"Nor of that next to it—Emanuel Swedenborg," said he. "Were ever two men of transcendent imagination more unlike?"

In the centre of the hall springs an ornamental fountain, the water of which continually throws itself into new shapes, and snatches the most diversified hues from the stained atmosphere around. It is impossible to conceive what a strange vivacity is imparted to the scene by the magic dance of this fountain, with its endless transformations, in which the imaginative beholder may discern what form he will. The water is supposed by some to flow from the same source as the Castalian spring, and is extolled by others as uniting the virtues of the Fountain of Youth with those of many other enchanted wells, long celebrated in tale and song. Having never tasted it, I can bear no testimony to its quality.

"Did you ever drink this water?" I inquired of my friend.

"A few sips, now and then," answered he. "But there are men here who make it their constant beverage—or, at least, have the credit of doing so. In some instances, it is known to have intoxicating qualities."

"Pray let us look at these water-drinkers," said I.

So we passed among the fantastic pillars, till we came to a spot where a number of persons were clustered together, in the light of one of the great stained windows, which seemed to glorify the whole group, as well as the marble that they trod on. Most of them were men of broad foreheads, meditative countenances, and thoughtful, inward eyes; yet it required but a trifle to summon up mirth, peeping out from the very midst of grave and lofty musings. Some strode about, or leaned against the pillars of the hall, alone and in silence; their faces wore a rapt expression, as if sweet music were in the air around them, or as if their inmost souls were about to float away in song. One or two, perhaps, stole a glance at the bystanders, to watch if their poetic absorption were observed. Others stood talking in groups, with a liveliness of expression, a ready smile, and a light, intellectual laughter, which showed how rapidly the shafts of wit were glancing to-and-fro among them.

A few held higher converse, which caused their calm and melancholy souls to beam moonlight from their eyes. As I lingered near them—for I felt an inward attraction towards these men, as if the sympathy of feeling, if not of genius, had united me to their order—my friend mentioned several of their names. The world has likewise heard those names; with some it has been familiar for years; and others are daily making their way deeper into the universal heart.

"Thank heaven," observed I to my companion, as we passed to another part of the hall, "we have done with this techy, wayward, shy, proud, unreasonable set of laurel-gatherers. I love them in their works, but have little desire to meet them elsewhere."

"You have adopted an old prejudice, I see," replied my friend, who was familiar with most of these worthies, being himself a student of poetry, and not without the poetic flame. "But so far as my experience goes, men of genius are fairly gifted with the social qualities; and in this age, there appears to be a fellow-feeling among them, which had not heretofore been developed. As men, they ask nothing better than to be on equal terms with their fellow-men; and as authors, they have thrown aside their proverbial jealousy, and acknowledge a generous brotherhood."

"The world does not think so," answered I. "An author is received in general society pretty much as we honest citizens are in the Hall of Fantasy. We gaze at him as if he had no business among us, and question whether he is fit for any of our pursuits."

"Then it is a very foolish question," said he. "Now, here are a class of men, whom we may daily meet on 'Change. Yet what poet in the hall is more a fool of fancy than the sagest of them?"

He pointed to a number of persons, who, manifest as the fact was, would have deemed it an insult to be told that they stood in the Hall of Fantasy. Their visages were traced into wrinkles and furrows, each of which seemed the record of some actual experience in life. Their eyes had the shrewd, calculating glance, which detects so quickly and so surely all that it concerns a man of business to know, about the characters and purposes of his fellow-men. Judging them as they stood, they might be honored and trusted members of the Chamber of Commerce, who had found the genuine secret of wealth, and whose sagacity gave them the command of fortune. There was a character of detail and matter-of-fact in their talk, which concealed the extravagance of its purport, insomuch that the wildest schemes had the aspect of every-day realities. Thus the listener was not startled at the idea of cities to be built, as if by magic, in the heart of pathless forests; and of streets to be laid out, where now the sea was tossing; and of mighty rivers to be staid in their courses, in order to turn the machinery of a cotton-mill. It was only by an effort—and scarcely then—that the mind convinced itself that such speculations were as much matter of fantasy as the old dream of Eldorado, or as Mammon's Cave, or any other vision of gold, ever conjured up by the imagination of needy poet or romantic adventurer.

"Upon my word," said I, "it is dangerous to listen to such dreamers as these! Their madness is contagious."

"Yes," said my friend, "because they mistake the Hall of Fantasy for actual brick and mortar, and its purple atmosphere for unsophisticated sunshine. But the poet knows his whereabout, and therefore is less likely to make a fool of himself in real life."

"Here again," observed I, as we advanced a little further, "we see another order of dreamers—peculiarly characteristic, too, of the genius of our country."

These were the inventors of fantastic machines. Models of their contrivances were placed against some of the pillars of the hall, and afforded good emblems of the result generally to be anticipated from an attempt to reduce day-dreams to practice. The analogy may hold in morals, as well as physics. For instance, here was the model of a railroad through the air, and a tunnel under the sea. Here was a machine—stolen, I believe—for the distillation of heat from moonshine; and another for the condensation of morning-mist into square blocks of granite, wherewith it was proposed to rebuild the entire Hall of Fantasy. One man exhibited a sort of lens, whereby he had succeeded in making sunshine out of a lady's smile; and it was his purpose wholly to irradiate the earth, by means of this wonderful invention.

"It is nothing new," said I, "for most of our sunshine comes from woman's smile already."

"True," answered the inventor; "but my machine will secure a constant supply for domestic use—whereas, hitherto, it has been very precarious."

Another person had a scheme for fixing the reflections of objects in a pool of water, and thus taking the most life-like portraits imaginable; and the same gentleman demonstrated the practicability of giving a permanent dye to ladies' dresses, in the gorgeous clouds of sunset. There were at least fifty kinds of perpetual motion, one of which was applicable to the wits of newspaper editors and writers of every description. Professor Espy was here, with a tremendous storm in a gum-elastic bag. I could enumerate many more of these Utopian inventions; but, after all, a more imaginative collection is to be found in the Patent Office at Washington.

Turning from the inventors, we took a more general survey of the inmates of the hall. Many persons were present, whose

right of entrance appeared to consist in some crochet of the
brain, which, so long as it might operate, produced a change
in their relation to the actual world. It is singular how very few
there are, who do not occasionally gain admittance on such a
score, either in abstracted musings, or momentary thoughts,
or bright anticipations, or vivid remembrances; for even the actual becomes ideal, whether in hope or memory, and beguiles
the dreamer into the Hall of Fantasy. Some unfortunates make
their whole abode and business here, and contract habits which
unfit them for all the real employments of life. Others—but
these are few—possess the faculty, in their occasional visits, of
discovering a purer truth than the world can impart, among
the lights and shadows of these pictured windows.

And with all its dangerous influences, we have reason to
thank God, that there is such a place of refuge from the gloom
and chillness of actual life. Hither may come the prisoner, es-
caping from his dark and narrow cell, and cankerous chain, to
breathe free air in this enchanted atmosphere. The sick man
leaves his weary pillow, and finds strength to wander hither,
though his wasted limbs might not support him even to the
threshold of his chamber. The exile passes through the Hall of
Fantasy, to revisit his native soil. The burthen of years rolls
down from the old man's shoulders, the moment that the door
uncloses. Mourners leave their heavy sorrows at the entrance,
and here rejoin the lost ones, whose faces would else be seen no
more, until thought shall have become the only fact. It may be
said, in truth, that there is but half a life—the meaner and
earthlier half—for those who never find their way into the hall.
Nor must I fail to mention, that, in the observatory of the edifice, is kept that wonderful perspective glass, through which
the shepherds of the Delectable Mountains showed Christian
the far-off gleam of the Celestial City. The eye of Faith still
loves to gaze through it.

"I observe some men here," said I to my friend, "who might

set up a strong claim to be reckoned among the most real personages of the day."

"Certainly," he replied. "If a man be in advance of his age, he must be content to make his abode in this hall, until the lingering generations of his fellow-men come up with him. He can find no other shelter in the universe. But the fantasies of one day are the deepest realities of a future one."

"It is difficult to distinguish them apart, amid the gorgeous and bewildering light of this hall," rejoined I. "The white sunshine of actual life is necessary in order to test them. I am rather apt to doubt both men and their reasonings, till I meet them in that truthful medium."

"Perhaps your faith in the ideal is deeper than you are aware," said my friend. "You are at least a Democrat; and methinks no scanty share of such faith is essential to the adoption of that creed."

Among the characters who had elicited these remarks, were most of the noted reformers of the day, whether in physics, politics, morals, or religion. There is no surer method of arriving at the Hall of Fantasy, than to throw oneself into the current of a theory; for, whatever landmarks of fact may be set up along the stream, there is a law of nature that impels it thither. And let it be so; for here the wise head and capacious heart may do their work; and what is good and true becomes gradually hardened into fact, while error melts away and vanishes among the shadows of the hall. Therefore may none, who believe and rejoice in the progress of mankind, be angry with me because I recognized their apostles and leaders, amid the fantastic radiance of those pictured windows. I love and honor such men, as well as they.

It would be endless to describe the herd of real or self-styled reformers, that peopled this place of refuge. They were the representatives of an unquiet period, when mankind is seeking to cast off the whole tissue of ancient custom, like a tattered gar-

ment. Many of them had got possession of some crystal fragment of truth, the brightness of which so dazzled them, that
they could see nothing else in the wide universe. Here were
men, whose faith had embodied itself in the form of a potatoe;
and others whose long beards had a deep spiritual significance.
Here was the abolitionist, brandishing his one idea like an iron
flail. In a word, there were a thousand shapes of good and evil,
faith and infidelity, wisdom and nonsense,—a most incongru-
ous throng.

Yet, withal, the heart of the stanchest conservative, unless
he abjured his fellowship with man, could hardly have helped
throbbing in sympathy with the spirit that pervaded these innumerable theorists. It was good for the man of unquickened
heart to listen even to their folly. Far down, beyond the fathom
of the intellect, the soul acknowledged that all these varying
and conflicting developments of humanity were united in one
sentiment. Be the individual theory as wild as fancy could
make it, still the wiser spirit would recognize the struggle of
the race after a better and purer life, than had yet been realized
on earth. My faith revived, even while I rejected all their
schemes. It could not be, that the world should continue forever what it has been; a soil where Happiness is so rare a
flower, and Virtue so often a blighted fruit; a battle-field
where the good principle, with its shield flung above its head,
can hardly save itself amid the rush of adverse influences. In
the enthusiasm of such thoughts, I gazed through one of the
pictured windows; and, behold! the whole external world was
tinged with the dimly glorious aspect that is peculiar to the
Hall of Fantasy; insomuch that it seemed practicable, at that
very instant, to realize some plan for the perfection of mankind. But, alas! if reformers would understand the sphere in
which their lot is cast, they must cease to look through pictured windows. Yet they not only use this medium, but mistake it for the whitest sunshine.

"Come," said I to my friend, starting from a deep reverie,—

"let us hasten hence, or I shall be tempted to make a theory—after which, there is little hope of any man."

"Come hither, then," answered he. "Here is one theory, that swallows up and annihilates all others."

He led me to a distant part of the hall, where a crowd of deeply attentive auditors were assembled round an elderly man, of plain, honest, trustworthy aspect. With an earnestness that betokened the sincerest faith in his own doctrine, he announced that the destruction of the world was close at hand.

"It is Father Miller himself!" exclaimed I.

"No less a man," said my friend, "and observe how picturesque a contrast between his dogma, and those of the reformers whom we have just glanced at. They look for the earthly perfection of mankind, and are forming schemes, which imply that the immortal spirit will be connected with a physical nature, for innumerable ages of futurity. On the other hand, here comes good Father Miller, and, with one puff of his relentless theory, scatters all their dreams like so many withered leaves upon the blast."

"It is, perhaps, the only method of getting mankind out of the various perplexities, into which they have fallen," I replied. "Yet I could wish that the world might be permitted to endure, until some great moral shall have been evolved. A riddle is propounded. Where is the solution? The sphinx did not slay herself, until her riddle had been guessed. Will it not be so with the world? Now, if it should be burnt to-morrow morning, I am at a loss to know what purpose will have been accomplished, or how the universe will be wiser or better for our existence and destruction."

"We cannot tell what mighty truths may have been embodied in act, through the existence of the globe and its inhabitants," rejoined my companion. "Perhaps it may be revealed to us, after the fall of the curtain over our catastrophe; or not impossibly, the whole drama, in which we are involuntary actors, may have been performed for the instruction of another set of spectators. I cannot perceive that our own comprehension of it is at all essential to the matter. At any rate, while our view is so ridiculously narrow and superficial, it would be absurd to argue the continuance of the world from the fact, that it seems to have existed hitherto in vain."

"The poor old Earth," murmured I. "She has faults enough, in all conscience; but I cannot bear to have her perish."

"It is no great matter," said my friend. "The happiest of us has been weary of her, many a time and oft."

"I doubt it," answered I, pertinaciously; "the root of human nature strikes down deep into this earthly soil; and it is but reluctantly that we submit to be transplanted, even for a higher cultivation in Heaven. I query whether the destruction of the earth would gratify any one individual; except, perhaps, some embarrassed man of business, whose notes fall due a day after the day of doom."

Then, methought, I heard the expostulating cry of a multitude against the consummation, prophesied by Father Miller. The lover wrestled with Providence for his fore-shadowed bliss. Parents entreated that the earth's span of endurance might be prolonged by some seventy years, so that their newborn infant should not be defrauded of his life-time. A youthful poet murmured, because there would be no posterity to recognize the inspiration of his song. The reformers, one and all, demanded a few thousand years, to test their theories, after which the universe might go to wreck. A mechanician, who was busied with an improvement of the steam-engine, asked merely time to perfect his model. A miser insisted that the world's destruction would be a personal wrong to himself, unless he should first be permitted to add a specified sum to his enormous heap of gold. A little boy made dolorous inquiry whether the last day would come before Christmas, and thus deprive him of his anticipated dainties. In short, nobody seemed satisfied that this mortal scene of things should have its close just now. Yet, it must be confessed, the motives of the crowd for desiring its continuance were mostly so absurd, that, unless Infinite Wisdom had been aware of much better reasons, the solid Earth must have melted away at once.

For my own part, not to speak of a few private and personal ends, I really desired our old Mother's prolonged existence, for her own dear sake.

"The poor old Earth!" I repeated. "What I should chiefly regret in her destruction would be that very earthliness, which no other sphere or state of existence can renew or compensate. The fragrance of flowers, and of new-mown hay; the genial warmth of sunshine, and the beauty of a sunset among clouds; the comfort and cheerful glow of the fireside; the deliciousness of fruits, and of all good cheer; the magnificence of mountains, and seas, and cataracts, and the softer charm of rural scenery; even the fast-falling snow, and the gray atmosphere through which it descends—all these, and innumerable other enjoyable things of earth, must perish with her. Then the country frolics; the homely humor; the broad, open-mouthed roar of laughter, in which body and soul conjoin so heartily! I fear that no other world can show us anything just like this. As for purely moral enjoyments, the good will find them in every state of being. But where the material and the moral exist together, what is to happen then? And then our mute four-footed friends, and the winged songsters of our woods! Might it not be lawful to regret them, even in the hallowed groves of Paradise?"

"You speak like the very spirit of earth, imbued with a scent of freshly-turned soil!" exclaimed my friend.

"It is not that I so much object to giving up these enjoyments, on my own account," continued I; "but I hate to think that they will have been eternally annihilated from the list of joys."

"Nor need they be," he replied. "I see no real force in what you say. Standing in this Hall of Fantasy, we perceive what even the earth-clogged intellect of man can do, in creating circumstances, which, though we call them shadowy and visionary, are scarcely more so than those that surround us in actual life. Doubt not, then, that man's disembodied spirit may recreate Time and the World for itself, with all their peculiar enjoyments, should there still be human yearnings amid life eternal and infinite. But I doubt whether we shall be inclined to play such a poor scene over again."

"Oh, you are ungrateful to our Mother Earth!" rejoined I. "Come what may, I never will forget her! Neither will it satisfy me to have her exist merely in idea. I want her great, round, solid self to endure interminably, and still to be peopled with the kindly race of man, whom I uphold to be much better than he thinks himself. Nevertheless, I confide the whole matter to Providence, and shall endeavor so to live, that the world may come to an end at any moment, without leaving me at a loss to find foothold somewhere else."

"It is an excellent resolve," said my companion, looking at his watch. "But come; it is the dinner hour. Will you partake of my vegetable diet?"

A thing so matter-of-fact as an invitation to dinner, even when the fare was to be nothing more substantial than vegetables and fruit, compelled us forthwith to remove from the Hall of Fantasy. As we passed out of the portal, we met the spirits of several persons, who had been sent thither in magnetic sleep. I looked back among the sculptured pillars, and at the transformations of the gleaming fountain, and almost desired that the whole of life might be spent in that visionary scene, where the actual world, with its hard angles, should never rub against me, and only be viewed through the medium of pictured windows. But, for those who waste all their days in the Hall of Fantasy, good Father Miller's prophecy is already accomplished, and the solid earth has come to an untimely end. Let us be content, therefore, with merely an occasional visit, for the sake of spiritualizing the grossness of this actual life, and prefiguring to ourselves a state, in which the Idea shall be all in all.

The Birth-mark

In the latter part of the last century, there lived a man of science—an eminent proficient in every branch of natural philosophy—who, not long before our story opens, had made experience of a spiritual affinity, more attractive than any chemical one. He had left his laboratory to the care of an assistant, cleared his fine countenance from the furnace-smoke, washed the stain of acids from his fingers, and persuaded a beautiful woman to become his wife. In those days, when the comparatively recent discovery of electricity, and other kindred mysteries of nature, seemed to open paths into the region of miracle, it was not unusual for the love of science to rival the love of woman, in its depth and absorbing energy. The higher intellect, the imagination, the spirit, and even the heart, might all find their congenial aliment in pursuits which, as some of their ardent votaries believed, would ascend from one step of powerful intelligence to another, until the philosopher should lay his hand on the secret of creative force, and perhaps make new worlds for himself. We know not whether Aylmer possessed this degree of faith in man's ultimate control over nature. He had devoted himself, however, too unreservedly to scientific studies, ever to be weaned from them by any second passion. His love for his young wife might prove the stronger of the two; but it could only be by intertwining itself with his love of science, and uniting the strength of the latter to its own.

Such a union accordingly took place, and was attended with

truly remarkable consequences, and a deeply impressive moral. One day, very soon after their marriage, Aylmer sat gazing at his wife, with a trouble in his countenance that grew stronger, until he spoke.

"Georgiana," said he, "has it never occurred to you that the mark upon your cheek might be removed?"

"No, indeed," said she, smiling; but perceiving the seriousness of his manner, she blushed deeply. "To tell you the truth, it has been so often called a charm, that I was simple enough to imagine it might be so."

"Ah, upon another face, perhaps it might," replied her husband. "But never on yours! No, dearest Georgiana, you came so nearly perfect from the hand of Nature, that this slightest possible defect—which we hesitate whether to term a defect or a beauty—shocks me, as being the visible mark of earthly imperfection."

"Shocks you, my husband!" cried Georgiana, deeply hurt; at first reddening with momentary anger, but then bursting into tears. "Then why did you take me from my mother's side? You cannot love what shocks you!"

To explain this conversation, it must be mentioned, that, in the centre of Georgiana's left cheek, there was a singular mark, deeply interwoven, as it were, with the texture and substance of her face. In the usual state of her complexion,—a healthy, though delicate bloom,—the mark wore a tint of deeper crimson, which imperfectly defined its shape amid the surrounding rosiness. When she blushed, it gradually became more indistinct, and finally vanished amid the triumphant rush of blood, that bathed the whole cheek with its brilliant glow. But, if any shifting emotion caused her to turn pale, there was the mark again, a crimson stain upon the snow, in what Aylmer sometimes deemed an almost fearful distinctness. Its shape bore not a little similarity to the human hand, though of the smallest pigmy size. Georgiana's lovers were wont to say, that some fairy, at her birth-hour, had laid her tiny hand upon the infant's cheek, and left this impress there, in token of the magic endowments that were to give her such sway over all hearts. Many a desperate swain would have risked life for the privilege of pressing his lips to the mysterious hand. It must not be concealed, however, that the impression wrought by this fairy sign-manual varied exceedingly, according to the difference of temperament in the beholders. Some fastidious persons—but they were exclusively of her own sex—affirmed that the Bloody Hand, as they chose to call it, quite destroyed the effect of Georgiana's beauty, and rendered her countenance even hideous. But it would be as reasonable to say, that one of those small blue stains, which sometimes occur in the purest statuary marble, would convert the Eve of Powers to a monster. Masculine observers, if the birth-mark did not heighten their admiration, contented themselves with wishing it away, that the world might possess one living specimen of ideal loveliness, without the semblance of a flaw. After his marriage—for he thought little or nothing of the matter before—Aylmer discovered that this was the case with himself.

Had she been less beautiful—if Envy's self could have found aught else to sneer at—he might have felt his affection heightened by the prettiness of this mimic hand, now vaguely portrayed, now lost, now stealing forth again, and glimmering to-and-fro with every pulse of emotion that throbbed within her heart. But, seeing her otherwise so perfect, he found this one defect grow more and more intolerable, with every moment of their united lives. It was the fatal flaw of humanity, which Nature, in one shape or another, stamps ineffaceably on all her productions, either to imply that they are temporary and finite, or that their perfection must be wrought by toil and pain. The Crimson Hand expressed the ineludible gripe, in which mortality clutches the highest and purest of earthly mould, degrading them into kindred with the lowest, and even with the very brutes, like whom their visible frames return to dust. In this manner, selecting it as the symbol of his wife's liability to sin, sorrow, decay, and death, Alymer's sombre imagination was not long in rendering the birth-mark a frightful object, causing him more trouble and horror than ever Georgiana's beauty, whether of soul or sense, had given him delight.

At all the seasons which should have been their happiest, he invariably, and without intending it—nay, in spite of a purpose to the contrary—reverted to this one disastrous topic. Trifling as it at first appeared, it so connected itself with innumerable trains of thought, and modes of feeling, that it became the central point of all. With the morning twilight, Aylmer opened his eyes upon his wife's face, and recognized the symbol of imperfection; and when they sat together at the evening hearth, his eyes wandered stealthily to her cheek, and beheld, flickering with the blaze of the wood fire, the spectral Hand that wrote mortality, where he would fain have worshipped. Georgiana soon learned to shudder at his gaze. It needed but a glance, with the peculiar expression that his face often wore, to change the roses of her cheek into a deathlike paleness, amid which the Crimson Hand was brought strongly out, like a bas-relief of ruby on the whitest marble.

Late, one night, when the lights were growing dim, so as hardly to betray the stain on the poor wife's cheek, she herself, for the first time, voluntarily took up the subject.

"Do you remember, my dear Aylmer," said she, with a feeble attempt at a smile—"have you any recollection of a dream, last night, about this odious Hand?"

"None!—none whatever!" replied Aylmer, starting; but then he added in a dry, cold tone, affected for the sake of concealing the real depth of his emotion:—"I might well dream of it; for before I fell asleep, it had taken a pretty firm hold of my fancy."

"And you did dream of it," continued Georgiana, hastily; for she dreaded lest a gush of tears should interrupt what she had to say—"A terrible dream! I wonder that you can forget it. Is it possible to forget this one expression?—'It is in her heart now—we must have it out!'—Reflect, my husband; for by all means I would have you recall that dream."

The mind is in a sad note, when Sleep, the all-involving, cannot confine her spectres within the dim region of her sway, but suffers them to break forth, affrighting this actual life with secrets that perchance belong to a deeper one. Aylmer now remembered his dream. He had fancied himself, with his servant Aminadab, attempting an operation for the removal of the birth-mark. But the deeper went the knife, the deeper sank the Hand, until at length its tiny grasp appeared to have caught hold of Georgiana's heart; whence, however, her husband was inexorably resolved to cut or wrench it away.

When the dream had shaped itself perfectly in his memory, Aylmer sat in his wife's presence with a guilty feeling. Truth often finds its way to the mind close-muffled in robes of sleep, and then speaks with uncompromising directness of matters in regard to which we practise an unconscious self-deception, during our waking moments. Until now, he had not been aware of the tyrannizing influence acquired by one idea over his mind, and of the lengths which he might find in his heart to go, for the sake of giving himself peace.

"Aylmer," resumed Georgiana, solemnly, "I know not what may be the cost to both of us, to rid me of this fatal birthmark. Perhaps its removal may cause cureless deformity. Or, it may be, the stain goes as deep as life itself. Again, do we know that there is a possibility, on any terms, of unclasping the firm gripe of this little Hand, which was laid upon me before I came into the world?"

"Dearest Georgiana, I have spent much thought upon the subject," hastily interrupted Aylmer—"I am convinced of the perfect practicability of its removal."

"If there be the remotest possibility of it," continued Georgiana, "let the attempt be made, at whatever risk. Danger is nothing to me; for life—while this hateful mark makes me the object of your horror and disgust—life is a burthen which I would fling down with joy. Either remove this dreadful Hand, or take my wretched life! You have deep science! All the world bears witness of it. You have achieved great wonders! Cannot you remove this little, little mark, which I cover with the tips of two small fingers? Is this beyond your power, for the sake of your own peace, and to save your poor wife from madness?"

"Noblest—dearest—tenderest wife!" cried Aylmer, rapturously. "Doubt not my power. I have already given this matter the deepest thought—thought which might almost have enlightened me to create a being less perfect than yourself. Georgiana, you have led me deeper than ever into the heart of science. I feel myself fully competent to render this dear cheek as faultless as its fellow; and then, most beloved, what will be my triumph, when I shall have corrected what Nature left imperfect, in her fairest work! Even Pygmalion, when his sculptured woman assumed life, felt not greater ecstasy than mine will be."

"It is resolved, then," said Georgiana, faintly smiling,—"And, Aylmer, spare me not, though you should find the birth-mark take refuge in my heart at last."

Her husband tenderly kissed her cheek—her right cheek—not that which bore the impress of the Crimson Hand.

The next day, Aylmer apprized his wife of a plan that he had formed, whereby he might have opportunity for the intense thought and constant watchfulness, which the proposed operation would require; while Georgiana, likewise, would enjoy the perfect repose essential to its success. They were to seclude themselves in the extensive apartments occupied by Aylmer as a laboratory, and where, during his toilsome youth, he had made discoveries in the elemental powers of nature, that had roused the admiration of all the learned societies in Europe. Seated calmly in this laboratory, the pale philosopher had investigated the secrets of the highest cloud-region, and of the profoundest mines; he had satisfied himself of the causes that kindled and kept alive the fires of the volcano; and had explained the mystery of fountains, and how it is that they gush forth, some so bright and pure, and others with such rich medicinal virtues, from the dark bosom of the earth. Here, too, at an earlier period, he had studied the wonders of the human frame, and attempted to fathom the very process by which Nature assimilates all her precious influences from earth and air, and from the spiritual world, to create and foster Man, her masterpiece. The latter pursuit, however, Aylmer had long laid aside, in unwilling recognition of the truth, against which all seekers sooner or later stumble, that our great creative Mother, while she amuses us with apparently working in the broadest sunshine, is yet severely careful to keep her own secrets, and, in spite of her pretended openness, shows us nothing but results. She permits us indeed, to mar, but seldom to mend, and, like a jealous patentee, on no account to make. Now, however, Aylmer resumed these half-forgotten investigations; not, of course, with such hopes or wishes as first suggested them; but because they involved much physiological truth, and lay in the path of his proposed scheme for the treatment of Georgiana.

As he led her over the threshold of the laboratory, Georgiana was cold and tremulous. Aylmer looked cheerfully into her face, with intent to reassure her, but was so startled with the intense glow of the birth-mark upon the whiteness of her cheek, that he could not restrain a strong convulsive shudder. His wife fainted.

"Aminadab! Aminadab!" shouted Aylmer, stamping violently on the floor.

Forthwith, there issued from an inner apartment a man of low stature, but bulky frame, with shaggy hair hanging about his visage, which was grimed with the vapors of the furnace. This personage had been Aylmer's under-worker during his whole scientific career, and was admirably fitted for that office by his great mechanical readiness, and the skill with which, while incapable of comprehending a single principle, he executed all the practical details of his master's experiments. With his vast strength, his shaggy hair, his smoky aspect, and the indescribable earthiness that incrusted him, he seemed to represent man's physical nature; while Aylmer's slender figure, and pale, intellectual face, were no less apt a type of the spiritual element.

"Throw open the door of the boudoir, Aminadab," said Aylmer, "and burn a pastille."

"Yes, master," answered Aminadab, looking intently at the lifeless form of Georgiana; and then he muttered to himself:—"If she were my wife, I'd never part with that birth-mark."

When Georgiana recovered consciousness, she found herself breathing an atmosphere of penetrating fragrance, the gentle potency of which had recalled her from her deathlike faintness. The scene around her looked like enchantment. Aylmer had converted those smoky, dingy, sombre rooms, where he had spent his brightest years in recondite pursuits, into a series of beautiful apartments, not unfit to be the secluded abode of a lovely woman. The walls were hung with gorgeous curtains, which imparted the combination of grandeur and grace, that no other species of adornment can achieve; and as they fell from the ceiling to the floor, their rich and ponderous folds, concealing all angles and straight lines, appeared to shut in the scene from infinite space. For aught Georgiana knew, it might be a pavilion among the clouds. And Aylmer, excluding the sunshine, which would have interfered with his chemical processes, had supplied its place with perfumed lamps, emitting flames of various hue, but all uniting in a soft, empurpled radiance. He now knelt by his wife's side, watching her earnestly, but without alarm; for he was confident in his science, and felt that he could draw a magic circle round her, within which no evil might intrude.

"Where am I?—Ah, I remember!" said Georgiana, faintly; and she placed her hand over her cheek, to hide the terrible mark from her husband's eyes.

"Fear not, dearest!" exclaimed he. "Do not shrink from me! Believe me, Georgiana, I even rejoice in this single imperfection, since it will be such rapture to remove it."

"Oh, spare me!" sadly replied his wife—"Pray do not look at it again. I never can forget that convulsive shudder."

In order to soothe Georgiana, and, as it were, to release her mind from the burthen of actual things, Aylmer now put in practice some of the light and playful secrets, which science had taught him among its profounder lore. Airy figures, absolutely bodiless ideas, and forms of unsubstantial beauty, came and danced before her, imprinting their momentary footsteps on beams of light. Though she had some indistinct idea of the method of these optical phenomena, still the illusion was almost perfect enough to warrant the belief, that her husband possessed sway over the spiritual world. Then again, when she felt a wish to look forth from her seclusion, immediately, as if her thoughts were answered, the procession of external existence flitted across a screen. The scenery and the figures of actual life were perfectly represented, but with that bewitching, yet indescribable difference, which always makes a picture, an image, or a shadow, so much more attractive than the original. When wearied of this, Aylmer bade her cast her eyes upon a vessel, containing a quantity of earth. She did so, with little interest at first, but was soon startled, to perceive the germ of a plant, shooting upward from the soil. Then came the slender stalk—the leaves gradually unfolded themselves—and amid them was a perfect and lovely flower.

"It is magical!" cried Georgiana, "I dare not touch it."

"Nay, pluck it," answered Aylmer, "pluck it, and inhale its brief perfume while you may. The flower will wither in a few moments, and leave nothing save its brown seed-vessels—but thence may be perpetuated a race as ephemeral as itself."

But Georgiana had no sooner touched the flower than the whole plant suffered a blight, its leaves turning coal-black, as if by the agency of fire.

"There was too powerful a stimulus," said Aylmer thoughtfully.

To make up for this abortive experiment, he proposed to take her portrait by a scientific process of his own invention. It was to be effected by rays of light striking upon a polished plate of metal. Georgiana assented—but, on looking at the result, was affrighted to find the features of the portrait blurred and indefinable; while the minute figure of a hand appeared where the cheek should have been. Aylmer snatched the metallic plate, and threw it into a jar of corrosive acid.

Soon, however, he forgot these mortifying failures. In the intervals of study and chemical experiment, he came to her, flushed and exhausted, but seemed invigorated by her presence, and spoke in glowing language of the resources of his art. He gave a history of the long dynasty of the Alchemists, who spent so many ages in quest of the universal solvent, by which the Golden Principle might be elicted from all things vile and base. Aylmer appeared to believe, that, by the plainest scientific logic, it was altogether within the limits of possibility to discover this long-sought medium; but, he added, a philosopher who should go deep enough to acquire the power, would attain too lofty a wisdom to stoop to the exercise of it. Not less singular were his opinions in regard to the Elixir Vitæ. He more than intimated, that it was his option to concoct a liquid that should prolong life for years—perhaps interminably—but that it would produce a discord in nature, which all the world, and chiefly the quaffer of the immortal nostrum, would find cause to curse.

"Aylmer, are you in earnest?" asked Georgiana, looking at

him with amazement and fear; "it is terrible to possess such power, or even to dream of possessing it!"

"Oh, do not tremble, my love!" said her husband, "I would not wrong either you or myself by working such inharmonious effects upon our lives. But I would have you consider how trifling, in comparison, is the skill requisite to remove this little Hand."

At the mention of the birth-mark, Georgiana, as usual, shrank, as if a red-hot iron had touched her cheek.

Again Aylmer applied himself to his labors. She could hear his voice in the distant furnace-room, giving directions to Aminadab, whose harsh, uncouth, misshapen tones were audible in response, more like the grunt or growl of a brute than human speech. After hours of absence, Aylmer reappeared, and proposed that she should now examine his cabinet of chemical products, and natural treasures of the earth. Among the former he showed her a small vial, in which, he remarked, was contained a gentle yet most powerful fragrance, capable of impregnating all the breezes that blow across a kingdom. They were of inestimable value, the contents of that little vial; and, as he said so, he threw some of the perfume into the air, and filled the room with piercing and invigorating delight.

"And what is this?" asked Georgiana, pointing to a small crystal globe, containing a gold-colored liquid. "It is so beautiful to the eye, that I could imagine it the Elixir of Life."

"In one sense it is," replied Aylmer, "or rather the Elixir of Immortality. It is the most precious poison that ever was concocted in this world. By its aid, I could apportion the lifetime of any mortal at whom you might point your finger. The strength of the dose would determine whether he were to linger out years, or drop dead in the midst of a breath. No king, on his guarded throne, could keep his life, if I, in my private station, should deem that the welfare of millions justified me in depriving him of it."

"Why do you keep such a terrific drug?" inquired Georgiana in horror.

"Do not mistrust me, dearest!" said her husband, smiling; "its virtuous potency is yet greater than its harmful one. But, see! here is a powerful cosmetic. With a few drops of this, in a vase of water, freckles may be washed away as easily as the hands are cleansed. A stronger infusion would take the blood out of the cheek, and leave the rosiest beauty a pale ghost."

"Is it with this lotion that you intend to bathe my cheek?" asked Georgiana anxiously.

"Oh, no!" hastily replied her husband—"this is merely superficial. Your case demands a remedy that shall go deeper."

In his interviews with Georgiana, Aylmer generally made minute inquiries as to her sensations, and whether the confinement of the rooms, and the temperature of the atmosphere, agreed with her. These questions had such a particular drift, that Georgiana began to conjecture that she was already subjected to certain physical influences, either breathed in with the fragrant air, or taken with her food. She fancied, likewise—but it might be altogether fancy—that there was a stirring up of her system,—a strange indefinite sensation creeping through her veins, and tingling, half painfully, half pleasurably, at her heart. Still, whenever she dared to look into the mirror, there she beheld herself, pale as a white rose, and with the crimson birth-mark stamped upon her cheek. Not even Aylmer now hated it so much as she.

To dispel the tedium of the hours which her husband found it necessary to devote to the processes of combination and analysis, Georgiana turned over the volumes of his scientific library. In many dark old tomes, she met with chapters full of romance and poetry. They were the works of the philosophers of the middle ages, such as Albertus Magnus, Cornelius Agrippa, Paracelsus, and the famous friar who created the prophetic Brazen Head. All these antique naturalists stood in advance of their centuries, yet were imbued with some of their credulity, and therefore were believed, and perhaps imagined themselves, to have acquired from the investigation of nature a power above nature, and from physics a sway over the spiritual world. Hardly less curious and imaginative were the early volumes of the Transactions of the Royal Society, in which the members, knowing little of the limits of natural possibility, were continually recording wonders, or proposing methods whereby wonders might be wrought.

But, to Georgiana, the most engrossing volume was a large folio from her husband's own hand, in which he had recorded every experiment of his scientific career, with its original aim, the methods adopted for its development, and its final success or failure, with the circumstances to which either event was attributable. The book, in truth, was both the history and emblem of his ardent, ambitious, imaginative, yet practical and laborious, life. He handled physical details, as if there were nothing beyond them; yet spiritualized them all, and redeemed himself from materialism, by his strong and eager aspiration towards the infinite. In his grasp, the veriest clod of earth assumed a soul. Georgiana, as she read, reverenced Aylmer, and loved him more profoundly than ever, but with a less entire dependence on his judgment than heretofore. Much as he had accomplished, she could not but observe that his most splendid successes were almost invariably failures, if compared with the ideal at which he aimed. His brightest diamonds were the merest pebbles, and felt to be so by himself, in comparison with the inestimable gems which lay hidden beyond his reach. The volume, rich with achievements that had won renown for its author, was yet as melancholy a record as ever mortal hand had penned. It was the sad confession, and continual exemplification, of the short-comings of the composite man—the spirit burthened with clay and working in matter—and of the despair that assails the higher nature, at finding itself so miserably thwarted by the earthly part. Perhaps every man of genius, in whatever sphere, might recognize the image of his own experience in Aylmer's journal.

So deeply did these reflections affect Georgiana, that she laid her face upon the open volume, and burst into tears. In this situation she was found by her husband.

"It is dangerous to read in a sorcerer's books," said he, with a smile, though his countenance was uneasy and displeased. "Georgiana, there are pages in that volume, which I can scarcely glance over and keep my senses. Take heed lest it prove as detrimental to you!"

"It has made me worship you more than ever," said she.

"Ah! wait for this one success," rejoined he, "then worship me if you will. I shall deem myself hardly unworthy of it. But, come! I have sought you for the luxury of your voice. Sing to me, dearest!"

So she poured out the liquid music of her voice to quench the thirst of his spirit. He then took his leave, with a boyish exuberance of gaiety, assuring her that her seclusion would endure but a little longer, and that the result was already certain. Scarcely had he departed, when Georgiana felt irresistibly impelled to follow him. She had forgotten to inform Aylmer of a symptom, which, for two or three hours past, had begun to excite her attention. It was a sensation in the fatal birth-mark, not painful, but which induced a restlessness throughout her system. Hastening after her husband, she intruded, for the first time, into the laboratory.

The first thing that struck her eye was the furnace, that hot and feverish worker, with the intense glow of its fire, which, by the quantities of soot clustered above it, seemed to have been burning for ages. There was a distilling apparatus in full operation. Around the room were retorts, tubes, cylinders, crucibles, and other apparatus of chemical research. An electrical machine stood ready for immediate use. The atmosphere felt oppressively close, and was tainted with gaseous odors, which had been tormented forth by the processes of science. The severe and homely simplicity of the apartment, with its naked walls and brick pavement, looked strange, accustomed as Georgiana had become to the fantastic elegance of her boudoir. But what chiefly, indeed almost solely, drew her attention, was the aspect of Aylmer himself.

He was pale as death, anxious, and absorbed, and hung over the furnace as if it depended upon his utmost watchfulness whether the liquid, which it was distilling, should be the draught of immortal happiness or misery. How different from the sanguine and joyous mien that he had assumed for Georgiana's encouragement!

"Carefully now, Aminadab! Carefully, thou human machine! Carefully, thou man of clay!" muttered Aylmer, more to himself than his assistant. "Now, if there be a thought too much or too little, it is all over!"

"Hoh! hoh!" mumbled Aminadab—"look, master, look!"

Aylmer raised his eyes hastily, and at first reddened, then grew paler than ever, on beholding Georgiana. He rushed towards her, and seized her arm with a gripe that left the print of his fingers upon it.

"Why do you come hither? Have you no trust in your husband?" cried he impetuously. "Would you throw the blight of that fatal birth-mark over my labors? It is not well done. Go, prying woman, go!"

"Nay, Aylmer," said Georgiana, with the firmness of which she possessed no stinted endowment, "it is not you that have a right to complain. You mistrust your wife! You have concealed the anxiety with which you watch the development of this experiment. Think not so unworthily of me, my husband! Tell me all the risk we run; and fear not that I shall shrink, for my share in it is far less than your own!"

"No, no, Georgiana!" said Aylmer impatiently, "it must not be."

"I submit," replied she calmly. "And, Aylmer, I shall quaff

whatever draught you bring me; but it will be on the same principle that would induce me to take a dose of poison, if offered by your hand."

"My noble wife," said Aylmer, deeply moved, "I knew not the height and depth of your nature, until now. Nothing shall be concealed. Know, then, that this Crimson Hand, superficial as it seems, has clutched its grasp into your being, with a strength of which I had no previous conception. I have already administered agents powerful enough to do aught except to change your entire physical system. Only one thing remains to be tried. If that fail us, we are ruined!"

"Why did you hesitate to tell me this?" asked she.

"Because, Georgiana," said Aylmer, in a low voice, "there is danger!"

"Danger? There is but one danger—that this horrible stigma shall be left upon my cheek!" cried Georgiana. "Remove it! remove it!—whatever be the cost—or we shall both go mad!"

"Heaven knows, your words are too true," said Aylmer, sadly. "And now, dearest, return to your boudoir. In a little while, all will be tested."

He conducted her back, and took leave of her with a solemn tenderness, which spoke far more than his words how much was now at stake. After his departure, Georgiana became wrapt in musings. She considered the character of Aylmer, and did it completer justice than at any previous moment. Her heart exulted, while it trembled, at his honorable love, so pure and lofty that it would accept nothing less than perfection, nor miserably make itself contented with an earthlier nature than he had dreamed of. She felt how much more precious was such a sentiment, than that meaner kind which would have borne with the imperfection for her sake, and have been guilty of treason to holy love, by degrading its perfect idea to the level of the actual. And, with her whole spirit, she prayed, that, for a single moment, she might satisfy his highest and deepest conception. Longer than one moment, she well knew, it could not be; for his spirit was ever on the march—ever ascending—and each instant required something that was beyond the scope of the instant before.

The sound of her husband's footsteps aroused her. He bore a crystal goblet, containing a liquor colorless as water, but bright enough to be the draught of immortality. Aylmer was pale; but it seemed rather the consequence of a highly wrought state of mind, and tension of spirit, than of fear or doubt.

"The concoction of the draught has been perfect," said he, in answer to Georgiana's look. "Unless all my science have deceived me, it cannot fail."

"Save on your account, my dearest Aylmer," observed his wife, "I might wish to put off this birth-mark of mortality by relinquishing mortality itself, in preference to any other mode. Life is but a sad possession to those who have attained precisely the degree of moral advancement at which I stand. Were I weaker and blinder, it might be happiness. Were I stronger, it might be endured hopefully. But, being what I find myself, methinks I am of all mortals the most fit to die."

"You are fit for heaven without tasting death!" replied her husband. "But why do we speak of dying? The draught cannot fail. Behold its effect upon this plant!"

On the window-seat there stood a geranium, diseased with yellow blotches, which had overspread all its leaves. Aylmer poured a small quantity of the liquid upon the soil in which it grew. In a little time, when the roots of the plant had taken up the moisture, the unsightly blotches began to be extinguished in a living verdure.

"There needed no proof," said Georgiana, quietly. "Give me the goblet. I joyfully stake all upon your word."

"Drink, then, thou lofty creature!" exclaimed Aylmer, with fervid admiration. "There is no taint of imperfection on thy spirit. Thy sensible frame, too, shall soon be all perfect!"

She quaffed the liquid, and returned the goblet to his hand.

"It is grateful," said she, with a placid smile. "Methinks it is like water from a heavenly fountain; for it contains I know not what of unobtrusive fragrance and deliciousness. It allays a feverish thirst, that had parched me for many days. Now, dearest, let me sleep. My earthly senses are closing over my spirit, like the leaves round the heart of a rose, at sunset."

She spoke the last words with a gentle reluctance, as if it required almost more energy than she could command to pronounce the faint and lingering syllables. Scarcely had they loitered through her lips, ere she was lost in slumber. Aylmer sat by her side, watching her aspect with the emotions proper to a man, the whole value of whose existence was involved in the process now to be tested. Mingled with this mood, however, was the philosophic investigation, characteristic of the man of science. Not the minutest symptom escaped him. A heightened flush of the cheek—a slight irregularity of breath—a quiver of the eyelid—a hardly perceptible tremor through the frame—such were the details which, as the moments passed, he wrote down in his folio volume. Intense thought had set its stamp upon every previous page of that volume; but the thoughts of years were all concentrated upon the last.

While thus employed, he failed not to gaze often at the fatal Hand, and not without a shudder. Yet once, by a strange and unaccountable impulse, he pressed it with his lips. His spirit recoiled, however, in the very act, and Georgiana, out of the midst of her deep sleep, moved uneasily and murmured, as if in remonstrance. Again, Aylmer resumed his watch. Nor was it without avail. The Crimson Hand, which at first had been strongly visible upon the marble paleness of Georgiana's cheek now grew more faintly outlined. She remained not less pale than ever; but the birth-mark, with every breath that came and went, lost somewhat of its former distinctness. Its presence had been awful; its departure was more awful still. Watch the stain of the rainbow fading out of the sky; and you will know how that mysterious symbol passed away.

"By Heaven, it is well nigh gone!" said Aylmer to himself, in almost irrepressible ecstasy. "I can scarcely trace it now. Success! Success! And now it is like the faintest rose-color. The slightest flush of blood across her cheek would overcome it. But she is so pale!"

He drew aside the window-curtain, and suffered the light of natural day to fall into the room, and rest upon her cheek. At the same time, he heard a gross, hoarse chuckle, which he had long known as his servant Aminadab's expression of delight.

"Ah, clod! Ah, earthly mass!" cried Aylmer, laughing in a sort of frenzy. "You have served me well! Matter and Spirit— Earth and Heaven—have both done their part in this! Laugh, thing of senses! You have earned the right to laugh."

These exclamations broke Georgiana's sleep. She slowly unclosed her eyes, and gazed into the mirror, which her husband had arranged for that purpose. A faint smile flitted over her lips, when she recognized how barely perceptible was now that Crimson Hand, which had once blazed forth with such disastrous brilliancy as to scare away all their happiness. But then her eyes sought Aylmer's face, with a trouble and anxiety that he could by no means account for.

"My poor Aylmer!" murmured she.

"Poor? Nay, richest! Happiest! Most favored!" exclaimed he. "My peerless bride, it is successful! You are perfect!"

"My poor Aylmer!" she repeated, with a more than human tenderness. "You have aimed loftily!—you have done nobly! Do not repent, that, with so high and pure a feeling, you have rejected the best that earth could offer. Aylmer—dearest Aylmer—I am dying!"

Alas, it was too true! The fatal Hand had grappled with the mystery of life, and was the bond by which an angelic spirit kept itself in union with a mortal frame. As the last crimson

tint of the birth-mark—that sole token of human imperfection—faded from her cheek, the parting breath of the now perfect woman passed into the atmosphere, and her soul, lingering a moment near her husband, took its heavenward flight.
Then a hoarse, chuckling laugh was heard again! Thus ever
does the gross Fatality of Earth exult in its invariable triumph
over the immortal essence, which, in this dim sphere of half-
development, demands the completeness of a higher state.
Yet, had Aylmer reached a profounder wisdom, he need not
thus have flung away the happiness, which would have woven
his mortal life of the self-same texture with the celestial. The
momentary circumstance was too strong for him; he failed to
look beyond the shadowy scope of Time, and living once for all
in Eternity, to find the perfect Future in the present.

Egotism;* or, The Bosom-Serpent

FROM THE UNPUBLISHED
"ALLEGORIES OF THE HEART"

"Here he comes!" shouted the boys along the street.—
"Here comes the man with a snake in his bosom!"

This outcry, saluting Herkimer's ears, as he was about to enter the iron gate of the Elliston mansion, made him pause. It
was not without a shudder that he found himself on the point
of meeting his former acquaintance, whom he had known in
the glory of youth, and whom now, after an interval of five
years, he was to find the victim either of a diseased fancy, or a
horrible physical misfortune.

"A snake in his bosom!" repeated the young sculptor to himself. "It must be he. No second man on earth has such a
bosom-friend! And now, my poor Rosina, Heaven grant me
wisdom to discharge my errand aright! Woman's faith must be
strong indeed, since thine has not yet failed."

Thus musing, he took his stand at the entrance of the gate,
and waited until the personage, so singularly announced,
should make his appearance. After an instant or two, he beheld
the figure of a lean man, of unwholesome look, with glittering
eyes and long black hair, who seemed to imitate the motion of
a snake; for, instead of walking straight forward with open
front, he undulated along the pavement in a curved line. It
may be too fanciful to say, that something, either in his

*The physical fact, to which it is here attempted to give a moral signification, has been
known to occur in more than one instance.

moral or material aspect, suggested the idea that a miracle had been wrought, by transforming a serpent into a man; but so imperfectly, that the snaky nature was yet hidden, and scarcely hidden, under the mere outward guise of humanity. Herkimer remarked that his complexion had a greenish tinge over its sickly white, reminding him of a species of marble out of which he had once wrought a head of Envy, with her snaky locks.

The wretched being approached the gate, but, instead of entering, stopt short, and fixed the glitter of his eye full upon the compassionate, yet steady countenance of the sculptor.

"It gnaws me! It gnaws me!" he exclaimed.

And then there was an audible hiss, but whether it came from the apparent lunatic's own lips, or was the real hiss of a serpent, might admit of discussion. At all events, it made Herkimer shudder to his heart's core.

"Do you know me, George Herkimer?" asked the snake-possessed.

Herkimer did know him. But it demanded all the intimate and practical acquaintance with the human face, acquired by modelling actual likenesses in clay, to recognize the features of Roderick Elliston in the visage that now met the sculptor's gaze. Yet it was he. It added nothing to the wonder, to reflect that the once brilliant young man had undergone this odious and fearful change, during the no more than five brief years of Herkimer's abode at Florence. The possibility of such a transformation being granted, it was as easy to conceive it effected in a moment as in an age. Inexpressibly shocked and startled, it was still the keenest pang, when Herkimer remembered that the fate of his cousin Rosina, the ideal of gentle womanhood, was indissolubly interwoven with that of a being whom Providence seemed to have unhumanized.

"Elliston! Roderick!" cried he, "I had heard of this; but my conception came far short of the truth. What has befallen you? Why do I find you thus?"

"Oh, 'tis a mere nothing! A snake! A snake! The commonest thing in the world. A snake in the bosom—that's all," answered Roderick Elliston. "But how is your own breast?" continued he, looking the sculptor in the eye, with the most acute and penetrating glance that it had ever been his fortune to encounter. "All pure and wholesome? No reptile there? By my faith and conscience, and by the devil within me, here is a wonder! A man without a serpent in his bosom!"

"Be calm, Elliston," whispered George Herkimer, laying his hand upon the shoulder of the snake-possessed. "I have crossed the ocean to meet you. Listen!—let us be private—I bring a message from Rosina!—from your wife!"

"It gnaws me! It gnaws me!" muttered Roderick.

With this exclamation, the most frequent in his mouth, the unfortunate man clutched both hands upon his breast, as if an intolerable sting or torture impelled him to rend it open, and let out the living mischief, even were it intertwined with his own life. He then freed himself from Herkimer's grasp, by a subtle motion, and gliding through the gate, took refuge in his antiquated family residence. The sculptor did not pursue him. He saw that no available intercourse could be expected at such a moment, and was desirous, before another meeting, to inquire closely into the nature of Roderick's disease, and the circumstances that had reduced him to so lamentable a condition. He succeeded in obtaining the necessary information from an eminent medical gentleman.

Shortly after Elliston's separation from his wife—now nearly four years ago—his associates had observed a singular gloom spreading over his daily life, like those chill, grey mists that sometimes steal away the sunshine from a summer's morning. The symptoms caused them endless perplexity. They knew not whether ill health were robbing his spirits of elasticity; or whether a canker of the mind was gradually eating, as such cankers do, from his moral system into the physical frame, which is but the shadow of the former. They looked for

the root of this trouble in his shattered schemes of domestic
bliss—wilfully shattered by himself—but could not be satisfied of its existence there. Some thought that their once brilliant friend was in an incipient stage of insanity, of which his
passionate impulses had perhaps been the forerunners; others
prognosticated a general blight and gradual decline. From
Roderick's own lips, they could learn nothing. More than
once, it is true, he had been heard to say, clutching his hands
convulsively upon his breast—"It gnaws me! It gnaws me!"—
but, by different auditors, a great diversity of explanation was
assigned to this ominous expression. What could it be, that
gnawed the breast of Roderick Elliston? Was it sorrow? Was it
merely the tooth of physical disease? Or, in his reckless course,
often verging upon profligacy, if not plunging into its depths,
had he been guilty of some deed, which made his bosom a
prey to the deadlier fangs of remorse? There was plausible
ground for each of these conjectures; but it must not be concealed that more than one elderly gentleman, the victim of
good cheer and slothful habits, magisterially pronounced the
secret of the whole matter to be Dyspepsia!

Meanwhile, Roderick seemed aware how generally he had
become the subject of curiosity and conjecture, and, with a
morbid repugnance to such notice, or to any notice whatso-
ever, estranged himself from all companionship. Not merely
the eye of man was a horror to him; not merely the light of a
friend's countenance; but even the blessed sunshine, likewise,
which, in its universal beneficence, typifies the radiance of the
Creator's face, expressing his love for all the creatures of his
hand. The dusky twilight was now too transparent for Roderick Elliston; the blackest midnight was his chosen hour to steal
abroad; and if ever he were seen, it was when the watchman's
lantern gleamed upon his figure, gliding along the street, with
his hands clutched upon his bosom, still muttering:—"It
gnaws me! It gnaws me!" What could it be that gnawed him?

After a time, it became known that Elliston was in the habit of resorting to all the noted quacks that infested the city, or whom money would tempt to journey thither from a distance. By one of these persons, in the exultation of a supposed cure, it was proclaimed far and wide, by dint of hand-bills and little pamphlets on dingy paper, that a distinguished gentleman, Roderick Elliston, Esq., had been relieved of a Snake in his stomach! So here was the monstrous secret, ejected from its lurking-place into public view, in all its horrible deformity. The mystery was out; but not so the bosom-serpent. He, if it were anything but a delusion, still lay coiled in his living den. The empiric's cure had been a sham, the effect, it was supposed, of some stupefying drug, which more nearly caused the death of the patient than of the odious reptile that possessed him. When Roderick Elliston regained entire sensibility, it was to find his misfortune the town talk—the more than nine days' wonder and horror—while, at his bosom, he felt the sickening motion of a thing alive, and the gnawing of that restless fang, which seemed to gratify at once a physical appetite and a fiendish spite.

He summoned the old black servant, who had been bred up in his father's house, and was a middle-aged man while Roderick lay in his cradle.

"Scipio!" he began; and then paused, with his arms folded over his heart—"What do people say of me, Scipio?"

"Sir! my poor master! that you had a serpent in your bosom," answered the servant, with hesitation.

"And what else?" asked Roderick, with a ghastly look at the man.

"Nothing else, dear master," replied Scipio;—"only that the Doctor gave you a powder, and that the snake leapt out upon the floor."

"No, no!" muttered Roderick to himself, as he shook his head, and pressed his hands with a more convulsive force upon his breast,—"I feel him still. It gnaws me! It gnaws me!"

From this time, the miserable sufferer ceased to shun the

world, but rather solicited and forced himself upon the notice
of acquaintances and strangers. It was partly the result of desperation, on finding that the cavern of his own bosom had not
proved deep and dark enough to hide the secret, even while it
was so secure a fortress for the loathsome fiend that had crept
into it. But still more, this craving for notoriety was a symptom of the intense morbidness which now pervaded his nature.
All persons, chronically diseased, are egotists, whether the disease be of the mind or body; whether it be sin, sorrow, or
merely the more tolerable calamity of some endless pain, or
mischief among the cords of mortal life. Such individuals are
made acutely conscious of a self, by the torture in which it
dwells. Self, therefore, grows to be so prominent an object
with them, that they cannot but present it to the face of every
casual passer-by. There is a pleasure—perhaps the greatest of
which the sufferer is susceptible—in displaying the wasted or
ulcerated limb, or the cancer in the breast; and the fouler the
crime, with so much the more difficulty does the perpetrator
prevent it from thrusting up its snake-like head, to frighten
the world; for it is that cancer, or that crime, which constitutes
their respective individuality. Roderick Elliston, who, a little
while before, had held himself so scornfully above the common
lot of men, now paid full allegiance to this humiliating law.
The snake in his bosom seemed the symbol of a monstrous egotism, to which everything was referred, and which he pampered, night and day, with a continual and exclusive sacrifice
of devil-worship.

He soon exhibited what most people considered indubitable
tokens of insanity. In some of his moods, strange to say, he
prided and gloried himself on being marked out from the ordinary experience of mankind, by the possession of a double nature, and a life within a life. He appeared to imagine that the
snake was a divinity—not celestial, it is true, but darkly infernal—and that he thence derived an eminence and a sanctity,

horrid, indeed, yet more desirable than whatever ambition aims at. Thus he drew his misery around him like a regal mantle, and looked down triumphantly upon those whose vitals nourished no deadly monster. Oftener, however, his human nature asserted its empire over him, in the shape of a yearning for fellowship. It grew to be his custom to spend the whole day in wandering about the streets, aimlessly, unless it might be called an aim, to establish a species of brotherhood between himself and the world. With cankered ingenuity, he sought out his own disease in every breast. Whether insane or not, he showed so keen a perception of frailty, error, and vice, that many persons gave him credit for being possessed not merely with a serpent, but with an actual fiend, who imparted this evil faculty of recognizing whatever was ugliest in man's heart.

For instance, he met an individual, who, for thirty years, had cherished a hatred against his own brother. Roderick, amidst the throng of the street, laid his hand on this man's chest, and looking full into his forbidding face,

"How is the snake to-day?"—he inquired, with a mock expression of sympathy.

"The snake!" exclaimed the brother-hater—"What do you mean?"

"The snake! The snake! Does he gnaw you?" persisted Roderick. "Did you take counsel with him, this morning, when you should have been saying your prayers? Did he sting, when you thought of your brother's health, wealth, and good repute? Did he caper for joy, when you remembered the profligacy of his only son? And whether he stung, or whether he frolicked, did you feel his poison throughout your body and soul, converting everything to sourness and bitterness? That is the way of such serpents. I have learned the whole nature of them from my own!"

"Where is the police?" roared the object of Roderick's persecution, at the same time giving an instinctive clutch to his breast. "Why is this lunatic allowed to go at large?"

"Ha, ha!" chuckled Roderick, releasing his grasp of the man.—"His bosom-serpent has stung him then!"

Often, it pleased the unfortunate young man to vex people with a lighter satire, yet still characterized by somewhat of snake-like virulence. One day, he encountered an ambitious statesman, and gravely inquired after the welfare of his boa constrictor; for of that species, Roderick affirmed, this gentleman's serpent must needs be, since its appetite was enormous enough to devour the whole country and constitution. At another time, he stopped a close-fisted old fellow, of great wealth, but who skulked about the city, in the guise of a scare-crow, with a patched blue surtout, brown hat, and mouldy boots, scraping pence together, and picking up rusty nails. Pretending to look earnestly at this respectable person's stomach, Roderick assured him that his snake was a copperhead, and had been generated by the immense quantities of that base metal, with which he daily defiled his fingers. Again, he assaulted a man of rubicund visage, and told him that few bosom-serpents had more of the devil in them, than those that breed in the vats of a distillery. The next whom Roderick honored with his attention was a distinguished clergyman, who happened just then to be engaged in a theological controversy, where human wrath was more perceptible than divine inspiration.

"You have swallowed a snake, in a cup of sacramental wine," quoth he.

"Profane wretch!" exclaimed the divine; but nevertheless, his hand stole to his breast.

He met a person of sickly sensibility, who, on some early disappointment, had retired from the world, and thereafter held no intercourse with his fellow-men, but brooded sullenly or passionately over the irrevocable past. This man's very heart, if Roderick might be believed, had been changed into a serpent, which would finally torment both him and itself to death. Observing a married couple, whose domestic troubles were matter of notoriety, he condoled with both on having mutually taken a house-adder to their bosoms. To an envious author, who depreciated works which he could never equal, he said, that his snake was the slimiest and filthiest of all the reptile tribe, but was fortunately without a sting. A man of impure life, and a brazen face, asking Roderick if there were any serpent in his breast, he told him that there was, and of the same species that once tortured Don Rodrigo, the Goth. He took a fair young girl by the hand, and gazing sadly into her eyes, warned her that she cherished a serpent of the deadliest kind within her gentle breast; and the world found the truth of those ominous words, when, a few months afterwards, the poor girl died of love and shame. Two ladies, rivals in fashionable life, who tormented one another with a thousand little stings of womanish spite, were given to understand, that each of their hearts was a nest of diminutive snakes, which did quite as much mischief as one great one.

But nothing seemed to please Roderick better, than to lay hold of a person infected with jealousy, which he represented as an enormous green reptile, with an ice-cold length of body, and the sharpest sting of any snake save one.

"And what one is that?" asked a bystander, overhearing him.

It was a dark-browed man, who put the question; he had an evasive eye, which, in the course of a dozen years, had looked no mortal directly in the face. There was an ambiguity about this person's character—a stain upon his reputation—yet none could tell precisely of what nature; although the city-gossips, male and female, whispered the most atrocious surmises. Until a recent period, he had followed the sea, and was, in fact, the very ship-master whom George Herkimer had encountered, under such singular circumstances, in the Grecian Archipelago.

"What bosom-serpent has the sharpest sting?" repeated this

man; but he put the question as if by a reluctant necessity, and grew pale while he was uttering it.

"Why need you ask?" replied Roderick, with a look of dark intelligence. "Look into your own breast! Hark, my serpent bestirs himself! He acknowledges the presence of a master-fiend!"

And then, as the bystanders afterwards affirmed, a hissing sound was heard, apparently in Roderick Elliston's breast. It was said, too, that an answering hiss came from the vitals of the shipmaster, as if a snake were actually lurking there, and had been aroused by the call of its brother-reptile. If there were in fact any such sound, it might have been caused by a malicious exercise of ventriloquism, on the part of Roderick.

Thus, making his own actual serpent—if a serpent there actually was in his bosom—the type of each man's fatal error, or hoarded sin, or unquiet conscience, and striking his sting so unremorsefully into the sorest spot, we may well imagine that Roderick became the pest of the city. Nobody could elude him; none could withstand him. He grappled with the ugliest truth that he could lay his hand on, and compelled his adversary to do the same. Strange spectacle in human life, where it is the instinctive effort of one and all to hide those sad realities, and leave them undisturbed beneath a heap of superficial topics, which constitute the materials of intercourse between man and man! It was not to be tolerated that Roderick Elliston should break through the tacit compact, by which the world has done its best to secure repose, without relinquishing evil. The victims of his malicious remarks, it is true, had brothers enough to keep them in countenance; for, by Roderick's theory, every mortal bosom harbored either a brood of small serpents, or one overgrown monster, that had devoured all the rest. Still, the city could not bear this new apostle. It was demanded by nearly all, and particularly by the most respectable inhabitants, that Roderick should no longer be permitted to violate the received rules of decorum, by obtruding his own bosom-serpent to the public gaze, and dragging those of decent people from their lurking-places.

Accordingly, his relatives interfered, and placed him in a private asylum for the insane. When the news was noised abroad, it was observed that many persons walked the streets with freer countenances, and covered their breasts less carefully with their hands.

His confinement, however, although it contributed not a little to the peace of the town, operated unfavorably upon Roderick himself. In solitude, his melancholy grew more black and sullen. He spent whole days—indeed, it was his sole occupation—in communing with the serpent. A conversation was sustained, in which as it seemed, the hidden monster bore a part, though unintelligibly to the listeners, and inaudible, except in a hiss. Singular as it may appear, the sufferer had now contracted a sort of affection for his tormentor; mingled, however, with the intensest loathing and horror. Nor were such discordant emotions incompatible; each, on the contrary, imparted strength and poignancy to its opposite. Horrible love—horrible antipathy—embracing one another in his bosom, and both concentrating themselves upon a being that had crept into his vitals, or been engendered there, and which was nourished with his food, and lived upon his life, and was as intimate with him as his own heart, and yet was the foulest of all created things! But not the less was it the true type of a morbid nature.

Sometimes, in his moments of rage and bitter hatred against the snake and himself, Roderick determined to be the death of him, even at the expense of his own life. Once he attempted it by starvation. But, while the wretched man was on the point of famishing, the monster seemed to feed upon his heart, and to thrive and wax gamesome, as if it were his sweetest and most congenial diet. Then he privily took a dose of active poison, imagining that it would not fail to kill either himself, or the devil that possessed him, or both together. Another mistake; for if Roderick had not yet been destroyed by his own poisoned heart, nor the snake by gnawing it, they had little to fear from arsenic or corrosive sublimate. Indeed, the venomous pest appeared to operate as an antidote against all other poisons. The physicians tried to suffocate the fiend with tobaccosmoke. He breathed it as freely as if it were his native atmosphere. Again, they drugged their patient with opium, and drenched him with intoxicating liquors, hoping that the snake might thus be reduced to stupor, and perhaps be ejected from the stomach. They succeeded in rendering Roderick insensible; but, placing their hands upon his breast, they were inexpressibly horror-stricken to feel the monster wriggling, twining, and darting to and fro, within his narrow limits, evidently enlivened by the opium or alcohol, and incited to unusual feats of activity. Thenceforth, they gave up all attempts at cure or palliation. The doomed sufferer submitted to his fate, resumed his former loathsome affection for the bosom-fiend, and spent whole miserable days before a looking glass, with his mouth wide open, watching, in hope and horror, to catch a glimpse of the snake's head, far down within his throat. It is supposed that he succeeded; for the attendants once heard a frenzied shout, and rushing into the room, found Roderick lifeless upon the floor.

He was kept but little longer under restraint. After minute investigation, the medical directors of the asylum decided that his mental disease did not amount to insanity, nor would warrant his confinement; especially as its influence upon his spirits was unfavorable, and might produce the evil which it was meant to remedy. His eccentricities were doubtless great—he had habitually violated many of the customs and prejudices of society; but the world was not, without surer ground, entitled to treat him as a madman. On this decision of such competent authority, Roderick was released, and had returned to his native city, the very day before his encounter with George Herkimer.

As soon as possible after learning these particulars, the sculptor, together with a sad and tremulous companion, sought Elliston at his own house. It was a large, sombre edifice of wood with pilasters and a balcony, and was divided from one of the principal streets by a terrace of three elevations, which was ascended by successive flights of stone steps. Some immense old elms almost concealed the front of the mansion. This spacious and once magnificent family-residence was built by a grandee of the race, early in the past century; at which epoch, land being of small comparative value, the garden and other grounds had formed quite an extensive domain. Although a portion of the ancestral heritage had been alienated, there was still a shadowy enclosure in the rear of the mansion, where a student, or a dreamer, or a man of stricken heart, might lie all day upon the grass, amid the solitude of murmuring boughs, and forget that a city had grown up around him.

Into this retirement, the sculptor and his companion were ushered by Scipio, the old black servant, whose wrinkled visage grew almost sunny with intelligence and joy, as he paid his humble greetings to one of the two visitors.

"Remain in the arbor," whispered the sculptor to the figure that leaned upon his arm, "you will know whether, and when, to make your appearance."

"God will teach me," was the reply. "May he support me too!"

Roderick was reclining on the margin of a fountain, which gushed into the fleckered sunshine with the same clear sparkle, and the same voice of airy quietude, as when trees of primeval growth flung their shadows across its bosom. How strange is the life of a fountain, born at every moment, yet of an age coeval with the rocks, and far surpassing the venerable antiquity of a forest!

"You are come! I have expected you," said Elliston, when he became aware of the sculptor's presence.

His manner was very different from that of the preceding

day—quiet, courteous, and, as Herkimer thought, watchful both over his guest and himself. This unnatural restraint was almost the only trait that betokened anything amiss. He had just thrown a book upon the grass, where it lay half-opened, thus disclosing itself to be a natural history of the serpent-tribe, illustrated by life-like plates. Near it lay that bulky volume, the Ductor Dubitantium of Jeremy Taylor, full of cases of conscience, and in which most men, possessed of a conscience, may find something applicable to their purpose.

"You see," observed Elliston, pointing to the book of serpents, while a smile gleamed upon his lips, "I am making an effort to become better acquainted with my bosom-friend. But I find nothing satisfactory in this volume. If I mistake not, he will prove to be *sui generis,* and akin to no other reptile in creation."

"Whence came this strange calamity?" inquired the sculptor.

"My sable friend, Scipio, has a story," replied Roderick, "of a snake that had lurked in this fountain—pure and innocent as it looks—ever since it was known to the first settlers. This insinuating personage once crept into the vitals of my great-grandfather, and dwelt there many years, tormenting the old gentleman beyond mortal endurance. In short, it is a family peculiarity. But, to tell you the truth, I have no faith in this idea of the snake's being an heir-loom. He is my own snake, and no man's else."

"But what was his origin?" demanded Herkimer.

"Oh! there is poisonous stuff in any man's heart, sufficient to generate a brood of serpents," said Elliston, with a hollow laugh. "You should have heard my homilies to the good townspeople. Positively, I deem myself fortunate in having bred but a single serpent. You, however, have none in your bosom, and therefore, cannot sympathize with the rest of the world. It gnaws me! It gnaws me!"

With this exclamation, Roderick lost his self-control and threw himself upon the grass, testifying his agony by intricate writhings, in which Herkimer could not but fancy a resemblance to the motions of a snake. Then, likewise, was heard that frightful hiss, which often ran through the sufferer's speech, and crept between the words and syllables, without interrupting their succession.

"This is awful indeed!" exclaimed the sculptor—"an awful infliction, whether it be actual or imaginary! Tell me, Roderick Elliston, is there any remedy for this loathsome evil?"

"Yes, but an impossible one," muttered Roderick, as he lay wallowing with his face in the grass. "Could I, for one instant, forget myself, the serpent might not abide within me. It is my diseased self-contemplation that has engendered and nourished him!"

"Then forget yourself, my husband," said a gentle voice above him—"forget yourself in the idea of another!"

Rosina had emerged from the arbor, and was bending over him, with the shadow of his anguish reflected in her countenance, yet so mingled with hope and unselfish love, that all anguish seemed but an earthly shadow and a dream. She touched Roderick with her hand. A tremor shivered through his frame. At that moment, if report be trustworthy, the sculptor beheld a waving motion through the grass, and heard a tinkling sound, as if something had plunged into the fountain. Be the truth as it might, it is certain that Roderick Elliston sat up, like a man renewed, restored to his right mind, and rescued from the fiend, which had so miserably overcome him in the battle-field of his own breast.

"Rosina!" cried he, in broken and passionate tones, but with nothing of the wild wail that had haunted his voice so long. "Forgive! Forgive!"

Her happy tears bedewed his face.

"The punishment has been severe," observed the sculptor. "Even Justice might now forgive—how much more a woman's tenderness! Roderick Elliston, whether the serpent was a physical reptile, or whether the morbidness of your nature suggested that symbol to your fancy, the moral of the story is not the less true and strong. A tremendous Egotism—manifesting itself, in your case, in the form of jealousy—is as fearful a fiend as ever stole into the human heart. Can a breast, where it has dwelt so long, be purified?"

"Oh, yes!" said Rosina, with a heavenly smile. "The serpent was but a dark fantasy, and what it typified was as shadowy as itself. The past, dismal as it seems, shall fling no gloom upon the future. To give it its due importance, we must think of it but as an anecdote in our Eternity!"

The Christmas Banquet

FROM THE UNPUBLISHED
"ALLEGORIES OF THE HEART"

"I HAVE here attempted," said Roderick, unfolding a few sheets of manuscript, as he sat with Rosina and the sculptor in the summer-house——"I have attempted to seize hold of a personage who glides past me, occasionally, in my walk through life. My former sad experience, as you know, has gifted me with some degree of insight into the gloomy mysteries of the human heart, through which I have wandered like one astray in a dark cavern, with his torch fast flickering to extinction. But this man——this class of men——is a hopeless puzzle."

"Well, but propound him," said the sculptor. "Let us have an idea of him, to begin with."

"Why, indeed," replied Roderick, "he is such a being as I could conceive you to carve out of marble, and some yet unrealized perfection of human science to endow with an exquisite mockery of intellect; but still there lacks the last inestimable touch of a divine Creator. He looks like a man, and, perchance, like a better specimen of man than you ordinarily meet. You might esteem him wise——he is capable of cultivation and refinement, and has at least an external conscience—— but the demands that spirit makes upon spirit, are precisely those to which he cannot respond. When, at last, you come close to him, you find him chill and unsubstantial——a mere vapor."

"I believe," said Rosina, "I have a glimmering idea of what you mean."

"Then be thankful," answered her husband, smiling; "but do not anticipate any further illumination from what I am about to read. I have here imagined such a man to be—what, probably, he never is—conscious of the deficiency in his spiritual organization. Methinks the result would be a sense of cold unreality, wherewith he would go shivering through the world, longing to exchange his load of ice for any burthen of real grief that fate could fling upon a human being."

Contenting himself with this preface, Roderick began to read.

In a certain old gentleman's last will and testament, there appeared a bequest, which, as his final thought and deed, was singularly in keeping with a long life of melancholy eccentricity. He devised a considerable sum for establishing a fund, the interest of which was to be expended, annually forever, in preparing a Christmas Banquet for ten of the most miserable persons that could be found. It seemed not to be the testator's purpose to make these half-a-score of sad hearts merry, but to provide that the stern or fierce expression of human discontent should not be drowned, even for that one holy and joyful day, amid the acclamations of festal gratitude which all Christendom sends up. And he desired, likewise, to perpetuate his own remonstrance against the earthly course of Providence, and his sad and sour dissent from those systems of religion or philosophy which either find sunshine in the world, or draw it down from heaven.

The task of inviting the guests, or of selecting among such as might advance their claims to partake of this dismal hospitality, was confided to the two trustees or stewards of the fund. These gentlemen, like their deceased friend, were sombre humorists, who made it their principal occupation to number the sable threads in the web of human life, and drop all the golden ones out of the reckoning. They performed their present office with integrity and judgment. The aspect of the assembled company, on the day of the first festival, might not, it is true, have satisfied every beholder that these were especially the individuals, chosen forth from all the world, whose griefs were worthy to stand as indicators of the mass of human suffering. Yet, after due consideration, it could not be disputed that here was a variety of hopeless discomfort, which, if it sometimes arose from causes apparently inadequate, was thereby only the shrewder imputation against the nature and mechanism of life.

The arrangements and decorations of the banquet were probably intended to signify that death-in-life which had been the testator's definition of existence. The hall, illuminated by torches, was hung round with curtains of deep and dusky purple, and adorned with branches of cypress and wreaths of artificial flowers, imitative of such as used to be strewn over the dead. A sprig of parsley was laid by every plate. The main reservoir of wine was a sepulchral urn of silver, whence the liquor was distributed around the table in small vases, accurately copied from those that held the tears of ancient mourners. Neither had the stewards—if it were their taste that arranged these details—forgotten the fantasy of the old Egyptians, who seated a skeleton at every festive board, and mocked their own merriment with the imperturbable grin of a death's-head. Such a fearful guest, shrouded in a black mantle, sat now at the head of the table. It was whispered, I know not with what truth, that the testator himself had once walked the visible world with the machinery of that same skeleton, and that it was one of the stipulations of his will, that he should thus be permitted to sit, from year to year, at the banquet which he had instituted. If so, it was perhaps covertly implied that he had cherished no hopes of bliss beyond the grave to compensate for the evils which he felt or imagined here. And if, in their bewildered conjectures as to the purpose of earthly existence, the banqueters should throw aside the veil, and cast an inquiring glance at this figure of death, as seeking thence the solution otherwise unattainable, the only reply would be a stare of the vacant eye-caverns, and a grin of the skeleton-jaws. Such was the response that the dead man had fancied himself to receive, when he asked of Death to solve the riddle of his life; and it was his desire to repeat it when the guests of his dismal hospitality should find themselves perplexed with the same question.

"What means that wreath?" asked several of the company, while viewing the decorations of the table.

They alluded to a wreath of cypress, which was held on high by a skeleton-arm, protruding from within the black mantle.

"It is a crown," said one of the stewards, "not for the worthiest, but for the wofullest, when he shall prove his claim to it."

The guest earliest bidden to the festival, was a man of soft and gentle character, who had not energy to struggle against the heavy despondency to which his temperament rendered him liable; and therefore, with nothing outwardly to excuse him from happiness, he had spent a life of quiet misery, that made his blood torpid, and weighed upon his breath, and sat like a ponderous night-fiend upon every throb of his unresisting heart. His wretchedness seemed as deep as his original nature, if not identical with it. It was the misfortune of a second guest to cherish within his bosom a diseased heart, which had become so wretchedly sore, that the continual and unavoidable rubs of the world, the blow of an enemy, the careless jostle of a stranger, and even the faithful and loving touch of a friend, alike made ulcers in it. As is the habit of people thus afflicted, he found his chief employment in exhibiting these miserable sores to any who would give themselves the pain of viewing them. A third guest was a hypochondriac, whose imagination wrought necromancy in his outward and inward world, and caused him to see monstrous faces in the household fire, and dragons in the clouds of sunset, and fiends in the guise of beautiful women, and something ugly or wicked beneath all the pleasant surfaces of nature. His neighbor at table was one who, in his early youth, had trusted mankind too much, and hoped too highly in their behalf, and, in meeting with many disappointments, had become desperately soured. For several years back, this misanthrope had employed himself in accumulating motives for hating and despising his race—such as murder, lust, treachery, ingratitude, faithlessness of trusted friends, instinctive vices of children, impurity of women, hidden guilt in men of saint-like aspect—and, in short, all manner of black realities that sought to decorate themselves with outward grace or glory. But, at every atrocious fact that was added to his catalogue—at every increase of the sad knowledge which he spent his life to collect—the native impulses of the poor man's loving and confiding heart made him groan with anguish. Next, with his heavy brow bent downward, there stole into the hall a man naturally earnest and impassioned, who, from his immemorial infancy, had felt the consciousness of a high message to the world, but, essaying to deliver it, had found either no voice or form of speech, or else no ears to listen. Therefore his whole life was a bitter questioning of himself—"Why have not men acknowledged my mission? Am I not a self-deluding fool? What business have I on earth? Where is my grave?" Throughout the festival, he quaffed frequent draughts from the sepulchral urn of wine, hoping thus to quench the celestial fire that tortured his own breast, and could not benefit his race.

Then there entered—having flung away a ticket for a ball— a gay gallant of yesterday, who had found four or five wrinkles in his brow, and more grey hairs than he could well number, on his head. Endowed with sense and feeling, he had nevertheless spent his youth in folly, but had reached at last that dreary point in life, where Folly quits us of her own accord, leaving us to make friends with Wisdom if we can. Thus, cold and desolate, he had come to seek Wisdom at the banquet, and wondered if the skeleton were she. To eke out the company, the stewards had invited a distressed poet from his home in the alms-house, and a melancholy idiot from the street corner. The latter had just the glimmering of sense that was sufficient to make him conscious of a vacancy, which the poor fellow, all his life long, had mistily sought to fill up with intelligence, wandering up and down the streets, and groaning miserably, because his attempts were ineffectual. The only lady in the hall was one who had fallen short of absolute and perfect beauty, merely by the trifling defect of a slight cast in her left eye. But this blemish, minute as it was, so shocked the pure ideal of her soul, rather than her vanity, that she passed her life in solitude, and veiled her countenance even from her own gaze. So the skeleton sat shrouded at one end of the table, and this poor lady at the other.

One other guest remains to be described. He was a young man of smooth brow, fair cheek, and fashionable mien. So far as his exterior developed him, he might much more suitably have found a place at some merry Christmas table, than have been numbered among the blighted, fate-stricken, fancy-tortured set of ill-starred banqueters. Murmurs arose among the guests, as they noted the glance of general scrutiny which the intruder threw over his companions. What had he to do among them? Why did not the skeleton of the dead founder of the feast unbend its rattling joints, arise, and motion the unwelcome stranger from the board?

"Shameful!" said the morbid man, while a new ulcer broke out in his heart. "He comes to mock us!—we shall be the jest of his tavern friends!—he will make a farce of our miseries, and bring it out upon the stage!"

"Oh, never mind him!" said the hypochondriac, smiling sourly. "He shall feast from yonder tureen of viper soup, and if there is a fricassee of scorpions on the table, pray let him have his share of it. For the dessert, he shall taste the apples of Sodom. Then, if he like our Christmas fare, let him return again next year!"

"Trouble him not," murmured the melancholy man, with gentleness. "What matters it whether the consciousness of misery come a few years sooner or later? If this youth deem himself happy now, yet let him sit with us, for the sake of the wretch-edness to come."

The poor idiot approached the young man, with that mourn-ful aspect of vacant inquiry which his face continually wore, and which caused people to say that he was always in search of his missing wits. After no little examination, he touched the stranger's hand, but immediately drew back his own, shaking his head and shivering.

"Cold, cold, cold!" muttered the idiot.

The young man shivered too—and smiled.

"Gentlemen—and you, madam,"—said one of the stewards of the festival, "do not conceive so ill, either of our caution or judgment, as to imagine that we have admitted this young stranger—Gervayse Hastings by name—without a full investi-gation and thoughtful balance of his claims. Trust me, not a guest at the table is better entitled to his seat."

The steward's guarantee was perforce satisfactory. The com-pany, therefore, took their places, and addressed themselves to the serious business of the feast, but were soon disturbed by the hypochondriac, who thrust back his chair, complaining that a dish of stewed toads and vipers was set before him, and that there was green ditch-water in his cup of wine. This mistake be-ing amended, he quietly resumed his seat. The wine, as it flowed freely from the sepulchral urn, seemed to come imbued with all gloomy inspirations; so that its influence was not to cheer, but either to sink the revellers into a deeper melancholy, or elevate their spirits to an enthusiasm of wretchedness. The conversation was various. They told sad stories about people who might have been worthy guests at such a festival as the present. They talked of grisly incidents in human history; of strange crimes, which, if truly considered, were but convul-sions of agony; of some lives that had been altogether wretched, and of others, which, wearing a general semblance of happi-ness, had yet been deformed, sooner or later, by misfortune, as by the intrusion of a grim face at a banquet; of death-bed scenes, and what dark intimations might be gathered from the words of dying men; of suicide, and whether the more eligible mode were by halter, knife, poison, drowning, gradual starvation, or the fumes of charcoal. The majority of the guests, as is the custom with people thoroughly and profoundly sick at heart, were anxious to make their own woes the theme of discussion, and prove themselves most excellent in anguish. The misanthropist went deep into the philosophy of evil, and wandered about in the darkness, with now and then a gleam of discolored light hovering on ghastly shapes and horrid scenery. Many a miserable thought, such as men have stumbled upon from age to age, did he now rake up again, and gloat over it as an inestimable gem, a diamond, a treasure far preferable to those bright, spiritual revelations of a better world, which are like precious stones from heaven's pavement. And then, amid his lore of wretchedness, he hid his face and wept.

It was a festival at which the woful man of Uz might suitably have been a guest, together with all, in each succeeding age, who have tasted deepest of the bitterness of life. And be it said, too, that every son or daughter of woman, however favored with happy fortune, might, at one sad moment or another, have claimed the privilege of a stricken heart, to sit down at this table. But, throughout the feast, it was remarked that the young stranger, Gervayse Hastings, was unsuccessful in his attempts to catch its pervading spirit. At any deep, strong thought that found utterance, and which was torn out, as it were, from the saddest recesses of human consciousness, he looked mystified and bewildered; even more than the poor idiot, who seemed to grasp at such things with his earnest heart, and thus occasionally to comprehend them. The young man's conversation was of a colder and lighter kind, often brilliant, but lacking the powerful characteristics of a nature that had been developed by suffering.

"Sir," said the misanthropist, bluntly, in reply to some observation by Gervayse Hastings, "pray do not address me again. We have no right to talk together. Our minds have nothing in common. By what claim you appear at this banquet, I cannot guess; but methinks, to a man who could say what you have just now said, my companions and myself must seem no more than shadows, flickering on the wall. And precisely such a shadow are you to us!"

The young man smiled and bowed, but drawing himself back in his chair, he buttoned his coat over his breast, as if the banqueting-hall were growing chill. Again the idiot fixed his melancholy stare upon the youth, and murmured—"Cold! cold! cold!"

The banquet drew to its conclusion, and the guests departed. Scarcely had they stepped across the threshold of the hall, when the scene that had there passed seemed like the vision of a sick fancy, or an exhalation from a stagnant heart. Now and then, however, during the year that ensued, these melancholy people caught glimpses of one another, transient, indeed, but enough to prove that they walked the earth with the ordinary allotment of reality. Sometimes, a pair of them came face to face, while stealing through the evening twilight, enveloped in their sable cloaks. Sometimes, they casually met in church-yards. Once, also, it happened, that two of the dismal banqueters mutually started, at recognizing each other in the noon-day sunshine of a crowded street, stalking there like ghosts astray. Doubtless, they wondered why the skeleton did not come abroad at noon-day, too!

But, whenever the necessity of their affairs compelled these Christmas guests into the bustling world, they were sure to encounter the young man, who had so unaccountably been admitted to the festival. They saw him among the gay and fortunate; they caught the sunny sparkle of his eye; they heard the light and careless tones of his voice—and muttered to themselves, with such indignation as only the aristocracy of wretchedness could kindle:—"The traitor! The vile impostor! Providence, in its own good time, may give him a right to feast among us!" But the young man's unabashed eye dwelt upon their gloomy figures, as they passed him, seeming to say, perchance with somewhat of a sneer—"First, know my secret!—then, measure your claims with mine!"

The step of Time stole onward, and soon brought merry Christmas round again, with glad and solemn worship in the churches, and sports, games, festivals, and everywhere the bright face of Joy beside the household fire. Again, likewise, the hall, with its curtains of dusky purple, was illuminated by the death-torches, gleaming on the sepulchral decorations of the banquet. The veiled skeleton sat in state, lifting the cypress wreath above its head, as the guerdon of some guest, illustrious in the qualifications which there claimed precedence. As the stewards deemed the world inexhaustible in misery, and were desirous of recognizing it in all its forms, they had not seen fit to re-assemble the company of the former year. New faces now threw their gloom across the table.

There was a man of nice conscience, who bore a blood-stain in his heart—the death of a fellow-creature—which, for his more exquisite torture, had chanced with such a peculiarity of circumstances, that he could not absolutely determine whether his will had entered into the deed, or not. Therefore, his whole life was spent in the agony of an inward trial for murder, with a continual sifting of the details of his terrible calamity, until his mind had no longer any thought, nor his soul any emotion, disconnected with it. There was a mother, too—a mother once, but a desolation now—who, many years before, had gone out on a pleasure-party, and, returning, found her infant smothered in its little bed. And ever since she had been tortured with the fantasy, that her buried baby lay smothering in its coffin. Then there was an aged lady, who had lived from time immemorial with a constant tremor quivering through her frame. It was terrible to discern her dark shadow tremulous upon the wall; her lips, likewise, were tremulous; and the expression of her eyes seemed to indicate that her soul was trembling too. Owing to the bewilderment and confusion which made almost a chaos of her intellect, it was impossible to discover what dire misfortune had thus shaken her nature to its depths; so that the stewards had admitted her to the table, not from any acquaintance with her history, but on the safe testimony of her miserable aspect. Some surprise was expressed at the presence of a bluff, red-faced gentleman, a certain Mr. Smith, who had evidently the fat of many a rich feast within him, and the habitual twinkle of whose eye betrayed a disposition to break forth into uproarious laughter, for little cause or none. It turned out, however, that, with the best possible flow of spirits, our poor friend was afflicted with a physical disease of the heart, which threatened instant death on the slightest cachinnatory indulgence, or even that titillation of the bodily frame, produced by merry thoughts. In this dilemma, he had sought admittance to the banquet, on the ostensible plea of his irksome and miserable state, but, in reality, with the hope of imbibing a life-preserving melancholy.

A married couple had been invited, from a motive of bitter humor; it being well understood, that they rendered each other unutterably miserable whenever they chanced to meet, and therefore must necessarily be fit associates at the festival. In contrast with these, was another couple, still unmarried, who had interchanged their hearts in early life, but had been divided by circumstances as impalpable as morning mist, and kept apart so long, that their spirits now found it impossible to meet. Therefore, yearning for communion, yet shrinking from one another, and choosing none beside, they felt themselves companionless in life, and looked upon eternity as a boundless desert. Next to the skeleton sat a mere son of earth—a haunter of the Exchange—a gatherer of shining dust—a man whose life's record was in his leger, and whose soul's prison-house, the vaults of the bank where he kept his deposits. This person had been greatly perplexed at his invitation, deeming himself one of the most fortunate men in the city; but the stewards persisted in demanding his presence, assuring him that he had no conception how miserable he was.

And now appeared a figure, which we must acknowledge as our acquaintance of the former festival. It was Gervayse Hastings, whose presence had then caused so much question and criticism, and who now took his place with the composure of one whose claims were satisfactory to himself, and must needs be allowed by others. Yet his easy and unruffled face betrayed no sorrow. The well-skilled beholders gazed a moment into his eyes, and shook their heads, to miss the unuttered sympathy—the countersign, never to be falsified—of those whose hearts are cavern-mouths, through which they descend into a region of illimitable wo, and recognize other wanderers there.

"Who is this youth?" asked the man with a blood-stain on his conscience. "Surely he has never gone down into the depths! I know all the aspects of those who have passed through the dark valley. By what right is he among us?"

"Ah, it is a sinful thing to come hither without a sorrow," murmured the aged lady, in accents that partook of the eternal tremor which pervaded her whole being. "Depart, young man! Your soul has never been shaken; and therefore I tremble so much the more to look at you."

"His soul shaken! No; I'll answer for it," said bluff Mr. Smith, pressing his hand upon his heart, and making himself as melancholy as he could, for fear of a fatal explosion of laughter. "I know the lad well; he has as fair prospects as any young man about town, and has no more right among us, miserable creatures, than the child unborn. He never was miserable, and probably never will be!"

"Our honored guests," interposed the stewards, "pray have patience with us, and believe, at least, that our deep veneration for the sacredness of this solemnity would preclude any wilful violation of it. Receive this young man to your table. It may not be too much to say, that no guest here would exchange his own heart for the one that beats within that youthful bosom!"

"I'd call it a bargain, and gladly too," muttered Mr. Smith, with a perplexing mixture of sadness and mirthful conceit. "A plague upon their nonsense! My own heart is the only really miserable one in the company—it will certainly be the death of me at last!"

Nevertheless, as on the former occasion, the judgment of the stewards being without appeal, the company sat down. The obnoxious guest made no more attempt to obtrude his conversation on those about him, but appeared to listen to the table-talk with peculiar assiduity, as if some inestimable secret, otherwise beyond his reach, might be conveyed in a casual word. And, in truth, to those who could understand and value it, there was rich matter in the upgushings and outpourings of these initiated souls, to whom sorrow had been a talisman, admitting them into spiritual depths which no other spell can open. Sometimes, out of the midst of densest gloom, there flashed a momentary radiance, pure as crystal, bright as the flame of stars, and shedding such a glow upon the mystery of life, that the guests were ready to exclaim, "Surely the riddle is on the point of being solved!" At such illuminated intervals, the saddest mourners felt it to be revealed, that mortal griefs are but shadowy and external; no more than the sable robes, voluminously shrouding a certain divine reality, and thus indicating what might otherwise be altogether invisible to mortal eye.

"Just now," remarked the trembling old woman, "I seemed to see beyond the outside. And then my everlasting tremor passed away!"

"Would that I could dwell always in these momentary gleams of light!" said the man of stricken conscience. "Then the blood-stain in my heart would be washed clean away."

This strain of conversation appeared so unintelligibly absurd to good Mr. Smith, that he burst into precisely the fit of laughter which his physicians had warned him against, as likely to prove instantaneously fatal. In effect, he fell back in his chair, a corpse with a broad grin upon his face; while his ghost, perchance, remained beside it, bewildered at its unpremeditated exit. This catastrophe, of course, broke up the festival.

"How is this? You do not tremble?" observed the tremulous old woman to Gervayse Hastings, who was gazing at the dead man with singular intentness. "Is it not awful to see him so suddenly vanish out of the midst of life—this man of flesh and blood, whose earthly nature was so warm and strong? There is a never-ending tremor in my soul; but it trembles afresh at this! And you are calm!"

"Would that he could teach me somewhat!" said Gervayse Hastings, drawing a long breath. "Men pass before me like shadows on the wall—their actions, passions, feelings, are flickerings of the light—and then they vanish! Neither the corpse, nor yonder skeleton, nor this old woman's everlasting tremor, can give me what I seek."

And then the company departed.

We cannot linger to narrate, in such detail, more circumstances of these singular festivals, which, in accordance with the founder's will, continued to be kept with the regularity of an established institution. In process of time, the stewards adopted the custom of inviting, from far and near, those individuals whose misfortunes were prominent above other men's, and whose mental and moral development might, therefore, be supposed to possess a corresponding interest. The exiled noble of the French Revolution, and the broken soldier of the Empire, were alike represented at the table. Fallen monarchs, wandering about the earth, have found places at that forlorn and miserable feast. The statesman, when his party flung him off, might, if he chose it, be once more a great man for the space of a single banquet. Aaron Burr's name appears on the record, at a period when his ruin—the profoundest and most striking, with more of moral circumstance in it than that of almost any other man—was complete, in his lonely age. Stephen Girard, when his wealth weighed upon him like a mountain, once sought admittance of his own accord. It is not probable, however, that these men had any lessons to teach in the lore of discontent and misery, which might not equally well have been studied in the common walks of life. Illustrious unfortunates attract a wider sympathy, not because their griefs are more intense, but because, being set on lofty pedestals, they the better serve mankind as instances and by-words of calamity.

It concerns our present purpose to say that, at each successive festival, Gervayse Hastings showed his face, gradually changing from the smooth beauty of his youth to the thoughtful comeliness of manhood, and thence to the bald, impressive dignity of age. He was the only individual invariably present. Yet, on every occasion, there were murmurs, both from those who knew his character and position, and from them whose hearts shrank back, as denying his companionship in their mystic fraternity.

"Who is this impassive man?" had been asked a hundred times. "Has he suffered? Has he sinned? There are no traces of either. Then wherefore is he here?"

"You must inquire of the stewards, or of himself," was the constant reply. "We seem to know him well, here in our city, and know nothing of him but what is creditable and fortunate. Yet hither he comes, year after year, to this gloomy banquet, and sits among the guests like a marble statue. Ask yonder skeleton—perhaps that may solve the riddle!"

It was, in truth, a wonder. The life of Gervayse Hastings was not merely a prosperous, but a brilliant one. Everything had gone well with him. He was wealthy, far beyond the expenditure that was required by habits of magnificence, a taste of rare purity and cultivation, a love of travel, a scholar's instinct to collect a splendid library, and, moreover, what seemed a munificent liberality to the distressed. He had sought domestic happiness, and not vainly, if a lovely and tender wife, and children of fair promise, could insure it. He had, besides, ascended above the limit which separates the obscure from the distinguished, and had won a stainless reputation in affairs of the widest public importance. Not that he was a popular character, or had within him the mysterious attributes which are essential to that species of success. To the public, he was a cold abstraction, wholly destitute of those rich hues of personality, that living warmth, and the peculiar faculty of stamping his own heart's impression on a multitude of hearts, by which the people recognize their favorites. And it must be owned that, after his most intimate associates had done their best to know him thoroughly, and love him warmly, they were startled to find how little hold he had upon their affections. They approved—they admired—but still, in those moments when the human spirit most craves reality, they shrank back from Gervayse Hastings, as powerless to give them what they sought. It was the feeling of distrustful regret, with which we should draw back the hand, after extending it, in an illusive twilight, to grasp the hand of a shadow upon the wall.

As the superficial fervency of youth decayed, this peculiar effect of Gervayse Hastings' character grew more perceptible. His children, when he extended his arms, came coldly to his knees, but never climbed them of their own accord. His wife wept secretly, and almost adjudged herself a criminal, because she shivered in the chill of his bosom. He, too, occasionally appeared not unconscious of the chillness of his moral atmosphere, and willing, if it might be so, to warm himself at a kindly fire. But age stole onward, and benumbed him more and more. As the hoar-frost began to gather on him, his wife went to her grave, and was doubtless warmer there; his children either died, or were scattered to different homes of their own; and old Gervayse Hastings, unscathed by grief—alone, but needing no companionship—continued his steady walk through life, and still, on every Christmas-day, attended at the dismal banquet. His privilege as a guest had become prescriptive now. Had he claimed the head of the table, even the skeleton would have been ejected from its seat.

Finally, at the merry Christmas-tide, when he had numbered four-score years complete, this pale, high-browed, marble-featured old man once more entered the long-frequented hall, with the same impassive aspect that had called forth so much dissatisfied remark at his first attendance. Time, except in matters merely external, had done nothing for him, either of good or evil. As he took his place, he threw a calm, inquiring glance around the table, as if to ascertain whether any guest had yet appeared, after so many unsuccessful banquets, who might impart to him the mystery—the deep, warm secret—the life within the life—which, whether manifested in joy or sorrow, is what gives substance to a world of shadows.

"My friends," said Gervayse Hastings, assuming a position which his long conversance with the festival caused to appear natural, "you are welcome! I drink to you all in this cup of sepulchral wine."

The guests replied courteously, but still in a manner that proved them unable to receive the old man as a member of their sad fraternity. It may be well to give the reader an idea of the present company at the banquet.

One was formerly a clergyman, enthusiastic in his profession, and apparently of the genuine dynasty of those old Puritan divines whose faith in their calling, and stern exercise of it, had placed them among the mighty of the earth. But, yielding to the speculative tendency of the age, he had gone astray from the firm foundation of an ancient faith, and wandered into a cloud region, where everything was misty and deceptive, ever mocking him with a semblance of reality, but still dissolving when he flung himself upon it for support and rest. His instinct and early training demanded something steadfast; but, looking forward, he beheld vapors piled on vapors, and, behind him, an impassable gulf between the man of yesterday and to-day; on the borders of which he paced to and fro, sometimes wringing his hands in agony, and often making his own wo a theme of scornful merriment. This, surely, was a miserable man. Next, there was a theorist—one of a numerous tribe, although he deemed himself unique since the creation—a theorist, who had conceived a plan by which all the wretchedness of earth, moral and physical, might be done away, and the bliss of the millennium at once accomplished. But, the incredulity of mankind debarring him from action, he was smitten with as much grief as if the whole mass of wo which he was denied the opportunity to remedy, were crowded into his own bosom. A plain old man in black attracted much of the company's notice, on the supposition that he was no other than Father Miller, who, it seemed, had given himself up to despair at the tedious delay of the final conflagration. Then there was a man distinguished for native pride and obstinacy, who, a little while before, had possessed immense wealth, and held the control of a vast moneyed interest, which he had wielded in the same spirit as a despotic monarch would wield the power of his empire, carrying on a tremendous moral warfare, the roar and tremor of which was felt at every fireside in the land. At length came a crushing ruin—a total overthrow of fortune, power, and character—the effect of which on his imperious, and, in many respects, noble and lofty nature, might have entitled him to a place, not merely at our festival, but among the peers of Pandemonium.

There was a modern philanthropist, who had become so deeply sensible of the calamities of thousands and millions of his fellow creatures, and of the impracticableness of any general measures for their relief, that he had no heart to do what little good lay immediately within his power, but contented himself with being miserable for sympathy. Near him sat a gentleman in a predicament hitherto unprecedented, but of which the present epoch, probably, affords numerous examples. Ever since he was of capacity to read a newspaper, this person had prided himself on his consistent adherence to one political party, but, in the confusion of these latter days, had got bewildered, and knew not whereabouts his party was. This wretched condition, so morally desolate and disheartening to a man who has long accustomed himself to merge his individuality in the mass of a great body, can only be conceived by such as have experienced it. His next companion was a popular orator who had lost his voice, and—as it was pretty much all that he had to lose—had fallen into a state of hopeless melancholy. The table was likewise graced by two of the gentler sex—one, a half-starved, consumptive seamstress, the representative of thousands just as wretched; the other, a woman of unemployed energy, who found herself in the world with nothing to achieve, nothing to enjoy, and nothing even to suffer. She had, therefore, driven herself to the verge of madness by dark broodings over the wrongs of her sex, and its exclusion from a proper field of action. The roll of guests being thus complete, a side-table had been set for three or four disappointed office-seekers, with hearts as sick as death, whom the stewards had admitted, partly because their calamities really entitled them to entrance here, and partly that they were in especial need of a good dinner. There was likewise a homeless dog, with his tail between his legs, licking up the crumbs and gnawing the fragments of the feast—such a melancholy cur as one sometimes sees about the streets, without a master, and willing to follow the first that will accept his service.

In their own way, these were as wretched a set of people as ever had assembled at the festival. There they sat, with the veiled skeleton of the founder, holding aloft the cypress wreath, at one end of the table; and at the other, wrapt in furs, the withered figure of Gervayse Hastings, stately, calm, and cold, impressing the company with awe, yet so little interesting their sympathy, that he might have vanished into thin air, without their once exclaiming—"Whither is he gone?"

"Sir," said the philanthropist, addressing the old man, "you have been so long a guest at this annual festival, and have thus been conversant with so many varieties of human affliction, that, not improbably, you have thence derived some great and important lessons. How blessed were your lot, could you reveal a secret by which all this mass of wo might be removed!"

"I know of but one misfortune," answered Gervayse Hastings, quietly, "and that is my own."

"Your own!" rejoined the philanthropist. "And, looking back on your serene and prosperous life, how can you claim to be the sole unfortunate of the human race?"

"You will not understand it," replied Gervayse Hastings, feebly, and with a singular inefficiency of pronunciation, and sometimes putting one word for another. "None have understood it—not even those who experience the like. It is a chillness—a want of earnestness—a feeling as if what should be my heart were a thing of vapor—a haunting perception of unreality! Thus, seeming to possess all that other men have—all that men aim at—I have really possessed nothing, neither joys nor griefs. All things—all persons—as was truly said to me at this table long and long ago—have been like shadows flickering on the wall. It was so with my wife and children—with those who seemed my friends: it is so with yourselves, whom I see now before me. Neither have I myself any real existence, but am a shadow like the rest!"

"And how is it with your views of a future life?" inquired the speculative clergyman.

"Worse than with you," said the old man, in a hollow and feeble tone; "for I cannot conceive it earnestly enough to feel either hope or fear. Mine—mine is the wretchedness! This cold heart—this unreal life! Ah! it grows colder still."

It so chanced, that at this juncture the decayed ligaments of the skeleton gave way, and the dry bones fell together in a heap, thus causing the dusty wreath of cypress to drop upon the table. The attention of the company being thus diverted, for a single instant, from Gervayse Hastings, they perceived, on turning again towards him, that the old man had undergone a change. His shadow had ceased to flicker on the wall.

"Well, Rosina, what is your criticism?" asked Roderick, as he rolled up the manuscript.

"Frankly, your success is by no means complete," replied she. "It is true, I have an idea of the character you endeavor to describe; but it is rather by dint of my own thought than your expression."

"That is unavoidable," observed the sculptor, "because the characteristics are all negative. If Gervayse Hastings could have imbibed one human grief at the gloomy banquet, the task of describing him would have been infinitely easier. Of such persons—and we do meet with these moral monsters now and then—it is difficult to conceive how they came to exist here, or what there is in them capable of existence hereafter. They seem to be on the outside of everything; and nothing wearies the soul more than an attempt to comprehend them within its grasp."

The Celestial Rail-road

Not a great while ago, passing through the gate of dreams, I visited that region of the earth in which lies the famous city of Destruction. It interested me much to learn, that, by the public spirit of some of the inhabitants, a rail-road has recently been established between this populous and flourishing town, and the Celestial City. Having a little time upon my hands, I resolved to gratify a liberal curiosity by making a trip thither. Accordingly, one fine morning, after paying my bill at the hotel, and directing the porter to stow my luggage behind a coach, I took my seat in the vehicle, and set out for the Station House. It was my good fortune to enjoy the company of a gentleman—one Mr. Smooth-it-away—who, though he had never actually visited the Celestial City, yet seemed as well acquainted with its laws, customs, policy, and statistics, as with those of the city of Destruction, of which he was a native townsman. Being, moreover, a director of the rail-road corporation, and one of its largest stockholders, he had it in his power to give me all desirable information respecting that praiseworthy enterprise.

Our coach rattled out of the city, and, at a short distance from its outskirts, passed over a bridge, of elegant construction, but somewhat too slight, as I imagined, to sustain any considerable weight. On both sides lay an extensive quagmire, which could not have been more disagreeable either to sight or smell, had all the kennels of the earth emptied their pollution there.

"This," remarked Mr. Smooth-it-away, "is the famous Slough of Despond—a disgrace to all the neighborhood; and the greater, that it might so easily be converted into firm ground."

"I have understood," said I, "that efforts have been made for that purpose, from time immemorial. Bunyan mentions that above twenty thousand cart-loads of wholesome instructions had been thrown in here, without effect."

"Very probably!—and what effect could be anticipated from such unsubstantial stuff?" cried Mr. Smooth-it-away. "You observe this convenient bridge. We obtained a sufficient foundation for it by throwing into the slough some editions of books of morality, volumes of French philosophy and German rationalism, tracts, sermons, and essays of modern clergymen, extracts from Plato, Confucius, and various Hindoo sages, together with a few ingenious commentaries upon texts of Scripture—all of which, by some scientific process, have been converted into a mass like granite. The whole bog might be filled up with similar matter."

It really seemed to me, however, that the bridge vibrated and heaved up and down, in a very formidable manner; and, spite of Mr. Smooth-it-away's testimony to the solidity of its foundation, I should be loth to cross it in a crowded omnibus; especially if each passenger were encumbered with as heavy luggage as that gentleman and myself. Nevertheless, we got over without accident, and soon found ourselves at the Station House. This very neat and spacious edifice is erected on the site of the little Wicket-Gate, which formerly, as all old pilgrims will recollect, stood directly across the highway, and, by its inconvenient narrowness, was a great obstruction to the traveller of liberal mind and expansive stomach. The reader of John Bunyan will be glad to know, that Christian's old friend

Evangelist, who was accustomed to supply each pilgrim with a mystic roll, now presides at the ticket-office. Some malicious persons, it is true, deny the identity of this reputable character with the Evangelist of old times, and even pretend to bring competent evidence of an imposture. Without involving myself in the dispute, I shall merely observe, that, so far as my experience goes, the square pieces of pasteboard, now delivered to passengers, are much more convenient and useful along the road, than the antique roll of parchment. Whether they will be as readily received at the gate of the Celestial City, I decline giving an opinion.

A large number of passengers were already at the Station House, awaiting the departure of the cars. By the aspect and demeanor of these persons, it was easy to judge that the feelings of the community had undergone a very favorable change, in reference to the Celestial pilgrimage. It would have done Bunyan's heart good to see it. Instead of a lonely and ragged man, with a huge burthen on his back, plodding along sorrowfully on foot, while the whole city hooted after him, here were parties of the first gentry and most respectable people in the neighborhood, setting forth towards the Celestial City, as cheerfully as if the pilgrimage were merely a summer tour. Among the gentlemen were characters of deserved eminence, magistrates, politicians, and men of wealth, by whose example religion could not but be greatly recommended to their meaner brethren. In the ladies' apartment, too, I rejoiced to distinguish some of those flowers of fashionable society, who are so well fitted to adorn the most elevated circles of the Celestial City. There was much pleasant conversation about the news of the day, topics of business, politics, or the lighter matters of amusement; while religion, though indubitably the main thing at heart, was thrown tastefully into the back-ground. Even an infidel would have heard little or nothing to shock his sensibility.

One great convenience of the new method of going on pil-

grimage, I must not forget to mention. Our enormous burthens, instead of being carried on our shoulders, as had been
the custom of old, were all snugly deposited in the baggage-
car, and, as I was assured, would be delivered to their respective owners, at the journey's end. Another thing, likewise,
the benevolent reader will be delighted to understand. It may
be remembered that there was an ancient feud between Prince
Beelzebub and the keeper of the Wicket-Gate, and that the
adherents of the former distinguished personage were accustomed to shoot deadly arrows at honest pilgrims, while knocking at the door. This dispute, much to the credit as well of
the illustrious potentate above-mentioned as of the worthy
and enlightened Directors of the rail-road, has been pacifi-
cally arranged, on the principle of mutual compromise. The
prince's subjects are now pretty numerously employed about
the Station House, some in taking care of the baggage, others
in collecting fuel, feeding the engines, and such congenial occupations; and I can conscientiously affirm, that persons more
attentive to their business, more willing to accommodate, or
more generally agreeable to the passengers, are not to be
found on any rail-road. Every good heart must surely exult at
so satisfactory an arrangement of an immemorial difficulty.

  "Where is Mr. Greatheart?" inquired I. "Beyond a doubt,
the Directors have engaged that famous old champion to be
chief engineer on the rail-road?"

  "Why, no," said Mr. Smooth-it-away, with a dry cough.
"He was offered the situation of brake-man; but, to tell you the
truth, our friend Greatheart has grown preposterously stiff and
narrow, in his old age. He has so often guided pilgrims over
the road, on foot, that he considers it a sin to travel in any
other fashion. Besides, the old fellow had entered so heartily
into the ancient feud with Prince Beelzebub, that he would
have been perpetually at blows or ill language with some of the
prince's subjects, and thus have embroiled us anew. So, on the
whole, we were not sorry when honest Greatheart went off to

the Celestial City in a huff, and left us at liberty to choose a more suitable and accommodating man. Yonder comes the engineer of the train. You will probably recognize him at once."

The engine at this moment took its station in advance of the cars, looking, I must confess, much more like a sort of mechanical demon, that would hurry us to the infernal regions, than a laudable contrivance for smoothing our way to the Celestial City. On its top sat a personage almost enveloped in smoke and flame, which—not to startle the reader—appeared to gush from his own mouth and stomach, as well as from the engine's brazen abdomen.

"Do my eyes deceive me?" cried I. "What on earth is this! A living creature?—if so, he is own brother to the engine that he rides upon!"

"Poh, poh; you are obtuse!" said Mr. Smooth-it-away, with a hearty laugh. "Don't you know Apollyon, Christian's old enemy, with whom he fought so fierce a battle in the Valley of Humiliation? He was the very fellow to manage the engine; and so we have reconciled him to the custom of going on pilgrimage, and engaged him as chief engineer."

"Bravo, bravo!" exclaimed I, with irrepressible enthusiasm. "This shows the liberality of the age; this proves, if anything can, that all musty prejudices are in a fair way to be obliterated. And how will Christian rejoice to hear of this happy transformation of his old antagonist! I promise myself great pleasure in informing him of it, when we reach the Celestial City."

The passengers being all comfortably seated, we now rattled away merrily, accomplishing a greater distance in ten minutes, than Christian probably trudged over, in a day. It was laughable, while we glanced along, as it were, at the tail of a thunder-bolt, to observe two dusty foot-travellers, in the old pilgrim-guise, with cockle-shell and staff, their mystic rolls of parchment in their hands, and their intolerable burthens on their backs. The preposterous obstinacy of these honest people, in persisting to groan and stumble along the

difficult pathway, rather than take advantage of modern improvements, excited great mirth among our wiser brotherhood. We greeted the two pilgrims with many pleasant gibes
and a roar of laughter; whereupon, they gazed at us with such
woeful and absurdly compassionate visages, that our merriment grew tenfold more obstreperous. Apollyon, also, entered heartily into the fun, and contrived to flirt the smoke
and flame of the engine, or of his own breath, into their
faces, and enveloped them in an atmosphere of scalding
steam. These little practical jokes amused us mightily, and
doubtless afforded the pilgrims the gratification of considering themselves martyrs.

At some distance from the rail-road, Mr. Smooth-it-away
pointed to a large, antique edifice, which, he observed, was a
tavern of long standing, and had formerly been a noted stopping-place for pilgrims. In Bunyan's road-book, it is mentioned as the Interpreter's House.

"I have long had a curiosity to visit that old mansion," remarked I.

"It is not one of our stations, as you perceive," said my companion. "The keeper was violently opposed to the rail-road;
and well he might be, as the track left his house of entertainment on one side, and thus was pretty certain to deprive him of
all his reputable customers. But the foot-path still passes his
door; and the old gentleman now and then receives a call from
some simple traveller, and entertains him with fare as old-fashioned as himself."

Before our talk on this subject came to a conclusion, we
were rushing by the place where Christian's burthen fell from
his shoulders, at the sight of the cross. This served as a theme
for Mr. Smooth-it-away, Mr. Live-for-the-world, Mr. Hide-
sin-in-the-heart, Mr. Scaly Conscience, and a knot of gentlemen from the town of Shun Repentance, to descant upon the
inestimable advantages resulting from the safety of our baggage. Myself, and all the passengers indeed, joined with great

unanimity in this view of the matter; for our burthens were rich in many things, esteemed precious throughout the world; and, especially, we each of us possessed a great variety of favorite Habits, which we trusted would not be out of fashion, even in the polite circles of the Celestial City. It would have been a sad spectacle, to see such an assortment of valuable articles tumbling into the sepulchre. Thus pleasantly conversing on the favorable circumstances of our position, as compared with those of past pilgrims, and of narrow-minded ones at the present day, we soon found ourselves at the foot of the Hill Difficulty. Through the very heart of this rocky mountain a tunnel has been constructed, of most admirable architecture, with a lofty arch and a spacious double-track; so that, unless the earth and rocks should chance to crumble down, it will remain an eternal monument of the builder's skill and enterprise. It is a great, though incidental advantage, that the materials from the heart of the Hill Difficulty have been employed in filling up the Valley of Humiliation; thus obviating the necessity of descending into that disagreeable and unwholesome hollow.

"This is a wonderful improvement, indeed," said I. "Yet I should have been glad of an opportunity to visit the Palace Beautiful, and be introduced to the charming young ladies—Miss Prudence, Miss Piety, Miss Charity, and the rest—who have the kindness to entertain pilgrims there."

"Young ladies!" cried Mr. Smooth-it-away, as soon as he could speak for laughing. "And charming young ladies! Why, my dear fellow, they are old maids, every soul of them—prim, starched, dry, and angular—and not one of them, I will venture to say, has altered so much as the fashion of her gown, since the days of Christian's pilgrimage."

"Ah, well," said I, much comforted. "Then I can very readily dispense with their acquaintance."

The respectable Apollyon was now putting on the steam at a prodigious rate, anxious, perhaps, to get rid of the unpleasant reminiscences, connected with the spot where he had so disastrously encountered Christian. Consulting Mr. Bunyan's road-book, I perceived that we must now be within a few miles of the Valley of the Shadow of Death; into which doleful region, at our present speed, we should plunge much sooner than seemed at all desirable. In truth, I expected nothing better than to find myself in the ditch on one side, or the quag on the other. But, on communicating my apprehensions to Mr. Smooth-it-away, he assured me that the difficulties of this passage, even in its worst condition, had been vastly exaggerated, and that, in its present state of improvement, I might consider myself as safe as on any rail-road in Christendom.

Even while we were speaking, the train shot into the entrance of this dreaded Valley. Though I plead guilty to some foolish palpitations of the heart, during our headlong rush over the causeway here constructed, yet it were unjust to withhold the highest encomiums on the boldness of its original conception, and the ingenuity of those who executed it. It was gratifying, likewise, to observe how much care had been taken to dispel the everlasting gloom, and supply the defect of cheerful sunshine; not a ray of which has ever penetrated among these awful shadows. For this purpose, the inflammable gas, which exudes plentifully from the soil, is collected by means of pipes, and thence communicated to a quadruple row of lamps, along the whole extent of the passage. Thus a radiance has been created, even out of the fiery and sulphurous curse that rests forever upon the Valley; a radiance hurtful, however, to the eyes, and somewhat bewildering, as I discovered by the changes which it wrought in the visages of my companions. In this respect, as compared with natural daylight, there is the same difference as between truth and falsehood; but, if the reader have ever travelled through the Dark Valley, he will have learned to be thankful for any light that he could get; if not from the sky above, then from the blasted soil beneath. Such was the red brilliancy of these lamps, that they appeared to build walls of fire on both sides of the track, between which we held our course at lightning-speed, while a reverberating thunder filled the Valley with its echoes. Had the engine run off the track—a catastrophe, it is whispered, by no means unprecedented—the bottomless pit, if there be any such place, would undoubtedly have received us. Just as some dismal fooleries of this nature had made my heart quake, there came a tremendous shriek, careering along the Valley as if a thousand devils had burst their lungs to utter it, but which proved to be merely the whistle of the engine, on arriving at a stopping-place.

The spot, where we had now paused, is the same that our friend Bunyan—a truthful man, but infected with many fantastic notions—has designated, in terms plainer than I like to repeat, as the mouth of the infernal region. This, however, must be a mistake; inasmuch as Mr. Smooth-it-away, while we remained in the smoky and lurid cavern, took occasion to prove that Tophet has not even a metaphorical existence. The place, he assured us, is no other than the crater of a half-extinct volcano, in which the Directors had caused forges to be set up, for the manufacture of rail-road iron. Hence, also, is obtained a plentiful supply of fuel for the use of the engines. Whoever had gazed into the dismal obscurity of the broad cavern-mouth, whence, ever and anon, darted huge tongues of dusky flame,—and had seen the strange, half-shaped monsters, and visions of faces horribly grotesque, into which the smoke seemed to wreathe itself,—and had heard the awful murmurs, and shrieks, and deep shuddering whispers of the blast, sometimes forming itself into words almost articulate,—he would have seized upon Mr. Smooth-it-away's comfortable explanation, as greedily as we did. The inhabitants of the cavern, moreover, were unlovely personages, dark, smoke-begrimed, generally deformed, with misshapen feet, and a glow of dusky redness in their eyes; as if their hearts had caught fire, and were blazing out of the upper windows. It struck me as a peculiarity, that the laborers at the forge, and those who brought

fuel to the engine, when they began to draw short breath, positively emitted smoke from their mouth and nostrils.

Among the idlers about the train, most of whom were puffing cigars which they had lighted at the flame of the crater, I
was perplexed to notice several, who, to my certain knowledge, had heretofore set forth by rail-road for the Celestial
City. They looked dark, wild, and smoky, with a singular resemblance, indeed, to the native inhabitants; like whom, also,
they had a disagreeable propensity to ill-natured gibes and
sneers; the habit of which had wrought a settled contortion of
their visages. Having been on speaking terms with one of these
persons—an indolent, good-for-nothing fellow, who went by
the name of Take-it-easy—I called to him, and inquired what
was his business there.

"Did you not start," said I, "for the Celestial City?"

"That's a fact," said Mr. Take-it-easy, carelessly puffing
some smoke into my eyes. "But I heard such bad accounts, that
I never took pains to climb the hill, on which the city stands.
No business doing—no fun going on—nothing to drink, and
no smoking allowed—and a thrumming of church-music from
morning till night! I would not stay in such a place, if they offered me house-room and living free."

"But, my good Mr. Take-it-easy," cried I, "why take up
your residence here, of all places in the world?"

"Oh," said the loafer, with a grin, "it is very warm hereabouts, and I meet with plenty of old acquaintances, and altogether the place suits me. I hope to see you back again, some
day soon. A pleasant journey to you!"

While he was speaking, the bell of the engine rang, and we
dashed away, after dropping a few passengers, but receiving no
new ones. Rattling onward through the Valley, we were dazzled with the fiercely gleaming gas-lamps, as before. But sometimes, in the dark of intense brightness, grim faces, that bore
the aspect and expression of individual sins, or evil passions,

seemed to thrust themselves through the veil of light, glaring upon us, and stretching forth a great dusky hand, as if to impede our progress. I almost thought, that they were my own sins that appalled me there. These were freaks of imagination—nothing more, certainly,—mere delusions, which I ought to be heartily ashamed of—but, all through the Dark Valley, I was tormented, and pestered, and dolefully bewildered, with the same kind of waking dreams. The mephitic gasses of that region intoxicate the brain. As the light of natural day, however, began to struggle with the glow of the lanterns, these vain imaginations lost their vividness, and finally vanished with the first ray of sunshine that greeted our escape from the Valley of the Shadow of Death. Ere we had gone a mile beyond it, I could well nigh have taken my oath that this whole gloomy passage was a dream.

At the end of the Valley, as John Bunyan mentions, is a cavern, where, in his days, dwelt two cruel giants, Pope and Pagan, who had strewn the ground about their residence with the bones of slaughtered pilgrims. These vile old troglodytes are no longer there; but into their deserted cave another terrible giant has thrust himself, and makes it his business to seize upon honest travellers, and fat them for his table with plentiful meals of smoke, mist, moonshine, raw potatoes, and saw-dust. He is a German by birth, and is called Giant Transcendentalist; but as to his form, his features, his substance, and his nature generally, it is the chief peculiarity of this huge miscreant, that neither he for himself, nor anybody for him, has ever been able to describe them. As we rushed by the cavern's mouth, we caught a hasty glimpse of him, looking somewhat like an ill-proportioned figure, but considerably more like a heap of fog and duskiness. He shouted after us, but in so strange a phraseology that we knew not what he meant, nor whether to be encouraged or affrighted.

It was late in the day, when the train thundered into the ancient city of Vanity, where Vanity Fair is still at the height of prosperity, and exhibits an epitome of whatever is brilliant, gay, and fascinating, beneath the sun. As I purposed to make a considerable stay here, it gratified me to learn that there is no longer the want of harmony between the townspeople and pilgrims, which impelled the former to such lamentably mistaken measures as the persecution of Christian, and the fiery martyrdom of Faithful. On the contrary, as the new rail-road brings with it great trade and a constant influx of strangers, the lord of Vanity Fair is its chief patron, and the capitalists of the city are among the largest stockholders. Many passengers stop to take their pleasure or make their profit in the Fair, instead of going onward to the Celestial City. Indeed, such are the charms of the place, that people often affirm it to be the true and only heaven; stoutly contending that there is no other, that those who seek further are mere dreamers, and that, if the fabled brightness of the Celestial City lay but a bare mile beyond the gates of Vanity, they would not be fools enough to go thither. Without subscribing to these, perhaps, exaggerated encomiums, I can truly say, that my abode in the city was mainly agreeable, and my intercourse with the inhabitants productive of much amusement and instruction.

Being naturally of a serious turn, my attention was directed to the solid advantages derivable from a residence here, rather than to the effervescent pleasures, which are the grand object with too many visitants. The Christian reader, if he have had no accounts of the city later than Bunyan's time, will be surprised to hear that almost every street has its church, and that the reverend clergy are nowhere held in higher respect than at Vanity Fair. And well do they deserve such honorable estimation; for the maxims of wisdom and virtue, which fall from their lips, come from as deep a spiritual source, and tend to us as lofty a religious aim, as those of the sagest philosophers of old. In justification of this high praise, I need only mention the names of the Rev. Mr. Shallow-deep; the Rev. Mr. Stumble-at-truth; that fine old clerical character, the Rev. Mr. This-to-day, who expects shortly to re-sign his pulpit to the Rev. Mr. That-to-morrow; together with the Rev. Mr. Bewilderment; the Rev. Mr. Clog-the-spirit; and, last and greatest, the Rev. Dr. Wind-of-doctrine. The labors of these eminent divines are aided by those of innu-merable lecturers, who diffuse such a various profundity, in all subjects of human or celestial science, that any man may acquire an omnigenous erudition, without the trouble of even learning to read. Thus literature is etherealized by assuming for its medium the human voice; and knowledge, depositing all its heavier particles—except, doubtless, its gold—be-comes exhaled into a sound, which forthwith steals into the ever-open ear of the community. These ingenious methods constitute a sort of machinery, by which thought and study are done to every person's hand, without his putting himself to the slightest inconvenience in the matter. There is another species of machine for the wholesale manufacture of individ-ual morality. This excellent result is effected by societies for all manner of virtuous purposes; with which a man has merely to connect himself, throwing, as it were, his quota of virtue into the common stock; and the president and directors will take care that the aggregate amount be well applied. All these, and other wonderful improvements in ethics, religion, and literature, being made plain to my comprehension by the ingenious Mr. Smooth-it-away, inspired me with a vast admi-ration of Vanity Fair.

It would fill a volume, in an age of pamphlets, were I to re-cord all my observations in this great capital of human business and pleasure. There was an unlimited range of society—the powerful, the wise, the witty, and the famous in every walk of life—princes, presidents, poets, generals, artists, actors, and philanthropists, all making their own market at the Fair, and deeming no price too exorbitant for such commodities as hit their fancy. It was well worth one's while, even if he had no idea of buying or selling, to loiter through the bazaars, and observe the various sorts of traffic that were going forward.

Some of the purchasers, I thought, made very foolish bargains. For instance, a young man, having inherited a splendid fortune, laid out a considerable portion of it in the purchase of diseases, and finally spent all the rest for a heavy lot of repentance and a suit of rags. A very pretty girl bartered a heart as clear as crystal, and which seemed her most valuable possession, for another jewel of the same kind, but so worn and defaced as to be utterly worthless. In one shop, there were a great many crowns of laurel and myrtle, which soldiers, authors, statesmen, and various other people, pressed eagerly to buy; some purchased these paltry wreaths with their lives; others by a toilsome servitude of years; and many sacrificed whatever was most valuable, yet finally slunk away without the crown. There was a sort of stock or scrip, called Conscience, which seemed to be in great demand, and would purchase almost anything. Indeed, few rich commodities were to be obtained without paying a heavy sum in this particular stock; and a man's business was seldom very lucrative, unless he knew precisely when and how to throw his hoard of Conscience into the market. Yet, as this stock was the only thing of permanent value, whoever parted with it was sure to find himself a loser, in the long run. Several of the speculations were of a questionable character. Occasionally, a member of congress recruited his pocket by the sale of his constituents; and I was assured that public officers have often sold their country, at very moderate prices. Thousands sold their happiness for a whim. Gilded chains were in great demand, and purchased with almost any sacrifice. In truth, those who desired, according to the old adage, to sell anything valuable for a song, might find customers all over the Fair; and there were innumerable messes of pottage, piping hot, for such as chose to buy them with their birth-rights. A few articles, however, could not be found genuine, at Vanity Fair. If a customer wished to renew his stock of youth, the dealers offered him a set of false teeth and an auburn wig; if he demanded peace of mind, they recommended opium or a brandy-bottle.

Tracts of land and golden mansions, situate in the Celestial City, were often exchanged, at very disadvantageous rates, for a few years lease of small, dismal, inconvenient tenements in Vanity Fair. Prince Beelzebub himself took great interest in this sort of traffic, and sometimes condescended to meddle with smaller matters. I once had the pleasure to see him bargaining with a miser for his soul, which, after much ingenious skirmishing on both sides, his Highness succeeded in obtaining at about the value of sixpence. The prince remarked, with a smile, that he was a loser by the transaction.

Day after day, as I walked the streets of Vanity, my manners and deportment became more and more like those of the inhabitants. The place began to seem like home; the idea of pursuing my travels to the Celestial City was almost obliterated from my mind. I was reminded of it, however, by the sight of the same pair of simple pilgrims at whom we had laughed so heartily, when Apollyon puffed smoke and steam into their faces, at the commencement of our journey. There they stood amid the densest bustle of Vanity—the dealers offering them their purple, and fine linen, and jewels; the men of wit and humor gibing at them; a pair of buxom ladies ogling them askance; while the benevolent Mr. Smooth-it-away whispered some of his wisdom at their elbows, and pointed to a newly erected temple—but there were these worthy simpletons, making the scene look wild and monstrous, merely by their sturdy repudiation of all part in its business or pleasures.

One of them—his name was Stick-to-the-right—perceived in my face, I suppose, a species of sympathy and almost admiration, which, to my own great surprise, I could not help feeling for this pragmatic couple. It prompted him to address me.

"Sir," inquired he, with a sad, yet mild and kindly voice, "do you call yourself a pilgrim?"

"Yes," I replied. "My right to that appellation is indubitable. I am merely a sojourner here in Vanity Fair, being bound for the Celestial City, by the new rail-road."

"Alas, friend," rejoined Mr. Stick-to-the-right, "I do assure you, and beseech you to receive the truth of my words, that that whole concern is a bubble. You may travel on it all your life-time, were you to live thousands of years, and yet never get beyond the limits of Vanity Fair! Yea; though you should deem yourself entering the gates of the Blessed City, it will be nothing but a miserable delusion."

"The Lord of the Celestial City," began the other pilgrim, whose name was Mr. Foot-it-to-Heaven, "has refused, and will ever refuse, to grant an act of incorporation for this rail-road; and unless that be obtained, no passenger can ever hope to enter his dominions. Wherefore, every man, who buys a ticket, must lay his account with losing the purchase-money—which is the value of his own soul."

"Poh, nonsense!" said Mr. Smooth-it-away, taking my arm and leading me off. "These fellows ought to be indicted for a libel. If the law stood as it once did in Vanity Fair, we should see them grinning through the iron-bars of the prison-window."

This incident made a considerable impression on my mind, and contributed with other circumstances to indispose me to a permanent residence in the city of Vanity; although, of course, I was not simple enough to give up my original plan of gliding along easily and commodiously by rail-road. Still, I grew anxious to be gone. There was one strange thing that troubled me; amid the occupations or amusements of the Fair, nothing was more common than for a person—whether at a feast, theatre, or church, or trafficking for wealth and honors, or whatever he might be doing, and however unseasonable the interruption— suddenly to vanish like a soap-bubble, and be never more seen of his fellows; and so accustomed were the latter to such little accidents, that they went on with their business, as quietly as if nothing had happened. But it was otherwise with me.

Finally, after a pretty long residence at the Fair, I resumed my journey towards the Celestial City, still with Mr. Smooth-it-away at my side. At a short distance beyond the suburbs of Vanity, we passed the ancient silver-mine, of which Demas was the first discoverer, and which is now wrought to great advantage, supplying nearly all the coined currency of the world. A little further onward was the spot where Lot's wife had stood for ages, under the semblance of a pillar of salt. Curious travellers have long since carried it away piece-meal. Had all regrets been punished as rigorously as this poor dame's were, my yearning for the relinquished delights of Vanity Fair might have produced a similar change in my own corporeal substance, and left me a warning to future pilgrims.

The next remarkable object was a large edifice, constructed of moss-grown stone, but in a modern and airy style of architecture. The engine came to a pause in its vicinity, with the usual tremendous shriek.

"This was formerly the castle of the redoubted giant Despair," observed Mr. Smooth-it-away; "but, since his death, Mr. Flimsy-faith has repaired it, and now keeps an excellent house of entertainment here. It is one of our stopping-places."

"It seems but slightly put together," remarked I, looking at the frail, yet ponderous walls. "I do not envy Mr. Flimsy-faith his habitation. Some day, it will thunder down upon the heads of the occupants."

"We shall escape, at all events," said Mr. Smooth-it-away; "for Apollyon is putting on the steam again."

The road now plunged into a gorge of the Delectable Mountains, and traversed the field where, in former ages, the blind men wandered and stumbled among the tombs. One of these ancient tomb-stones had been thrust across the track, by some malicious person, and gave the train of cars a terrible jolt. Far up the rugged side of a mountain, I perceived a rusty iron-door, half-overgrown with bushes and creeping-plants, but with smoke issuing from its crevices.

"Is that," inquired I, "the very door in the hill-side, which the shepherds assured Christian was a by-way to hell?"

"That was a joke on the part of the shepherds," said Mr. Smooth-it-away, with a smile. "It is neither more nor less than the door of a cavern, which they use as a smoke-house for the preparation of mutton-hams."

My recollections of the journey are now, for a little space, dim and confused; inasmuch as a singular drowsiness here overcame me, owing to the fact that we were passing over the Enchanted Ground, the air of which encourages a disposition to sleep. I awoke, however, as soon as we crossed the borders of the pleasant land of Beulah. All the passengers were rubbing their eyes, comparing watches, and congratulating one another on the prospect of arriving so seasonably at the journey's end. The sweet breezes of this happy clime came refreshingly to our nostrils; we beheld the glimmering gush of silver fountains, overhung by trees of beautiful foliage and delicious fruit, which were propagated by grafts from the Celestial gardens. Once, as we dashed onward like a hurricane, there was a flutter of wings, and the bright appearance of an angel in the air, speeding forth on some heavenly mission. The engine now announced the close vicinity of the final Station House, by one last and horrible scream, in which there seemed to be distinguishable every kind of wailing and woe, and bitter fierceness of wrath, all mixed up with the wild laughter of a devil or a madman. Throughout our journey, at every stopping-place, Apollyon had exercised his ingenuity in screwing the most abominable sounds out of the whistle of the steam-engine; but, in this closing effort, he outdid himself, and created an infernal uproar, which, besides disturbing the peaceful inhabitants of Beulah, must have sent its discord even through the Celestial gates.

While the horrid clamor was still ringing in our ears, we heard an exulting strain, as if a thousand instruments of music, with height, and depth, and sweetness in their tones, at once tender and triumphant, were struck in unison, to greet the approach of some illustrious hero, who had fought the good fight, and won a glorious victory, and was come to lay aside his battered arms forever. Looking to ascertain what might be the occasion of this glad harmony, I perceived, on alighting from the cars, that a multitude of Shining Ones had assembled on the other side of the river, to welcome two poor pilgrims, who were just emerging from its depths. They were the same whom Apollyon and ourselves had persecuted with taunts and gibes, and scalding steam, at the commencement of our journey; the same whose unworldly aspect and impressive words had stirred my conscience, amid the wild revellers of Vanity Fair.

"How amazingly well those men have got on!" cried I to Mr. Smooth-it-away. "I wish we were secure of as good a reception."

"Never fear—never fear!" answered my friend. "Come!—make haste!—the ferry-boat will be off directly; and in three minutes you will be on the other side of the river. No doubt you will find coaches to carry you up to the city-gates."

A steam ferry-boat, the last improvement on this important route, lay at the river-side, puffing, snorting, and emitting all those other disagreeable utterances, which betoken the departure to be immediate. I hurried on board, with the rest of the passengers, most of whom were in great perturbation; some bawling out for their baggage; some tearing their hair, and exclaiming that the boat would explode or sink; some already pale with the heaving of the stream; some gazing affrighted at the ugly aspect of the steersman; and some still dizzy with the slumberous influences of the Enchanted Ground. Looking back to the shore, I was amazed to discern Mr. Smooth-it-away, waving his hand in token of farewell!

"Don't you go over to the Celestial City?" exclaimed I.

"Oh, no!" answered he with a queer smile, and that same disagreeable contortion of visage, which I had remarked in the inhabitants of the Dark Valley. "Oh, no! I have come thus far only for the sake of your pleasant company. Good bye! We shall meet again."

And then did my excellent friend, Mr. Smooth-it-away, laugh outright; in the midst of which cachinnation, a smoke-wreath issued from his mouth and nostrils; while a twinkle of lurid flame darted out of either eye, proving indubitably that his heart was all of a red blaze. The impudent Fiend! To deny the existence of Tophet, when he felt its fiery tortures raging within his breast! I rushed to the side of the boat, intending to fling myself on shore. But the wheels, as they began their revolutions, threw a dash of spray over me, so cold—so deadly cold, with the chill that will never leave those waters, until Death be drowned in his own river—that, with a shiver and a heart-quake, I awoke. Thank Heaven, it was a Dream!

Earth's Holocaust

ONCE upon a time—but whether in time past or time to come, is a matter of little or no moment—this wide world had become so overburthened with an accumulation of worn-out trumpery, that the inhabitants determined to rid themselves of it by a general bonfire. The site fixed upon, at the representation of the Insurance Companies, and as being as central a spot as any other on the globe, was one of the broadest prairies of the West, where no human habitation would be endangered by the flames, and where a vast assemblage of spectators might commodiously admire the show. Having a taste for sights of this kind, and imagining, likewise, that the illumination of the bonfire might reveal some profundity of moral truth, heretofore hidden in mist or darkness, I made it convenient to journey thither and be present. At my arrival, although the heap of condemned rubbish was as yet comparatively small, the torch had already been applied. Amid that boundless plain, in the dusk of evening, like a far-off star alone in the firmament, there was merely visible one tremulous gleam, whence none could have anticipated so fierce a blaze as was destined to ensue. With every moment, however, there came foot-travellers, women holding up their aprons, men on horseback, wheelbarrows, lumbering baggage-wagons, and other vehicles great and small, and from far and near, laden with articles that were judged fit for nothing but to be burnt.

"What materials have been used to kindle the flames?" inquired I of a bystander; for I was desirous of knowing the whole process of the affair, from beginning to end.

The person whom I addressed was a grave man, fifty years old or thereabout, who had evidently come thither as a looker-on; he struck me immediately as having weighed for himself the true value of life and its circumstances, and therefore as feeling little personal interest in whatever judgment the world might form of them. Before answering my question, he looked me in the face, by the kindling light of the fire.

"Oh, some very dry combustibles," replied he, "and extremely suitable to the purpose—no other, in fact, than yesterday's newspapers, last month's magazines, and last year's withered leaves. Here, now, comes some antiquated trash, that will take fire like a handfull of shavings."

As he spoke, some rough-looking men advanced to the verge of the bonfire, and threw in, as it appeared, all the rubbish of the Herald's Office; the blazonry of coat-armor; the crests and devices of illustrious families; pedigrees that extended back, like lines of light, into the mist of the dark ages; together with stars, garters, and embroidered collars; each of which, as paltry a bauble as it might appear to the uninstructed eye, had once possessed vast significance, and was still, in truth, reckoned among the most precious of moral or material facts, by the worshippers of the gorgeous past. Mingled with this confused heap, which was tossed into the flames by armsfull at once, were innumerable badges of knighthood; comprising those of all the European sovereignties, and Napoleon's decoration of the Legion of Honor, the ribands of which were entangled with those of the ancient order of St. Louis. There, too, were the medals of our own society of Cincinnati, by means of which, as history tells us, an order of hereditary knights came near being constituted out of the king-quellers of the Revolution. And, besides, there were the patents of nobility of German counts and barons, Spanish grandees, and English peers, from the worm-eaten instrument signed by William the Conqueror, down to the bran-new parchment of the latest lord, who has received his honors from the fair hand of Victoria.

At sight of the dense volumes of smoke, mingled with vivid jets of flame, that gushed and eddied forth from this immense pile of earthly distinctions, the multitude of plebeian spectators set up a joyous shout, and clapt their hands with an emphasis that made the welkin echo. That was their moment of triumph, achieved after long ages, over creatures of the same clay and same spiritual infirmities, who had dared to assume the privileges due only to Heaven's better workmanship. But now there rushed towards the blazing heap a gray-haired man, of stately presence, wearing a coat from the breast of which some star, or other badge of rank, seemed to have been forcibly wrenched away. He had not the tokens of intellectual power in his face; but still there was the demeanor—the habitual, and almost native dignity—of one who had been born to the idea of his own social superiority, and had never felt it questioned, till that moment.

"People," cried he, gazing at the ruin of what was dearest in his eyes, with grief and wonder, but, nevertheless, with a degree of stateliness—"people, what have you done! This fire is consuming all that marked your advance from barbarism, or that could have prevented your relapse thither. We—the men of the privileged orders—were those who kept alive, from age to age, the old chivalrous spirit; the gentle and generous thought; the higher, the purer, the more refined and delicate life! With the nobles, too, you cast off the poet, the painter, the sculptor—all the beautiful arts;—for we were their patrons, and created the atmosphere in which they flourish. In abolishing the majestic distinctions of rank, society loses not only its grace, but its steadfastness—"

More he would doubtless have spoken; but here there arose an outcry, sportive, contemptuous, and indignant, that altogether drowned the appeal of the fallen nobleman; insomuch that, casting one look of despair at his own half-burnt pedigree, he shrunk back into the crowd, glad to shelter himself under his new-found insignificance.

"Let him thank his stars that we have not flung him into the same fire!" shouted a rude figure, spurning the embers with his foot. "And, henceforth, let no man dare to show a piece of musty parchment, as his warrant for lording it over his fellows! If he have strength of arm, well and good; it is one species of superiority. If he have wit, wisdom, courage, force of character, let these attributes do for him what they may. But, from this day forward, no mortal must hope for place and consideration, by reckoning up the mouldy bones of his ancestors! That non-sense is done away."

"And in good time," remarked the grave observer by my side—in a low voice however—"if no worse nonsense come in its place. But at all events, this species of nonsense has fairly lived out its life."

There was little space to muse or moralize over the embers of this time-honored rubbish; for, before it was half burnt out, there came another multitude from beyond the sea, bearing the purple robes of royalty, and the crowns, globes, and sceptres of emperors and kings. All these had been condemned as useless baubles; playthings, at best, fit only for the infancy of the world, or rods to govern and chastise it in its nonage; but with which universal manhood, at its full-grown stature, could no longer brook to be insulted. Into such contempt had these re-gal insignia now fallen, that the gilded crown and tinselled robes of the player-king, from Drury Lane Theatre, had been thrown in among the rest, doubtless as a mockery of his brother-monarchs, on the great stage of the world. It was a strange sight, to discern the crown-jewels of England, glowing and flashing in the midst of the fire. Some of them had been de-livered down from the times of the Saxon princes; others were purchased with vast revenues, or, perchance, ravished from the dead brows of the native potentates of Hindostan; and the whole now blazed with a dazzling lustre, as if a star had fallen in that spot, and been shattered into fragments. The splendor of the ruined monarchy had no reflection, save in those inestimable precious-stones. But, enough on this subject! It were but tedious to describe how the Emperor of Austria's mantle was converted to tinder, and how the posts and pillars of the French throne became a heap of coals, which it was impossible to distinguish from those of any other wood. Let me add, however, that I noticed one of the exiled Poles, stirring up the bonfire with the Czar of Russia's sceptre, which he afterwards flung into the flames.

"The smell of singed garments is quite intolerable here," observed my new acquaintance, as the breeze enveloped us in the smoke of a royal wardrobe. "Let us get to windward, and see what they are doing on the other side of the bonfire."

We accordingly passed round, and were just in time to witness the arrival of a vast procession of Washingtonians—as the votaries of temperance call themselves now-a-days—accompanied by thousands of the Irish disciples of Father Mathew, with that great apostle at their head. They brought a rich contribution to the bonfire; being nothing less than all the hogsheads and barrels of liquor in the world, which they rolled before them across the prairie.

"Now, my children," cried Father Mathew, when they reached the verge of the fire—"one shove more, and the work is done! And now let us stand off, and see Satan deal with his own liquor!"

Accordingly, having placed their wooden vessels within reach of the flames, the procession stood off at a safe distance, and soon beheld them burst into a blaze that reached the clouds, and threatened to set the sky itself on fire. And well it might. For here was the whole world's stock of spirituous liquors, which, instead of kindling a frenzied light in the eyes of individual topers as of yore, soared upward with a bewildering gleam that startled all mankind. It was the aggregate of that fierce fire, which would otherwise have scorched the hearts of millions. Meantime, numberless bottles of precious wine were flung into the blaze; which lapped up the contents as if it loved them, and grew, like other drunkards, the merrier and fiercer for what it quaffed. Never again will the insatiable thirst of the fire-fiend be so pampered! Here were the treasures of famous bon-vivants—liquors that had been tossed on ocean, and mellowed in the sun, and hoarded long in the recesses of the earth—the pale, the gold, the ruddy juice of whatever vineyards were most delicate—the entire vintage of Tokay—all mingling in one stream with the vile fluids of the common pot-house, and contributing to heighten the self-same blaze. And while it rose in a gigantic spire, that seemed to wave against the arch of the firmament, and combine itself with the light of stars, the multitude gave a shout, as if the broad earth were exulting in its deliverance from the curse of ages.

But the joy was not universal. Many deemed that human life would be gloomier than ever, when that brief illumination should sink down. While the reformers were at work, I had overheard muttered expostulations from several respectable gentlemen with red noses, and wearing gouty shoes; and a ragged worthy, whose face looked like a hearth where the fire is burnt out, now expressed his discontent more openly and boldly.

"What is this world good for," said the Last Toper, "now that we can never be jolly any more? What is to comfort the poor man in sorrow and perplexity?—how is he to keep his heart warm against the cold winds of this cheerless earth?—and what do you propose to give him, in exchange for the solace that you take away? How are old friends to sit together by the fireside, without a cheerful glass between them? A plague upon your reformation! It is a sad world, a cold world, a selfish world, a low world, not worth an honest fellow's living in, now that good-fellowship is gone forever!"

This harangue excited great mirth among the bystanders. But, preposterous as was the sentiment, I could not help commiserating the forlorn condition of the Last Toper, whose boon-companions had dwindled away from his side, leaving the poor fellow without a soul to countenance him in sipping his liquor, nor, indeed, any liquor to sip. Not that this was quite the true state of the case; for I had observed him, at a critical moment, filch a bottle of fourth-proof brandy that fell beside the bonfire, and hide it in his pocket.

The spirituous and fermented liquors being thus disposed of, the zeal of the reformers next induced them to replenish the fire with all the boxes of tea and bags of coffee in the world. And now came the planters of Virginia, bringing their crops of tobacco. These, being cast upon the heap of inutility, aggregated it to the size of a mountain, and incensed the atmosphere with such potent fragrance, that methought we should never draw pure breath again. The present sacrifice seemed to startle the lovers of the weed, more than any that they had hitherto witnessed.

"Well;—they've put my pipe out," said an old gentleman, flinging it into the flames in a pet. "What is this world coming to? Everything rich and racy—all the spice of life—is to be condemned as useless. Now that they have kindled the bonfire, if these nonsensical reformers would fling themselves into it, all would be well enough!"

"Be patient," responded a staunch conservative;—"it will come to that in the end. They will first fling us in, and finally themselves."

From the general and systematic measures of reform, I now turned to consider the individual contributions to this memorable bonfire. In many instances, these were of a very amusing character. One poor fellow threw in his empty purse, and another, a bundle of counterfeit or insolvable banknotes. Fashionable ladies threw in their last season's bonnets, together with heaps of ribbon, yellow lace, and much other half-worn milliner's ware; all of which proved even more evanescent in the fire, than it had been in the fashion. A multitude of lovers, of both sexes—discarded maids or bachelors, and couples, mutually weary of one another—tossed in bundles of perfumed letters and enamored sonnets. A hack-politician, being deprived of bread by the loss of office, threw in his teeth, which happened to be false ones. The Rev. Sydney Smith—having voyaged across the Atlantic for that sole purpose—came up to the bonfire, with a bitter grin, and threw in certain repudiated bonds, fortified though they were with the broad seal of a sovereign state. A little boy of five years old, in the premature manliness of the present epoch, threw in his playthings; a college-graduate, his diploma; an apothecary, ruined by the spread of homœopathy, his whole stock of drugs and medicines; a physician, his library; a parson, his old sermons; and a fine gentleman of the old school, his code of manners, which he had formerly written down for the benefit of the next generation. A widow, resolving on a second marriage, slily threw in her dead husband's miniature. A young man, jilted by his mistress, would willingly have flung his own desperate heart into the flames, but could find no means to wrench it out of his bosom. An American author, whose works were neglected by the public, threw his pen and paper into the bonfire, and betook himself to some less discouraging occupation. It somewhat startled me to overhear a number of ladies, highly respectable in appearance, proposing to fling their gowns and petticoats into the flames, and assume the garb, together with the manners, duties, offices, and responsibilities, of the opposite sex.

What favor was accorded to this scheme, I am unable to say; my attention being suddenly drawn to a poor, deceived, and half-delirious girl, who, exclaiming that she was the most worthless thing alive or dead, attempted to cast herself into the fire, amid all that wrecked and broken trumpery of the world. A good man, however, ran to her rescue.

"Patience, my poor girl!" said he, as he drew her back from the fierce embrace of the destroying angel. "Be patient, and abide Heaven's will. So long as you possess a living soul, all may be restored to its first freshness. These things of matter, and creations of human fantasy, are fit for nothing but to be burnt, when once they have had their day. But your day is Eternity!"

"Yes," said the wretched girl, whose frenzy seemed now to have sunk down into deep despondency;—"yes; and the sunshine is blotted out of it!"

It was now rumored among the spectators, that all the weapons and munitions of war were to be thrown into the bonfire; with the exception of the world's stock of gunpowder, which, as the safest mode of disposing of it, had already been drowned in the sea. This intelligence seemed to awaken great diversity of opinion. The hopeful philanthropist esteemed it a token that the millennium was already come; while persons of another stamp, in whose view mankind was a breed of bull-dogs, prophesied that all the old stoutness, fervor, nobleness, generosity, and magnanimity of the race, would disappear; these qualities, as they affirmed, requiring blood for their nourishment. They comforted themselves, however, in the belief that the proposed abolition of war was impracticable, for any length of time together.

Be that as it might, numberless great guns, whose thunder had long been the voice of battle—the artillery of the Armada, the battering-trains of Marlborough, and the adverse cannon of Napoleon and Wellington—were trundled into the midst of the fire. By the continual addition of dry combustibles, it had now waxed so intense, that neither brass nor iron could withstand it. It was wonderful to behold, how those terrible instruments of slaughter melted away like playthings of wax. Then the armies of the earth wheeled around the mighty furnace, with their military music playing triumphant marches, and flung in their muskets and swords. The standard-bearers, likewise, cast one look upward at their banners, all tattered with shot-holes, and inscribed with the names of victorious fields; and giving them a last flourish on the breeze, they lowered them into the flame, which snatched them upward in its rush towards the clouds. This ceremony being over, the world was left without a single weapon in its hands, except, possibly, a few old King's arms and rusty swords, and other trophies of the Revolution, in some of our state-armories. And now the drums were beaten and the trumpets brayed all together, as a prelude to the proclamation of universal and eternal peace, and the announcement that glory was no longer to be won by blood; but that it would henceforth be the contention of the human race, to work out the greatest mutual good; and that beneficence, in the future annals of the earth, would claim the praise of valor. The blessed tidings were accordingly promulgated, and caused infinite rejoicings among those who had stood aghast at the horror and absurdity of war.

But I saw a grim smile pass over the scarred visage of a stately old commander—by his war-worn figure and rich military dress, he might have been one of Napoleon's famous marshals—who, with the rest of the world's soldiery, had just flung away the sword, that had been familiar to his right hand for half-a-century.

"Aye, aye!" grumbled he. "Let them proclaim what they please; but, in the end, we shall find that all this foolery has only made more work for the armorers and cannon-founderies."

"Why, Sir," exclaimed I, in astonishment, "do you imagine that the human race will ever so far return on the steps of its past madness, as to weld another sword, or cast another cannon?"

"There will be no need," observed, with a sneer, one who neither felt benevolence, nor had faith in it. "When Cain wished to slay his brother, he was at no loss for a weapon."

"We shall see," replied the veteran commander.—"If I am mistaken, so much the better; but, in my opinion—without pretending to philosophize about the matter—the necessity of war lies far deeper than these honest gentlemen suppose.

What! Is there a field for all the petty disputes of individuals, and shall there be no great law-court for the settlement of national difficulties? The battle-field is the only court where such suits can be tried!"

"You forget, General," rejoined I, "that, in this advanced stage of civilization, Reason and Philanthropy combined will constitute just such a tribunal as is requisite."

"Ah, I had forgotten that, indeed!" said the old warrior, as he limped away.

The fire was now to be replenished with materials that had hitherto been considered of even greater importance to the well-being of society, than the warlike munitions which we had already seen consumed. A body of reformers had travelled all over the earth, in quest of the machinery by which the different nations were accustomed to inflict the punishment of death. A shudder passed through the multitude, as these ghastly emblems were dragged forward. Even the flames seemed at first to shrink away, displaying the shape and murderous contrivance of each in a full blaze of light, which, of itself, was sufficient to convince mankind of the long and deadly error of human law. Those old implements of cruelty—those horrible monsters of mechanism—those inventions which it seemed to demand something worse than man's natural heart to contrive, and which had lurked in the dusky nooks of ancient prisons, the subject of terror-stricken legends—were now brought forth to view. Headsmen's axes, with the rust of noble and royal blood upon them, and a vast collection of halters that had choked the breath of plebeian victims, were thrown in together. A shout greeted the arrival of the guillotine, which was thrust forward on the same wheels that had borne it from one to another of the blood-stained streets of Paris. But the loudest roar of applause went up, telling the distant sky of the triumph of the earth's redemption, when the gallows made its appearance. An ill-looking fellow, however, rushed forward, and putting himself in the path of the reformers, bellowed hoarsely, and fought with brute fury to stay their progress.

It was little matter of surprise, perhaps, that the executioner should thus do his best to vindicate and uphold the machinery by which he himself had his livelihood, and worthier individuals their death. But it deserved special note, that men of a far different sphere—even of that consecrated class in whose guardianship the world is apt to trust its benevolence—were found to take the hangman's view of the question.

"Stay, my brethren!" cried one of them. "You are misled by a false philanthropy!—you know not what you do. The gallows is a heaven-oriented instrument! Bear it back, then, reverently, and set it up in its old place; else the world will fall to speedy ruin and desolation!"

"Onward, onward!" shouted a leader in the reform. "Into the flames with the accursed instrument of man's bloody policy! How can human law inculcate benevolence and love, while it persists in setting up the gallows as its chief symbol? One heave more, good friends; and the world will be redeemed from its greatest error!"

A thousand hands, that, nevertheless, loathed the touch, now lent their assistance, and thrust the ominous burthen far, far, into the centre of the raging furnace. There its fatal and abhorred image was beheld, first black, then a red coal, then ashes.

"That was well done!" exclaimed I.

"Yes; it was well done," replied—but with less enthusiasm than I expected—the thoughtful observer who was still at my side; "well done, if the world be good enough for the measure. Death, however, is an idea that cannot easily be dispensed with, in any condition between the primal innocence and that other purity and perfection, which, perchance, we are destined to attain, after travelling round the full circle. But, at all events, it is well that the experiment should now be tried."

"Too cold!—too cold!" impatiently exclaimed the young and ardent leader in this triumph. "Let the heart have its voice here, as well as the intellect. And as for ripeness—and as for progress—let mankind always do the highest, kindest, noblest thing, that, at any given period, it has attained to the perception of; and surely that thing cannot be wrong, nor wrongly timed!"

I know not whether it were the excitement of the scene, or whether the good people around the bonfire were really growing more enlightened, every instant; but they now proceeded to measures, in the full length of which I was hardly prepared to keep them company. For instance, some threw their marriage-certificates into the flames, and declared themselves candidates for a higher, holier, and more comprehensive union than that which had subsisted from the birth of time, under the form of the connubial tie. Others hastened to the vaults of banks, and to the coffers of the rich—all of which were open to the first-comer, on this fated occasion—and brought entire bales of paper-money to enliven the blaze, and tons of coin to be melted down by its intensity. Henceforth, they said, universal benevolence, uncoined and exhaustless, was to be the golden currency of the world. At this intelligence, the bankers, and speculators in the stocks, grew pale; and a pickpocket, who had reaped a rich harvest among the crowd, fell down in a deadly fainting-fit. A few men of business burnt their day-books and legers, the notes and obligations of their creditors, and all other evidences of debts due to themselves; while perhaps a somewhat larger number satisfied their zeal for reform with the sacrifice of any uncomfortable recollection of their own indebtment. There was then a cry, that the period was arrived, when the title-deeds of landed property should be given to the flames, and the whole soil of the earth revert to the public, from whom it had been wrongfully abstracted, and most unequally distributed among individuals. Another party demanded, that all written constitutions, set forms of government, legislative acts, statute-books, and everything else on which human invention had endeavored to stamp its arbitrary laws, should at once be destroyed, leaving the consummated world as free as the man first created.

Whether any ultimate action was taken with regard to these propositions, is beyond my knowledge; for, just then, some matters were in progress that concerned my sympathies more nearly.

"See!—see!—what heaps of books and pamphlets," cried a fellow, who did not seem to be a lover of literature. "Now we shall have a glorious blaze!"

"That's just the thing," said a modern philosopher. "Now we shall get rid of the weight of dead men's thought, which has hitherto pressed so heavily on the living intellect, that it has been incompetent to any effectual self-exertion. Well done, my lads! Into the fire with them! Now you are enlightening the world, indeed!"

"But what is to become of the Trade?" cried a frantic bookseller.

"Oh, by all means, let them accompany their merchandise," coolly observed an author. "It will be a noble funeral-pile!"

The truth was, that the human race had now reached a stage of progress, so far beyond what the wisest and wittiest men of former ages had ever dreamed of, that it would have been a manifest absurdity to allow the earth to be any longer encumbered with their poor achievements in the literary line. Accordingly, a thorough and searching investigation had swept the booksellers' shops, hawkers' stands, public and private libraries, and even the little book-shelf by the country fireside, and had brought the world's entire mass of printed paper, bound or in sheets, to swell the already mountain-bulk of our illustrious bonfire. Thick, heavy folios, containing the labors of lexicographers, commentators, and encyclopediasts, were flung in, and, falling among the embers with a leaden thump, smouldered away to ashes, like rotten wood. The small, richly-gilt, French tomes, of the last age, with the hundred volumes of Voltaire among them, went off in a brilliant shower of sparkles, and little jets of flame; while the current literature of the same nation burnt red and blue, and threw an infernal light over the visages of the spectators, converting them all to the aspect of parti-colored fiends. A collection of German stories emitted a scent of brimstone. The English standard authors made excellent fuel, generally exhibiting the properties of sound oak logs. Milton's works, in particular, sent up a powerful blaze, gradually reddening into a coal, which promised to endure longer than almost any other material of the pile. From Shakspeare there gushed a flame of such marvellous splendor, that men shaded their eyes as against the sun's meridian glory; nor, even when the works of his own elucidators were flung upon him, did he cease to flash forth a dazzling radiance, from beneath the ponderous heap. It is my belief, that he is still blazing as fervidly as ever.

"Could a poet but light a lamp at that glorious flame," remarked I, "he might then consume the midnight oil to some good purpose."

"That is the very thing which modern poets have been too apt to do—or, at least, to attempt," answered a critic. "The chief benefit to be expected from this conflagration of past literature, undoubtedly is, that writers will henceforth be compelled to light their lamps at the sun or stars."

"If they can reach so high," said I. "But that task requires a giant, who may afterwards distribute the light among inferior men. It is not every one that can steal the fire from Heaven, like Prometheus; but when once he had done the deed, a thousand hearths were kindled by it."

It amazed me much to observe, how indefinite was the proportion between the physical mass of any given author, and the property of brilliant and long-continued combustion. For instance, there was not a quarto volume of the last century—nor, indeed, of the present—that could compete, in that particular, with a child's little gilt-covered book, containing Mother

Goose's Melodies. The Life and Death of Tom Thumb out-
lasted the biography of Marlborough. An epic indeed, a dozen
of them—was converted to white ashes, before the single sheet
of an old ballad was half-consumed. In more than one case,
too, when volumes of applauded verse proved incapable of anything better than a stifling smoke, an unregarded ditty of some
nameless bard—perchance, in the corner of a newspaper—
soared up among the stars, with a flame as brilliant as their
own. Speaking of the properties of flame, methought Shelley's
poetry emitted a purer light than almost any other productions
of his day; contrasting beautifully with the fitful and lurid
gleams, and gushes of black vapor, that flashed and eddied
from the volumes of Lord Byron. As for Tom Moore, some of
his songs diffused an odor like a burning pastille.

I felt particular interest in watching the combustion of
American authors, and scrupulously noted, by my watch, the
precise number of moments that changed most of them from
shabbily-printed books to indistinguishable ashes. It would be
invidious, however, if not perilous, to betray these awful secrets; so that I shall content myself with observing, that it was
not invariably the writer most frequent in the public mouth,
that made the most splendid appearance in the bonfire. I especially remember, that a great deal of excellent inflammability
was exhibited in a thin volume of poems by Ellery Channing;
although, to speak the truth, there were certain portions that
hissed and spluttered in a very disagreeable fashion. A curious
phenomenon occurred, in reference to several writers, native as
well as foreign. Their books, though of highly respectable figure, instead of bursting into a blaze, or even smouldering out
their substance in smoke, suddenly melted away, in a manner
that proved them to be ice.

If it be no lack of modesty to mention my own works, it
must here be confessed, that I looked for them with fatherly interest, but in vain. Too probably, they were changed to vapor
by the first action of the heat; at best, I can only hope, that, in

their quiet way, they contributed a glimmering spark or two to the splendor of the evening.

"Alas, and woe is me!" thus bemoaned himself a heavy-looking gentleman in green spectacles. "The world is utterly ruined, and there is nothing to live for any longer! The business of my life is snatched from me. Not a volume to be had for love or money!"

"This," remarked the sedate observer beside me, "is a book-worm—one of those men who are born to gnaw dead thoughts. His clothes, you see, are covered with the dust of libraries. He has no inward fountain of ideas; and, in good earnest, now that the old stock is abolished, I do not see what is to become of the poor fellow. Have you no word of comfort for him?"

"My dear Sir," said I to the desperate book-worm, "is not Nature better than a book?—is not the human heart deeper than any system of philosophy?—is not life replete with more instruction than past observers have found it possible to write down in maxims? Be of good cheer! The great book of Time is still spread wide open before us; and, if we read it aright, it will be to us a volume of eternal Truth."

"Oh, my books, my books, my precious, printed books!" reiterated the forlorn book-worm. "My only reality was a bound volume; and now they will not leave me even a shadowy pamphlet!"

In fact, the last remnant of the literature of all the ages was now descending upon the blazing heap, in the shape of a cloud of pamphlets from the press of the New World. These, likewise, were consumed in the twinkling of an eye, leaving the earth, for the first time since the days of Cadmus, free from the plague of letters—an enviable field for the authors of the next generation!

"Well!—and does anything remain to be done?" inquired I, somewhat anxiously. "Unless we set fire to the earth itself, and then leap boldly off into infinite space, I know not that we can carry reform to any further point."

"You are vastly mistaken, my good friend," said the observer. "Believe me, the fire will not be allowed to settle down, without the addition of fuel that will startle many persons, who have lent a willing hand thus far."

Nevertheless, there appeared to be a relaxation of effort, for a little time, during which, probably, the leaders of the movement were considering what should be done next. In the interval, a philosopher threw his theory into the flames; a sacrifice, which, by those who knew how to estimate it, was pronounced the most remarkable that had yet been made. The combustion, however, was by no means brilliant. Some indefatigable people, scorning to take a moment's ease, now employed themselves in collecting all the withered leaves and fallen boughs of the forest, and thereby recruited the bonfire to a greater height than ever. But this was mere by-play.

"Here comes the fresh fuel that I spoke of," said my companion.

To my astonishment, the persons who now advanced into the vacant space, around the mountain of fire, bore surplices and other priestly garments, mitres, crosiers, and a confusion of popish and protestant emblems, with which it seemed their purpose to consummate this great Act of Faith. Crosses, from the spires of old cathedrals, were cast upon the heap, with as little remorse as if the reverence of centuries, passing in long array beneath the lofty towers, had not looked up to them as the holiest of symbols. The font, in which infants were consecrated to God; the sacramental vessels, whence Piety had received the hallowed draught; were given to the same destruction. Perhaps it most nearly touched my heart, to see, among these devoted relics, fragments of the humble communion-tables and undecorated pulpits, which I recognized as having been torn from the meeting-houses of New-England. Those simple edifices might have been permitted to retain all of sacred embellishment that their Puritan founders had bestowed, even though the mighty structure of St. Peter's had sent its spoils to the fire of this terrible sacrifice. Yet I felt that these were but the externals of religion, and might most safely be relinquished by spirits that best knew their deep significance.

"All is well," said I, cheerfully. "The wood-paths shall be the aisles of our cathedral—the firmament itself shall be its ceiling! What needs an earthly roof between the Deity and his worshipper? Our faith can well afford to lose all the drapery that even the holiest men have thrown around it, and be only the more sublime in its simplicity."

"True," said my companion. "But will they pause here?"

The doubt, implied in his question, was well-founded. In the general destruction of books, already described, a holy volume—that stood apart from the catalogue of human literature, and yet, in one sense, was at its head—had been spared. But the Titan of innovation—angel or fiend, double in his nature, and capable of deeds befitting both characters—at first shaking down only the old and rotten shapes of things, had now, as it appeared, laid his terrible hand upon the main pillars, which supported the whole edifice of our moral and spiritual state. The inhabitants of the earth had grown too enlightened to define their faith within a form of words, or to limit the spiritual by any analogy to our material existence. Truths, which the Heavens trembled at, were now but a fable of the world's infancy. Therefore, as the final sacrifice of human error, what else remained, to be thrown upon the embers of that awful pile, except the Book, which, though a celestial revelation to past ages, was but a voice from a lower sphere, as regarded the present race of man? It was done! Upon the blazing heap of falsehood and worn-out truth—things that the earth had never needed, or had ceased to need, or had grown childishly weary of—fell the ponderous church-Bible, the great old volume, that had lain so long on the cushions of the pulpit, and whence the pastor's solemn voice had given holy utterances, on so many a Sabbath-day. There, likewise, fell the family-Bible, which the long-buried patriarch had read to his children—in prosperity or sorrow, by the fireside, and in the summer-shade of trees—and had bequeathed downward, as the heirloom of generations. There fell the bosom-Bible, the little volume that had been the soul's friend of some sorely tried Child of Dust, who thence took courage, whether his trial were for life or death, steadfastly confronting both, in the strong assurance of Immortality.

All these were flung into the fierce and riotous blaze; and then a mighty wind came roaring across the plain, with a desolate howl, as if it were the angry lamentation of the Earth for the loss of Heaven's sunshine; and it shook the gigantic pyramid of flame, and scattered the cinders of half-consumed abominations around upon the spectators.

"This is terrible!" said I, feeling that my cheek grew pale, and seeing a like change in the visages about me.

"Be of good courage yet," answered the man with whom I had so often spoken. He continued to gaze steadily at the spectacle, with a singular calmness, as if it concerned him merely as an observer.—"Be of good courage—nor yet exult too much; for there is far less both of good and evil, in the effect of this bonfire, than the world might be willing to believe."

"How can that be?" exclaimed I, impatiently.—"Has it not consumed everything? Has it not swallowed up, or melted down, every human or divine appendage of our mortal state, that had substance enough to be acted on by fire? Will there be anything left us, tomorrow morning, better or worse than a heap of embers and ashes?"

"Assuredly there will," said my grave friend. "Come hither tomorrow morning—or whenever the combustible portion of the pile shall be quite burnt out—and you will find among the ashes everything really valuable that you have seen cast into the flames. Trust me; the world of tomorrow will again enrich itself with the gold and diamonds, which have been cast off by the world of to-day. Not a truth is destroyed—nor buried so deep among the ashes, but it will be raked up at last."

This was a strange assurance. Yet I felt inclined to credit it; the more especially as I beheld, among the wallowing flames, a copy of the Holy Scriptures, the pages of which, instead of being blackened into tinder, only assumed a more dazzling whiteness, as the finger-marks of human imperfection were purified away. Certain marginal notes and commentaries, it is true, yielded to the intensity of the fiery test, but without detriment to the smallest syllable that had flamed from the pen of inspiration.

"Yes;—there is the proof of what you say," answered I, turning to the observer. "But, if only what is evil can feel the action of the fire, then, surely, the conflagration has been of inestimable utility. Yet, if I understand aright, you intimate a doubt whether the world's expectation of benefit will be realized by it."

"Listen to the talk of these worthies," said he, pointing to a group in front of the blazing pile.—"Possibly, they may teach you something useful, without intending it."

The persons, whom he indicated, consisted of that brutal and most earthy figure, who had stood forth so furiously in defence of the gallows—the hangman, in short—together with the Last Thief and the Last Murderer; all three of whom were clustered about the Last Toper. The latter was liberally passing the brandy-bottle, which he had rescued from the general destruction of wines and spirits. This little convivial party seemed at the lowest pitch of despondency; as considering that the purified world must needs be utterly unlike, the sphere that they had hitherto known, and therefore but a strange and desolate abode for gentlemen of their kidney.

"The best counsel for all of us, is," remarked the hangman, "that—as soon as we have finished the last drop of liquor—I help you, my three friends, to a comfortable end upon the nearest tree, and then hang myself on the same bough. This is no world for us, any longer."

"Poh, poh, my good fellows!" said a dark-complexioned personage, who now joined the group—his complexion was indeed fearfully dark; and his eyes glowed with a redder light than that of the bonfire—"Be not so cast down, my dear friends; you shall see good days yet. There is one thing that these wiseacres have forgotten to throw into the fire, and without which all the rest of the conflagration is just nothing at all—yes; though they had burnt the earth itself to a cinder!"

"And what may that be?" eagerly demanded the Last Murderer.

"What, but the human heart itself!" said the dark-visaged stranger, with a portentous grin. "And, unless they hit upon some method of purifying that foul cavern, forth from it will re-issue all the shapes of wrong and misery—the same old shapes, or worse ones—which they have taken such a vast deal of trouble to consume to ashes. I have stood by, this live-long night, and laughed in my sleeve at the whole business. Oh, take my word for it, it will be the old world yet!"

This brief conversation supplied me with a theme for lengthened thought. How sad a truth—if true it were—that Man's age-long endeavor for perfection had served only to render him the mockery of the Evil Principle, from the fatal circumstance of an error at the very root of the matter! The Heart—the Heart—there was the little, yet boundless sphere, wherein existed the original wrong, of which the crime and misery of this outward world were merely types. Purify that inner sphere; and the many shapes of evil that haunt the outward, and which now seem almost our only realities, will turn to shadowy phantoms, and vanish of their own accord. But, if we go no deeper than the Intellect, and strive, with merely that feeble instrument, to discern and rectify what is wrong, our whole accomplishment will be a dream; so unsubstantial, that it matters little whether the bonfire, which I have so faithfully described, were what we choose to call a real event, and a flame that would scorch the finger—or only a phosphoric radiance, and a parable of my own brain!

The Artist of the Beautiful

AN elderly man, with his pretty daughter on his arm, was passing along the street, and emerged from the gloom of the cloudy evening into the light that fell across the pavement from the window of a small shop. It was a projecting window; and on the inside were suspended a variety of watches,—pinchbeck, silver, and one or two of gold,—all with their faces turned from the street, as if churlishly disinclined to inform the wayfarers what o'clock it was. Seated within the shop, sidelong to the window, with his pale face bent earnestly over some delicate piece of mechanism, on which was thrown the concentrated lustre of a shade-lamp, appeared a young man.

"What can Owen Warland be about?" muttered old Peter Hovenden,—himself a retired watchmaker, and the former master of this same young man, whose occupation he was now wondering at. "What can the fellow be about? These six months past, I have never come by his shop without seeing him just as steadily at work as now. It would be a flight beyond his usual foolery to seek for the Perpetual Motion. And yet I know enough of my old business to be certain, that what he is now so busy with is no part of the machinery of a watch."

"Perhaps, father," said Annie, without showing much interest in the question, "Owen is inventing a new kind of timekeeper. I am sure he has ingenuity enough."

"Poh, child! he has not the sort of ingenuity to invent anything better than a Dutch toy," answered her father, who had formerly been put to much vexation by Owen Warland's irregular genius. "A plague on such ingenuity! All the effect that ever I knew of it, was to spoil the accuracy of some of the best watches in my shop. He would turn the sun out of its orbit, and derange the whole course of time, if, as I said before, his ingenuity could grasp anything bigger than a child's toy!"

"Hush, father! he hears you," whispered Annie, pressing the old man's arm. "His ears are as delicate as his feelings, and you know how easily disturbed they are. Do let us move on."

So Peter Hovenden and his daughter Annie plodded on, without further conversation, until, in a by-street of the town, they found themselves passing the open door of a blacksmith's shop. Within was seen the forge, now blazing up, and illuminating the high and dusky roof, and now confining its lustre to a narrow precinct of the coal-strewn floor, according as the breath of the bellows was puffed forth, or again inhaled into its vast leathern lungs. In the intervals of brightness, it was easy to distinguish objects in remote corners of the shop, and the horse-shoes that hung upon the wall; in the momentary gloom, the fire seemed to be glimmering amidst the vagueness of unenclosed space. Moving about in this red glare and alternate dusk, was the figure of the blacksmith, well worthy to be viewed in so picturesque an aspect of light and shade, where the bright blaze struggled with the black night, as if each would have snatched his comely strength from the other. Anon, he drew a white-hot bar of iron from the coals, laid it on the anvil, uplifted his arm of might, and was soon enveloped in the myriads of sparks which the strokes of his hammer scattered into the surrounding gloom.

"Now, that is a pleasant sight," said the old watchmaker. "I know what it is to work in gold, but give me the worker in iron, after all is said and done. He spends his labor upon a reality. What say you, daughter Annie?"

"Pray don't speak so loud, father," whispered Annie. "Robert Danforth will hear you."

"And what if he should hear me?" said Peter Hovenden; "I say again, it is a good and a wholesome thing to depend upon main strength and reality, and to earn one's bread with the bare and brawny arm of a blacksmith. A watchmaker gets his brain puzzled by his wheels within a wheel, or loses his health or the nicety of his eyesight, as was my case; and finds himself, at middle age, or a little after, past labor at his own trade, and fit for nothing else, yet too poor to live at his ease. So, I say once again, give me main strength for my money. And then, how it takes the nonsense out of a man! Did you ever hear of a blacksmith being such a fool as Owen Warland, yonder?"

"Well said, uncle Hovenden!" shouted Robert Danforth, from the forge, in a full, deep, merry voice, that made the roof re-echo. "And what says Miss Annie to that doctrine? She, I suppose, will think it a genteeler business to tinker up a lady's watch, than to forge a horse-shoe or make a grid-iron!"

Annie drew her father onward, without giving him time for reply.

But we must return to Owen Warland's shop, and spend more meditation upon his history and character than either Peter Hovenden, or probably his daughter Annie, or Owen's old schoolfellow, Robert Danforth, would have thought due to so slight a subject. From the time that his little fingers could grasp a pen-knife, Owen had been remarkable for a delicate ingenuity, which sometimes produced pretty shapes in wood, principally figures of flowers and birds, and sometimes seemed to aim at the hidden mysteries of mechanism. But it was always for purposes of grace, and never with any mockery of the useful. He did not, like the crowd of school-boy artizans, construct little windmills on the angle of a barn, or watermills across the neighboring brook. Those who discovered such peculiarity in the boy, as to think it worth their while to observe him closely, sometimes saw reason to suppose that he was attempting to imitate the beautiful movements of Nature, as exemplified in the flight of birds or the activity of little animals. It seemed, in fact, a new development of the love of the Beautiful, such as might have made him a poet, a painter, or a sculptor, and which was as completely refined from all utilitarian coarseness, as it could have been in either of the fine arts. He looked with singular distaste at the stiff and regular processes of ordinary machinery. Being once carried to see a steam-engine, in the expectation that his intuitive comprehension of mechanical principles would be gratified, he turned pale, and grew sick, as if something monstrous and unnatural had been presented to him. This horror was partly owing to the size and terrible energy of the Iron Laborer; for the character of Owen's mind was microscopic, and tended naturally to the minute, in accordance with his diminutive frame, and the marvellous smallness and delicate power of his fingers. Not that his sense of beauty was thereby diminished into a sense of prettiness. The Beautiful Idea has no relation to size, and may be as perfectly developed in a space too minute for any but microscopic investigation, as within the ample verge that is measured by the arc of the rainbow. But, at all events, this characteristic minuteness in his objects and accomplishments made the world even more incapable, than it might otherwise have been, of appreciating Owen Warland's genius. The boy's relatives saw nothing better to be done—as perhaps there was not—than to bind him apprentice to a watchmaker, hoping that his strange ingenuity might thus be regulated, and put to utilitarian purposes.

Peter Hovenden's opinion of his apprentice has already been expressed. He could make nothing of the lad. Owen's apprehension of the professional mysteries, it is true, was inconceivably quick. But he altogether forgot or despised the grand object of a watchmaker's business, and cared no more for the measurement of time than if it had been merged into eternity. So long, however, as he remained under his old master's care, Owen's lack of sturdiness made it possible, by strict injunctions and sharp oversight, to restrain his creative eccentricity within bounds. But when his apprenticeship was served out, and he had taken the little shop which Peter Hovenden's failing eye-sight compelled him to relinquish, then did people recognize how unfit a person was Owen Warland to lead old blind Father Time along his daily course. One of his most rational projects was, to connect a musical operation with the machinery of his watches, so that all the harsh dissonances of life might be rendered tuneful, and each flitting moment fall into the abyss of the Past in golden drops of harmony. If a family-clock was entrusted to him for repair—one of those tall, ancient clocks that have grown nearly allied to human nature, by measuring out the lifetime of many generations he would take upon himself to arrange a dance or funeral procession of figures, across its venerable face, representing twelve mirthful or melancholy hours. Several freaks of this kind quite destroyed the young watchmaker's credit with that steady and matter-of-fact class of people who hold the opinion that time is not to be trifled with, whether considered as the medium of advancement and prosperity in this world, or preparation for the next. His custom rapidly diminished—a misfortune, however, that was probably reckoned among his better accidents by Owen Warland, who was becoming more and more absorbed in a secret occupation, which drew all his science and manual dexterity into itself, and likewise gave full employment to the characteristic tendencies of his genius. This pursuit had already consumed many months.

After the old watchmaker and his pretty daughter had gazed at him, out of the obscurity of the street, Owen Warland was seized with a fluttering of the nerves, which made his hand tremble too violently to proceed with such delicate labor as he was now engaged upon.

"It was Annie herself!" murmured he. "I should have known it, by this throbbing of my heart, before I heard her father's voice. Ah, how it throbs! I shall scarcely be able to work again on this exquisite mechanism to-night. Annie—dearest Annie—thou shouldst give firmness to my heart and hand, and not shake them thus; for if I strive to put the very spirit of Beauty into form, and give it motion, it is for thy sake alone. Oh, throbbing heart, be quiet! If my labor be thus thwarted, there will come vague and unsatisfied dreams, which will leave me spiritless to-morrow."

As he was endeavoring to settle himself again to his task, the shop-door opened, and gave admittance to no other than the stalwart figure which Peter Hovenden had paused to admire, as seen amid the light and shadow of the blacksmith's shop. Robert Danforth had brought a little anvil of his own manufacture, and peculiarly constructed, which the young artist had recently bespoken. Owen examined the article, and pronounced it fashioned according to his wish.

"Why, yes," said Robert Danforth, his strong voice filling the shop as with the sound of a bass-viol, "I consider myself equal to anything in the way of my own trade; though I should have made but a poor figure at yours, with such a fist as this,"—added he, laughing, as he laid his vast hand beside the delicate one of Owen. "But what then? I put more main strength into one blow of my sledge-hammer, than all that you have expended since you were a 'prentice. Is not that the truth?"

"Very probably," answered the low and slender voice of Owen. "Strength is an earthly monster. I make no pretensions to it. My force, whatever there may be of it, is altogether spiritual."

"Well; but, Owen, what are you about!" asked his old schoolfellow, still in such a hearty volume of tone that it made the artist shrink; especially as the question related to a subject so sacred as the absorbing dream of his imagination. "Folks do say, that you are trying to discover the Perpetual Motion."

"The Perpetual Motion?—nonsense!" replied Owen Warland, with a movement of digust; for he was full of little petulances. "It can never be discovered! It is a dream that may delude men whose brains are mystified with matter, but not me. Besides, if such a discovery were possible, it would not be worth my while to make it, only to have the secret turned to such purposes as are now effected by steam and water-power. I am not ambitious to be honored with the paternity of a new kind of cotton-machine."

"That would be droll enough!" cried the blacksmith, breaking out into such an uproar of laughter, that Owen himself, and the bell-glasses on his work-board, quivered in unison. "No, no, Owen! No child of yours will have iron joints and sinews. Well, I won't hinder you any more. Good night, Owen, and success; and if you need any assistance, so far as a downright blow of hammer upon anvil will answer the purpose, I'm your man!"

And with another laugh, the man of main strength left the shop.

"How strange it is," whispered Owen Warland to himself, leaning his head upon his hand, "that all my musings, my purposes, my passion for the Beautiful, my consciousness of power to create it—a finer, more ethereal power, of which this earthly giant can have no conception—all, all, look so vain and idle, whenever my path is crossed by Robert Danforth! He would drive me mad, were I to meet him often. His hard, brute force darkens and confuses the spiritual element within me. But I, too, will be strong in my own way. I will not yield to him!"

He took from beneath a glass, a piece of minute machinery, which he set in the condensed light of his lamp, and, looking intently at it through a magnifying glass, proceeded to operate with a delicate instrument of steel. In an instant, however, he fell back in his chair, and clasped his hands, with a look of horror on his face, that made its small features as impressive as those of a giant would have been.

"Heaven! What have I done!" exclaimed he. "The vapor!— the influence of that brute force!—it has bewildered me, and obscured my perception. I have made the very stroke—the fa-

tal stroke—that I have dreaded from the first! It is all over—
the toil of months—the object of my life! I am ruined!"

And there he sat, in strange despair, until his lamp flickered
in the socket, and left the Artist of the Beautiful in darkness.

Thus it is, that ideas which grow up within the imagination, and appear so lovely to it, and of a value beyond whatever
men call valuable, are exposed to be shattered and annihilated
by contact with the Practical. It is requisite for the ideal artist
to possess a force of character that seems hardly compatible
with its delicacy; he must keep his faith in himself, while the
incredulous world assails him with its utter disbelief; he must
stand up against mankind and be his own sole disciple, both as
respects his genius, and the objects to which it is directed.

For a time, Owen Warland succumbed to this severe, but inevitable test. He spent a few sluggish weeks, with his head so
continually resting in his hands, that the townspeople had
scarcely an opportunity to see his countenance. When, at last,
it was again uplifted to the light of day, a cold, dull, nameless
change was perceptible upon it. In the opinion of Peter
Hovenden, however, and that order of sagacious understand-
ings who think that life should be regulated, like clock-work,
with leaden weights, the alteration was entirely for the better.
Owen now indeed, applied himself to business with dogged in-
dustry. It was marvellous to witness the obtuse gravity with
which he would inspect the wheels of a great, old silver watch;
thereby delighting the owner, in whose fob it had been worn
till he deemed it a portion of his own life, and was accordingly
jealous of its treatment. In consequence of the good report thus
acquired, Owen Warland was invited by the proper authorities
to regulate the clock in the church-steeple. He succeeded so admirably in this matter of public interest, that the merchants
gruffly acknowledged his merits on 'Change; the nurse whispered his praises, as she gave the potion in the sick-chamber;
the lover blessed him at the hour of appointed interview; and
the town in general thanked Owen for the punctuality of din-

ner-time. In a word, the heavy weight upon his spirits kept everything in order, not merely within his own system, but wheresoever the iron accents of the church-clock were audible. It was a circumstance, though minute, yet characteristic of his present state, that, when employed to engrave names or initials on silver spoons, he now wrote the requisite letters in the plainest possible style; omitting a variety of fanciful flourishes, that had heretofore distinguished his work in this kind.

One day, during the era of this happy transformation, old Peter Hovenden came to visit his former apprentice.

"Well, Owen," said he, "I am glad to hear such good accounts of you from all quarters; and especially from the town-clock yonder, which speaks in your commendation every hour of the twenty-four. Only get rid altogether of your nonsensical trash about the Beautiful—which I, nor nobody else, nor yourself to boot, could never understand—only free yourself of that, and your success in life is as sure as daylight. Why, if you go on in this way, I should even venture to let you doctor this precious old watch of mine; though, except my daughter Annie, I have nothing else so valuable in the world."

"I should hardly dare touch it, sir," replied Owen in a depressed tone; for he was weighed down by his old master's presence.

"In time," said the latter, "in time, you will be capable of it."

The old watchmaker, with the freedom naturally consequent on his former authority, went on inspecting the work which Owen had in hand at the moment, together with other matters that were in progress. The artist, meanwhile, could scarcely lift his head. There was nothing so antipodal to his nature as this man's cold, unimaginative sagacity, by contact with which everything was converted into a dream, except the densest matter of the physical world. Owen groaned in spirit, and prayed fervently to be delivered from him.

"But what is this?" cried Peter Hovenden abruptly, taking

up a dusty bell-glass, beneath which appeared a mechanical something, as delicate and minute as the system of a butterfly's anatomy. "What have we here! Owen, Owen! there is witchcraft in these little chains, and wheels, and paddles! See! with one pinch of my finger and thumb, I am going to deliver you from all future peril."

"For Heaven's sake," screamed Owen Warland, springing up with wonderful energy, "as you would not drive me mad—do not touch it! The slightest pressure of your finger would ruin me for ever."

"Aha, young man! And is it so?" said the old watchmaker, looking at him with just enough of penetration to torture Owen's soul with the bitterness of worldly criticism. "Well; take your own course. But I warn you again, that in this small piece of mechanism lives your evil spirit. Shall I exorcise him?"

"You are my Evil Spirit," answered Owen, much excited—"you, and the hard, coarse world! The leaden thoughts and the despondency that you fling upon me are my clogs. Else, I should long ago have achieved the task that I was created for."

Peter Hovenden shook his head, with the mixture of contempt and indignation which mankind, of whom he was partly a representative, deem themselves entitled to feel towards all simpletons who seek other prizes than the dusty ones along the highway. He then took his leave with an uplifted finger, and a sneer upon his face, that haunted the artist's dreams for many a night afterwards. At the time of his old master's visit, Owen was probably on the point of taking up the relinquished task; but, by this sinister event, he was thrown back into the state whence he had been slowly emerging.

But the innate tendency of his soul had only been accumulating fresh vigor, during its apparent sluggishness. As the summer advanced, he almost totally relinquished his business, and permitted Father Time, so far as the old gentleman was represented by the clocks and watches under his control, to stray at random through human life, making infinite confusion among the train of bewildered hours. He wasted the sunshine, as people said, in wandering through the woods and fields, and along the banks of streams. There, like a child, he found amusement in chasing butterflies, or watching the motions of water-insects. There was something truly mysterious in the intentness with which he contemplated these living playthings, as they sported on the breeze; or examined the structure of an imperial insect whom he had imprisoned. The chase of butterflies was an apt emblem of the ideal pursuit in which he had spent so many golden hours. But, would the Beautiful Idea ever be yielded to his hand, like the butterfly that symbolized it? Sweet, doubtless, were these days, and congenial to the artist's soul. They were full of bright conceptions, which gleamed through his intellectual world, as the butterflies gleamed through the outward atmosphere, and were real to him for the instant, without the toil, and perplexity, and many disappointments, of attempting to make them visible to the sensual eye. Alas, that the artist, whether in poetry or whatever other material, may not content himself with the inward enjoyment of the Beautiful, but must chase the flitting mystery beyond the verge of his ethereal domain, and crush its frail being in seizing it with a material grasp! Owen Warland felt the impulse to give external reality to his ideas, as irresistibly as any of the poets or painters, who have arrayed the world in a dimmer and fainter beauty, imperfectly copied from the richness of their visions.

The night was now his time for the slow process of recreating the one Idea, to which all his intellectual activity referred itself. Always at the approach of dusk, he stole into the town, locked himself within his shop, and wrought with patient delicacy of touch, for many hours. Sometimes he was startled by the rap of the watchman, who, when all the world should be asleep, had caught the gleam of lamp-light through the crevices of Owen Warland's shutters. Daylight, to the morbid sensibility of his mind, seemed to have an intrusiveness that interfered with his pursuits. On cloudy and inclement days, therefore, he sat with his head upon his hands, muffling, as it were, his sensitive brain in a mist of indefinite musings; for it was a relief to escape from the sharp distinctness with which he was compelled to shape out his thoughts, during his nightly toil.

From one of these fits of torpor, he was aroused by the entrance of Annie Hovenden, who came into the shop with the freedom of a customer, and also with something of the familiarity of a childish friend. She had worn a hole through her silver thimble, and wanted Owen to repair it.

"But I don't know whether you will condescend to such a task," said she, laughing, "now that you are so taken up with the notion of putting spirit into machinery."

"Where did you get that idea, Annie?" said Owen, starting in surprise.

"Oh, out of my own head," answered she, "and from something that I heard you say, long ago, when you were but a boy, and I a little child. But, come! will you mend this poor thimble of mine?"

"Anything for your sake, Annie," said Owen Warland—"anything; even were it to work at Robert Danforth's forge."

"And that would be a pretty sight!" retorted Annie, glancing with imperceptible slightness at the artist's small and slender frame. "Well; here is the thimble."

"But that is a strange idea of yours," said Owen, "about the spiritualization of matter!"

And then the thought stole into his mind, that this young girl possessed the gift to comprehend him, better than all the world beside. And what a help and strength would it be to him, in his lonely toil, if he could gain the sympathy of the only being whom he loved! To persons whose pursuits are insulated from the common business of life—who are either in advance of mankind, or apart from it—there often comes a sensation of moral cold, that makes the spirit shiver, as if it had reached the frozen solitudes around the pole. What the prophet, the poet, the reformer, the criminal, or any other man, with human yearnings, but separated from the multitude by a peculiar lot, might feel, poor Owen Warland felt.

"Annie," cried he, growing pale as death at the thought, "how gladly would I tell you the secret of my pursuit! You, methinks, would estimate it rightly. You, I know, would hear it with a reverence that I must not expect from the harsh, material world."

"Would I not? to be sure I would!" replied Annie Hovenden, lightly laughing. "Come; explain to me quickly what is the meaning of this little whirligig, so delicately wrought that it might be a plaything for Queen Mab. See; I will put it in motion."

"Hold," exclaimed Owen, "hold!"

Annie had but given the slightest possible touch, with the point of a needle, to the same minute portion of complicated machinery which has been more than once mentioned, when the artist seized her by the wrist with a force that made her scream aloud. She was affrighted at the convulsion of intense rage and anguish that writhed across his features. The next instant he let his head sink upon his hands.

"Go, Annie," murmured he, "I have deceived myself, and must suffer for it. I yearned for sympathy—and thought—and fancied—and dreamed—that you might give it me. But you lack the talisman, Annie, that should admit you into my secrets. That touch has undone the toil of months, and the thought of a lifetime! It was not your fault, Annie—but you have ruined me!"

Poor Owen Warland! He had indeed erred, yet pardonably; for if any human spirit could have sufficiently reverenced the processes so sacred in his eyes, it must have been a woman's. Even Annie Hovenden, possibly, might not have disappointed him, had she been enlightened by the deep intelligence of love.

The artist spent the ensuing winter in a way that satisfied any persons, who had hitherto retained a hopeful opinion of him, that he was, in truth, irrevocably doomed to inutility as regarded the world, and to an evil destiny on his own part. The decease of a relative had put him in possession of a small inheritance. Thus freed from the necessity of toil, and having lost the steadfast influence of a great purpose—great, at least to him—he abandoned himself to habits from which, it might have been supposed, the mere delicacy of his organization would have availed to secure him. But when the ethereal portion of a man of genius is obscured, the earthly part assumes an influence the more uncontrollable, because the character is now thrown off the balance to which Providence had so nicely adjusted it, and which, in coarser natures, is adjusted by some other method. Owen Warland made proof of whatever show of bliss may be found in riot. He looked at the world through the golden medium of wine, and contemplated the visions that bubble up so gaily around the brim of the glass, and that people the air with shapes of pleasant madness, which so soon grow ghostly and forlorn. Even when this dismal and inevitable change had taken place, the young man might still have continued to quaff the cup of enchantments, though its vapor did but shroud life in gloom, and fill the gloom with spectres that mocked at him. There was a certain irksomeness of spirit, which, being real, and the deepest sensation of which the artist was now conscious, was more intolerable than any fantastic miseries and horrors that the abuse of wine could summon up. In the latter case, he could remember, even out of the midst of his trouble, that all was but a delusion; in the former, the heavy anguish was his actual life.

From this perilous state, he was redeemed by an incident which more than one person witnessed, but of which the shrewdest could not explain nor conjecture the operation on Owen Warland's mind. It was very simple. On a warm afternoon of spring, as the artist sat among his riotous companions, with a glass of wine before him, a splendid butterfly flew in at the open window, and fluttered about his head.

"Ah!" exclaimed Owen, who had drank freely, "Are you alive again, child of the sun, and playmate of the summer breeze, after your dismal winter's nap! Then it is time for me to be at work!"

And leaving his unemptied glass upon the table, he departed, and was never known to sip another drop of wine.

And now, again, he resumed his wanderings in the woods and fields. It might be fancied that the bright butterfly, which had come so spiritlike into the window, as Owen sat with the rude revellers, was indeed a spirit, commissioned to recall him to the pure, ideal life that had so etherealized him among men. It might be fancied, that he went forth to seek this spirit, in its sunny haunts; for still, as in the summer-time gone by, he was seen to steal gently up, wherever a butterfly had alighted, and lose himself in contemplation of it. When it took flight, his eyes followed the winged vision, as if its airy track would show the path to heaven. But what could be the purpose of the unseasonable toil, which was again resumed, as the watchman knew by the lines of lamp-light through the crevices of Owen Warland's shutters? The townspeople had one comprehensive explanation of all these singularities. Owen Warland had gone mad! How universally efficacious—how satisfactory, too, and soothing to the injured sensibility of narrowness and dullness—is this easy method of accounting for whatever lies beyond the world's most ordinary scope! From Saint Paul's days, down to our poor little Artist of the Beautiful, the same talisman has been applied to the elucidation of all mysteries in the words or deeds of men, who spoke or acted too wisely or too well. In Owen Warland's case, the judgment of his townspeople may have been correct. Perhaps he was mad. The lack of sympathy—that contrast between himself and his neighbors, which took away the restraint of example—was enough to make him so. Or, possibly, he had caught just so much of ethereal radiance as served to bewilder him, in an earthly sense, by its intermixture with the common daylight.

One evening, when the artist had returned from a customary ramble, and had just thrown the lustre of his lamp on the delicate piece of work, so often interrupted, but still taken up again, as if his fate were embodied in its mechanism, he was surprised by the entrance of old Peter Hovenden. Owen never met this man without a shrinking of the heart. Of all the world, he was most terrible, by reason of a keen understanding, which saw so distinctly what it did see, and disbelieved so uncompromisingly in what it could not see. On this occasion, the old watchmaker had merely a gracious word or two to say.

"Owen, my lad," said he, "we must see you at my house to-morrow night."

The artist began to mutter some excuse.

"Oh, but it must be so," quoth Peter Hovenden, "for the sake of the days when you were one of the household. What, my boy, don't you know that my daughter Annie is engaged to Robert Danforth? We are making an entertainment, in our humble way, to celebrate the event."

"Ah!" said Owen.

That little monosyllable was all he uttered; its tone seemed cold and unconcerned, to an ear like Peter Hovenden's; and yet there was in it the stifled outcry of the poor artist's heart, which he compressed within him like a man holding down an evil spirit. One slight outbreak, however, imperceptible to the old watchmaker, he allowed himself. Raising the instrument with which he was about to begin his work, he let it fall upon the little system of machinery that had, anew, cost him months of thought and toil. It was shattered by the stroke!

Owen Warland's story would have been no tolerable representation of the troubled life of those who strive to create the Beautiful, if, amid all other thwarting influences, love had not interposed to steal the cunning from his hand. Out-

wardly, he had been no ardent or enterprising lover; the career
of his passion had confined its tumults and vicissitudes so entirely within the artist's imagination, that Annie herself had
scarcely more than a woman's intuitive perception of it. But,
in Owen's view, it covered the whole field of his life. Forget-
ful of the time when she had shown herself incapable of any
deep response, he had persisted in connecting all his dreams
of artistical success with Annie's image; she was the visible
shape in which the spiritual power that he worshipped, and
on whose altar he hoped to lay a not unworthy offering, was
made manifest to him. Of course he had deceived himself;
there were no such attributes in Annie Hovenden as his imagination had endowed her with. She, in the aspect which she
wore to his inward vision, was as much a creation of his own,
as the mysterious piece of mechanism would be were it ever realized. Had he become convinced of his mistake through the
medium of successful love; had he won Annie to his bosom,
and there beheld her fade from angel into ordinary woman,
the disappointment might have driven him back, with concentrated energy, upon his sole remaining object. On the other
hand, had he found Annie what he fancied, his lot would have
been so rich in beauty, that, out of its mere redundancy, he
might have wrought the Beautiful into many a worthier type
than he had toiled for. But the guise in which his sorrow
came to him, the sense that the angel of his life had been
snatched away and given to a rude man of earth and iron, who
could neither need nor appreciate her ministrations; this was
the very perversity of fate, that makes human existence appear
too absurd and contradictory to be the scene of one other hope
or one other fear. There was nothing left for Owen Warland
but to sit down like a man that had been stunned.

He went through a fit of illness. After his recovery, his
small and slender frame assumed an obtuser garniture of flesh
than it had ever before worn. His thin cheeks became round;

his delicate little hand, so spiritually fashioned to achieve fairy task-work, grew plumper than the hand of a thriving infant. His aspect had a childishness, such as might have induced a stranger to pat him on the head—pausing, however, in the act, to wonder what manner of child was here. It was as if the spirit had gone out of him, leaving the body to flourish in a sort of vegetable existence. Not that Owen Warland was idiotic. He could talk, and not irrationally. Somewhat of a babbler, indeed, did people begin to think him; for he was apt to discourse at wearisome length, of marvels of mechanism that he had read about in books, but which he had learned to consider as absolutely fabulous. Among them he enumerated the Man of Brass, constructed by Albertus Magnus, and the Brazen Head of Friar Bacon; and, coming down to later times, the automata of a little coach and horses, which, it was pretended, had been manufactured for the Dauphin of France; together with an insect that buzzed about the ear like a living fly, and yet was but a contrivance of minute steel springs. There was a story, too, of a duck that waddled, and quacked, and ate; though, had any honest citizen purchased it for dinner, he would have found himself cheated with the mere mechanical apparition of a duck.

"But all these accounts," said Owen Warland, "I am now satisfied, are mere impositions."

Then, in a mysterious way, he would confess that he once thought differently. In his idle and dreamy days, he had considered it possible, in a certain sense, to spiritualize machinery; and to combine with the new species of life and motion, thus produced, a beauty that should attain to the ideal which Nature has proposed to herself, in all her creatures, but has never taken pains to realize. He seemed, however, to retain no very distinct perception either of the process of achieving this object, or of the design itself.

"I have thrown it all aside now," he would say. "It was a

dream, such as young men are always mystifying themselves with. Now that I have acquired a little common sense, it makes me laugh to think of it."

Poor, poor, and fallen Owen Warland! These were the symptoms that he had ceased to be an inhabitant of the better sphere that lies unseen around us. He had lost his faith in the invisible, and now prided himself, as such unfortunates invariably do, in the wisdom which rejected much that even his eye could see, and trusted confidently in nothing but what his hand could touch. This is the calamity of men whose spiritual part dies out of them, and leaves the grosser understanding to assimilate them more and more to the things of which alone it can take cognizance. But, in Owen Warland, the spirit was not dead, nor past away; it only slept.

How it awoke again, is not recorded. Perhaps, the torpid slumber was broken by a convulsive pain. Perhaps, as in a former instance, the butterfly came and hovered about his head, and reinspired him—as, indeed, this creature of the sunshine had always a mysterious mission for the artist—reinspired him with the former purpose of his life. Whether it were pain or happiness that thrilled through his veins, his first impulse was to thank Heaven for rendering him again the being of thought, imagination, and keenest sensibility, that he had long ceased to be.

"Now for my task," said he. "Never did I feel such strength for it as now."

Yet, strong as he felt himself, he was incited to toil the more diligently, by an anxiety lest death should surprise him in the midst of his labors. This anxiety, perhaps, is common to all men who set their hearts upon anything so high, in their own view of it, that life becomes of importance only as conditional to its accomplishment. So long as we love life for itself, we seldom dread the losing it. When we desire life for the attainment of an object, we recognize the frailty of its texture. But, side by side with this sense of insecurity, there is a vital faith in our invulnerability to the shaft of death, while engaged in any task that seems assigned by Providence as our proper thing to do, and which the world would have cause to mourn for, should we leave it unaccomplished. Can the philosopher, big with the inspiration of an idea that is to reform mankind, believe that he is to be beckoned from this sensible existence, at the very instant when he is mustering his breath to speak the word of light? Should he perish so, the weary ages may pass away—the world's whole life-sand may fall, drop by drop—before another intellect is prepared to develop the truth that might have been uttered then. But history affords many an example, where the most precious spirit, at any particular epoch manifested in human shape, has gone hence untimely, without space allowed him, so far as mortal judgment could discern, to perform his mission on the earth. The prophet dies; and the man of torpid heart and sluggish brain lives on. The poet leaves his song half sung, or finishes it, beyond the scope of mortal ears, in a celestial choir. The painter—as Allston did—leaves half his conception on the canvass, to sadden us with its imperfect beauty, and goes to picture forth the whole, if it be no irreverence to say so, in the hues of Heaven. But, rather, such incomplete designs of this life will be perfected nowhere. This so frequent abortion of man's dearest projects must be taken as a proof, that the deeds of earth, however etherealized by piety or genius, are without value, except as exercises and manifestations of the spirit. In Heaven, all ordinary thought is higher and more melodious than Milton's song. Then, would he add another verse to any strain that he had left unfinished here?

But to return to Owen Warland. It was his fortune, good or ill, to achieve the purpose of his life. Pass we over a long space of intense thought, yearning effort, minute toil, and wasting anxiety, succeeded by an instant of solitary triumph; let all this be imagined; and then behold the artist, on a winter evening, seeking admittance to Robert Danforth's fireside circle. There he found the Man of Iron, with his massive substance thoroughly warmed and attempered by domestic influences. And there was Annie, too, now transformed into a matron, with much of her husband's plain and sturdy nature, but imbued, as Owen Warland still believed, with a finer grace, that might enable her to be the interpreter between Strength and Beauty. It happened, likewise, that old Peter Hovenden was a guest, this evening, at his daughter's fireside; and it was his well-remembered expression of keen, cold criticism, that first encountered the artist's glance.

"My old friend Owen!" cried Robert Danforth, starting up, and compressing the artist's delicate fingers within a hand that was accustomed to gripe bars of iron. "This is kind and neighborly, to come to us at last! I was afraid your Perpetual Motion had bewitched you out of the remembrance of old times."

"We are glad to see you!" said Annie, while a blush reddened her matronly cheek. "It was not like a friend, to stay from us so long."

"Well, Owen," inquired the old watchmaker, as his first greeting, "how comes on the Beautiful? Have you created it at last?"

The artist did not immediately reply, being startled by the apparition of a young child of strength, that was tumbling about on the carpet; a little personage who had come mysteriously out of the infinite, but with something so sturdy and real in his composition that he seemed moulded out of the densest substance which earth could supply. This hopeful infant crawled towards the new-comer, and setting himself on end—as Robert Danforth expressed the posture—stared at Owen with a look of such sagacious observation, that the mother could not help exchanging a proud glance with her husband. But the artist was disturbed by the child's look, as imagining a resemblance between it and Peter Hovenden's habitual expression. He could have fancied that the old watchmaker was compressed into this baby-shape, and was looking out of those baby-eyes, and repeating—as he now did—the malicious question:

"The Beautiful, Owen! How comes on the Beautiful? Have you succeeded in creating the Beautiful?"

"I have succeeded," replied the artist, with a momentary light of triumph in his eyes, and a smile of sunshine, yet steeped in such depth of thought that it was almost sadness. "Yes, my friends, it is the truth. I have succeeded!"

"Indeed!" cried Annie, a look of maiden mirthfulness peeping out of her face again. "And it is lawful, now, to inquire what the secret is?"

"Surely; it is to disclose it, that I have come," answered Owen Warland. "You shall know, and see, and touch, and possess, the secret! For Annie—if by that name I may still address the friend of my boyish years—Annie, it is for your bridal gift that I have wrought this spiritualized mechanism, this harmony of motion, this Mystery of Beauty! It comes late, indeed; but it is as we go onward in life, when objects begin to lose their freshness of hue, and our souls their delicacy of perception, that the spirit of Beauty is most needed. If—forgive me, Annie—if you know how to value this gift, it can never come too late!"

He produced, as he spoke, what seemed a jewel-box. It was carved richly out of ebony by his own hand, and inlaid with a fanciful tracery of pearl, representing a boy in pursuit of a butterfly, which, elsewhere, had become a winged spirit, and was flying heavenward; while the boy, or youth, had found such efficacy in his strong desire, that he ascended from earth to cloud, and from cloud to celestial atmosphere, to win the Beautiful. This case of ebony the artist opened, and bade Annie place her finger on its edge. She did so, but almost screamed, as a butterfly fluttered forth, and alighting on her finger's tip, sat waving the ample magnificence of its purple and gold-speckled wings, as if in prelude to a flight. It is impossible to

express by words the glory, the splendor, the delicate gorgeousness, which were softened into the beauty of this object. Nature's ideal butterfly was here realized in all its perfection; not
in the pattern of such faded insects as flit among earthly flowers, but of those which hover across the meads of Paradise, for
child-angels and the spirits of departed infants to disport themselves with. The rich down was visible upon its wings; the
lustre of its eyes seemed instinct with spirit. The firelight glimmered around this wonder—the candles gleamed upon it—but
it glistened apparently by its own radiance, and illuminated
the finger and outstretched hand on which it rested, with a
white gleam like that of precious stones. In its perfect beauty,
the consideration of size was entirely lost. Had its wings
overarched the firmament, the mind could not have been more
filled or satisfied.

"Beautiful! Beautiful!" exclaimed Annie. "Is it alive? Is it
alive?"

"Alive? To be sure it is," answered her husband. "Do you
suppose any mortal has skill enough to make a butterfly,—or
would put himself to the trouble of making one, when any
child may catch a score of them in a summer's afternoon?
Alive? Certainly! But this pretty box is undoubtedly of our
friend Owen's manufacture; and really it does him credit."

At this moment, the butterfly waved its wings anew, with a
motion so absolutely lifelike that Annie was startled, and even
awe-stricken; for, in spite of her husband's opinion, she could
not satisfy herself whether it was indeed a living creature, or a
piece of wondrous mechanism.

"Is it alive?" she repeated, more earnestly than before.

"Judge for yourself," said Owen Warland, who stood gazing
in her face with fixed attention.

The butterfly now flung itself upon the air, fluttered round
Annie's head, and soared into a distant region of the parlor,
still making itself perceptible to sight by the starry gleam in
which the motion of its wings enveloped it. The infant on the

floor, followed its course with his sagacious little eyes. After flying about the room, it returned, in a spiral curve, and settled again on Annie's finger.

"But is it alive?" exclaimed she again; and the finger, on which the gorgeous mystery had alighted, was so tremulous that the butterfly was forced to balance himself with his wings. "Tell me if it be alive, or whether you created it?"

"Wherefore ask who created it, so it be beautiful?" replied Owen Warland. "Alive? Yes, Annie; it may well be said to possess life, for it absorbed my own being into itself; and in the secret of that butterfly, and in its beauty—which is not merely outward, but deep as its whole system—is represented the intellect, the imagination, the sensibility, the soul, of an Artist of the Beautiful! Yes, I created it. But"—and here his countenance somewhat changed—"this butterfly is not now to me what it was when I beheld it afar off, in the day-dreams of my youth."

"Be it what it may, it is a pretty plaything," said the blacksmith, grinning with childlike delight. "I wonder whether it would condescend to alight on such a great clumsy finger as mine? Hold it hither, Annie!"

By the artist's direction, Annie touched her finger's tip to that of her husband; and, after a momentary delay, the butterfly fluttered from one to the other. It preluded a second flight by a similar, yet not precisely the same waving of wings, as in the first experiment; then, ascending from the blacksmith's stalwart finger, it rose in a gradually enlarging curve to the ceiling, made one wide sweep around the room, and returned with an undulating movement to the point whence it had started.

"Well, that does beat all nature!" cried Robert Danforth, bestowing the heartiest praise that he could find expression for; and, indeed, had he paused there, a man of finer words and nicer perception, could not easily have said more. "That goes beyond me, I confess! But what then? There is more real use in one downright blow of my sledge-hammer, than in the whole five years' labor that our friend Owen has wasted on this butter-fly!"

Here the child clapped his hands, and made a great babble of indistinct utterance, apparently demanding that the butter-fly should be given him for a plaything.

Owen Warland, meanwhile, glanced sidelong at Annie, to discover whether she sympathized in her husband's estimate of the comparative value of the Beautiful and the Practical. There was, amid all her kindness towards himself, amid all the won-der and admiration with which she contemplated the marvel-ous work of his hands, and incarnation of his idea, a secret scorn; too secret, perhaps, for her own consciousness, and per-ceptible only to such intuitive discernment as that of the artist. But Owen, in the latter stages of his pursuit, had risen out of the region in which such a discovery might have been torture. He knew that the world, and Annie as the representative of the world, whatever praise might be bestowed, could never say the fitting word, nor feel the fitting sentiment which should be the perfect recompense of an artist who, symbolizing a lofty moral by a material trifle—converting what was earthly, to spiritual gold—had won the Beautiful into his handiwork. Not at this latest moment, was he to learn that the reward of all high performance must be sought within itself, or sought in vain. There was, however, a view of the matter, which Annie, and her husband, and even Peter Hovenden, might fully have understood, and which would have satisfied them that the toil of years had here been worthily bestowed. Owen Warland might have told them, that this butterfly, this plaything, this bridal-gift of a poor watchmaker to a blacksmith's wife, was, in truth, a gem of art that a monarch would have purchased with honors and abundant wealth, and have treasured it among the jewels of his kingdom, as the most unique and wondrous of them all! But the artist smiled, and kept the secret to himself.

"Father," said Annie, thinking that a word of praise from

the old watchmaker might gratify his former apprentice, "do come and admire this pretty butterfly!"

"Let us see," said Peter Hovenden, rising from his chair, with the sneer upon his face that always made people doubt, as he himself did, in everything but a material existence. "Here is my finger for it to alight upon. I shall understand it better when once I have touched it."

But, to the increased astonishment of Annie, when the tip of her father's finger was pressed against that of her husband, on which the butterfly still rested, the insect drooped its wings, and seemed on the point of falling to the floor. Even the bright spots of gold upon its wings and body, unless her eyes deceived her, grew dim, and the glowing purple took a dusky hue, and the starry lustre that gleamed around the blacksmith's hand, became faint, and vanished.

"It is dying! it is dying!" cried Annie, in alarm.

"It has been delicately wrought," said the artist calmly. "As I told you, it has imbibed a spiritual essence—call it magnetism, or what you will. In an atmosphere of doubt and mockery, its exquisite susceptibility suffers torture, as does the soul of him who instilled his own life into it. It has already lost its beauty; in a few moments more, its mechanism would be irreparably injured."

"Take away your hand, father!" entreated Annie, turning pale. "Here is my child; let it rest on his innocent hand. There, perhaps, its life will revive, and its colors grow brighter than ever."

Her father, with an acrid smile, withdrew his finger. The butterfly then appeared to recover the power of voluntary motion; while its hues assumed much of their original lustre, and the gleam of starlight, which was its most ethereal attribute, again formed a halo round about it. At first, when transferred from Robert Danforth's hand to the small finger of the child, this radiance grew so powerful that it positively threw the little fellow's shadow back against the wall. He, meanwhile, extended his plump hand as he had seen his father and mother do, and watched the waving of the insect's wings, with infantine delight. Nevertheless, there was a certain odd expression of sagacity, that made Owen Warland feel as if here were old Peter Hovenden, partially, and but partially, redeemed from his hard scepticism into childish faith.

"How wise the little monkey looks!" whispered Robert Danforth to his wife.

"I never saw such a look on a child's face," answered Annie, admiring her own infant, and with good reason, far more than the artistic butterfly. "The darling knows more of the mystery than we do."

As if the butterfly, like the artist, were conscious of something not entirely congenial in the child's nature, it alternately sparkled and grew dim. At length, it arose from the small hand of the infant with an airy motion, that seemed to bear it upward without an effort; as if the ethereal instincts, with which its master's spirit had endowed it, impelled this fair vision involuntarily to a higher sphere. Had there been no obstruction, it might have soared into the sky, and grown immortal. But its lustre gleamed upon the ceiling; the exquisite texture of its wings brushed against that earthly medium; and a sparkle or two, as of star-dust, floated downward and lay glimmering on the carpet. Then the butterfly came fluttering down, and instead of returning to the infant, was apparently attracted towards the artist's hand.

"Not so, not so!" murmured Owen Warland, as if his handiwork could have understood him. "Thou hast gone forth out of thy master's heart. There is no return for thee!"

With a wavering movement, and emitting a tremulous radiance, the butterfly struggled, as it were, towards the infant, and was about to alight upon his finger. But, while it still hovered in the air, the little Child of Strength, with his grandsire's sharp and shrewd expression in his face, made a snatch at the marvellous insect, and compressed it in his hand. Annie screamed! Old Peter Hovenden burst into a cold and scornful laugh. The blacksmith, by main force, unclosed the infant's hand, and found within the palm a small heap of glittering fragments, whence the Mystery of Beauty had fled for ever. And as for Owen Warland, he looked placidly at what seemed the ruin of his life's labor, and which was yet no ruin. He had caught a far other butterfly than this. When the artist rose high enough to achieve the Beautiful, the symbol by which he made it perceptible to mortal senses became of little value in his eyes, while his spirit possessed itself in the enjoyment of the Reality.

Rappaccini's Daughter

FROM THE WRITINGS OF AUBÉPINE

WE do not remember to have seen any translated specimens of the productions of M. de l'Aubépine; a fact the less to be wondered at, as his very name is unknown to many of his own countrymen, as well as to the student of foreign literature. As a writer, he seems to occupy an unfortunate position between the Transcendentalists (who, under one name or another, have their share in all the current literature of the world), and the great body of pen-and-ink men who address the intellect and sympathies of the multitude. If not too refined, at all events too remote, too shadowy and unsubstantial in his modes of development, to suit the taste of the latter class, and yet too popular to satisfy the spiritual or metaphysical requisitions of the former, he must necessarily find himself without an audience; except here and there an individual, or possibly an isolated clique. His writings, to do them justice, are not altogether destitute of fancy and originality; they might have won him greater reputation but for an inveterate love of allegory, which is apt to invest his plots and characters with the aspect of scenery and people in the clouds, and to steal away the human warmth out of his conceptions. His fictions are sometimes historical, sometimes of the present day, and sometimes, so far as can be discovered, have little or no reference either to time or space. In any case, he generally contents himself with a very slight embroidery of outward manners,—the faintest possible counterfeit of real life,—and endeavors to create an interest by some less obvious peculiarity of the subject. Occasionally, a breath of nature, a rain-drop of pathos and tenderness, or a gleam of humor, will find its way into the midst of his fantastic imagery, and make us feel as if, after all, we were yet within the limits of our native earth. We will only add to this very cursory notice, that M. de l'Aubépine's productions, if the reader chance to take them in precisely the proper point of view, may amuse a leisure hour as well as those of a brighter man; if otherwise, they can hardly fail to look excessively like nonsense.

Our author is voluminous; he continues to write and publish with as much praiseworthy and indefatigable prolixity, as if his efforts were crowned with the brilliant success that so justly attends those of Eugene Sue. His first appearance was by a collection of stories, in a long series of volumes, entitled *"Contes deux fois racontées."* The titles of some of his more recent works (we quote from memory) are as follows:—*"Le Voyage Céleste à Chemin de Fer,"* 3 tom. 1838. *"Le nouveau Père Adam et la nouvelle Mère Eve,"* 2 tom. 1839. *"Roderic; ou le Serpent à l'estomac,"* 2 tom. 1840. *"Le Culte du Feu,"* a folio volume of ponderous research into the religion and ritual of the old Persian Ghebers, published in 1841. *"La Soirée du Château en Espagne,"* 1 tom. 8 vo. 1842; and *"L'Artiste du Beau; ou le Papillon Mécanique,"* 5 tom. 4to. 1843. Our somewhat wearisome perusal of this startling catalogue of volumes has left behind it a certain personal affection and sympathy, though by no means admiration, for M. de l'Aubépine; and we would fain do the little in our power towards introducing him favorably to the American public. The ensuing tale is a translation of his *"Beatrice; ou la Belle Empoisonneuse,"* recently published in *"La Revue Anti-Aristocratique."* This journal, edited by the Comte de Bearhaven, has, for some years past, led the defence of liberal principles and popular rights, with a faithfulness and ability worthy of all praise.

A young man, named Giovanni Guasconti, came, very long ago, from the more southern region of Italy, to pursue his studies at the University of Padua. Giovanni, who had but a scanty supply of gold ducats in his pocket, took lodgings in a high and gloomy chamber of an old edifice, which looked not unworthy to have been the palace of a Paduan noble, and which, in fact, exhibited over its entrance the armorial bearings of a family long since extinct. The young stranger, who was not unstudied in the great poem of his country, recollected that one of the ancestors of this family, and perhaps an occupant of this very mansion, had been pictured by Dante as a partaker of the immortal agonies of his Inferno. These reminiscences and associations, together with the tendency to heart-break natural to a young man for the first time out of his native sphere, caused Giovanni to sigh heavily, as he looked around the desolate and ill-furnished apartment.

"Holy Virgin, Signor," cried old dame Lisabetta, who, won by the youth's remarkable beauty of person, was kindly endeavoring to give the chamber a habitable air, "what a sigh was that to come out of a young man's heart! Do you find this old mansion gloomy? For the love of heaven, then, put your head out of the window, and you will see as bright sunshine as you have left in Naples."

Guasconti mechanically did as the old woman advised, but could not quite agree with her that the Paduan sunshine was as cheerful as that of southern Italy. Such as it was, however, it fell upon a garden beneath the window, and expended its fostering influences on a variety of plants, which seemed to have been cultivated with exceeding care.

"Does this garden belong to the house?" asked Giovanni.

"Heaven forbid, Signor!—unless it were fruitful of better pot-herbs than any that grow there now," answered old Lisabetta. "No; that garden is cultivated by the own hands of Signor Giacomo Rappaccini, the famous Doctor, who, I warrant him, has been heard of as far as Naples. It is said that he distils these plants into medicines that are as potent as a charm. Oftentimes you may see the Signor Doctor at work, and perchance the Signora his daughter, too, gathering the strange flowers that grow in the garden."

The old woman had now done what she could for the aspect of the chamber, and, commending the young man to the protection of the saints, took her departure.

Giovanni still found no better occupation than to look down into the garden beneath his window. From its appearance, he judged it to be one of those botanic gardens, which were of earlier date in Padua than elsewhere in Italy, or in the world. Or, not improbably, it might once have been the pleasure-place of an opulent family; for there was the ruin of a marble fountain in the centre, sculptured with rare art, but so wofully shattered that it was impossible to trace the original design from the chaos of remaining fragments. The water, however, continued to gush and sparkle into the sunbeams as cheerfully as ever. A little gurgling sound ascended to the young man's window, and made him feel as if the fountain were an immortal spirit, that sung its song unceasingly, and without heeding the vicissitudes around it; while one century embodied it in marble, and another scattered the perishable garniture on the soil. All about the pool into which the water subsided, grew various plants, that seemed to require a plentiful supply of moisture for the nourishment of gigantic leaves, and, in some instances, flowers gorgeously magnificent. There was one shrub in particular, set in a marble vase in the midst of the pool, that bore a profusion of purple blossoms, each of which had the lustre and richness of a gem; and the whole together made a show so resplendent that it seemed enough to illuminate the garden, even had there been no sunshine. Every portion of the soil was peopled with plants and herbs, which, if less beautiful, still bore tokens of assiduous care; as if all had their individual virtues, known to the scientific mind that fostered them. Some were placed in urns, rich with old carving, and others in common garden-pots; some crept serpent-like along the ground, or climbed on high, using whatever means of ascent was offered them. One plant had wreathed itself round a statue of Vertumnus, which was thus quite veiled and shrouded in a drapery of hanging foliage, so happily arranged that it might have served a sculptor for a study.

While Giovanni stood at the window, he heard a rustling behind a screen of leaves, and became aware that a person was at work in the garden. His figure soon emerged into view, and showed itself to be that of no common laborer, but a tall, emaciated, sallow, and sickly-looking man, dressed in a scholar's garb of black. He was beyond the middle term of life, with grey hair, a thin grey beard, and a face singularly marked with intellect and cultivation, but which could never, even in his more youthful days, have expressed much warmth of heart.

Nothing could exceed the intentness with which this scientific gardener examined every shrub which grew in his path; it seemed as if he was looking into their inmost nature, making observations in regard to their creative essence, and discovering why one leaf grew in this shape, and another in that, and wherefore such and such flowers differed among themselves in hue and perfume. Nevertheless, in spite of this deep intelligence on his part, there was no approach to intimacy between himself and these vegetable existences. On the contrary, he avoided their actual touch, or the direct inhaling of their odors, with a caution that impressed Giovanni most disagreeably; for the man's demeanor was that of one walking among malignant influences, such as savage beasts, or deadly snakes, or evil spirits, which, should he allow them one moment of license, would wreak upon him some terrible fatality. It was strangely frightful to the young man's imagination, to see this air of insecurity in a person cultivating a garden, that most simple and innocent of human toils, and which had been alike the joy and labor of the unfallen parents of the race. Was this garden, then, the Eden of the present world?—and this man, with such a perception of harm in what his own hands caused to grow, was he the Adam?

The distrustful gardener, while plucking away the dead leaves or pruning the too luxuriant growth of the shrubs, defended his hands with a pair of thick gloves. Nor were these his only armor. When, in his walk through the garden, he came to the magnificent plant that hung its purple gems beside the marble fountain, he placed a kind of mask over his mouth and nostrils, as if all this beauty did but conceal a deadlier malice. But finding his task still too dangerous, he drew back, removed the mask, and called loudly, but in the infirm voice of a person affected with inward disease:

"Beatrice!—Beatrice!"

"Here am I, my father! What would you?" cried a rich and youthful voice from the window of the opposite house; a voice as rich as a tropical sunset, and which made Giovanni, though he knew not why, think of deep hues of purple or crimson, and of perfumes heavily delectable.—"Are you in the garden?"

"Yes, Beatrice," answered the gardener, "and I need your help."

Soon there emerged from under a sculptured portal the figure of a young girl, arrayed with as much richness of taste as the most splendid of the flowers, beautiful as the day, and with a bloom so deep and vivid that one shade more would have been too much. She looked redundant with life, health, and energy; all of which attributes were bound down and compressed, as it were, and girdled tensely, in their luxuriance, by her virgin zone. Yet Giovanni's fancy must have grown morbid, while he looked down into the garden; for the impression which the fair stranger made upon him was as if here were another flower, the human sister of those vegetable ones, as beautiful as they—more beautiful than the richest of them—but still to be touched only with a glove, nor to be approached without a mask. As Beatrice came down the garden path, it was observable that she handled and inhaled the odor of several of the plants, which her father had most sedulously avoided.

"Here, Beatrice," said the latter,—"see how many needful offices require to be done to our chief treasure. Yet, shattered as I am, my life might pay the penalty of approaching it so closely as circumstances demand. Henceforth, I fear, this plant must be consigned to your sole charge."

"And gladly will I undertake it," cried again the rich tones of the young lady, as she bent towards the magnificent plant, and opened her arms as if to embrace it. "Yes, my sister, my splendor, it shall be Beatrice's task to nurse and serve thee; and thou shalt reward her with thy kisses and perfumed breath, which to her is as the breath of life!"

Then, with all the tenderness in her manner that was so strikingly expressed in her words, she busied herself with such attentions as the plant seemed to require; and Giovanni, at his lofty window, rubbed his eyes, and almost doubted whether it were a girl tending her favorite flower, or one sister performing the duties of affection to another. The scene soon terminated. Whether Doctor Rappaccini had finished his labors in the garden, or that his watchful eye had caught the stranger's face, he now took his daughter's arm and retired. Night was already closing in; oppressive exhalations seemed to proceed from the plants, and steal upward past the open window; and Giovanni, closing the lattice, went to his couch, and dreamed of a rich flower and beautiful girl. Flower and maiden were different and yet the same, and fraught with some strange peril in either shape.

But there is an influence in the light of morning that tends to rectify whatever errors of fancy, or even of judgment, we may have incurred during the sun's decline, or among the shadows of the night, or in the less wholesome glow of moonshine. Giovanni's first movement on starting from sleep, was to throw open the window, and gaze down into the garden which his dreams had made so fertile of mysteries. He was surprised, and a little ashamed, to find how real and matter-of-fact an affair it proved to be, in the first rays of the sun, which gilded the dew-drops that hung upon leaf and blossom, and, while giving a brighter beauty to each rare flower, brought everything within the limits of ordinary experience. The young man rejoiced, that, in the heart of the barren city, he had the privilege of over-looking this spot of lovely and luxuriant vegetation. It would serve, he said to himself, as a symbolic language, to keep him in communion with Nature. Neither the sickly and thought-worn Doctor Giacomo Rappaccini, it is true, nor his brilliant daughter, were now visible; so that Giovanni could not deter-mine how much of the singularity which he attributed to both, was due to their own qualities, and how much to his wonder-working fancy. But he was inclined to take a most rational view of the whole matter.

In the course of the day, he paid his respects to Signor Pietro Baglioni, professor of medicine in the University, a physician of eminent repute, to whom Giovanni had brought a letter of introduction. The Professor was an elderly personage, appar-ently of genial nature, and habits that might almost be called jovial; he kept the young man to dinner, and made himself very agreeable by the freedom and liveliness of his conversa-tion, especially when warmed by a flask or two of Tuscan wine. Giovanni, conceiving that men of science, inhabitants of the same city, must needs be on familiar terms with one another, took an opportunity to mention the name of Doctor Rappaccini. But the Professor did not respond with so much cordiality as he had anticipated.

"Ill would it become a teacher of the divine art of medicine," said Professor Pietro Baglioni, in answer to a question of Gio-vanni, "to withhold due and well-considered praise of a physi-cian so eminently skilled as Rappaccini. But, on the other hand, I should answer it but scantily to my conscience, were I to permit a worthy youth like yourself, Signor Giovanni, the son of an ancient friend, to imbibe erroneous ideas respecting a man who might hereafter chance to hold your life and death in his hands. The truth is, our worshipful Doctor Rappaccini has as much science as any member of the faculty—with perhaps one single exception—in Padua, or all Italy. But there are certain grave objections to his professional character."

"And what are they?" asked the young man.

"Has my friend Giovanni any disease of body or heart, that he is so inquisitive about physicians?" said the Professor, with a smile. "But as for Rappaccini, it is said of him—and I, who know the man well, can answer for its truth—that he cares infinitely more for science than for mankind. His patients are interesting to him only as subjects for some new experiment. He would sacrifice human life, his own among the rest, or whatever else was dearest to him, for the sake of adding so much as a grain of mustard-seed to the great heap of his accumulated knowledge."

"Methinks he is an awful man, indeed," remarked Guasconti, mentally recalling the cold and purely intellectual aspect of Rappaccini. "And yet, worshipful Professor, is it not a noble spirit? Are there many men capable of so spiritual a love of science?"

"God forbid," answered the Professor, somewhat testily—"at least, unless they take sounder views of the healing art than those adopted by Rappaccini. It is his theory, that all medicinal virtues are comprised within those substances which we term vegetable poisons. These he cultivates with his own hands, and is said even to have produced new varieties of poison, more horribly deleterious than Nature, without the assistance of this learned person, would ever have plagued the world withal. That the Signor Doctor does less mischief than might be expected, with such dangerous substances, is undeniable. Now and then, it must be owned, he has effected—or seemed to effect—a marvellous cure. But, to tell you my private mind, Signor Giovanni, he should receive little credit for such instances of success—they being probably the work of chance—but should be held strictly accountable for his failures, which may justly be considered his own work."

The youth might have taken Baglioni's opinions with many grains of allowance, had he known that there was a professional warfare of long continuance between him and Doctor Rappaccini, in which the latter was generally thought to have gained the advantage. If the reader be inclined to judge for himself, we refer him to certain black-letter tracts on both sides, preserved in the medical department of the University of Padua.

"I know not, most learned Professor," returned Giovanni, after musing on what had been said of Rappaccini's exclusive zeal for science—"I know not how dearly this physician may love his art; but surely there is one object more dear to him. He has a daughter."

"Aha!" cried the Professor with a laugh. "So now our friend Giovanni's secret is out. You have heard of this daughter, whom all the young men in Padua are wild about, though not half a dozen have ever had the good hap to see her face. I know little of the Signora Beatrice, save that Rappaccini is said to have instructed her deeply in his science, and that, young and beautiful as fame reports her, she is already qualified to fill a professor's chair. Perchance her father destines her for mine! Other absurd rumors there be, not worth talking about, or listening to. So now, Signor Giovanni, drink off your glass of Lacryma."

Guasconti returned to his lodgings somewhat heated with the wine he had quaffed, and which caused his brain to swim with strange fantasies in reference to Doctor Rappaccini and the beautiful Beatrice. On his way, happening to pass by a florist's, he bought a fresh bouquet of flowers.

Ascending to his chamber, he seated himself near the window, but within the shadow thrown by the depth of the wall, so that he could look down into the garden with little risk of being discovered. All beneath his eye was a solitude. The strange plants were basking in the sunshine, and now and then nodding gently to one another, as if in acknowledgment of sympathy and kindred. In the midst, by the shattered fountain, grew the magnificent shrub, with its purple gems clustering all over it; they glowed in the air, and gleamed back again out of the depths of the pool, which thus seemed to overflow with colored radiance from the rich reflection that was steeped in it. At first, as we have said, the garden was a solitude. Soon, however,—as Giovanni had half-hoped, half-feared, would be the case,—a figure appeared beneath the antique sculptured portal, and came down between the rows of plants, inhaling their various perfumes, as if she were one of those beings of old classic fable, that lived upon sweet odors. On again beholding Beatrice, the young man was even startled to perceive how much her beauty exceeded his recollection of it; so brilliant, so vivid was its character, that she glowed amid the sunlight, and, as Giovanni whispered to himself, positively illuminated the more shadowy intervals of the garden path. Her face being now more revealed than on the former occasion, he was struck by its expression of simplicity and sweetness; qualities that had not entered into his idea of her character, and which made him ask anew, what manner of mortal she might be. Nor did he fail again to observe, or imagine, an analogy between the beautiful girl and the gorgeous shrub that hung its gem-like flowers over the fountain; a resemblance which Beatrice seemed to have indulged a fantastic humor in heightening, both by the arrangement of her dress and the selection of its hues.

Approaching the shrub, she threw open her arms, as with a passionate ardor, and drew its branches into an intimate embrace; so intimate, that her features were hidden in its leafy bosom, and her glistening ringlets all intermingled with the flowers.

"Give me thy breath, my sister," exclaimed Beatrice; "for I am faint with common air! And give me this flower of thine, which I separate with gentlest fingers from the stem, and place it close beside my heart."

With these words, the beautiful daughter of Rappaccini plucked one of the richest blossoms of the shrub, and was about to fasten it in her bosom. But now, unless Giovanni's draughts of wine had bewildered his senses, a singular incident occurred. A small orange-colored reptile, of the lizard or chameleon species, chanced to be creeping along the path, just at the feet of Beatrice. It appeared to Giovanni—but, at the distance from which he gazed, he could scarcely have seen anything so minute—it appeared to him, however, that a drop or two of moisture from the broken stem of the flower descended upon the lizard's head. For an instant, the reptile contorted itself violently, and then lay motionless in the sunshine. Beatrice observed this remarkable phenomenon, and crossed herself, sadly, but without surprise; nor did she therefore hesitate to arrange the fatal flower in her bosom. There it blushed, and almost glimmered with the dazzling effect of a precious stone, adding to her dress and aspect the one appropriate charm, which nothing else in the world could have supplied. But Giovanni, out of the shadow of his window, bent forward and shrank back, and murmured and trembled.

"Am I awake? Have I my senses?" said he to himself. "What is this being?—beautiful, shall I call her?—or inexpressibly terrible?"

Beatrice now strayed carelessly through the garden, approaching closer beneath Giovanni's window, so that he was compelled to thrust his head quite out of its concealment in order to gratify the intense and painful curiosity which she excited. At this moment, there came a beautiful insect over the garden wall; it had perhaps wandered through the city and found no flowers nor verdure among those antique haunts of men, until the heavy perfumes of Doctor Rappaccini's shrubs had lured it from afar. Without alighting on the flowers, this winged brightness seemed to be attracted by Beatrice, and lingered in the air and fluttered about her head. Now, here it could not be but that Giovanni Guasconti's eyes deceived him. Be that as it might, he fancied that while Beatrice was gazing at the insect with childish delight, it grew faint and fell at her feet;—its bright wings shivered; it was dead—from no cause that he could discern, unless it were the atmosphere of her breath. Again Beatrice crossed herself and sighed heavily, as she bent over the dead insect.

An impulsive movement of Giovanni drew her eyes to the window. There she beheld the beautiful head of the young man—rather a Grecian than an Italian head, with fair, regular features, and a glistening of gold among his ringlets—gazing down upon her like a being that hovered in midair. Scarcely knowing what he did, Giovanni threw down the bouquet which he had hitherto held in his hand.

"Signora," said he, "there are pure and healthful flowers. Wear them for the sake of Giovanni Guasconti!"

"Thanks, Signor," replied Beatrice, with her rich voice, that came forth as it were like a gush of music; and with a mirthful expression half childish and half woman-like. "I accept your gift, and would fain recompense it with this precious purple flower; but if I toss it into the air, it will not reach you. So Signor Guasconti must even content himself with my thanks."

She lifted the bouquet from the ground, and then as if inwardly ashamed at having stepped aside from her maidenly reserve to respond to a stranger's greeting, passed swiftly homeward through the garden. But, few as the moments were, it seemed to Giovanni when she was on the point of vanishing beneath the sculptured portal, that his beautiful bouquet was already beginning to wither in her grasp. It was an idle thought; there could be no possibility of distinguishing a faded flower from a fresh one at so great a distance.

For many days after this incident, the young man avoided the window that looked into Doctor Rappaccini's garden, as if something ugly and monstrous would have blasted his eye-sight, had he been betrayed into a glance. He felt conscious of having put himself, to a certain extent, within the influence of an unintelligible power, by the communication which he had opened with Beatrice. The wisest course would have been, if his heart were in any real danger, to quit his lodgings and Padua itself, at once; the next wiser, to have accustomed himself, as far as possible, to the familiar and day-light view of Beatrice; thus bringing her rigidly and systematically within the limits of ordinary experience. Least of all, while avoiding her sight, ought Giovanni to have remained so near this extraordinary being, that the proximity and possibility even of intercourse, should give a kind of substance and reality to the wild vagaries which his imagination ran riot continually in producing. Guasconti had not a deep heart—or at all events, its depths were not sounded now—but he had a quick fancy, and an ardent southern temperament, which rose every instant to a higher fever-pitch. Whether or no Beatrice possessed those terrible attributes—that fatal breath—the affinity with those so beautiful and deadly flowers—which were indicated by what Giovanni had witnessed, she had at least instilled a fierce and subtle poison into his system. It was not love, although her rich beauty was a madness to him; nor horror, even while he fancied her spirit to be imbued with the same baneful essence that seemed to pervade her physical frame; but a wild offspring of both love and horror that had each parent in it, and burned like one and shivered like the other. Giovanni knew not what to dread; still less did he know what to hope; yet hope and dread kept a continual warfare in his breast, alternately vanquishing one another and starting up afresh to renew the contest. Blessed are all simple emotions, be they dark or bright! It is the lurid intermixture of the two that produces the illuminating blaze of the infernal regions.

Sometimes he endeavored to assuage the fever of his spirit by a rapid walk through the streets of Padua, or beyond its gates;

his footsteps kept time with the throbbings of his brain, so that the walk was apt to accelerate itself to a race. One day, he found himself arrested; his arm was seized by a portly personage who had turned back on recognizing the young man, and expended much breath in overtaking him.

"Signor Giovanni!—stay, my young friend!" cried he. "Have you forgotten me? That might well be the case, if I were as much altered as yourself."

It was Baglioni, whom Giovanni had avoided, ever since their first meeting, from a doubt that the Professor's sagacity would look too deeply into his secrets. Endeavoring to recover himself, he stared forth wildly from his inner world into the outer one, and spoke like a man in a dream:

"Yes; I am Giovanni Guasconti. You are Professor Pietro Baglioni. Now let me pass!"

"Not yet—not yet, Signor Giovanni Guasconti," said the Professor, smiling, but at the same time scrutinizing the youth with an earnest glance.—"What; did I grow up side by side with your father, and shall his son pass me like a stranger, in these old streets of Padua? Stand still, Signor Giovanni; for we must have a word or two, before we part."

"Speedily, then, most worshipful Professor, speedily!" said Giovanni, with feverish impatience. "Does not your worship see that I am in haste?"

Now, while he was speaking, there came a man in black along the street, stooping and moving feebly, like a person in inferior health. His face was all overspread with a most sickly and sallow hue, but yet so pervaded with an expression of piercing and active intellect, that an observer might easily have overlooked the merely physical attributes, and have seen only this wonderful energy. As he passed, this person exchanged a cold and distant salutation with Baglioni, but fixed his eyes upon Giovanni with an intentness that seemed to bring out whatever was within him worthy of notice. Nevertheless, there was a peculiar quietness in the look, as if taking merely a speculative, not a human, interest in the young man.

"It is Doctor Rappaccini!" whispered the Professor, when the stranger had passed.—"Has he ever seen your face before?"

"Not that I know," answered Giovanni, starting at the name.

"He *has* seen you!—he must have seen you!" said Baglioni, hastily. "For some purpose or other, this man of science is making a study of you. I know that look of his! It is the same that coldly illuminates his face, as he bends over a bird, a mouse, or a butterfly, which, in pursuance of some experiment, he has killed by the perfume of a flower;—a look as deep as Nature itself, but without Nature's warmth of love. Signor Giovanni, I will stake my life upon it, you are the subject of one of Rappaccini's experiments!"

"Will you make a fool of me?" cried Giovanni, passionately. "*That,* Signor Professor, were an untoward experiment."

"Patience, patience!" replied the imperturbable Professor.— "I tell thee, my poor Giovanni, that Rappaccini has a scientific interest in thee. Thou hast fallen into fearful hands! And the Signora Beatrice? What part does she act in this mystery?"

But Guasconti, finding Baglioni's pertinacity intolerable, here broke away, and was gone before the Professor could again seize his arm. He looked after the young man intently, and shook his head.

"This must not be," said Baglioni to himself. "The youth is the son of my old friend, and shall not come to any harm from which the arcana of medical science can preserve him. Besides, it is too insufferable an impertinence in Rappaccini, thus to snatch the lad out of my own hands, as I may say, and make use of him for his infernal experiments. This daughter of his! It shall be looked to. Perchance, most learned Rappaccini, I may foil you where you little dream of it!"

Meanwhile, Giovanni had pursued a circuitous route, and at

length found himself at the door of his lodgings. As he crossed the threshold, he was met by old Lisabetta, who smirked and smiled, and was evidently desirous to attract his attention; vainly, however, as the ebullition of his feelings had momentarily subsided into a cold and dull vacuity. He turned his eyes full upon the withered face that was puckering itself into a smile, but seemed to behold it not. The old dame, therefore, laid her grasp upon his cloak.

"Signor!—Signor!" whispered she, still with a smile over the whole breadth of her visage, so that it looked not unlike a grotesque carving in wood, darkened by centuries—"Listen, Signor! There is a private entrance into the garden!"

"What do you say?" exclaimed Giovanni, turning quickly about, as if an inanimate thing should start into feverish life.—"A private entrance into Doctor Rappaccini's garden!"

"Hush! hush!—not so loud!" whispered Lisabetta, putting her hand over his mouth. "Yes; into the worshipful Doctor's garden, where you may see all his fine shrubbery. Many a young man in Padua would give gold to be admitted among those flowers."

Giovanni put a piece of gold into her hand.

"Show me the way," said he.

A surmise, probably excited by his conversation with Baglioni, crossed his mind, that this interposition of old Lisabetta might perchance be connected with the intrigue, whatever were its nature, in which the Professor seemed to suppose that Doctor Rappaccini was involving him. But such a suspicion, though it disturbed Giovanni, was inadequate to restrain him. The instant that he was aware of the possibility of approaching Beatrice, it seemed an absolute necessity of his existence to do so. It mattered not whether she were angel or demon; he was irrevocably within her sphere, and must obey the law that whirled him onward, in ever lessening circles, towards a result which he did not attempt to foreshadow. And yet, strange to say, there came across him a sudden doubt, whether this intense interest on his part were not delusory—whether it were really of so deep and positive a nature as to justify him in now thrusting himself into an incalculable position—whether it were not merely the fantasy of a young man's brain, only slightly, or not at all, connected with his heart!

He paused—hesitated—turned half about—but again went on. His withered guide led him along several obscure passages, and finally undid a door, through which, as it was opened, there came the sight and sound of rustling leaves, with the broken sunshine glimmering among them. Giovanni stepped forth, and forcing himself through the entanglement of a shrub that wreathed its tendrils over the hidden entrance, he stood beneath his own window, in the open area of Doctor Rappaccini's garden.

How often is it the case, that, when impossibilities have come to pass, and dreams have condensed their misty substance into tangible realities, we find ourselves calm, and even coldly self-possessed, amid circumstances which it would have been a delirium of joy or agony to anticipate! Fate delights to thwart us thus. Passion will choose his own time to rush upon the scene, and lingers sluggishly behind, when an appropriate adjustment of events would seem to summon his appearance. So was it now with Giovanni. Day after day, his pulses had throbbed with feverish blood, at the improbable idea of an interview with Beatrice, and of standing with her, face to face, in this very garden, basking in the Oriental sunshine of her beauty, and snatching from her full gaze the mystery which he deemed the riddle of his own existence. But now there was a singular and untimely equanimity within his breast. He threw a glance around the garden to discover if Beatrice or her father were present, and perceiving that he was alone, began a critical observation of the plants.

The aspect of one and all of them dissatisfied him; their gorgeousness seemed fierce, passionate, and even unnatural. There was hardly an individual shrub which a wanderer, straying by himself through a forest, would not have been startled to find growing wild, as if an unearthly face had glared at him out of the thicket. Several, also, would have shocked a delicate instinct by an appearance of artificialness, indicating that there had been such commixture, and, as it were, adultery of various vegetable species, that the production was no longer of God's making, but the monstrous offspring of man's depraved fancy, glowing with only an evil mockery of beauty. They were probably the result of experiment, which, in one or two cases, had succeeded in mingling plants individually lovely into a compound possessing the questionable and ominous character that distinguished the whole growth of the garden. In fine, Giovanni recognized but two or three plants in the collection, and those of a kind that he well knew to be poisonous. While busy with these contemplations, he heard the rustling of a silken garment, and turning, beheld Beatrice emerging from beneath the sculptured portal.

Giovanni had not considered with himself what should be his deportment; whether he should apologize for his intrusion into the garden, or assume that he was there with the privity, at least, if not by the desire, of Doctor Rappaccini or his daughter. But Beatrice's manner placed him at his ease, though leaving him still in doubt by what agency he had gained admittance. She came lightly along the path, and met him near the broken fountain. There was surprise in her face, but brightened by a simple and kind expression of pleasure.

"You are a connoisseur in flowers, Signor," said Beatrice with a smile, alluding to the bouquet which he had flung her from the window. "It is no marvel, therefore, if the sight of my father's rare collection has tempted you to take a nearer view. If he were here, he could tell you many strange and interesting facts as to the nature and habits of these shrubs, for he has spent a life-time in such studies, and this garden is his world."

"And yourself, lady"—observed Giovanni—"if fame says

true—you, likewise, are deeply skilled in the virtues indicated by these rich blossoms, and these spicy perfumes. Would you deign to be my instructress, I should prove an apter scholar than if taught by Signor Rappaccini himself."

"Are there such idle rumors?" asked Beatrice, with the music of a pleasant laugh. "Do people say that I am skilled in my father's science of plants? What a jest is there! No; though I have grown up among these flowers, I know no more of them than their hues and perfume; and sometimes, methinks I would fain rid myself of even that small knowledge. There are many flowers here, and those not the least brilliant, that shock and offend me, when they meet my eye. But, pray, Signor, do not believe these stories about my science. Believe nothing of me save what you see with your own eyes."

"And must I believe all that I have seen with my own eyes?" asked Giovanni pointedly, while the recollection of former scenes made him shrink. "No, Signora, you demand too little of me. Bid me believe nothing, save what comes from your own lips."

It would appear that Beatrice understood him. There came a deep flush to her cheek; but she looked full into Giovanni's eyes, and responded to his gaze of uneasy suspicion with a queen-like haughtiness.

"I do so bid you, Signor!" she replied. "Forget whatever you may have fancied in regard to me. If true to the outward senses, still it may be false in its essence. But the words of Beatrice Rappaccini's lips are true from the depths of the heart outward. Those you may believe!"

A fervor glowed in her whole aspect, and beamed upon Giovanni's consciousness like the light of truth itself. But while she spoke, there was a fragrance in the atmosphere around her, rich and delightful, though evanescent, yet which the young man, from an indefinable reluctance, scarcely dared to draw into his lungs. It might be the odor of the flowers. Could it be Beatrice's breath, which thus embalmed her words with a

strange richness, as if by steeping them in her heart? A faintness passed like a shadow over Giovanni, and flitted away; he
seemed to gaze through the beautiful girl's eyes into her transparent soul, and felt no more doubt or fear.

The tinge of passion that had colored Beatrice's manner vanished; she became gay, and appeared to derive a pure delight
from her communion with the youth, not unlike what the
maiden of a lonely island might have felt, conversing with a
voyager from the civilized world. Evidently her experience of
life had been confined within the limits of that garden. She
talked now about matters as simple as the day-light or sum-
mer-clouds, and now asked questions in reference to the city,
or Giovanni's distant home, his friends, his mother, and his sisters; questions indicating such seclusion, and such lack of familiarity with modes and forms, that Giovanni responded as if
to an infant. Her spirit gushed out before him like a fresh rill,
that was just catching its first glimpse of the sunlight, and
wondering at the reflections of earth and sky which were flung
into its bosom. There came thoughts, too, from a deep source,
and fantasies of a gem-like brilliancy, as if diamonds and rubies sparkled upward among the bubbles of the fountain. Ever
and anon, there gleamed across the young man's mind a sense
of wonder, that he should be walking side by side with the being who had so wrought upon his imagination—whom he had
idealized in such hues of terror—in whom he had positively
witnessed such manifestations of dreadful attributes—that he
should be conversing with Beatrice like a brother, and should
find her so human and so maiden-like. But such reflections
were only momentary; the effect of her character was too real,
not to make itself familiar at once.

In this free intercourse, they had strayed through the garden, and now, after many turns among its avenues, were come
to the shattered fountain, beside which grew the magnificent
shrub with its treasury of glowing blossoms. A fragrance was
diffused from it, which Giovanni recognized as identical with

that which he had attributed to Beatrice's breath, but incomparably more powerful. As her eyes fell upon it, Giovanni beheld her press her hand to her bosom, as if her heart were throbbing suddenly and painfully.

"For the first time in my life," murmured she, addressing the shrub, "I had forgotten thee!"

"I remember, Signora," said Giovanni, "that you once promised to reward me with one of these living gems for the bouquet, which I had the happy boldness to fling to your feet. Permit me now to pluck it as a memorial of this interview."

He made a step towards the shrub, with extended hand. But Beatrice darted forward, uttering a shriek that went through his heart like a dagger. She caught his hand, and drew it back with the whole force of her slender figure. Giovanni felt her touch thrilling through his fibres.

"Touch it not!" exclaimed she, in a voice of agony. "Not for thy life! It is fatal!"

Then, hiding her face, she fled from him, and vanished beneath the sculptured portal. As Giovanni followed her with his eyes, he beheld the emaciated figure and pale intelligence of Doctor Rappaccini, who had been watching the scene, he knew not how long, within the shadow of the entrance.

No sooner was Guasconti alone in his chamber, than the image of Beatrice came back to his passionate musings, invested with all the witchery that had been gathering around it ever since his first glimpse of her, and now likewise imbued with a tender warmth of girlish womanhood. She was human: her nature was endowed with all gentle and feminine qualities; she was worthiest to be worshipped; she was capable, surely, on her part, of the height and heroism of love. Those tokens, which he had hitherto considered as proofs of a frightful peculiarity in her physical and moral system, were now either forgotten, or, by the subtle sophistry of passion, transmuted into a golden crown of enchantment, rendering Beatrice the more admirable, by so much as she was the more unique. Whatever had looked ugly, was now beautiful; or, if incapable of such a change, it stole away and hid itself among those shapeless half-ideas, which throng the dim region beyond the daylight of our perfect consciousness. Thus did he spend the night, nor fell asleep, until the dawn had begun to awake the slumbering flowers in Doctor Rappaccini's garden, whither Giovanni's dreams doubtless led him. Up rose the sun in his due season, and flinging his beams upon the young man's eyelids, awoke him to a sense of pain. When thoroughly aroused, he became sensible of a burning and tingling agony in his hand—in his right hand—the very hand which Beatrice had grasped in her own, when he was on the point of plucking one of the gem-like flowers. On the back of that hand there was now a purple print, like that of four small fingers, and the likeness of a slender thumb upon his wrist.

Oh, how stubbornly does love—or even that cunning semblance of love which flourishes in the imagination, but strikes no depth of root into the heart—how stubbornly does it hold its faith, until the moment come, when it is doomed to vanish into thin mist! Giovanni wrapt a handkerchief about his hand, and wondered what evil thing had stung him, and soon forgot his pain in a reverie of Beatrice.

After the first interview, a second was in the inevitable course of what we call fate. A third; a fourth; and a meeting with Beatrice in the garden was no longer an incident in Giovanni's daily life, but the whole space in which he might be said to live; for the anticipation and memory of that ecstatic hour made up the remainder. Nor was it otherwise with the daughter of Rappaccini. She watched for the youth's appearance, and flew to his side with confidence as unreserved as if they had been playmates from early infancy—as if they were such playmates still. If, by any unwonted chance, he failed to come at the appointed moment, she stood beneath the window, and sent up the rich sweetness of her tones to float around him in his chamber, and echo and reverberate throughout his heart—"Giovanni! Giovanni! Why tarriest thou? Come down!"—And down he hastened into that Eden of poisonous flowers.

But, with all this intimate familiarity, there was still a reserve in Beatrice's demeanor, so rigidly and invariably sustained, that the idea of infringing it scarcely occurred to his imagination. By all appreciable signs, they loved; they had looked love, with eyes that conveyed the holy secret from the depths of one soul into the depths of the other, as if it were too sacred to be whispered by the way; they had even spoken love, in those gushes of passion when their spirits darted forth in articulated breath, like tongues of long-hidden flame; and yet there had been no seal of lips, no clasp of hands, nor any slightest caress, such as love claims and hallows. He had never touched one of the gleaming ringlets of her hair; her garment—so marked was the physical barrier between them—had never been waved against him by a breeze. On the few occasions when Giovanni had seemed tempted to overstep the limit, Beatrice grew so sad, so stern, and withal wore such a look of desolate separation, shuddering at itself, that not a spoken word was requisite to repel him. At such times, he was startled at the horrible suspicions that rose, monster-like, out of the caverns of his heart, and stared him in the face; his love grew thin and faint as the morning-mist; his doubts alone had substance. But when Beatrice's face brightened again, after the momentary shadow, she was transformed at once from the mysterious, questionable being, whom he had watched with so much awe and horror; she was now the beautiful and unsophisticated girl, whom he felt that his spirit knew with a certainty beyond all other knowledge.

A considerable time had now passed since Giovanni's last meeting with Baglioni. One morning, however, he was disagreeably surprised by a visit from the Professor, whom he had scarcely thought of for whole weeks, and would willingly have forgotten still longer. Given up, as he had long been, to a pervading excitement, he could tolerate no companions, except upon condition of their perfect sympathy with his present state of feeling. Such sympathy was not to be expected from Professor Baglioni.

The visitor chatted carelessly, for a few moments, about the gossip of the city and the University, and then took up another topic.

"I have been reading an old classic author lately," said he, "and met with a story that strangely interested me. Possibly you may remember it. It is of an Indian prince, who sent a beautiful woman as a present to Alexander the Great. She was as lovely as the dawn, and gorgeous as the sunset; but what especially distinguished her was a certain rich perfume in her breath—richer than a garden of Persian roses. Alexander, as was natural to a youthful conqueror, fell in love at first sight with this magnificent stranger. But a certain sage physician, happening to be present, discovered a terrible secret in regard to her."

"And what was that?" asked Giovanni, turning his eyes downward to avoid those of the Professor.

"That this lovely woman," continued Baglioni, with emphasis, "had been nourished with poisons from her birth upward, until her whole nature was so imbued with them, that she herself had become the deadliest poison in existence. Poison was her element of life. With that rich perfume of her breath, she blasted the very air. Her love would have been poison!—her embrace death! Is not this a marvelous tale?"

"A childish fable," answered Giovanni, nervously starting from his chair. "I marvel how your worship finds time to read such nonsense, among your graver studies."

"By the bye," said the Professor, looking uneasily about him, "what singular fragrance is this in your apartment? Is it the perfume of your gloves? It is faint, but delicious, and yet, after all, by no means agreeable. Were I to breathe it long, methinks it would make me ill. It is like the breath of a flower—but I see no flowers in the chamber."

"Nor are there any," replied Giovanni, who had turned pale as the Professor spoke; "nor, I think, is there any fragrance, except in your worship's imagination. Odors, being a sort of element combined of the sensual and the spiritual, are apt to deceive us in this manner. The recollection of a perfume—the bare idea of it—may easily be mistaken for a present reality."

"Aye; but my sober imagination does not often play such tricks," said Baglioni; "and were I to fancy any kind of odor, it would be that of some vile apothecary drug, wherewith my fingers are likely enough to be imbued. Our worshipful friend Rappaccini, as I have heard, tinctures his medicaments with odors richer than those of Araby. Doubtless, likewise, the fair and learned Signora Beatrice would minister to her patients with draughts as sweet as a maiden's breath. But wo to him, that sips them!"

Giovanni's face evinced many contending emotions. The tone in which the Professor alluded to the pure and lovely daughter of Rappaccini was a torture to his soul; and yet, the intimation of a view of her character, opposite to his own, gave instantaneous distinctness to a thousand dim suspicions, which now grinned at him like so many demons. But he strove hard to quell them, and to respond to Baglioni with a true lover's perfect faith.

"Signor Professor," said he, "you were my father's friend—perchance, too, it is your purpose to act a friendly part towards his son. I would fain feel nothing towards you, save respect and deference. But I pray you to observe, Signor, that there is one subject on which we must not speak. You know not the Signora Beatrice. You cannot, therefore, estimate the wrong—the blasphemy, I may even say—that is offered to her character by a light or injurious word."

"Giovanni!—my poor Giovanni!" answered the Professor, with a calm expression of pity, "I know this wretched girl far better than yourself. You shall hear the truth in respect to the poisoner Rappaccini, and his poisonous daughter. Yes; poisonous as she is beautiful! Listen; for even should you do violence to my grey hairs, it shall not silence me. That old fable of the Indian woman has become a truth, by the deep and deadly science of Rappaccini, and in the person of the lovely Beatrice!"

Giovanni groaned and hid his face.

"Her father," continued Baglioni, "was not restrained by natural affection from offering up his child, in this horrible manner, as the victim of his insane zeal for science. For—let us do him justice—he is as true a man of science as ever distilled his own heart in an alembic. What, then, will be your fate? Beyond a doubt, you are selected as the material of some new experiment. Perhaps the result is to be death—perhaps a fate more awful still! Rappaccini, with what he calls the interest of science before his eyes, will hesitate at nothing."

"It is a dream!" muttered Giovanni to himself, "surely it is a dream!"

"But," resumed the Professor, "be of good cheer, son of my friend! It is not yet too late for the rescue. Possibly, we may even succeed in bringing back this miserable child within the limits of ordinary nature, from which her father's madness has estranged her. Behold this little silver vase! It was wrought by the hands of the renowned Benvenuto Cellini, and is well worthy to be a love-gift to the fairest dame in Italy. But its contents are invaluable. One little sip of this antidote would have rendered the most virulent poisons of the Borgias innocuous. Doubt not that it will be as efficacious against those of Rappaccini. Bestow the vase, and the precious liquid within it, on your Beatrice, and hopefully await the result."

Baglioni laid a small, exquisitely wrought silver phial on the table, and withdrew, leaving what he had said to produce its effect upon the young man's mind.

"We will thwart Rappaccini yet!" thought he, chuckling to himself, as he descended the stairs. "But, let us confess the truth of him, he is a wonderful man!—a wonderful man indeed! A vile empiric, however, in his practice, and therefore not to be tolerated by those who respect the good old rules of the medical profession!"

Throughout Giovanni's whole acquaintance with Beatrice, he had occasionally, as we have said, been haunted by dark surmises as to her character. Yet, so thoroughly had she made herself felt by him as a simple, natural, most affectionate and guileless creature, that the image now held up by Professor Baglioni, looked as strange and incredible, as if it were not in accordance with his own original conception. True, there were ugly recollections connected with his first glimpses of the beautiful girl; he could not quite forget the bouquet that withered in her grasp, and the insect that perished amid the sunny air, by no ostensible agency, save the fragrance of her breath. These incidents, however, dissolving in the pure light of her character, had no longer the efficacy of facts, but were acknowledged as mistaken fantasies, by whatever testimony of the senses they might appear to be substantiated. There is something truer and more real, than what we can see with the eyes, and touch with the finger. On such better evidence, had Giovanni founded his confidence in Beatrice, though rather by the necessary force of her high attributes, than by any deep and generous faith, on his part. But, now, his spirit was incapable of sustaining itself at the height to which the early enthusiasm of passion had exalted it; he fell down, grovelling among earthly doubts, and defiled therewith the pure whiteness of Beatrice's image. Not that he gave her up; he did but distrust. He resolved to institute some decisive test that should satisfy him, once for all, whether there were those dreadful peculiarities in her physical nature, which could not be supposed to exist without some corresponding monstrosity of soul. His eyes, gazing down afar, might have deceived him as to the lizard, the insect, and the flowers. But if he could witness, at the distance of a few paces, the sudden blight of one fresh and healthful flower in Beatrice's hand, there would be room for no further question. With this idea, he hastened to the florist's, and purchased a bouquet that was still gemmed with the morning dew-drops.

It was now the customary hour of his daily interview with Beatrice. Before descending into the garden, Giovanni failed not to look at his figure in the mirror; a vanity to be expected in a beautiful young man, yet, as displaying itself at that troubled and feverish moment, the token of a certain shallowness of feeling and insincerity of character. He did gaze, however, and said to himself, that his features had never before possessed so rich a grace, nor his eyes such vivacity, nor his cheeks so warm a hue of superabundant life.

"At least," thought he, "her poison has not yet insinuated itself into my system. I am no flower to perish in her grasp!"

With that thought, he turned his eyes on the bouquet, which he had never once laid aside from his hand. A thrill of indefinable horror shot through his frame, on perceiving that those dewy flowers were already beginning to droop; they wore the aspect of things that had been fresh and lovely, yesterday. Giovanni grew white as marble, and stood motionless before the mirror, staring at his own reflection there, as at the likeness of something frightful. He remembered Baglioni's remark about the fragrance that seemed to pervade the chamber. It must have been the poison in his breath! Then he shuddered—shuddered at himself! Recovering from his stupor, he began to watch, with curious eye, a spider that was busily at work, hanging its web from the antique cornice of the apartment, crossing and re-crossing the artful system of interwoven lines, as vigorous and active a spider as ever dangled from an old ceiling. Giovanni bent towards the insect, and emitted a deep, long breath. The spider suddenly ceased its toil; the web vibrated with a tremor originating in the body of the small artizan. Again Giovanni sent forth a breath, deeper, longer, and imbued with a venomous feeling out of his heart; he knew not whether he were wicked or only desperate. The spider made a convulsive gripe with his limbs, and hung dead across the window.

"Accursed! Accursed!" muttered Giovanni, addressing himself. "Hast thou grown so poisonous, that this deadly insect perishes by thy breath?"

At that moment, a rich, sweet voice came floating up from the garden:—

"Giovanni! Giovanni! It is past the hour! Why tarriest thou! Come down!"

"Yes," muttered Giovanni again. "She is the only being whom my breath may not slay! Would that it might!"

He rushed down, and in an instant, was standing before the bright and loving eyes of Beatrice. A moment ago, his wrath and despair had been so fierce that he could have desired nothing so much as to wither her by a glance. But, with her actual presence, there came influences which had too real an existence to be at once shaken off; recollections of the delicate and benign power of her feminine nature, which had so often enveloped him in a religious calm; recollections of many a holy and passionate outgush of her heart, when the pure fountain had been unsealed from its depths, and made visible in its transparency to his mental eye; recollections which, had Giovanni known how to estimate them, would have assured him that all this ugly mystery was but an earthly illusion, and that, whatever mist of evil might seem to have gathered over her, the real Beatrice was a heavenly angel. Incapable as he was of such high faith, still her presence had not utterly lost its magic. Giovanni's rage was quelled into an aspect of sullen insensibility. Beatrice, with a quick spiritual sense, immediately felt that there was a gulf of blackness between them, which neither he nor she could pass. They walked on together, sad and silent, and came thus to the marble fountain, and to its pool of water on the ground, in the midst of which grew the shrub that bore gem-

like blossoms. Giovanni was affrighted at the eager enjoyment—the appetite, as it were—with which he found himself
inhaling the fragrance of the flowers.

"Beatrice," asked he abruptly, "whence came this shrub?"

"My father created it," answered she, with simplicity.

"Created it! created it!" repeated Giovanni. "What mean
you, Beatrice?"

"He is a man fearfully acquainted with the secrets of nature,"
replied Beatrice; "and, at the hour when I first drew breath, this
plant sprang from the soil, the offspring of his science, of his intellect, while I was but his earthly child. Approach it not!" continued she, observing with terror that Giovanni was drawing
nearer to the shrub. "It has qualities that you little dream of.
But I, dearest Giovanni,—I grew up and blossomed with the
plant, and was nourished with its breath. It was my sister, and I
loved it with a human affection: for—alas! hast thou not suspected it? there was an awful doom."

Here Giovanni frowned so darkly upon her that Beatrice
paused and trembled. But her faith in his tenderness reassured
her, and made her blush that she had doubted for an instant.

"There was an awful doom," she continued,—"the effect of
my father's fatal love of science—which estranged me from all
society of my kind. Until Heaven sent thee, dearest Giovanni,
Oh! how lonely was thy poor Beatrice!"

"Was it a hard doom?" asked Giovanni, fixing his eyes upon
her.

"Only of late have I known how hard it was," answered she
tenderly. "Oh, yes; but my heart was torpid, and therefore
quiet."

Giovanni's rage broke forth from his sullen gloom like a
lightning-flash out of a dark cloud.

"Accursed one!" cried he, with venomous scorn and anger.
"And finding thy solitude wearisome, thou hast severed me,
likewise, from all the warmth of life, and enticed me into thy
region of unspeakable horror!"

"Giovanni!" exclaimed Beatrice, turning her large bright eyes upon his face. The force of his words had not found its way into her mind; she was merely thunder-struck.

"Yes, poisonous thing!" repeated Giovanni, beside himself with passion. "Thou hast done it! Thou hast blasted me! Thou hast filled my veins with poison! Thou hast made me as hateful, as ugly, as loathsome and deadly a creature as thyself,—a world's wonder of hideous monstrosity! Now—if our breath be happily as fatal to ourselves as to all others—let us join our lips in one kiss of unutterable hatred, and so die!"

"What has befallen me?" murmured Beatrice, with a low moan out of her heart. "Holy Virgin pity me, a poor heart-broken child!"

"Thou! Dost thou pray?" cried Giovanni, still with the same fiendish scorn. "Thy very prayers, as they come from thy lips, taint the atmosphere with death. Yes, yes; let us pray! Let us to church, and dip our fingers in the holy water at the portal! They that come after us will perish as by a pestilence. Let us sign crosses in the air! It will be scattering curses abroad in the likeness of holy symbols!"

"Giovanni," said Beatrice calmly, for her grief was beyond passion, "why dost thou join thyself with me thus in those terrible words? I, it is true, am the horrible thing thou namest me. But thou!—what hast thou to do, save with one other shudder at my hideous misery, to go forth out of the garden and mingle with thy race, and forget that there ever crawled on earth such a monster as poor Beatrice?"

"Dost thou pretend ignorance?" asked Giovanni, scowling upon her. "Behold! This power have I gained from the pure daughter of Rappaccini!"

There was a swarm of summer-insects flitting through the air, in search of the food promised by the flower-odors of the fatal garden. They circled round Giovanni's head, and were evidently attracted towards him by the same influence which had drawn them, for an instant, within the sphere of several of the shrubs. He sent forth a breath among them, and smiled bitterly at Beatrice, as at least a score of the insects fell dead upon the ground.

"I see it! I see it!" shrieked Beatrice. "It is my father's fatal science! No, no, Giovanni; it was not I! Never, never! I dreamed only to love thee, and be with thee a little time, and so to let thee pass away, leaving but thine image in mine heart. For, Giovanni—believe it—though my body be nourished with poison, my spirit is God's creature, and craves love as its daily food. But my father!—he has united us in this fearful sympathy. Yes; spurn me!—tread upon me!—kill me! Oh, what is death, after such words as thine? But it was not I! Not for a world of bliss would I have done it!"

Giovanni's passion had exhausted itself in its outburst from his lips. There now came across him a sense, mournful, and not without tenderness, of the intimate and peculiar relationship between Beatrice and himself. They stood, as it were, in an utter solitude, which would be made none the less solitary by the densest throng of human life. Ought not, then, the desert of humanity around them to press this insulated pair closer together? If they should be cruel to one another, who was there to be kind to them? Besides, thought Giovanni, might there not still be a hope of his returning within the limits of ordinary nature, and leading Beatrice—the redeemed Beatrice—by the hand? Oh, weak, and selfish, and unworthy spirit, that could dream of an earthly union and earthly happiness as possible, after such deep love had been so bitterly wronged as was Beatrice's love by Giovanni's blighting words! No, no; there could be no such hope. She must pass heavily, with that broken heart, across the borders of Time—she must bathe her hurts in some fount of Paradise, and forget her grief in the light of immortality—and *there* be well!

But Giovanni did not know it.

"Dear Beatrice," said he, approaching her, while she shrank

away, as always at his approach, but now with a different impulse—"dearest Beatrice, our fate is not yet so desperate. Behold! There is a medicine, potent, as a wise physician has assured me, and almost divine in its efficacy. It is composed of in-
gredients the most opposite to those by which thy awful father
has brought this calamity upon thee and me. It is distilled of
blessed herbs. Shall we not quaff it together, and thus be purified from evil?"

"Give it me!" said Beatrice, extending her hand to receive
the little silver phial which Giovanni took from his bosom. She
added, with a peculiar emphasis: "I will drink—but do thou
await the result."

She put Baglioni's antidote to her lips; and, at the same moment, the figure of Rappaccini emerged from the portal, and
came slowly towards the marble fountain. As he drew near, the
pale man of science seemed to gaze with a triumphant expression at the beautiful youth and maiden, as might an artist who
should spend his life in achieving a picture or a group of statuary, and finally be satisfied with his success. He paused—his
bent form grew erect with conscious power, he spread out his
hands over them, in the attitude of a father imploring a blessing upon his children. But those were the same hands that had
thrown poison into the stream of their lives! Giovanni trembled. Beatrice shuddered nervously, and pressed her hand upon
her heart.

"My daughter," said Rappaccini, "thou art no longer lonely
in the world! Pluck one of those precious gems from thy sister
shrub, and bid thy bridegroom wear it in his bosom. It will
not harm him now! My science, and the sympathy between
thee and him, have so wrought within his system, that he now
stands apart from common men, as thou dost, daughter of my
pride and triumph, from ordinary women. Pass on, then,
through the world, most dear to one another, and dreadful to
all besides!"

"My father," said Beatrice, feebly—and still, as she spoke, she kept her hand upon her heart—"wherefore didst thou inflict this miserable doom upon thy child?"

"Miserable!" exclaimed Rappaccini. "What mean you, foolish girl? Dost thou deem it misery to be endowed with marvellous gifts, against which no power nor strength could avail an enemy? Misery, to be able to quell the mightiest with a breath? Misery, to be as terrible as thou art beautiful? Wouldst thou, then, have preferred the condition of a weak woman, exposed to all evil, and capable of none?"

"I would fain have been loved, not feared," murmured Beatrice, sinking down upon the ground.—"But now it matters not; I am going, father, where the evil, which thou hast striven to mingle with my being, will pass away like a dream—like the fragrance of these poisonous flowers, which will no longer taint my breath among the flowers of Eden. Farewell, Giovanni! Thy words of hatred are like lead within my heart—but they, too, will fall away as I ascend. Oh, was there not, from the first, more poison in thy nature than in mine?"

To Beatrice—so radically had her earthly part been wrought upon by Rappaccini's skill—as poison had been life, so the powerful antidote was death. And thus the poor victim of man's ingenuity and of thwarted nature, and of the fatality that attends all such efforts of perverted wisdom, perished there, at the feet of her father and Giovanni. Just at that moment, Professor Pietro Baglioni looked forth from the window, and called loudly, in a tone of triumph mixed with horror, to the thunder-stricken man of science:

"Rappaccini! Rappaccini! And is *this* the upshot of your experiment?"

Ethan Brand

A CHAPTER FROM AN ABORTIVE ROMANCE

Bᴀʀᴛʀᴀᴍ, the lime-burner, a rough, heavy-looking man, be-grimed with charcoal, sat watching his kiln, at nightfall, while his little son played at building houses with the scattered fragments of marble; when, on the hill-side below them, they heard a roar of laughter, not mirthful, but slow, and even solemn, like a wind shaking the boughs of the forest.

"Father, what is that?" asked the little boy, leaving his play, and pressing betwixt his father's knees.

"Oh, some drunken man, I suppose," answered the lime-burner;—"some merry fellow from the bar-room in the village, who dared not laugh loud enough within doors, lest he should blow the roof of the house off. So here he is, shaking his jolly sides, at the foot of Graylock."

"But, father," said the child, more sensitive than the obtuse, middle-aged clown, "he does not laugh like a man that is glad. So the noise frightens me!"

"Don't be a fool, child!" cried his father, gruffly. "You will never make a man, I do believe; there is too much of your mother in you. I have known the rustling of a leaf startle you. Hark! Here comes the merry fellow now. You shall see that there is no harm in him."

Bartram and his little son, while they were talking thus, sat watching the same lime-kiln that had been the scene of Ethan Brand's solitary and meditative life, before he began his search for the Unpardonable Sin. Many years, as we have seen, had now elapsed, since that portentous night when the Idea was first developed. The kiln, however, on the mountain-side, stood unimpaired, and was in nothing changed, since he had thrown his dark thoughts into the intense glow of its furnace, and melted them, as it were, into the one thought that took possession of his life. It was a rude, round, tower-like structure, about twenty feet high, heavily built of rough stones, and with a hillock of earth heaped about the larger part of its circumference; so that blocks and fragments of marble might be drawn by cart-loads, and thrown in at the top. There was an opening at the bottom of the tower, like an oven-mouth, but large enough to admit a man in a stooping posture, and provided with a massive iron door. With the smoke and jets of flame issuing from the chinks and crevices of this door, which seemed to give admittance into the hill-side, it resembled nothing so much as the private entrance to the infernal regions, which the shepherds of the Delectable Mountains were accustomed to show to pilgrims.

There are many such lime-kilns in that tract of country, for the purpose of burning the white marble which composes a large part of the substance of the hills. Some of them, built years ago, and long deserted, with weeds growing in the vacant round of the interior, which is open to the sky, and grass and wild flowers rooting themselves into the chinks of the stones, look already like relics of antiquity, and may yet be overspread with the lichens of centuries to come. Others, where the lime-burner still feeds his daily and night-long fire, afford points of interest to the wanderer among the hills, who seats himself on a log of wood or a fragment of marble, to hold chat with the solitary man. It is a lonesome, and, when the character is inclined to thought, may be an intensely thoughtful occupation; as it proved in the case of Ethan Brand, who had mused to such strange purpose, in days gone by, while the fire in this very kiln was burning.

The man, who now watched the fire, was of a different order, and troubled himself with no thoughts save the very few that were requisite to his business. At frequent intervals he flung back the clashing weight of the iron door, and, turning his face from the insufferable glare, thrust in huge logs of oak, or stirred the immense brands with a long pole. Within the furnace, was seen the curling and riotous flames, and the burning marble, almost molten with the intensity of heat; while, without, the reflection of the fire quivered on the dark intricacy of the surrounding forest, and showed, in the foreground, a bright and ruddy little picture of the hut, the spring beside its door, the athletic and coal-begrimed figure of the lime-burner, and the half-frightened child, shrinking into the protection of his father's shadow. And when, again, the iron door was closed, then re-appeared the tender light of the half-full moon, which vainly strove to trace out the indistinct shapes of the neighboring mountains; and, in the upper sky, there was a flitting congregation of clouds, still faintly tinged with the rosy sunset, though, thus far down into the valley, the sunshine had vanished long and long ago.

The little boy now crept still closer to his father, as footsteps were heard ascending the hill-side, and a human form thrust aside the bushes that clustered beneath the trees.

"Halloo! who is it?" cried the lime-burner, vexed at his son's timidity, yet half-infected by it. "Come forward, and show yourself, like a man; or I'll fling this chunk of marble at your head!"

"You offer me a rough welcome," said a gloomy voice, as the unknown man drew nigh. "Yet I neither claim nor desire a kinder one, even at my own fireside."

To obtain a distincter view, Bartram threw open the iron door of the kiln, whence immediately issued a gush of fierce light, that smote full upon the stranger's face and figure. To a careless eye, there appeared nothing very remarkable in his aspect, which was that of a man in a coarse, brown, country-made suit of clothes, tall and thin, with the staff and heavy shoes of a wayfarer. As he advanced, he fixed his eyes, which were very bright, intently upon the brightness of the furnace, as if he beheld, or expected to behold, some object worthy of note within it.

"Good evening, stranger," said the lime-burner, "whence come you, so late in the day?"

"I come from my search," answered the wayfarer; "for, at last, it is finished."

"Drunk, or crazy!" muttered Bartram to himself. "I shall have trouble with the fellow. The sooner I drive him away, the better."

The little boy, all in a tremble, whispered to his father, and begged him to shut the door of the kiln, so that there might not be so much light; for that there was something in the man's face which he was afraid to look at, yet could not look away from. And, indeed, even the lime-burner's dull and torpid sense began to be impressed by an indescribable something in that thin, rugged, thoughtful visage, with the grizzled hair hanging wildly about it, and those deeply sunken eyes, which gleamed like fires within the entrance of a mysterious cavern. But, as he closed the door, the stranger turned towards him, and spoke in a quiet, familiar way, that made Bartram feel as if he were a sane and sensible man, after all.

"Your task draws to an end, I see," said he. "This marble has already been burning three days. A few hours more will convert the stone to lime."

"Why, who are you?" exclaimed the lime-burner. "You seem as well acquainted with my business as I myself."

"And well I may be," said the stranger, "for I followed the same craft, many a long year; and here, too, on this very spot. But you are a new comer in these parts. Did you never hear of Ethan Brand?"

"The man that went in search of the Unpardonable Sin?" asked Bartram, with a laugh.

"The same," answered the stranger. "He has found what he sought, and therefore he comes back again."

"What! then you are Ethan Brand, himself?" cried the lime-burner in amazement. "I am a new comer here, as you say; and they call it eighteen years since you left the foot of Graylock. But, I can tell you, the good folks still talk about Ethan Brand, in the village yonder, and what a strange errand took him away from his lime-kiln. Well, and so you have found the Unpardonable Sin?"

"Even so!" said the stranger, calmly.

"If the question is a fair one," proceeded Bartram, "where might it be?"

Ethan Brand laid his finger on his own heart. "Here!" replied he.

And then, without mirth in his countenance, but as if moved by an involuntary recognition of the infinite absurdity of seeking throughout the world for what was the closest of all things to himself, and looking into every heart, save his own, for what was hidden in no other breast, he broke into a laugh of scorn. It was the same slow, heavy laugh, that had almost appalled the lime-burner, when it heralded the wayfarer's approach.

The solitary mountain-side was made dismal by it. Laughter, when out of place, mistimed, or bursting forth from a disordered state of feeling, may be the most terrible modulation of the human voice. The laughter of one asleep, even if it be a little child—the madman's laugh—the wild, screaming laugh of a born idiot, are sounds that we sometimes tremble to hear, and would always willingly forget. Poets have imagined no utterance of fiends or hobgoblins so fearfully appropriate as a laugh. And even the obtuse lime-burner felt his nerves shaken, as this strange man looked inward at his own heart, and burst into laughter that rolled away into the night, and was indistinctly reverberated among the hills.

"Joe," said he to his little son, "scamper down to the tavern in the village, and tell the jolly fellows there that Ethan Brand has come back, and that he has found the Unpardonable Sin!"

The boy darted away on his errand, to which Ethan Brand made no objection, nor seemed hardly to notice it. He sat on a log of wood, looking steadfastly at the iron door of the kiln. When the child was out of sight, and his swift and light footsteps ceased to be heard, treading first on the fallen leaves, and then on the rocky mountain-path, the lime-burner began to regret his departure. He felt that the little fellow's presence had been a barrier between his guest and himself, and that he must now deal, heart to heart, with a man who, on his own confession, had committed the only crime for which Heaven could afford no mercy. That crime, in its indistinct blackness, seemed to overshadow him. The lime-burner's own sins rose up within him, and made his memory riotous with a throng of evil shapes that asserted their kindred with the Master Sin, whatever it might be, which it was within the scope of man's corrupted nature to conceive and cherish. They were all of one family; they went to and fro between his breast and Ethan Brand's, and carried dark greetings from one to the other.

Then Bartram remembered the stories which had grown traditionary in reference to this strange man, who had come upon him like a shadow of the night, and was making himself at home in his old place, after so long absence that the dead people, dead and buried for years, would have had more right to be at home, in any familiar spot, than he. Ethan Brand, it was said, had conversed with Satan himself, in the lurid blaze of this very kiln. The legend had been matter of mirth heretofore, but looked grisly now. According to this tale, before Ethan Brand departed on his search, he had been accustomed to evoke a fiend from the hot furnace of the lime-kiln, night after night, in order to confer with him about the Unpardonable Sin; the Man and the Fiend each laboring to frame the image of some mode of guilt, which could neither be atoned for, nor forgiven. And, with the first gleam of light upon the mountain-top, the fiend crept in at the iron door, there to abide in the intensest element of fire, until again summoned forth to share in the dreadful task of extending man's possible guilt beyond the scope of Heaven's else infinite mercy.

While the lime-burner was struggling with the horror of these thoughts, Ethan Brand rose from the log and flung open the door of the kiln. The action was in such accordance with the idea in Bartram's mind, that he almost expected to see the Evil One issue forth, red-hot from the raging furnace.

"Hold, hold!" cried he, with a tremulous attempt to laugh; for he was ashamed of his fears, although they overmastered him. "Don't, for mercy's sake, bring out your devil now!"

"Man!" sternly replied Ethan Brand, "what need have I of the devil? I have left him behind me on my track. It is with such half-way sinners as you that he busies himself. Fear not, because I open the door. I do but act by old custom, and am going to trim your fire, like a lime-burner, as I was once."

He stirred the vast coals, thrust in more wood, and bent forward to gaze into the hollow prison-house of the fire, regardless of the fierce glow that reddened upon his face. The lime-burner sat watching him, and half suspected his strange guest of a purpose, if not to evoke a fiend, at least to plunge bodily into the flames, and thus vanish from the sight of man. Ethan Brand, however, drew quietly back, and closed the door of the kiln.

"I have looked," said he, "into many a human heart that was seven times hotter with sinful passions than yonder furnace is with fire. But I found not there what I sought. No; not the Unpardonable Sin!"

"What is the Unpardonable Sin?" asked the lime-burner; and then he shrank farther from his companion, trembling lest his question should be answered.

"It is a sin that grew within my own breast," replied Ethan Brand, standing erect, with the pride that distinguishes all enthusiasts of his stamp. "A sin that grew nowhere else! The sin of an intellect that triumphed over the sense of brotherhood with man, and reverence for God, and sacrificed everything to its own mighty claims! The only sin that deserves a recompense of immortal agony! Freely, were it to do again, would I incur the guilt. Unshrinkingly, I accept the retribution!"

"The man's head is turned," muttered the lime-burner to himself. "He may be a sinner, like the rest of us—nothing more likely—but I'll be sworn, he is a madman, too."

Nevertheless, he felt uncomfortable at his situation, alone with Ethan Brand on the wild mountain-side, and was right glad to hear the rough murmur of tongues, and the footsteps of what seemed a pretty numerous party, stumbling over the stones, and rustling through the underbrush. Soon appeared the whole lazy regiment that was wont to infest the village tavern, comprehending three or four individuals who had drunk flip beside the bar-room fire, through all the winters, and smoked their pipes beneath the stoop, through all the summers since Ethan Brand's departure. Laughing boisterously, and mingling all their voices together in unceremonious talk, they now burst into the moonshine and narrow streaks of firelight that illuminated the open space before the lime-kiln. Bartram set the door ajar again, flooding the spot with light, that the whole company might get a fair view of Ethan Brand, and he of them.

There, among other old acquaintances, was a once ubiquitous man, now almost extinct, but whom we were formerly sure to encounter at the hotel of every thriving village throughout the country. It was the stage-agent. The present specimen of the genus was a wilted and smoke-dried man, wrinkled and red-nosed, in a smartly cut, brown, bob-tailed coat, with brass buttons, who, for a length of time unknown, had kept his desk and corner in the bar-room, and was still puffing what seemed to be the same cigar that he had lighted twenty years before. He had great fame as a dry joker, though, perhaps, less on account of any intrinsic humor, than from a certain flavor of brandy-toddy and tobacco-smoke, which impregnated all his ideas and expressions, as well as his person. Another well-re-membered, though strangely-altered face was that of Lawyer Giles, as people still called him in courtesy; an elderly ragamuf-fin, in his soiled shirt-sleeves and tow-cloth trowsers. This poor fellow had been an attorney, in what he called his better days, a sharp practitioner, and in great vogue among the village liti-gants; but flip, and sling, and toddy, and cocktails, imbibed at all hours, morning, noon, and night, had caused him to slide from intellectual, to various kinds and degrees of bodily labor, till, at last, to adopt his own phrase, he slid into a soap-vat. In other words, Giles was now a soap-boiler, in a small way. He had come to be but the fragment of a human being, a part of one foot having been chopped off by an axe, and an entire hand torn away by the devilish gripe of a steam-engine. Yet, though the corporeal hand was gone, a spiritual member remained; for, stretching forth the stump, Giles steadfastly averred, that he felt an invisible thumb and fingers, with as vivid a sensation as before the real ones were amputated. A maimed and miserable wretch he was; but one, nevertheless, whom the world could not trample on, and had no right to scorn, either in this or any previous stage of his misfortunes, since he had still kept up the courage and spirit of a man, asked nothing in charity, and, with his one hand—and that the left one—fought a stern battle against want and hostile circumstances.

Among the throng, too, came another personage, who, with certain points of similarity to Lawyer Giles, had more of differ-ence. It was the village Doctor, a man of some fifty years, whom, at an earlier period of his life, we should have intro-duced as paying a professional visit to Ethan Brand, during the latter's supposed insanity. He was now a purple-visaged, rude, and brutal, yet half-gentlemanly figure, with something wild, ruined, and desperate in his talk, and in all the details of his gesture and manners. Brandy possessed this man like an evil spirit, and made him as surly and savage as a wild beast, and as miserable as a lost soul; but there was supposed to be in him such wonderful skill, such native gifts of healing, beyond any which medical science could impart, that society caught hold of him, and would not let him sink out of its reach. So, swaying to and fro upon his horse, and grumbling thick accents at the bedside, he visited all the sick chambers for miles about among the mountain towns; and sometimes raised a dying man, as it were, by miracle, or, quite as often, no doubt, sent his patient to a grave that was dug many a year too soon. The Doctor had an everlasting pipe in his mouth, and, as somebody said, in allusion to his habit of swearing, it was always alight with hell-fire.

These three worthies pressed forward, and greeted Ethan Brand, each after his own fashion, earnestly inviting him to partake of the contents of a certain black bottle; in which, as they averred, he would find something far better worth seeking for, than the Unpardonable Sin. No mind, which has wrought itself, by intense and solitary meditation, into a high state of enthusiasm, can endure the kind of contact with low and vulgar modes of thought and feeling, to which Ethan Brand was now subjected. It made him doubt—and, strange to say, it was a painful doubt—whether he had indeed found the Unpardonable Sin, and found it within himself. The whole question on which he had exhausted life, and more than life, looked like a delusion.

"Leave me," he said bitterly, "ye brute beasts, that have made yourselves so, shrivelling up your souls with fiery liquors! I have done with you. Years and years ago, I groped into your hearts and found nothing there for my purpose. Get ye gone!"

"Why, you uncivil scoundrel," cried the fierce Doctor, "is that the way you respond to the kindness of your best friends? Then let me tell you the truth. You have no more found the Unpardonable Sin than yonder boy Joe has. You are but a crazy fellow—I told you so, twenty years ago—neither better nor worse than a crazy fellow, and the fit companion of old Humphrey, here!"

He pointed to an old man, shabbily dressed, with long white hair, thin visage, and unsteady eyes. For some years past, this aged person had been wandering about among the hills, inquiring of all travellers whom he met, for his daughter. The girl, it seemed, had gone off with a company of circus-performers; and, occasionally, tidings of her came to the village, and fine stories were told of her glittering appearance, as she rode on horseback in the ring, or performed marvellous feats on the tight-rope.

The white-haired father now approached Ethan Brand, and gazed unsteadily into his face.

"They tell me you have been all over the earth," said he, wringing his hands with earnestness. "You must have seen my daughter; for she makes a grand figure in the world, and everybody goes to see her. Did she send any word to her old father, or say when she is coming back?"

Ethan Brand's eye quailed beneath the old man's. That daughter, from whom he so earnestly desired a word of greeting, was the Esther of our tale; the very girl whom, with such cold and remorseless purpose, Ethan Brand had made the subject of a psychological experiment, and wasted, absorbed, and perhaps annihilated her soul, in the process.

"Yes," murmured he, turning away from the hoary wanderer; "it is no delusion. There is an Unpardonable Sin!"

While these things were passing, a merry scene was going forward in the area of cheerful light, besides the spring and before the door of the hut. A number of the youth of the village, young men and girls, had hurried up the hill-side, impelled by curiosity to see Ethan Brand, the hero of so many a legend familiar to their childhood. Finding nothing, however, very remarkable in his aspect—nothing but a sun-burnt wayfarer, in plain garb and dusty shoes, who sat looking into the fire, as if he fancied pictures among the coals—these young people speedily grew tired of observing him. As it happened, there was other amusement at hand. An old German Jew, travelling with a diorama on his back, was passing down the mountain-road towards the village, just as the party turned aside from it; and, in hopes of eking out the profits of the day, the showman had kept them company to the lime-kiln.

"Come, old Dutchman," cried one of the young men, "let us see your pictures, if you can swear they are worth looking at!"

"Oh, yes, Captain," answered the Jew—whether as a matter of courtesy or craft, he styled everybody Captain—"I shall show you, indeed, some very superb pictures!"

So, placing his box in a proper position, he invited the young men and girls to look through the glass orifices of the machine, and proceeded to exhibit a series of the most outrageous scratchings and daubings, as specimens of the fine arts, that ever an itinerant showman had the face to impose upon his circle of spectators. The pictures were worn out, moreover, tattered, full of cracks and wrinkles, dingy with tobacco-smoke, and otherwise in a most pitiable condition. Some purported to be cities, public edifices, and ruined castles, in Europe; others represented Napoleon's battles, and Nelson's sea-fights; and in the midst of these would be seen a gigantic, brown, hairy hand—which might have been mistaken for the Hand of Destiny, though, in truth, it was only the showman's—pointing its forefinger to various scenes of the conflict, while its owner gave historical illustrations. When, with much merriment at its abominable deficiency of merit, the exhibition was concluded, the German bade little Joe put his head into the box. Viewed through the magnifying glasses, the boy's round, rosy visage assumed the strangest imaginable aspect of an immense, Titanic child, the mouth grinning broadly, and the eyes, and every other feature, overflowing with fun at the joke. Suddenly, however, that merry face turned pale, and its expression changed to horror; for this easily impressed and excitable child had become sensible that the eye of Ethan Brand was fixed upon him through the glass.

"You make the little man to be afraid, Captain," said the German Jew, turning up the dark and strong outline of his visage, from his stooping posture. "But, look again; and, by chance, I shall cause you to see somewhat that is very fine, upon my word!"

Ethan Brand gazed into the box for an instant, and then starting back, looked fixedly at the German. What had he seen? Nothing, apparently; for a curious youth, who had peeped in, almost at the same moment, beheld only a vacant space of canvass.

"I remember you now," muttered Ethan Brand to the showman.

"Ah, Captain," whispered the Jew of Nuremberg, with a dark smile, "I find it to be a heavy matter in my show-box—this Unpardonable Sin! By my faith, Captain, it has wearied my shoulders, this long day, to carry it over the mountain."

"Peace!" answered Ethan Brand, sternly, "or get thee into the furnace yonder!"

The Jew's exhibition had scarcely concluded, when a great, elderly dog—who seemed to be his own master, as no person in the company laid claim to him—saw fit to render himself the object of public notice. Hitherto, he had shown himself a very quiet, well-disposed old dog, going round from one to another, and, by way of being sociable, offering his rough head to be patted by any kindly hand that would take so much trouble. But, now, all of a sudden, this grave and venerable quadruped, of his own mere notion, and without the slightest suggestion from anybody else, began to run round after his tail, which, to heighten the absurdity of the proceeding, was a great deal shorter than it should have been. Never was seen such headlong eagerness in pursuit of an object that could not possibly be attained; never was heard such a tremen-

dous outbreak of growling, snarling, barking, and snap-
ping—as if one end of the ridiculous brute's body were at
deadly and most unforgivable enmity with the other. Faster
and faster, roundabout went the cur; and faster and still faster
fled the unapproachable brevity of his tail; and louder and
fiercer grew his yells of rage and animosity; until, utterly exhausted, and as far from the goal as ever, the foolish old dog
ceased his performance as suddenly as he had begun it. The
next moment, he was as mild, quiet, sensible, and respectable in his deportment, as when he first scraped acquaintance
with the company.

As may be supposed, the exhibition was greeted with universal laughter, clapping of hands, and shouts of encore; to which
the canine performer responded by wagging all that there was
to wag of his tail, but appeared totally unable to repeat his very
successful effort to amuse the spectators.

Meanwhile, Ethan Brand had resumed his seat upon the log;
and, moved, it might be, by a perception of some remote analogy between his own case and that of this self-pursuing cur, he
broke into the awful laugh, which, more than any other token,
expressed the condition of his inward being. From that moment, the merriment of the party was at an end; they stood
aghast, dreading lest the inauspicious sound should be reverberated around the horizon, and that mountain would thunder it
to mountain, and so the horror be prolonged upon their ears.
Then, whispering one to another, that it was late—that the
moon was almost down—that the August night was growing
chill—they hurried homeward, leaving the lime-burner and little Joe to deal as they might with their unwelcome guest. Save
for these three human beings, the open space on the hill-side
was a solitude, set in a vast gloom of forest. Beyond that
darksome verge, the fire-light glimmered on the stately trunks
and almost black foliage of pines, intermixed with the lighter
verdure of sapling oaks, maples, and poplars, while, here and
there, lay the gigantic corpses of dead trees, decaying on the

leaf-strewn soil. And it seemed to little Joe—a timorous and imaginative child—that the silent forest was holding its breath, until some fearful thing should happen.

Ethan Brand thrust more wood into the fire, and closed the door of the kiln; then looking over his shoulder at the lime-burner and his son, he bade, rather than advised, them to retire to rest.

"For myself I cannot sleep," said he. "I have matters that it concerns me to meditate upon. I will watch the fire, as I used to do in the old time."

"And call the devil out of the furnace to keep you company, I suppose," muttered Bartram, who had been making intimate acquaintance with the black bottle above-mentioned. "But watch, if you like, and call as many devils as you like! For my part, I shall be all the better for a snooze. Come, Joe!"

As the boy followed his father into the hut, he looked back to the wayfarer, and the tears came into his eyes; for his tender spirit had an intuition of the bleak and terrible loneliness in which this man had enveloped himself.

When they had gone, Ethan Brand sat listening to the crackling of the kindled wood, and looking at the little spirts of fire that issued through the chinks of the door. These trifles, however, once so familiar, had but the slightest hold of his attention; while deep within his mind, he was reviewing the gradual, but marvellous change, that had been wrought upon him by the search to which he had devoted himself. He remembered how the night-dew had fallen upon him—how the dark forest had whispered to him—how the stars had gleamed upon him—a simple and loving man, watching his fire in the years gone by, and ever musing as it burned. He remembered with what tenderness, with what love and sympathy for mankind, and what pity for human guilt and wo, he had first begun to contemplate those ideas which afterwards became the inspiration of his life; with what reverence he had then looked into the heart of man, viewing it as a temple originally divine, and however desecrated, still to be held sacred by a brother; with what awful fear he had deprecated the success of his pursuit, and prayed that the Unpardonable Sin might never be revealed to him. Then ensued that vast intellectual development, which, in its progress, disturbed the counterpoise between his mind and heart. The Idea that possessed his life had operated as a means of education; it had gone on cultivating his powers to the highest point of which they were susceptible; it had raised him from the level of an unlettered laborer, to stand on a star-light eminence, whither the philosophers of the earth, laden with the lore of universities, might vainly strive to clamber after him. So much for the intellect! But where was the heart? That, indeed, had withered—had contracted—had hardened—had perished! It had ceased to partake of the universal throb. He had lost his hold of the magnetic chain of humanity. He was no longer a brother-man, opening the chambers or the dungeons of our common nature by the key of holy sympathy, which gave him a right to share in all its secrets; he was now a cold observer, looking on mankind as the subject of his experiment, and, at length, converting man and woman to be his puppets, and pulling the wires that moved them to such degrees of crime as were demanded for his study.

Thus Ethan Brand became a fiend. He began to be so from the moment that his moral nature had ceased to keep the pace of improvement with his intellect. And now, as his highest effort and inevitable development—as the bright and gorgeous flower, and rich, delicious fruit of his life's labor—he had produced the Unpardonable Sin!

"What more have I to seek? What more to achieve?" said Ethan Brand to himself. "My task is done, and well done!"

Starting from the log with a certain alacrity in his gait, and ascending the hillock of earth that was raised against the stone circumference of the lime-kiln, he thus reached the top of the structure. It was a space of perhaps ten feet across, from edge to edge, presenting a view of the upper surface of the immense mass of broken marble with which the kiln was heaped. All these innumerable blocks and fragments of marble were red-hot, and vividly on fire, sending up great spouts of blue flame, which quivered aloft and danced madly, as within a magic circle, and sank and rose again, with continual and multitudinous activity. As the lonely man bent forward over this terrible body of fire, the blasting heat smote up against his person with a breath that, it might be supposed, would have scorched and shrivelled him up in a moment.

Ethan Brand stood erect and raised his arms on high. The blue flames played upon his face, and imparted the wild and ghastly light which alone could have suited its expression; it was that of a fiend on the verge of plunging into his gulf of intensest torment.

"Oh, Mother Earth," cried he, "who art no more my Mother, and into whose bosom this frame shall never be re-solved! Oh, mankind, whose brotherhood I have cast off, and trampled thy great heart beneath my feet! Oh, stars of Heaven, that shone on me of old, as if to light me onward and up-ward!—farewell all, and forever! Come, deadly element of Fire—henceforth my familiar friend! Embrace me as I do thee!"

That night the sound of a fearful peal of laughter rolled heavily through the sleep of the lime-burner and his little son; dim shapes of horror and anguish haunted their dreams, and seemed still present in the rude hovel when they opened their eyes to the daylight.

"Up, boy, up!" cried the lime-burner, staring about him. "Thank Heaven, the night is gone at last; and rather than pass such another, I would watch my lime-kiln, wide awake, for a twelvemonth. This Ethan Brand, with his humbug of an Un-pardonable Sin, has done me no such mighty favor in taking my place!"

He issued from the hut, followed by little Joe, who kept fast hold of his father's hand. The early sunshine was already pouring its gold upon the mountain-tops, and though the valleys were still in shadow, they smiled cheerfully in the promise of the bright day that was hastening onward. The village, completely shut in by hills, which swelled away gently about it, looked as if it had rested peacefully in the hollow of the great hand of Providence. Every dwelling was distinctly visible; the little spires of the two churches pointed upward, and caught a fore-glimmering of brightness from the sun-gilt skies upon their gilded weathercocks. The tavern was astir, and the figure of the old, smoke-dried stage-agent, cigar in mouth, was seen beneath the stoop. Old Graylock was glorified with a golden cloud upon his head. Scattered, likewise, over the breasts of the surrounding mountains, there were heaps of hoary mist, in fantastic shapes, some of them far down into the valley, others high up towards the summits, and still others, of the same family of mist or cloud, hovering in the gold radiance of the upper atmosphere. Stepping from one to another of the clouds that rested on the hills, and thence to the loftier brotherhood that sailed in air, it seemed almost as if a mortal man might thus ascend into the heavenly regions. Earth was so mingled with sky that it was a daydream to look at it.

To supply that charm of the familiar and homely, which Nature so readily adopts into a scene like this, the stage-coach was rattling down the mountain-road, and the driver sounded his horn; while echo caught up the notes and intertwined them into a rich, and varied, and elaborate harmony, of which the original performer could lay claim to little share. The great hills played a concert among themselves, each contributing a strain of airy sweetness.

Little Joe's face brightened at once.

"Dear father," cried he, skipping cheerily to and fro, "that strange man is gone, and the sky and the mountains all seem glad of it!"

"Yes," growled the lime-burner with an oath, "but he has

let the fire go down, and no thanks to him, if five hundred bushels of lime are not spoilt. If I catch the fellow hereabouts again I shall feel like tossing him into the furnace!"

With his long pole in his hand he ascended to the top of the kiln. After a moment's pause he called to his son.

"Come up here, Joe!" said he.

So little Joe ran up the hillock and stood by his father's side. The marble was all burnt into perfect, snow-white lime. But on its surface, in the midst of the circle—snow-white too, and thoroughly converted into lime—lay a human skeleton, in the attitude of a person who, after long toil, lies down to long repose. Within the ribs—strange to say—was the shape of a human heart.

"Was the fellow's heart made of marble?" cried Bartram, in some perplexity at this phenomenon. "At any rate, it is burnt into what looks like special good lime; and, taking all the bones together, my kiln is half a bushel the richer for him."

So saying, the rude lime-burner lifted his pole, and letting it fall upon the skeleton, the relics of Ethan Brand were crumbled into fragments.

Suggestions for Further Reading

Randall Stewart, *Nathaniel Hawthorne: A Biography* (New Haven, Conn.: Yale University Press, 1948).

Richard Harter Fogle, *Hawthorne's Fiction: The Light and the Dark* (Norman: University of Oklahoma Press, 1952; rev. ed., 1964).

Hyatt H. Waggoner, *Hawthorne: A Critical Study* (Cambridge, Mass.: Harvard University Press, 1955; rev. ed., 1963).

Frederick C. Crews, *The Sins of the Fathers: Hawthorne's Psychological Themes* (New York: Oxford University Press, 1966).

Michael Davitt Bell, *Hawthorne and the Historical Romance of New England* (Princeton, N.J.: Princeton University Press, 1971).d

Neal Frank Doubleday, *Hawthorne's Early Tales: A Critical Study* (Durham, N.C.: Duke University Press, 1972).

Nina Baym, *The Shape of Hawthorne's Career* (Ithaca, N.Y.: Cornell University Press, 1976).

Kenneth Dauber, *Rediscovering Hawthorne* (Princeton, N.J.: Princeton University Press, 1977).

Taylor Stoehr, *Hawthorne's Mad Scientists* (Hamden, Conn.: Archon Books, 1978).

Arlin Turner, *Nathaniel Hawthorne: A Biography* (New York: Oxford University Press, 1980).

Michael J. Colacurcio, *The Province of Piety: Moral History in Hawthorne's Early Tales* (Cambridge, Mass.: Harvard University Press, 1984).

Carol Marie Bensick, *La Nouvelle Beatrice: Renaissance and Romance in "Rappaccini's Daughter"* (New Brunswick, N.J.: Rutgers University Press, 1985).